CW00556001

Edgar Allan Poe (born Edgar Poe; January 19, 1809 – October 7, 1849) was an American writer, editor, and literary critic. Poe is best known for his poetry and short stories, particularly his tales of mystery and the macabre. He is widely regarded as a central figure of Romanticism in the United States and of American literature as a whole, and he was one of the country's earliest practitioners of the short story. He is generally considered the inventor of the detective fiction genre and is further credited with contributing to the emerging genre of science fiction. He was the first well-known American writer to earn a living through writing alone, resulting in a financially difficult life and career. Poe was born in Boston, the second child of actors David and Elizabeth "Eliza" Arnold Hopkins Poe. His father abandoned the family in 1810, and his mother died the following year. Thus orphaned, the child was taken in by John and Frances Allan of Richmond, Virginia. They never formally adopted him, but he was with them well into young adulthood. (Source: Wikipedia)

Literary works:
The Black Cat
The Cask of Amontillado
A Descent into the Maelström
The Facts in the Case of M. Valdemar
The Fall of the House of Usher
The Gold-Bug
Hop-Frog
The Imp of the Perverse
Ligeia
The Masque of the Red Death
Morella
The Murders in the Rue Morgue

THE WORKS OF
EDGAR ALLAN POE
VOLUME 4

PRINCE CLASSICS

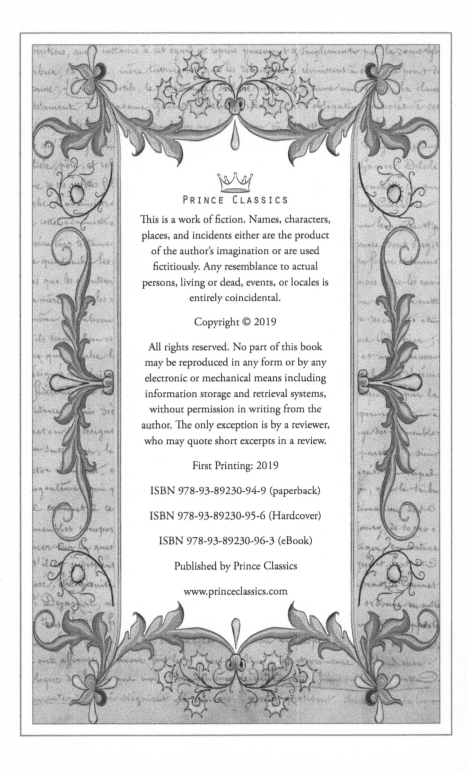

PRINCE CLASSICS

This is a work of fiction. Names, characters, places, and incidents either are the product of the author's imagination or are used fictitiously. Any resemblance to actual persons, living or dead, events, or locales is entirely coincidental.

Copyright © 2019

All rights reserved. No part of this book may be reproduced in any form or by any electronic or mechanical means including information storage and retrieval systems, without permission in writing from the author. The only exception is by a reviewer, who may quote short excerpts in a review.

First Printing: 2019

ISBN 978-93-89230-94-9 (paperback)

ISBN 978-93-89230-95-6 (Hardcover)

ISBN 978-93-89230-96-3 (eBook)

Published by Prince Classics

www.princeclassics.com

Contents

THE WORKS OF
EDGAR ALLAN POE
VOLUME 4

THE DEVIL IN THE BELFRY

What o'clock is it?—Old Saying.

EVERYBODY knows, in a general way, that the finest place in the world is—or, alas, was—the Dutch borough of Vondervotteimittiss. Yet as it lies some distance from any of the main roads, being in a somewhat out-of-the-way situation, there are perhaps very few of my readers who have ever paid it a visit. For the benefit of those who have not, therefore, it will be only proper that I should enter into some account of it. And this is indeed the more necessary, as with the hope of enlisting public sympathy in behalf of the inhabitants, I design here to give a history of the calamitous events which have so lately occurred within its limits. No one who knows me will doubt that the duty thus self-imposed will be executed to the best of my ability, with all that rigid impartiality, all that cautious examination into facts, and diligent collation of authorities, which should ever distinguish him who aspires to the title of historian.

By the united aid of medals, manuscripts, and inscriptions, I am enabled to say, positively, that the borough of Vondervotteimittiss has existed, from its origin, in precisely the same condition which it at present preserves. Of the date of this origin, however, I grieve that I can only speak with that species of indefinite definiteness which mathematicians are, at times, forced to put up with in certain algebraic formulae. The date, I may thus say, in regard to the remoteness of its antiquity, cannot be less than any assignable quantity whatsoever.

Touching the derivation of the name Vondervotteimittiss, I confess myself, with sorrow, equally at fault. Among a multitude of opinions upon this delicate point—some acute, some learned, some sufficiently the reverse—I am able to select nothing which ought to be considered satisfactory. Perhaps the idea of Grogswigg—nearly coincident with that of Kroutaplenttey—is to be cautiously preferred.—It runs:—"Vondervotteimittis—Vonder, lege Donder—Votteimittis, quasi und Bleitziz—Bleitziz obsol:—pro Blitzen."

This derivative, to say the truth, is still countenanced by some traces of the electric fluid evident on the summit of the steeple of the House of the Town-Council. I do not choose, however, to commit myself on a theme of such importance, and must refer the reader desirous of information to the "Oratiunculae de Rebus Praeter-Veteris," of Dundergutz. See, also, Blunderbuzzard "De Derivationibus," pp. 27 to 5010, Folio, Gothic edit., Red and Black character, Catch-word and No Cypher; wherein consult, also, marginal notes in the autograph of Stuffundpuff, with the Sub-Commentaries of Gruntundguzzell.

Notwithstanding the obscurity which thus envelops the date of the foundation of Vondervotteimittis, and the derivation of its name, there can be no doubt, as I said before, that it has always existed as we find it at this epoch. The oldest man in the borough can remember not the slightest difference in the appearance of any portion of it; and, indeed, the very suggestion of such a possibility is considered an insult. The site of the village is in a perfectly circular valley, about a quarter of a mile in circumference, and entirely surrounded by gentle hills, over whose summit the people have never yet ventured to pass. For this they assign the very good reason that they do not believe there is anything at all on the other side.

Round the skirts of the valley (which is quite level, and paved throughout with flat tiles), extends a continuous row of sixty little houses. These, having their backs on the hills, must look, of course, to the centre of the plain, which is just sixty yards from the front door of each dwelling. Every house has a small garden before it, with a circular path, a sun-dial, and twenty-four cabbages. The buildings themselves are so precisely alike, that one can in no manner be distinguished from the other. Owing to the vast antiquity, the style of architecture is somewhat odd, but it is not for that reason the less strikingly picturesque. They are fashioned of hard-burned little bricks, red, with black ends, so that the walls look like a chess-board upon a great scale. The gables are turned to the front, and there are cornices, as big as all the rest of the house, over the eaves and over the main doors. The windows are narrow and deep, with very tiny panes and a great deal of sash. On the roof is a vast quantity of tiles with long curly ears. The woodwork, throughout, is of a dark hue and there is much carving about it, with but a trifling variety of pattern for, time out of mind, the carvers of Vondervotteimittiss have never been able to carve more than two objects—a time-piece and a cabbage. But these they do exceedingly well, and intersperse them, with singular ingenuity, wherever they find room for the chisel.

The dwellings are as much alike inside as out, and the furniture is all upon one plan. The floors are of square tiles, the chairs and tables of black-looking wood with thin crooked legs and puppy feet. The mantelpieces are wide and high, and have not only time-pieces and cabbages sculptured over the front, but a real time-piece, which makes a prodigious ticking, on the top in the middle, with a flower-pot containing a cabbage standing on each extremity by way of outrider. Between each cabbage and the time-piece, again, is a little China man having a large stomach with a great round hole in it, through which is seen the dial-plate of a watch.

The fireplaces are large and deep, with fierce crooked-looking fire-dogs. There is constantly a rousing fire, and a huge pot over it, full of sauer-kraut and pork, to which the good woman of the house is always busy in attending. She is a little fat old lady, with blue eyes and a red face, and wears a huge cap like a sugar-loaf, ornamented with purple and yellow ribbons. Her dress is of orange-colored linsey-woolsey, made very full behind and very short in the waist—and indeed very short in other respects, not reaching below the middle of her leg. This is somewhat thick, and so are her ankles, but she has a fine pair of green stockings to cover them. Her shoes—of pink leather—are fastened each with a bunch of yellow ribbons puckered up in the shape of a cabbage. In her left hand she has a little heavy Dutch watch; in her right she wields a ladle for the sauerkraut and pork. By her side there stands a fat tabby cat, with a gilt toy-repeater tied to its tail, which "the boys" have there fastened by way of a quiz.

The boys themselves are, all three of them, in the garden attending the pig. They are each two feet in height. They have three-cornered cocked hats, purple waistcoats reaching down to their thighs, buckskin knee-breeches, red stockings, heavy shoes with big silver buckles, long surtout coats with large buttons of mother-of-pearl. Each, too, has a pipe in his mouth, and a

11

little dumpy watch in his right hand. He takes a puff and a look, and then a look and a puff. The pig—which is corpulent and lazy—is occupied now in picking up the stray leaves that fall from the cabbages, and now in giving a kick behind at the gilt repeater, which the urchins have also tied to his tail in order to make him look as handsome as the cat.

Right at the front door, in a high-backed leather-bottomed armed chair, with crooked legs and puppy feet like the tables, is seated the old man of the house himself. He is an exceedingly puffy little old gentleman, with big circular eyes and a huge double chin. His dress resembles that of the boys— and I need say nothing farther about it. All the difference is, that his pipe is somewhat bigger than theirs and he can make a greater smoke. Like them, he has a watch, but he carries his watch in his pocket. To say the truth, he has something of more importance than a watch to attend to—and what that is, I shall presently explain. He sits with his right leg upon his left knee, wears a grave countenance, and always keeps one of his eyes, at least, resolutely bent upon a certain remarkable object in the centre of the plain.

This object is situated in the steeple of the House of the Town Council. The Town Council are all very little, round, oily, intelligent men, with big saucer eyes and fat double chins, and have their coats much longer and their shoe-buckles much bigger than the ordinary inhabitants of Vondervotteimittiss. Since my sojourn in the borough, they have had several special meetings, and have adopted these three important resolutions:

"That it is wrong to alter the good old course of things:"

"That there is nothing tolerable out of Vondervotteimittiss:" and—

"That we will stick by our clocks and our cabbages."

Above the session-room of the Council is the steeple, and in the steeple is the belfry, where exists, and has existed time out of mind, the pride and wonder of the village—the great clock of the borough of Vondervotteimittiss. And this is the object to which the eyes of the old gentlemen are turned who sit in the leather-bottomed arm-chairs.

The great clock has seven faces—one in each of the seven sides of the steeple—so that it can be readily seen from all quarters. Its faces are large and white, and its hands heavy and black. There is a belfry-man whose sole duty is to attend to it; but this duty is the most perfect of sinecures—for the clock of Vondervotteimittis was never yet known to have anything the matter with it. Until lately, the bare supposition of such a thing was considered heretical. From the remotest period of antiquity to which the archives have reference, the hours have been regularly struck by the big bell. And, indeed the case was just the same with all the other clocks and watches in the borough. Never was such a place for keeping the true time. When the large clapper thought proper to say "Twelve o'clock!" all its obedient followers opened their throats simultaneously, and responded like a very echo. In short, the good burghers were fond of their sauer-kraut, but then they were proud of their clocks.

All people who hold sinecure offices are held in more or less respect, and as the belfry—man of Vondervotteimittiss has the most perfect of sinecures, he is the most perfectly respected of any man in the world. He is the chief dignitary of the borough, and the very pigs look up to him with a sentiment of reverence. His coat-tail is very far longer—his pipe, his shoe—buckles, his eyes, and his stomach, very far bigger—than those of any other old gentleman in the village; and as to his chin, it is not only double, but triple.

I have thus painted the happy estate of Vondervotteimittiss: alas, that so fair a picture should ever experience a reverse!

There has been long a saying among the wisest inhabitants, that "no good can come from over the hills"; and it really seemed that the words had in them something of the spirit of prophecy. It wanted five minutes of noon, on the day before yesterday, when there appeared a very odd-looking object on the summit of the ridge of the eastward. Such an occurrence, of course, attracted universal attention, and every little old gentleman who sat in a leather-bottomed arm-chair turned one of his eyes with a stare of dismay upon the phenomenon, still keeping the other upon the clock in the steeple.

By the time that it wanted only three minutes to noon, the droll object in question was perceived to be a very diminutive foreign-looking young man. He descended the hills at a great rate, so that every body had soon a good look at him. He was really the most finicky little personage that had ever been seen in Vondervotteimittiss. His countenance was of a dark snuff-color, and he had a long hooked nose, pea eyes, a wide mouth, and an excellent set of teeth, which latter he seemed anxious of displaying, as he was grinning from ear to ear. What with mustachios and whiskers, there was none of the rest of his face to be seen. His head was uncovered, and his hair neatly done up in papillotes. His dress was a tight-fitting swallow-tailed black coat (from one of whose pockets dangled a vast length of white handkerchief), black kerseymere knee-breeches, black stockings, and stumpy-looking pumps, with huge bunches of black satin ribbon for bows. Under one arm he carried a huge chapeau-de-bras, and under the other a fiddle nearly five times as big as himself. In his left hand was a gold snuff-box, from which, as he capered down the hill, cutting all manner of fantastic steps, he took snuff incessantly with an air of the greatest possible self-satisfaction. God bless me!—here was a sight for the honest burghers of Vondervotteimittiss!

To speak plainly, the fellow had, in spite of his grinning, an audacious and sinister kind of face; and as he curvetted right into the village, the old stumpy appearance of his pumps excited no little suspicion; and many a burgher who beheld him that day would have given a trifle for a peep beneath the white cambric handkerchief which hung so obtrusively from the pocket of his swallow-tailed coat. But what mainly occasioned a righteous indignation was, that the scoundrelly popinjay, while he cut a fandango here, and a whirligig there, did not seem to have the remotest idea in the world of such a thing as keeping time in his steps.

The good people of the borough had scarcely a chance, however, to get their eyes thoroughly open, when, just as it wanted half a minute of noon, the rascal bounced, as I say, right into the midst of them; gave a chassez here, and a balancez there; and then, after a pirouette and a pas-de-zephyr, pigeon-winged himself right up into the belfry of the House of the Town Council, where the wonder-stricken belfry-man sat smoking in a state of dignity and dismay. But the little chap seized him at once by the nose; gave it a swing and a pull; clapped the big chapeau de-bras upon his head; knocked it down over his eyes and mouth; and then, lifting up the big fiddle, beat him with it so long and so soundly, that what with the belfry-man being so fat, and the fiddle being so hollow, you would have sworn that there was a regiment of double-bass drummers all beating the devil's tattoo up in the belfry of the steeple of Vondervotteimittiss.

There is no knowing to what desperate act of vengeance this unprincipled attack might have aroused the inhabitants, but for the important fact that it now wanted only half a second of noon. The bell was about to strike, and it was a matter of absolute and pre-eminent necessity that every body should look well at his watch. It was evident, however, that just at this moment the fellow in the steeple was doing something that he had no business to do with the clock. But as it now began to strike, nobody had any time to attend to his manoeuvres, for they had all to count the strokes of the bell as it sounded.

"One!" said the clock.

"Von!" echoed every little old gentleman in every leather-bottomed arm-chair in Vondervotteimittiss. "Von!" said his watch also; "von!" said the watch of his vrow; and "von!" said the watches of the boys, and the little gilt repeaters on the tails of the cat and pig.

"Two!" continued the big bell; and

"Doo!" repeated all the repeaters.

"Three! Four! Five! Six! Seven! Eight! Nine! Ten!" said the bell.

"Dree! Vour! Fibe! Sax! Seben! Aight! Noin! Den!" answered the others.

"Eleven!" said the big one.

"Eleben!" assented the little ones.

"Twelve!" said the bell.

"Dvelf!" they replied perfectly satisfied, and dropping their voices.

"Und dvelf it is!" said all the little old gentlemen, putting up their watches. But the big bell had not done with them yet.

"Thirteen!" said he.

"Der Teufel!" gasped the little old gentlemen, turning pale, dropping their pipes, and putting down all their right legs from over their left knees.

"Der Teufel!" groaned they, "Dirteen! Dirteen!!—Mein Gott, it is Dirteen o'clock!!"

Why attempt to describe the terrible scene which ensued? All Vondervotteimittiss flew at once into a lamentable state of uproar.

"Vot is cum'd to mein pelly?" roared all the boys—"I've been ongry for dis hour!"

"Vot is com'd to mein kraut?" screamed all the vrows, "It has been done to rags for this hour!"

"Vot is cum'd to mein pipe?" swore all the little old gentlemen, "Donder and Blitzen; it has been smoked out for dis hour!"—and they filled them up again in a great rage, and sinking back in their arm-chairs, puffed away so fast and so fiercely that the whole valley was immediately filled with impenetrable smoke.

Meantime the cabbages all turned very red in the face, and it seemed as if old Nick himself had taken possession of every thing in the shape of a timepiece. The clocks carved upon the furniture took to dancing as if bewitched, while those upon the mantel-pieces could scarcely contain themselves for fury, and kept such a continual striking of thirteen, and such a frisking and wriggling of their pendulums as was really horrible to see. But, worse than all, neither the cats nor the pigs could put up any longer with the behavior of the little repeaters tied to their tails, and resented it by scampering all over the place, scratching and poking, and squeaking and screeching, and caterwauling and squalling, and flying into the faces, and running under the petticoats of the people, and creating altogether the most abominable din and confusion which it is possible for a reasonable person to conceive. And to make matters still more distressing, the rascally little scape-grace in the steeple was evidently exerting himself to the utmost. Every now and then one might catch a glimpse of the scoundrel through the smoke. There he sat in the belfry upon the belfry-man, who was lying flat upon his back. In his teeth the villain held the bell-rope, which he kept jerking about with his head, raising such a clatter that my ears ring again even to think of it. On his lap lay the big fiddle, at which he was scraping, out of all time and tune, with both hands, making a great show, the nincompoop! of playing "Judy O'Flannagan and Paddy O'Rafferty."

Affairs being thus miserably situated, I left the place in disgust, and now appeal for aid to all lovers of correct time and fine kraut. Let us proceed in a body to the borough, and restore the ancient order of things in Vondervotteimittiss by ejecting that little fellow from the steeple.

LIONIZING

———— *all people went*

Upon their ten toes in wild wonderment.

—*Bishop Hall's Satires.*

I am—that is to say I was—a great man; but I am neither the author of Junius nor the man in the mask; for my name, I believe, is Robert Jones, and I was born somewhere in the city of Fum-Fudge.

The first action of my life was the taking hold of my nose with both hands. My mother saw this and called me a genius: my father wept for joy and presented me with a treatise on Nosology. This I mastered before I was breeched.

I now began to feel my way in the science, and soon came to understand that, provided a man had a nose sufficiently conspicuous he might, by merely following it, arrive at a Lionship. But my attention was not confined to theories alone. Every morning I gave my proboscis a couple of pulls and swallowed a half dozen of drams.

When I came of age my father asked me, one day, If I would step with him into his study.

"My son," said he, when we were seated, "what is the chief end of your existence?"

"My father," I answered, "it is the study of Nosology."

"And what, Robert," he inquired, "is Nosology?"

"Sir," I said, "it is the Science of Noses."

"And can you tell me," he demanded, "what is the meaning of a nose?"

"A nose, my father;" I replied, greatly softened, "has been variously defined by about a thousand different authors." [Here I pulled out my watch.]

"It is now noon or thereabouts—we shall have time enough to get through with them all before midnight. To commence then:—The nose, according to Bartholinus, is that protuberance—that bump—that excrescence—that—"

"Will do, Robert," interrupted the good old gentleman. "I am thunderstruck at the extent of your information—I am positively—upon my soul." [Here he closed his eyes and placed his hand upon his heart.] "Come here!" [Here he took me by the arm.] "Your education may now be considered as finished—it is high time you should scuffle for yourself—and you cannot do a better thing than merely follow your nose—so—so—so—" [Here he kicked me down stairs and out of the door]—"so get out of my house, and God bless you!"

As I felt within me the divine afflatus, I considered this accident rather fortunate than otherwise. I resolved to be guided by the paternal advice. I determined to follow my nose. I gave it a pull or two upon the spot, and wrote a pamphlet on Nosology forthwith.

All Fum-Fudge was in an uproar.

"Wonderful genius!" said the Quarterly.

"Superb physiologist!" said the Westminster.

"Clever fellow!" said the Foreign.

"Fine writer!" said the Edinburgh.

"Profound thinker!" said the Dublin.

"Great man!" said Bentley.

"Divine soul!" said Fraser.

"One of us!" said Blackwood.

"Who can he be?" said Mrs. Bas-Bleu.

"What can he be?" said big Miss Bas-Bleu.

"Where can he be?" said little Miss Bas-Bleu.—But I paid these people no attention whatever—I just stepped into the shop of an artist.

The Duchess of Bless-my-Soul was sitting for her portrait; the Marquis of So-and-So was holding the Duchess' poodle; the Earl of This-and-That was flirting with her salts; and his Royal Highness of Touch-me-Not was leaning upon the back of her chair.

I approached the artist and turned up my nose.

"Oh, beautiful!" sighed her Grace.

"Oh my!" lisped the Marquis.

"Oh, shocking!" groaned the Earl.

"Oh, abominable!" growled his Royal Highness.

"What will you take for it?" asked the artist.

"For his nose!" shouted her Grace.

"A thousand pounds," said I, sitting down.

"A thousand pounds?" inquired the artist, musingly.

"A thousand pounds," said I.

"Beautiful!" said he, entranced.

"A thousand pounds," said I.

"Do you warrant it?" he asked, turning the nose to the light.

"I do," said I, blowing it well.

"Is it quite original?" he inquired; touching it with reverence.

"Humph!" said I, twisting it to one side.

"Has no copy been taken?" he demanded, surveying it through a microscope.

"None," said I, turning it up.

"Admirable!" he ejaculated, thrown quite off his guard by the beauty of the manoeuvre.

"A thousand pounds," said I.

"A thousand pounds?" said he.

"Precisely," said I.

"A thousand pounds?" said he.

"Just so," said I.

"You shall have them," said he. "What a piece of virtu!" So he drew me a check upon the spot, and took a sketch of my nose. I engaged rooms in Jermyn street, and sent her Majesty the ninety-ninth edition of the "Nosology," with a portrait of the proboscis.—That sad little rake, the Prince of Wales, invited me to dinner.

We were all lions and recherch?s.

There was a modern Platonist. He quoted Porphyry, Iamblicus, Plotinus, Proclus, Hierocles, Maximus Tyrius, and Syrianus.

There was a human-perfectibility man. He quoted Turgot, Price, Priestly, Condorcet, De Stael, and the "Ambitious Student in Ill Health."

There was Sir Positive Paradox. He observed that all fools were philosophers, and that all philosophers were fools.

There was ?stheticus Ethix. He spoke of fire, unity, and atoms; bi-part and pre-existent soul; affinity and discord; primitive intelligence and hom?omeria.

There was Theologos Theology. He talked of Eusebius and Arianus; heresy and the Council of Nice; Puseyism and consubstantialism; Homousios and Homouioisios.

There was Fricass?e from the Rocher de Cancale. He mentioned Muriton of red tongue; cauliflowers with velout? sauce; veal ? la St. Menehoult; marinade ? la St. Florentin; and orange jellies en mos?iques.

There was Bibulus O'Bumper. He touched upon Latour and

Markbr?nnen; upon Mousseux and Chambertin; upon Richbourg and St. George; upon Haubrion, Leonville, and Medoc; upon Barac and Preignac; upon Gr?ve, upon Sauterne, upon Lafitte, and upon St. Peray. He shook his head at Clos de Vougeot, and told, with his eyes shut, the difference between Sherry and Amontillado.

There was Signor Tintontintino from Florence. He discoursed of Cimabu?, Arpino, Carpaccio, and Argostino—of the gloom of Caravaggio, of the amenity of Albano, of the colors of Titian, of the frows of Rubens, and of the waggeries of Jan Steen.

There was the President of the Fum-Fudge University. He was of opinion that the moon was called Bendis in Thrace, Bubastis in Egypt, Dian in Rome, and Artemis in Greece. There was a Grand Turk from Stamboul. He could not help thinking that the angels were horses, cocks, and bulls; that somebody in the sixth heaven had seventy thousand heads; and that the earth was supported by a sky-blue cow with an incalculable number of green horns.

There was Delphinus Polyglott. He told us what had become of the eighty-three lost tragedies of ?schylus; of the fifty-four orations of Is?us; of the three hundred and ninety-one speeches of Lysias; of the hundred and eighty treatises of Theophrastus; of the eighth book of the conic sections of Apollonius; of Pindar's hymns and dithyrambics; and of the five and forty tragedies of Homer Junior.

There was Ferdinand Fitz-Fossillus Feltspar. He informed us all about internal fires and tertiary formations; about ?eriforms, fluidiforms, and solidiforms; about quartz and marl; about schist and schorl; about gypsum and trap; about talc and calc; about blende and horn-blende; about mica-slate and pudding-stone; about cyanite and lepidolite; about hematite and tremolite; about antimony and calcedony; about manganese and whatever you please.

There was myself. I spoke of myself;—of myself, of myself, of myself;—of Nosology, of my pamphlet, and of myself. I turned up my nose, and I spoke of myself.

"Marvellous clever man!" said the Prince.

"Superb!" said his guests:—and next morning her Grace of Bless-my-Soul paid me a visit.

"Will you go to Almack's, pretty creature?" she said, tapping me under the chin.

"Upon honor," said I.

"Nose and all?" she asked.

"As I live," I replied.

"Here then is a card, my life. Shall I say you will be there?"

"Dear Duchess, with all my heart."

"Pshaw, no!—but with all your nose?"

"Every bit of it, my love," said I: so I gave it a twist or two, and found myself at Almack's. The rooms were crowded to suffocation.

"He is coming!" said somebody on the staircase.

"He is coming!" said somebody farther up.

"He is coming!" said somebody farther still.

"He is come!" exclaimed the Duchess. "He is come, the little love!"—and, seizing me firmly by both hands, she kissed me thrice upon the nose. A marked sensation immediately ensued.

"Diavolo!" cried Count Capricornutti.

"Dios guarda!" muttered Don Stiletto.

"Mille tonnerres!" ejaculated the Prince de Grenouille.

"Tousand teufel!" growled the Elector of Bluddennuff.

It was not to be borne. I grew angry. I turned short upon Bluddennuff.

"Sir!" said I to him, "you are a baboon."

"Sir," he replied, after a pause, "Donner und Blitzen!"

This was all that could be desired. We exchanged cards. At Chalk-Farm, the next morning, I shot off his nose—and then called upon my friends.

"B?te!" said the first.

"Fool!" said the second.

"Dolt!" said the third.

"Ass!" said the fourth.

"Ninny!" said the fifth.

"Noodle!" said the sixth.

"Be off!" said the seventh.

At all this I felt mortified, and so called upon my father.

"Father," I asked, "what is the chief end of my existence?"

"My son," he replied, "it is still the study of Nosology; but in hitting the Elector upon the nose you have overshot your mark. You have a fine nose, it is true; but then Bluddennuff has none. You are damned, and he has become the hero of the day. I grant you that in Fum-Fudge the greatness of a lion is in proportion to the size of his proboscis—but, good heavens! there is no competing with a lion who has no proboscis at all."

X-ING A PARAGRAPH

AS it is well known that the 'wise men' came 'from the East,' and as Mr. Touch-and-go Bullet-head came from the East, it follows that Mr. Bullet-head was a wise man; and if collateral proof of the matter be needed, here we have it—Mr. B. was an editor. Irascibility was his sole foible, for in fact the obstinacy of which men accused him was anything but his foible, since he justly considered it his forte. It was his strong point—his virtue; and it would have required all the logic of a Brownson to convince him that it was 'anything else.'

I have shown that Touch-and-go Bullet-head was a wise man; and the only occasion on which he did not prove infallible, was when, abandoning that legitimate home for all wise men, the East, he migrated to the city of Alexander-the-Great-o-nopolis, or some place of a similar title, out West.

I must do him the justice to say, however, that when he made up his mind finally to settle in that town, it was under the impression that no newspaper, and consequently no editor, existed in that particular section of the country. In establishing 'The Tea-Pot' he expected to have the field all to himself. I feel confident he never would have dreamed of taking up his residence in Alexander-the-Great-o-nopolis had he been aware that, in Alexander-the-Great-o-nopolis, there lived a gentleman named John Smith (if I rightly remember), who for many years had there quietly grown fat in editing and publishing the 'Alexander-the-Great-o-nopolis Gazette.' It was solely, therefore, on account of having been misinformed, that Mr. Bullet-head found himself in Alex-suppose we call it Nopolis, 'for short'—but, as he did find himself there, he determined to keep up his character for obst—for firmness, and remain. So remain he did; and he did more; he unpacked his press, type, etc., etc., rented an office exactly opposite to that of the 'Gazette,' and, on the third morning after his arrival, issued the first number of 'The Alexan'—that is to say, of 'The Nopolis Tea-Pot'—as nearly as I can recollect, this was the name of the new paper.

The leading article, I must admit, was brilliant—not to say severe. It was especially bitter about things in general—and as for the editor of 'The Gazette,' he was torn all to pieces in particular. Some of Bullethead's remarks were really so fiery that I have always, since that time, been forced to look upon John Smith, who is still alive, in the light of a salamander. I cannot pretend to give all the 'Tea-Pot's' paragraphs verbatim, but one of them runs thus:

'Oh, yes!—Oh, we perceive! Oh, no doubt! The editor over the way is a genius—O, my! Oh, goodness, gracious!—what is this world coming to? Oh, tempora! Oh, Moses!'

A philippic at once so caustic and so classical, alighted like a bombshell among the hitherto peaceful citizens of Nopolis. Groups of excited individuals gathered at the corners of the streets. Every one awaited, with heartfelt anxiety, the reply of the dignified Smith. Next morning it appeared as follows:

'We quote from "The Tea-Pot" of yesterday the subjoined paragraph: "Oh, yes! Oh, we perceive! Oh, no doubt! Oh, my! Oh, goodness! Oh, tempora! Oh, Moses!" Why, the fellow is all O! That accounts for his reasoning in a circle, and explains why there is neither beginning nor end to him, nor to anything he says. We really do not believe the vagabond can write a word that hasn't an O in it. Wonder if this O-ing is a habit of his? By-the-by, he came away from Down-East in a great hurry. Wonder if he O's as much there as he does here? "O! it is pitiful."'

The indignation of Mr. Bullet-head at these scandalous insinuations, I shall not attempt to describe. On the eel-skinning principle, however, he did not seem to be so much incensed at the attack upon his integrity as one might have imagined. It was the sneer at his style that drove him to desperation. What!—he Touch-and-go Bullet-head!—not able to write a word without an O in it! He would soon let the jackanapes see that he was mistaken. Yes! he would let him see how much he was mistaken, the puppy! He, Touch-and-go Bullet-head, of Frogpondium, would let Mr. John Smith perceive that he, Bullet-head, could indite, if it so pleased him, a whole paragraph—aye! a whole article—in which that contemptible vowel should not once—not even once—make its appearance. But no;—that would be yielding a point to the said John Smith. He, Bullet-head, would make no alteration in his style, to suit the caprices of any Mr. Smith in Christendom. Perish so vile a thought! The O forever; He would persist in the O. He would be as O-wy as O-wy could be.

Burning with the chivalry of this determination, the great Touch-and-go, in the next 'Tea-Pot,' came out merely with this simple but resolute paragraph, in reference to this unhappy affair:

'The editor of the "Tea-Pot" has the honor of advising the editor of the "Gazette" that he (the "Tea-Pot") will take an opportunity in tomorrow morning's paper, of convincing him (the "Gazette") that he (the "Tea-Pot") both can and will be his own master, as regards style; he (the "Tea-Pot") intending to show him (the "Gazette") the supreme, and indeed the withering contempt with which the criticism of him (the "Gazette") inspires the independent bosom of him (the "TeaPot") by composing for the especial gratification (?) of him (the "Gazette") a leading article, of some extent, in which the beautiful vowel—the emblem of Eternity—yet so offensive to the hyper-exquisite delicacy of him (the "Gazette") shall most certainly not be avoided by his (the "Gazette's") most obedient, humble servant, the "Tea-Pot." "So much for Buckingham!"'

In fulfilment of the awful threat thus darkly intimated rather than decidedly enunciated, the great Bullet-head, turning a deaf ear to all entreaties for 'copy,' and simply requesting his foreman to 'go to the d——l,' when he (the foreman) assured him (the 'Tea-Pot'!) that it was high time to 'go to press': turning a deaf ear to everything, I say, the great Bullet-head sat up until day-break, consuming the midnight oil, and absorbed in the composition of the really unparalleled paragraph, which follows:—

'So ho, John! how now? Told you so, you know. Don't crow, another time, before you're out of the woods! Does your mother know you're out? Oh, no, no!—so go home at once, now, John, to your odious old woods of Concord! Go home to your woods, old owl—go! You won't! Oh, poh, poh, don't do so! You've got to go, you know! So go at once, and don't go slow, for nobody owns you here, you know! Oh! John, John, if you don't go you're no homo—no! You're only a fowl, an owl, a cow, a sow,—a doll, a poll; a poor, old, good-for-nothing-to-nobody, log, dog, hog, or frog, come out of a Concord bog. Cool, now—cool! Do be cool, you fool! None of your crowing, old cock! Don't frown so—don't! Don't hollo, nor howl nor growl, nor bow-wow-wow! Good Lord, John, how you do look! Told you so, you know—but stop rolling your goose of an old poll about so, and go and drown your sorrows in a bowl!'

Exhausted, very naturally, by so stupendous an effort, the great Touch-and-go could attend to nothing farther that night. Firmly, composedly, yet with an air of conscious power, he handed his MS. to the devil in waiting, and then, walking leisurely home, retired, with ineffable dignity to bed.

Meantime the devil, to whom the copy was entrusted, ran up stairs to his 'case,' in an unutterable hurry, and forthwith made a commencement at 'setting' the MS. 'up.'

In the first place, of course,—as the opening word was 'So,'—he made a plunge into the capital S hole and came out in triumph with a capital S. Elated by this success, he immediately threw himself upon the little-o box with a blindfold impetuosity—but who shall describe his horror when his fingers came up without the anticipated letter in their clutch? who shall paint his astonishment and rage at perceiving, as he rubbed his knuckles, that he had been only thumping them to no purpose, against the bottom of an empty box. Not a single little-o was in the little-o hole; and, glancing fearfully at the capital-O partition, he found that to his extreme terror, in a precisely similar predicament. Awe—stricken, his first impulse was to rush to the foreman.

'Sir!' said he, gasping for breath, 'I can't never set up nothing without no o's.'

'What do you mean by that?' growled the foreman, who was in a very ill humor at being kept so late.

'Why, sir, there beant an o in the office, neither a big un nor a little un!'

'What—what the d-l has become of all that were in the case?'

'I don't know, sir,' said the boy, 'but one of them ere "G'zette" devils is bin prowling 'bout here all night, and I spect he's gone and cabbaged 'em every one.'

'Dod rot him! I haven't a doubt of it,' replied the foreman, getting purple with rage 'but I tell you what you do, Bob, that's a good boy—you go over the first chance you get and hook every one of their i's and (d——n them!) their izzards.'

'Jist so,' replied Bob, with a wink and a frown—'I'll be into 'em, I'll let 'em know a thing or two; but in de meantime, that ere paragrab? Mus go in to-night, you know—else there'll be the d-l to pay, and-'

'And not a bit of pitch hot,' interrupted the foreman, with a deep sigh, and an emphasis on the 'bit.' 'Is it a long paragraph, Bob?'

'Shouldn't call it a wery long paragrab,' said Bob.

'Ah, well, then! do the best you can with it! We must get to press,' said the foreman, who was over head and ears in work; 'just stick in some other letter for o; nobody's going to read the fellow's trash anyhow.'

'Wery well,' replied Bob, 'here goes it!' and off he hurried to his case, muttering as he went: 'Considdeble vell, them ere expressions, perticcler for a man as doesn't swar. So I's to gouge out all their eyes, eh? and d-n all their gizzards! Vell! this here's the chap as is just able for to do it.' The fact is that although Bob was but twelve years old and four feet high, he was equal to any amount of fight, in a small way.

The exigency here described is by no means of rare occurrence in printing-offices; and I cannot tell how to account for it, but the fact is indisputable, that when the exigency does occur, it almost always happens that x is adopted as a substitute for the letter deficient. The true reason, perhaps, is that x is rather the most superabundant letter in the cases, or at least was so in the old times—long enough to render the substitution in question an habitual thing with printers. As for Bob, he would have considered it heretical to employ any other character, in a case of this kind, than the x to which he had been accustomed.

'I shell have to x this ere paragrab,' said he to himself, as he read it over in astonishment, 'but it's jest about the awfulest o-wy paragrab I ever did see': so x it he did, unflinchingly, and to press it went x-ed.

Next morning the population of Nopolis were taken all aback by reading in 'The Tea-Pot,' the following extraordinary leader:

'Sx hx, Jxhn! hxw nxw? Txld yxu sx, yxu knxw. Dxn't crxw, anxther time, befxre yxu're xut xf the wxxds! Dxes yxur mxther knxw yxu're xut? Xh, nx, nx!—sx gx hxme at xnce, nxw, Jxhn, tx yxur xdixus xld wxxds xf Cxncxrd! Gx hxme tx yxur wxxds, xld xwl,—gx! Yxu wxn't? Xh, pxh, pxh, Jxhn, dxn't dx sx! Yxu've gxt tx gx, yxu knxw, sx gx at xnce, and dxn't gx slxw; fxr nxbxdy xwns yxu here, yxu knxw. Xh, Jxhn, Jxhn, Jxhn, if yxu dxn't gx yxu're nx hxmx—nx! Yxu're xnly a fxwl, an xwl; a cxw, a sxw; a dxll, a pxll; a pxxr xld gxxd-fxr-nxthing-tx-nxbxdy, lxg, dxg, hxg, xr frxg, cxme xut xf a Cxncxrd bxg. Cxxl, nxw—cxxl! Dx be cxxl, yxu fxxl! Nxne xf yxur crxwing, xld cxck! Dxn't frxwn sx—dxn't! Dxn't hxllx, nxr hxwl, nxr grxwl, nxr bxw-wxw-wxw! Gxxd Lxrd, Jxhn, hxw yxu dx lxxk! Txld yxu sx, yxu knxw,—but stxp rxlling yxur gxxse xf an xld pxll abxut sx, and gx and drxwn yxur sxrrxws in a bxwl!'

The uproar occasioned by this mystical and cabalistical article, is not to be conceived. The first definite idea entertained by the populace was, that some diabolical treason lay concealed in the hieroglyphics; and there was a general rush to Bullet-head's residence, for the purpose of riding him on a rail; but that gentleman was nowhere to be found. He had vanished, no one could tell how; and not even the ghost of him has ever been seen since.

Unable to discover its legitimate object, the popular fury at length subsided; leaving behind it, by way of sediment, quite a medley of opinion about this unhappy affair.

One gentleman thought the whole an X-ellent joke.

Another said that, indeed, Bullet-head had shown much X-uberance of fancy.

A third admitted him X-entric, but no more.

A fourth could only suppose it the Yankee's design to X-press, in a general way, his X-asperation.

'Say, rather, to set an X-ample to posterity,' suggested a fifth.

That Bullet-head had been driven to an extremity, was clear to all; and in fact, since that editor could not be found, there was some talk about lynching the other one.

The more common conclusion, however, was that the affair was, simply, X-traordinary and in-X-plicable. Even the town mathematician confessed that he could make nothing of so dark a problem. X, every. body knew, was an unknown quantity; but in this case (as he properly observed), there was an unknown quantity of X.

The opinion of Bob, the devil (who kept dark about his having 'X-ed the paragrab'), did not meet with so much attention as I think it deserved, although it was very openly and very fearlessly expressed. He said that, for his part, he had no doubt about the matter at all, that it was a clear case, that Mr. Bullet-head 'never could be persuaded fur to drink like other folks, but vas continually a-svigging o' that ere blessed XXX ale, and as a naiteral consekvence, it just puffed him up savage, and made him X (cross) in the X-treme.'

METZENGERSTEIN

Pestis eram vivus—moriens tua mors ero.

—Martin Luther

HORROR and fatality have been stalking abroad in all ages. Why then give a date to this story I have to tell? Let it suffice to say, that at the period of which I speak, there existed, in the interior of Hungary, a settled although hidden belief in the doctrines of the Metempsychosis. Of the doctrines themselves—that is, of their falsity, or of their probability—I say nothing. I assert, however, that much of our incredulity—as La Bruy?re says of all our unhappiness—"vient de ne pouvoir ?tre seuls." {*1}

But there are some points in the Hungarian superstition which were fast verging to absurdity. They—the Hungarians—differed very essentially from their Eastern authorities. For example, "The soul," said the former—I give the words of an acute and intelligent Parisian—"ne demeure qu'un seul fois dans un corps sensible: au reste—un cheval, un chien, un homme m?me, n'est que la ressemblance peu tangible de ces animaux."

The families of Berlifitzing and Metzengerstein had been at variance for centuries. Never before were two houses so illustrious, mutually embittered by hostility so deadly. The origin of this enmity seems to be found in the words of an ancient prophecy—"A lofty name shall have a fearful fall when, as the rider over his horse, the mortality of Metzengerstein shall triumph over the immortality of Berlifitzing."

To be sure the words themselves had little or no meaning. But more trivial causes have given rise—and that no long while ago—to consequences equally eventful. Besides, the estates, which were contiguous, had long exercised a rival influence in the affairs of a busy government. Moreover, near neighbors are seldom friends; and the inhabitants of the Castle Berlifitzing might look, from their lofty buttresses, into the very windows of the palace Metzengerstein. Least of all had the more than feudal magnificence, thus discovered, a tendency to allay the irritable feelings of the less ancient and less wealthy Berlifitzings. What wonder then, that the words, however silly, of that prediction, should have succeeded in setting and keeping at variance two families already predisposed to quarrel by every instigation of hereditary jealousy? The prophecy seemed to imply—if it implied anything—a final triumph on the part of the already more powerful house; and was of course remembered with the more bitter animosity by the weaker and less influential.

Wilhelm, Count Berlifitzing, although loftily descended, was, at the epoch of this narrative, an infirm and doting old man, remarkable for nothing but an inordinate and inveterate personal antipathy to the family of his rival, and so passionate a love of horses, and of hunting, that neither bodily infirmity, great age, nor mental incapacity, prevented his daily participation in the dangers of the chase.

Frederick, Baron Metzengerstein, was, on the other hand, not yet of age. His father, the Minister G—, died young. His mother, the Lady Mary, followed him quickly after. Frederick was, at that time, in his fifteenth year. In a city, fifteen years are no long period—a child may be still a child in his third lustrum: but in a wilderness—in so magnificent a wilderness as that old principality, fifteen years have a far deeper meaning.

From some peculiar circumstances attending the administration of his father, the young Baron, at the decease of the former, entered immediately upon his vast possessions. Such estates were seldom held before by a nobleman of Hungary. His castles were without number. The chief in point of splendor and extent was the "Ch?teau Metzengerstein." The boundary line of his dominions was never clearly defined; but his principal park embraced a circuit of fifty miles.

Upon the succession of a proprietor so young, with a character so well known, to a fortune so unparalleled, little speculation was afloat in regard to his probable course of conduct. And, indeed, for the space of three days, the behavior of the heir out-heroded Herod, and fairly surpassed the expectations of his most enthusiastic admirers. Shameful debaucheries— flagrant treacheries—unheard-of atrocities—gave his trembling vassals quickly to understand that no servile submission on their part—no punctilios of conscience on his own—were thenceforward to prove any security against the remorseless fangs of a petty Caligula. On the night of the fourth day, the stables of the castle Berlifitzing were discovered to be on fire; and the unanimous opinion of the neighborhood added the crime of the incendiary to the already hideous list of the Baron's misdemeanors and enormities.

But during the tumult occasioned by this occurrence, the young nobleman himself sat apparently buried in meditation, in a vast and desolate upper apartment of the family palace of Metzengerstein. The rich although faded tapestry hangings which swung gloomily upon the walls, represented the shadowy and majestic forms of a thousand illustrious ancestors. Here, rich-ermined priests, and pontifical dignitaries, familiarly seated with the autocrat and the sovereign, put a veto on the wishes of a temporal king, or restrained with the fiat of papal supremacy the rebellious sceptre of the Arch-enemy. There, the dark, tall statures of the Princes Metzengerstein—their muscular war-coursers plunging over the carcasses of fallen foes—startled the steadiest nerves with their vigorous expression; and here, again, the voluptuous and swan-like figures of the dames of days gone by, floated away in the mazes of an unreal dance to the strains of imaginary melody.

But as the Baron listened, or affected to listen, to the gradually increasing uproar in the stables of Berlifitzing—or perhaps pondered upon some more novel, some more decided act of audacity—his eyes became unwittingly rivetted to the figure of an enormous, and unnaturally colored horse, represented in the tapestry as belonging to a Saracen ancestor of the family of his rival. The horse itself, in the foreground of the design, stood motionless and statue-like—while farther back, its discomfited rider perished by the dagger of a Metzengerstein.

On Frederick's lip arose a fiendish expression, as he became aware of the direction which his glance had, without his consciousness, assumed. Yet he did not remove it. On the contrary, he could by no means account for the overwhelming anxiety which appeared falling like a pall upon his senses. It was with difficulty that he reconciled his dreamy and incoherent feelings with the certainty of being awake. The longer he gazed the more absorbing became the spell—the more impossible did it appear that he could ever withdraw his glance from the fascination of that tapestry. But the tumult without becoming suddenly more violent, with a compulsory exertion he diverted his attention to the glare of ruddy light thrown full by the flaming stables upon the windows of the apartment.

The action, however, was but momentary, his gaze returned mechanically to the wall. To his extreme horror and astonishment, the head of the gigantic steed had, in the meantime, altered its position. The neck of the animal, before arched, as if in compassion, over the prostrate body of its lord, was now extended, at full length, in the direction of the Baron. The eyes, before invisible, now wore an energetic and human expression, while they gleamed with a fiery and unusual red; and the distended lips of the apparently enraged horse left in full view his gigantic and disgusting teeth.

Stupified with terror, the young nobleman tottered to the door. As he threw it open, a flash of red light, streaming far into the chamber, flung his shadow with a clear outline against the quivering tapestry, and he shuddered to perceive that shadow—as he staggered awhile upon the threshold—assuming the exact position, and precisely filling up the contour, of the relentless and triumphant murderer of the Saracen Berlifitzing.

To lighten the depression of his spirits, the Baron hurried into the open air. At the principal gate of the palace he encountered three equerries. With much difficulty, and at the imminent peril of their lives, they were restraining the convulsive plunges of a gigantic and fiery-colored horse.

"Whose horse? Where did you get him?" demanded the youth, in a querulous and husky tone of voice, as he became instantly aware that the mysterious steed in the tapestried chamber was the very counterpart of the furious animal before his eyes.

"He is your own property, sire," replied one of the equerries, "at least he is claimed by no other owner. We caught him flying, all smoking and foaming with rage, from the burning stables of the Castle Berlifitzing. Supposing him to have belonged to the old Count's stud of foreign horses, we led him back as an estray. But the grooms there disclaim any title to the creature; which is strange, since he bears evident marks of having made a narrow escape from the flames.

"The letters W. V. B. are also branded very distinctly on his forehead," interrupted a second equerry, "I supposed them, of course, to be the initials of Wilhelm Von Berlifitzing—but all at the castle are positive in denying any knowledge of the horse."

"Extremely singular!" said the young Baron, with a musing air, and apparently unconscious of the meaning of his words. "He is, as you say, a remarkable horse—a prodigious horse! although, as you very justly observe, of a suspicious and untractable character, let him be mine, however," he added, after a pause, "perhaps a rider like Frederick of Metzengerstein, may tame even the devil from the stables of Berlifitzing."

"You are mistaken, my lord; the horse, as I think we mentioned, is not from the stables of the Count. If such had been the case, we know our duty better than to bring him into the presence of a noble of your family."

"True!" observed the Baron, dryly, and at that instant a page of the bedchamber came from the palace with a heightened color, and a precipitate step. He whispered into his master's ear an account of the sudden disappearance of a small portion of the tapestry, in an apartment which he designated; entering, at the same time, into particulars of a minute and circumstantial character; but from the low tone of voice in which these latter were communicated, nothing escaped to gratify the excited curiosity of the equerries.

The young Frederick, during the conference, seemed agitated by a variety of emotions. He soon, however, recovered his composure, and an expression of determined malignancy settled upon his countenance, as he gave peremptory orders that a certain chamber should be immediately locked up, and the key placed in his own possession.

"Have you heard of the unhappy death of the old hunter Berlifitzing?" said one of his vassals to the Baron, as, after the departure of the page, the huge steed which that nobleman had adopted as his own, plunged and curvetted, with redoubled fury, down the long avenue which extended from the chateau to the stables of Metzengerstein.

"No!" said the Baron, turning abruptly toward the speaker, "dead! say you?"

"It is indeed true, my lord; and, to a noble of your name, will be, I imagine, no unwelcome intelligence."

A rapid smile shot over the countenance of the listener. "How died he?"

"In his rash exertions to rescue a favorite portion of his hunting stud, he has himself perished miserably in the flames."

"I-n-d-e-e-d-!" ejaculated the Baron, as if slowly and deliberately impressed with the truth of some exciting idea.

"Indeed;" repeated the vassal.

"Shocking!" said the youth, calmly, and turned quietly into the chateau.

From this date a marked alteration took place in the outward demeanor of the dissolute young Baron Frederick Von Metzengerstein. Indeed, his behavior disappointed every expectation, and proved little in accordance with the views of many a manoeuvering mamma; while his habits and manner, still less than formerly, offered any thing congenial with those of the neighboring aristocracy. He was never to be seen beyond the limits of his own domain, and, in this wide and social world, was utterly companionless—unless, indeed, that unnatural, impetuous, and fiery-colored horse, which he henceforward continually bestrode, had any mysterious right to the title of his friend.

Numerous invitations on the part of the neighborhood for a long time, however, periodically came in. "Will the Baron honor our festivals with his presence?" "Will the Baron join us in a hunting of the boar?"—"Metzengerstein does not hunt;" "Metzengerstein will not attend," were the haughty and laconic answers.

These repeated insults were not to be endured by an imperious nobility. Such invitations became less cordial—less frequent—in time they ceased altogether. The widow of the unfortunate Count Berlifitzing was even heard to express a hope "that the Baron might be at home when he did not wish to be at home, since he disdained the company of his equals; and ride when he did not wish to ride, since he preferred the society of a horse." This to be sure was a very silly explosion of hereditary pique; and merely proved how singularly unmeaning our sayings are apt to become, when we desire to be unusually energetic.

The charitable, nevertheless, attributed the alteration in the conduct of the young nobleman to the natural sorrow of a son for the untimely loss of his parents—forgetting, however, his atrocious and reckless behavior during the short period immediately succeeding that bereavement. Some there were, indeed, who suggested a too haughty idea of self-consequence and dignity. Others again (among them may be mentioned the family physician) did not hesitate in speaking of morbid melancholy, and hereditary ill-health; while dark hints, of a more equivocal nature, were current among the multitude.

Indeed, the Baron's perverse attachment to his lately-acquired charger—an attachment which seemed to attain new strength from every fresh example of the animal's ferocious and demon-like propensities—at length became, in the eyes of all reasonable men, a hideous and unnatural fervor. In the glare of noon—at the dead hour of night—in sickness or in health—in calm or in tempest—the young Metzengerstein seemed rivetted to the saddle of that colossal horse, whose intractable audacities so well accorded with his own spirit.

There were circumstances, moreover, which coupled with late events, gave an unearthly and portentous character to the mania of the rider, and to the capabilities of the steed. The space passed over in a single leap had been accurately measured, and was found to exceed, by an astounding difference, the wildest expectations of the most imaginative. The Baron, besides, had no particular name for the animal, although all the rest in his collection were distinguished by characteristic appellations. His stable, too, was appointed at a distance from the rest; and with regard to grooming and other necessary offices, none but the owner in person had ventured to officiate, or even to enter the enclosure of that particular stall. It was also to be observed, that although the three grooms, who had caught the steed as he fled from the conflagration at Berlifitzing, had succeeded in arresting his course, by means of a chain-bridle and noose—yet no one of the three could with any certainty affirm that he had, during that dangerous struggle, or at any period thereafter, actually placed his hand upon the body of the beast. Instances of peculiar intelligence in the demeanor of a noble and high-spirited horse are not to be supposed capable of exciting unreasonable attention—especially among men who, daily trained to the labors of the chase, might appear well acquainted with the sagacity of a horse—but there were certain circumstances which intruded themselves per force upon the most skeptical and phlegmatic; and it is said there were times when the animal caused the gaping crowd who stood around to recoil in horror from the deep and impressive meaning of his terrible stamp—times when the young Metzengerstein turned pale and shrunk away from the rapid and searching expression of his earnest and human-looking eye.

Among all the retinue of the Baron, however, none were found to doubt the ardor of that extraordinary affection which existed on the part of the young nobleman for the fiery qualities of his horse; at least, none but an insignificant and misshapen little page, whose deformities were in everybody's way, and whose opinions were of the least possible importance. He—if his ideas are worth mentioning at all—had the effrontery to assert that his master never vaulted into the saddle without an unaccountable and almost imperceptible shudder, and that, upon his return from every long-continued and habitual ride, an expression of triumphant malignity distorted every muscle in his countenance.

One tempestuous night, Metzengerstein, awaking from a heavy slumber, descended like a maniac from his chamber, and, mounting in hot haste, bounded away into the mazes of the forest. An occurrence so common attracted no particular attention, but his return was looked for with intense anxiety on the part of his domestics, when, after some hours' absence, the stupendous and magnificent battlements of the Chateau Metzengerstein, were discovered crackling and rocking to their very foundation, under the influence of a dense and livid mass of ungovernable fire.

As the flames, when first seen, had already made so terrible a progress that all efforts to save any portion of the building were evidently futile, the astonished neighborhood stood idly around in silent and pathetic wonder. But a new and fearful object soon rivetted the attention of the multitude, and proved how much more intense is the excitement wrought in the feelings of a crowd by the contemplation of human agony, than that brought about by the most appalling spectacles of inanimate matter.

Up the long avenue of aged oaks which led from the forest to the main entrance of the Ch?teau Metzengerstein, a steed, bearing an unbonneted and disordered rider, was seen leaping with an impetuosity which outstripped the very Demon of the Tempest.

The career of the horseman was indisputably, on his own part, uncontrollable. The agony of his countenance, the convulsive struggle of his frame, gave evidence of superhuman exertion: but no sound, save a solitary shriek, escaped from his lacerated lips, which were bitten through and through in the intensity of terror. One instant, and the clattering of hoofs resounded sharply and shrilly above the roaring of the flames and the shrieking of the winds—another, and, clearing at a single plunge the gate-way and the moat, the steed bounded far up the tottering staircases of the palace, and, with its rider, disappeared amid the whirlwind of chaotic fire.

The fury of the tempest immediately died away, and a dead calm sullenly succeeded. A white flame still enveloped the building like a shroud, and, streaming far away into the quiet atmosphere, shot forth a glare of preternatural light; while a cloud of smoke settled heavily over the battlements in the distinct colossal figure of—a horse.

THE SYSTEM OF DOCTOR TARR AND PROFESSOR FETHER

DURING the autumn of 18—, while on a tour through the extreme southern provinces of France, my route led me within a few miles of a certain Maison de Sante or private mad-house, about which I had heard much in Paris from my medical friends. As I had never visited a place of the kind, I thought the opportunity too good to be lost; and so proposed to my travelling companion (a gentleman with whom I had made casual acquaintance a few days before) that we should turn aside, for an hour or so, and look through the establishment. To this he objected—pleading haste in the first place, and, in the second, a very usual horror at the sight of a lunatic. He begged me, however, not to let any mere courtesy towards himself interfere with the gratification of my curiosity, and said that he would ride on leisurely, so that I might overtake him during the day, or, at all events, during the next. As he bade me good-bye, I bethought me that there might be some difficulty in obtaining access to the premises, and mentioned my fears on this point. He replied that, in fact, unless I had personal knowledge of the superintendent, Monsieur Maillard, or some credential in the way of a letter, a difficulty might be found to exist, as the regulations of these private mad-houses were more rigid than the public hospital laws. For himself, he added, he had, some years since, made the acquaintance of Maillard, and would so far assist me as to ride up to the door and introduce me; although his feelings on the subject of lunacy would not permit of his entering the house.

I thanked him, and, turning from the main road, we entered a grass-grown by-path, which, in half an hour, nearly lost itself in a dense forest, clothing the base of a mountain. Through this dank and gloomy wood we rode some two miles, when the Maison de Sante came in view. It was a fantastic chateau, much dilapidated, and indeed scarcely tenantable through age and neglect. Its aspect inspired me with absolute dread, and, checking my horse, I half resolved to turn back. I soon, however, grew ashamed of my weakness, and proceeded.

As we rode up to the gate-way, I perceived it slightly open, and the visage of a man peering through. In an instant afterward, this man came forth, accosted my companion by name, shook him cordially by the hand, and begged him to alight. It was Monsieur Maillard himself. He was a portly, fine-looking gentleman of the old school, with a polished manner, and a certain air of gravity, dignity, and authority which was very impressive.

My friend, having presented me, mentioned my desire to inspect the establishment, and received Monsieur Maillard's assurance that he would show me all attention, now took leave, and I saw him no more.

When he had gone, the superintendent ushered me into a small and exceedingly neat parlor, containing, among other indications of refined taste, many books, drawings, pots of flowers, and musical instruments. A cheerful fire blazed upon the hearth. At a piano, singing an aria from Bellini, sat a young and very beautiful woman, who, at my entrance, paused in her song, and received me with graceful courtesy. Her voice was low, and her whole manner subdued. I thought, too, that I perceived the traces of sorrow in her countenance, which was excessively, although to my taste, not unpleasingly, pale. She was attired in deep mourning, and excited in my bosom a feeling of mingled respect, interest, and admiration.

I had heard, at Paris, that the institution of Monsieur Maillard was managed upon what is vulgarly termed the "system of soothing"—that all punishments were avoided—that even confinement was seldom resorted to—that the patients, while secretly watched, were left much apparent liberty, and that most of them were permitted to roam about the house and grounds in the ordinary apparel of persons in right mind.

Keeping these impressions in view, I was cautious in what I said before the young lady; for I could not be sure that she was sane; and, in fact, there was a certain restless brilliancy about her eyes which half led me to imagine she was not. I confined my remarks, therefore, to general topics, and to such as I thought would not be displeasing or exciting even to a lunatic. She replied in a perfectly rational manner to all that I said; and even her original observations were marked with the soundest good sense, but a long acquaintance with the metaphysics of mania, had taught me to put no faith in such evidence of sanity, and I continued to practise, throughout the interview, the caution with which I commenced it.

Presently a smart footman in livery brought in a tray with fruit, wine, and other refreshments, of which I partook, the lady soon afterward leaving the room. As she departed I turned my eyes in an inquiring manner toward my host.

"No," he said, "oh, no—a member of my family—my niece, and a most accomplished woman."

"I beg a thousand pardons for the suspicion," I replied, "but of course you will know how to excuse me. The excellent administration of your affairs here is well understood in Paris, and I thought it just possible, you know—

"Yes, yes—say no more—or rather it is myself who should thank you for the commendable prudence you have displayed. We seldom find so much of forethought in young men; and, more than once, some unhappy contretemps has occurred in consequence of thoughtlessness on the part of our visitors. While my former system was in operation, and my patients were permitted the privilege of roaming to and fro at will, they were often aroused to a dangerous frenzy by injudicious persons who called to inspect the house. Hence I was obliged to enforce a rigid system of exclusion; and none obtained access to the premises upon whose discretion I could not rely."

"While your former system was in operation!" I said, repeating his words—"do I understand you, then, to say that the 'soothing system' of which I have heard so much is no longer in force?"

"It is now," he replied, "several weeks since we have concluded to renounce it forever."

"Indeed! you astonish me!"

"We found it, sir," he said, with a sigh, "absolutely necessary to return to the old usages. The danger of the soothing system was, at all times, appalling; and its advantages have been much overrated. I believe, sir, that in this house it has been given a fair trial, if ever in any. We did every thing that rational humanity could suggest. I am sorry that you could not have paid us a visit at an earlier period, that you might have judged for yourself. But I presume you are conversant with the soothing practice—with its details."

"Not altogether. What I have heard has been at third or fourth hand."

"I may state the system, then, in general terms, as one in which the patients were menages-humored. We contradicted no fancies which entered the brains of the mad. On the contrary, we not only indulged but encouraged them; and many of our most permanent cures have been thus effected. There is no argument which so touches the feeble reason of the madman as the argumentum ad absurdum. We have had men, for example, who fancied themselves chickens. The cure was, to insist upon the thing as a fact—to accuse the patient of stupidity in not sufficiently perceiving it to be a fact—and thus to refuse him any other diet for a week than that which properly appertains to a chicken. In this manner a little corn and gravel were made to perform wonders."

"But was this species of acquiescence all?"

"By no means. We put much faith in amusements of a simple kind, such as music, dancing, gymnastic exercises generally, cards, certain classes of books, and so forth. We affected to treat each individual as if for some ordinary physical disorder, and the word 'lunacy' was never employed. A great point was to set each lunatic to guard the actions of all the others. To repose confidence in the understanding or discretion of a madman, is to gain him body and soul. In this way we were enabled to dispens? with an expensive body of keepers."

"And you had no punishments of any kind?"

"None."

"And you never confined your patients?"

"Very rarely. Now and then, the malady of some individual growing to a crisis, or taking a sudden turn of fury, we conveyed him to a secret cell, lest his disorder should infect the rest, and there kept him until we could dismiss him to his friends—for with the raging maniac we have nothing to do. He is usually removed to the public hospitals."

"And you have now changed all this—and you think for the better?"

"Decidedly. The system had its disadvantages, and even its dangers. It is now, happily, exploded throughout all the Maisons de Sante of France."

"I am very much surprised," I said, "at what you tell me; for I made sure that, at this moment, no other method of treatment for mania existed in any portion of the country."

"You are young yet, my friend," replied my host, "but the time will arrive when you will learn to judge for yourself of what is going on in the world, without trusting to the gossip of others. Believe nothing you hear, and only one-half that you see. Now about our Maisons de Sante, it is clear that some ignoramus has misled you. After dinner, however, when you have sufficiently recovered from the fatigue of your ride, I will be happy to take you over the house, and introduce to you a system which, in my opinion, and in that of every one who has witnessed its operation, is incomparably the most effectual as yet devised."

"Your own?" I inquired—"one of your own invention?"

"I am proud," he replied, "to acknowledge that it is—at least in some measure."

In this manner I conversed with Monsieur Maillard for an hour or two, during which he showed me the gardens and conservatories of the place.

"I cannot let you see my patients," he said, "just at present. To a sensitive mind there is always more or less of the shocking in such exhibitions; and I do not wish to spoil your appetite for dinner. We will dine. I can give you some veal a la Menehoult, with cauliflowers in veloute sauce—after that a glass of Clos de Vougeot—then your nerves will be sufficiently steadied."

At six, dinner was announced; and my host conducted me into a large salle a manger, where a very numerous company were assembled—twenty-five or thirty in all. They were, apparently, people of rank-certainly of high breeding—although their habiliments, I thought, were extravagantly rich, partaking somewhat too much of the ostentatious finery of the vielle cour. I noticed that at least two-thirds of these guests were ladies; and some of the latter were by no means accoutred in what a Parisian would consider good taste at the present day. Many females, for example, whose age could not have been less than seventy were bedecked with a profusion of jewelry, such as rings, bracelets, and earrings, and wore their bosoms and arms shamefully bare. I observed, too, that very few of the dresses were well made—or, at least, that very few of them fitted the wearers. In looking about, I discovered the interesting girl to whom Monsieur Maillard had presented me in the little parlor; but my surprise was great to see her wearing a hoop and farthingale, with high-heeled shoes, and a dirty cap of Brussels lace, so much too large for her that it gave her face a ridiculously diminutive expression. When I had first seen her, she was attired, most becomingly, in deep mourning. There was an air of oddity, in short, about the dress of the whole party, which, at first, caused me to recur to my original idea of the "soothing system," and to fancy that Monsieur Maillard had been willing to deceive me until after dinner, that I might experience no uncomfortable feelings during the repast, at finding myself dining with lunatics; but I remembered having been informed, in Paris, that the southern provincialists were a peculiarly eccentric people, with a vast number of antiquated notions; and then, too, upon conversing with several members of the company, my apprehensions were immediately and fully dispelled.

The dining-room itself, although perhaps sufficiently comfortable and of good dimensions, had nothing too much of elegance about it. For example, the floor was uncarpeted; in France, however, a carpet is frequently dispensed with. The windows, too, were without curtains; the shutters, being shut, were securely fastened with iron bars, applied diagonally, after the fashion of our ordinary shop-shutters. The apartment, I observed, formed, in itself, a wing of the chateau, and thus the windows were on three sides of the parallelogram, the door being at the other. There were no less than ten windows in all.

The table was superbly set out. It was loaded with plate, and more than loaded with delicacies. The profusion was absolutely barbaric. There were meats enough to have feasted the Anakim. Never, in all my life, had I witnessed so lavish, so wasteful an expenditure of the good things of life. There seemed very little taste, however, in the arrangements; and my eyes, accustomed to quiet lights, were sadly offended by the prodigious glare of a multitude of wax candles, which, in silver candelabra, were deposited upon the table, and all about the room, wherever it was possible to find a place. There were several active servants in attendance; and, upon a large table, at the farther end of the apartment, were seated seven or eight people with fiddles, fifes, trombones, and a drum. These fellows annoyed me very much, at intervals, during the repast, by an infinite variety of noises, which were intended for music, and which appeared to afford much entertainment to all present, with the exception of myself.

Upon the whole, I could not help thinking that there was much of the bizarre about every thing I saw—but then the world is made up of all kinds of persons, with all modes of thought, and all sorts of conventional customs. I had travelled, too, so much, as to be quite an adept at the nil admirari; so I took my seat very coolly at the right hand of my host, and, having an excellent appetite, did justice to the good cheer set before me.

The conversation, in the meantime, was spirited and general. The ladies, as usual, talked a great deal. I soon found that nearly all the company were well educated; and my host was a world of good-humored anecdote in himself. He seemed quite willing to speak of his position as superintendent of a Maison de Sante; and, indeed, the topic of lunacy was, much to my surprise, a favorite one with all present. A great many amusing stories were told, having reference to the whims of the patients.

"We had a fellow here once," said a fat little gentleman, who sat at my right,—"a fellow that fancied himself a tea-pot; and by the way, is it not especially singular how often this particular crotchet has entered the brain of the lunatic? There is scarcely an insane asylum in France which cannot supply a human tea-pot. Our gentleman was a Britannia—ware tea-pot, and was careful to polish himself every morning with buckskin and whiting."

"And then," said a tall man just opposite, "we had here, not long ago, a person who had taken it into his head that he was a donkey—which allegorically speaking, you will say, was quite true. He was a troublesome patient; and we had much ado to keep him within bounds. For a long time he would eat nothing but thistles; but of this idea we soon cured him by insisting upon his eating nothing else. Then he was perpetually kicking out his heels-so-so-"

"Mr. De Kock! I will thank you to behave yourself!" here interrupted an old lady, who sat next to the speaker. "Please keep your feet to yourself! You have spoiled my brocade! Is it necessary, pray, to illustrate a remark in so practical a style? Our friend here can surely comprehend you without all this. Upon my word, you are nearly as great a donkey as the poor unfortunate imagined himself. Your acting is very natural, as I live."

"Mille pardons! Ma'm'selle!" replied Monsieur De Kock, thus addressed—"a thousand pardons! I had no intention of offending. Ma'm'selle Laplace—Monsieur De Kock will do himself the honor of taking wine with you."

Here Monsieur De Kock bowed low, kissed his hand with much ceremony, and took wine with Ma'm'selle Laplace.

"Allow me, mon ami," now said Monsieur Maillard, addressing myself, "allow me to send you a morsel of this veal a la St. Menhoult—you will find it particularly fine."

At this instant three sturdy waiters had just succeeded in depositing safely upon the table an enormous dish, or trencher, containing what I supposed to be the "monstrum horrendum, informe, ingens, cui lumen ademptum." A closer scrutiny assured me, however, that it was only a small calf roasted whole, and set upon its knees, with an apple in its mouth, as is the English fashion of dressing a hare.

"Thank you, no," I replied; "to say the truth, I am not particularly partial to veal a la St.—what is it?—for I do not find that it altogether agrees with me. I will change my plate, however, and try some of the rabbit."

There were several side-dishes on the table, containing what appeared to be the ordinary French rabbit—a very delicious morceau, which I can recommend.

"Pierre," cried the host, "change this gentleman's plate, and give him a side-piece of this rabbit au-chat."

"This what?" said I.

"This rabbit au-chat."

"Why, thank you—upon second thoughts, no. I will just help myself to some of the ham."

There is no knowing what one eats, thought I to myself, at the tables of these people of the province. I will have none of their rabbit au-chat—and, for the matter of that, none of their cat-au-rabbit either.

"And then," said a cadaverous looking personage, near the foot of the table, taking up the thread of the conversation where it had been broken off,—"and then, among other oddities, we had a patient, once upon a time, who very pertinaciously maintained himself to be a Cordova cheese, and went about, with a knife in his hand, soliciting his friends to try a small slice from the middle of his leg."

"He was a great fool, beyond doubt," interposed some one, "but not to be compared with a certain individual whom we all know, with the exception of this strange gentleman. I mean the man who took himself for a bottle of champagne, and always went off with a pop and a fizz, in this fashion."

Here the speaker, very rudely, as I thought, put his right thumb in his left cheek, withdrew it with a sound resembling the popping of a cork, and then, by a dexterous movement of the tongue upon the teeth, created a sharp hissing and fizzing, which lasted for several minutes, in imitation of the frothing of champagne. This behavior, I saw plainly, was not very pleasing to Monsieur Maillard; but that gentleman said nothing, and the conversation was resumed by a very lean little man in a big wig.

"And then there was an ignoramus," said he, "who mistook himself for a frog, which, by the way, he resembled in no little degree. I wish you could have seen him, sir,"—here the speaker addressed myself—"it would have done your heart good to see the natural airs that he put on. Sir, if that man was not a frog, I can only observe that it is a pity he was not. His croak thus—o-o-o-o-gh—o-o-o-o-gh! was the finest note in the world—B flat; and when he put his elbows upon the table thus—after taking a glass or two of wine—and distended his mouth, thus, and rolled up his eyes, thus, and winked them with excessive rapidity, thus, why then, sir, I take it upon myself to say, positively, that you would have been lost in admiration of the genius of the man."

"I have no doubt of it," I said.

"And then," said somebody else, "then there was Petit Gaillard, who thought himself a pinch of snuff, and was truly distressed because he could not take himself between his own finger and thumb."

"And then there was Jules Desoulieres, who was a very singular genius, indeed, and went mad with the idea that he was a pumpkin. He persecuted the cook to make him up into pies—a thing which the cook indignantly refused to do. For my part, I am by no means sure that a pumpkin pie a la Desoulieres would not have been very capital eating indeed!"

"You astonish me!" said I; and I looked inquisitively at Monsieur Maillard.

"Ha! ha! ha!" said that gentleman—"he! he! he!—hi! hi! hi!—ho! ho! ho!—hu! hu! hu! hu!—very good indeed! You must not be astonished, mon ami; our friend here is a wit—a drole—you must not understand him to the letter."

"And then," said some other one of the party,—"then there was Bouffon Le Grand—another extraordinary personage in his way. He grew deranged through love, and fancied himself possessed of two heads. One of these he maintained to be the head of Cicero; the other he imagined a composite one, being Demosthenes' from the top of the forehead to the mouth, and Lord Brougham's from the mouth to the chin. It is not impossible that he was wrong; but he would have convinced you of his being in the right; for he was a man of great eloquence. He had an absolute passion for oratory, and could not refrain from display. For example, he used to leap upon the dinner-table thus, and—and-"

Here a friend, at the side of the speaker, put a hand upon his shoulder and whispered a few words in his ear, upon which he ceased talking with great suddenness, and sank back within his chair.

"And then," said the friend who had whispered, "there was Boullard, the tee-totum. I call him the tee-totum because, in fact, he was seized with the droll but not altogether irrational crotchet, that he had been converted into a tee-totum. You would have roared with laughter to see him spin. He would turn round upon one heel by the hour, in this manner—so—"

Here the friend whom he had just interrupted by a whisper, performed an exactly similar office for himself.

"But then," cried the old lady, at the top of her voice, "your Monsieur Boullard was a madman, and a very silly madman at best; for who, allow me to ask you, ever heard of a human tee-totum? The thing is absurd. Madame Joyeuse was a more sensible person, as you know. She had a crotchet, but it was instinct with common sense, and gave pleasure to all who had the honor of her acquaintance. She found, upon mature deliberation, that, by some accident, she had been turned into a chicken-cock; but, as such, she behaved with propriety. She flapped her wings with prodigious effect—so—so—and, as for her crow, it was delicious!

Cock-a-doodle-doo!—cock-a-doodle-doo!—cock-a-doodle-de-doo dooo-do-o-o-o-o-o-o!"

"Madame Joyeuse, I will thank you to behave yourself!" here interrupted our host, very angrily. "You can either conduct yourself as a lady should do, or you can quit the table forthwith-take your choice."

The lady (whom I was much astonished to hear addressed as Madame Joyeuse, after the description of Madame Joyeuse she had just given) blushed up to the eyebrows, and seemed exceedingly abashed at the reproof. She hung down her head, and said not a syllable in reply. But another and younger lady resumed the theme. It was my beautiful girl of the little parlor.

"Oh, Madame Joyeuse was a fool!" she exclaimed, "but there was really much sound sense, after all, in the opinion of Eugenie Salsafette. She was a very beautiful and painfully modest young lady, who thought the ordinary mode of habiliment indecent, and wished to dress herself, always, by getting outside instead of inside of her clothes. It is a thing very easily done, after all. You have only to do so—and then so—so—so—and then so—so—so—and then so—so—and then—

"Mon dieu! Ma'm'selle Salsafette!" here cried a dozen voices at once. "What are you about?—forbear!—that is sufficient!—we see, very plainly, how it is done!—hold! hold!" and several persons were already leaping from their seats to withhold Ma'm'selle Salsafette from putting herself upon a par with the Medicean Venus, when the point was very effectually and suddenly accomplished by a series of loud screams, or yells, from some portion of the main body of the chateau.

My nerves were very much affected, indeed, by these yells; but the rest of the company I really pitied. I never saw any set of reasonable people so thoroughly frightened in my life. They all grew as pale as so many corpses, and, shrinking within their seats, sat quivering and gibbering with terror, and listening for a repetition of the sound. It came again—louder and seemingly nearer—and then a third time very loud, and then a fourth time with a vigor evidently diminished. At this apparent dying away of the noise, the spirits of the company were immediately regained, and all was life and anecdote as before. I now ventured to inquire the cause of the disturbance.

"A mere bagtelle," said Monsieur Maillard. "We are used to these things, and care really very little about them. The lunatics, every now and then, get up a howl in concert; one starting another, as is sometimes the case with a bevy of dogs at night. It occasionally happens, however, that the concerto yells are succeeded by a simultaneous effort at breaking loose, when, of course, some little danger is to be apprehended."

"And how many have you in charge?"

"At present we have not more than ten, altogether."

"Principally females, I presume?"

"Oh, no—every one of them men, and stout fellows, too, I can tell you."

"Indeed! I have always understood that the majority of lunatics were of the gentler sex."

"It is generally so, but not always. Some time ago, there were about twenty-seven patients here; and, of that number, no less than eighteen were women; but, lately, matters have changed very much, as you see."

"Yes—have changed very much, as you see," here interrupted the gentleman who had broken the shins of Ma'm'selle Laplace.

"Yes—have changed very much, as you see!" chimed in the whole company at once.

"Hold your tongues, every one of you!" said my host, in a great rage. Whereupon the whole company maintained a dead silence for nearly a minute. As for one lady, she obeyed Monsieur Maillard to the letter, and thrusting out her tongue, which was an excessively long one, held it very resignedly, with both hands, until the end of the entertainment.

"And this gentlewoman," said I, to Monsieur Maillard, bending over and addressing him in a whisper—"this good lady who has just spoken, and who gives us the cock-a-doodle-de-doo—she, I presume, is harmless—quite harmless, eh?"

"Harmless!" ejaculated he, in unfeigned surprise, "why—why, what can you mean?"

"Only slightly touched?" said I, touching my head. "I take it for granted that she is not particularly not dangerously affected, eh?"

"Mon dieu! what is it you imagine? This lady, my particular old friend Madame Joyeuse, is as absolutely sane as myself. She has her little eccentricities, to be sure—but then, you know, all old women—all very old women—are more or less eccentric!"

"To be sure," said I,—"to be sure—and then the rest of these ladies and gentlemen-"

"Are my friends and keepers," interupted Monsieur Maillard, drawing himself up with hauteur,—"my very good friends and assistants."

"What! all of them?" I asked,—"the women and all?"

"Assuredly," he said,—"we could not do at all without the women; they are the best lunatic nurses in the world; they have a way of their own, you know; their bright eyes have a marvellous effect;—something like the fascination of the snake, you know."

"To be sure," said I,—"to be sure! They behave a little odd, eh?—they are a little queer, eh?—don't you think so?"

"Odd!—queer!—why, do you really think so? We are not very prudish, to be sure, here in the South—do pretty much as we please—enjoy life, and all that sort of thing, you know-"

"To be sure," said I,—"to be sure."

"And then, perhaps, this Clos de Vougeot is a little heady, you know—a little strong—you understand, eh?"

"To be sure," said I,—"to be sure. By the bye, Monsieur, did I understand you to say that the system you have adopted, in place of the celebrated soothing system, was one of very rigorous severity?"

"By no means. Our confinement is necessarily close; but the treatment— the medical treatment, I mean—is rather agreeable to the patients than otherwise."

"And the new system is one of your own invention?"

"Not altogether. Some portions of it are referable to Professor Tarr, of whom you have, necessarily, heard; and, again, there are modifications in my plan which I am happy to acknowledge as belonging of right to the celebrated Fether, with whom, if I mistake not, you have the honor of an intimate acquaintance."

"I am quite ashamed to confess," I replied, "that I have never even heard the names of either gentleman before."

"Good heavens!" ejaculated my host, drawing back his chair abruptly, and uplifting his hands. "I surely do not hear you aright! You did not intend to say, eh? that you had never heard either of the learned Doctor Tarr, or of the celebrated Professor Fether?"

"I am forced to acknowledge my ignorance," I replied; "but the truth should be held inviolate above all things. Nevertheless, I feel humbled to the dust, not to be acquainted with the works of these, no doubt, extraordinary men. I will seek out their writings forthwith, and peruse them with deliberate care. Monsieur Maillard, you have really—I must confess it—you have really—made me ashamed of myself!"

And this was the fact.

"Say no more, my good young friend," he said kindly, pressing my hand,—"join me now in a glass of Sauterne."

We drank. The company followed our example without stint. They chatted—they jested—they laughed—they perpetrated a thousand absurdities—the fiddles shrieked—the drum row-de-dowed—the trombones bellowed like so many brazen bulls of Phalaris—and the whole scene, growing gradually worse and worse, as the wines gained the ascendancy, became at length a sort of pandemonium in petto. In the meantime, Monsieur Maillard and myself, with some bottles of Sauterne and Vougeot between us, continued our conversation at the top of the voice. A word spoken in an ordinary key stood no more chance of being heard than the voice of a fish from the bottom of Niagara Falls.

"And, sir," said I, screaming in his ear, "you mentioned something before dinner about the danger incurred in the old system of soothing. How is that?"

"Yes," he replied, "there was, occasionally, very great danger indeed. There is no accounting for the caprices of madmen; and, in my opinion as well as in that of Dr. Tarr and Professor Fether, it is never safe to permit them to run at large unattended. A lunatic may be 'soothed,' as it is called, for a time, but, in the end, he is very apt to become obstreperous. His cunning, too, is proverbial and great. If he has a project in view, he conceals his design with a marvellous wisdom; and the dexterity with which he counterfeits sanity, presents, to the metaphysician, one of the most singular problems in the study of mind. When a madman appears thoroughly sane, indeed, it is high time to put him in a straitjacket."

"But the danger, my dear sir, of which you were speaking, in your own experience—during your control of this house—have you had practical reason to think liberty hazardous in the case of a lunatic?"

"Here?—in my own experience?—why, I may say, yes. For example:—no very long while ago, a singular circumstance occurred in this very house. The 'soothing system,' you know, was then in operation, and the patients were at large. They behaved remarkably well-especially so, any one of sense might have known that some devilish scheme was brewing from that particular fact, that the fellows behaved so remarkably well. And, sure enough, one fine morning the keepers found themselves pinioned hand and foot, and thrown into the cells, where they were attended, as if they were the lunatics, by the lunatics themselves, who had usurped the offices of the keepers."

"You don't tell me so! I never heard of any thing so absurd in my life!"

"Fact—it all came to pass by means of a stupid fellow—a lunatic—who, by some means, had taken it into his head that he had invented a better system of government than any ever heard of before—of lunatic government, I mean. He wished to give his invention a trial, I suppose, and so he persuaded the rest of the patients to join him in a conspiracy for the overthrow of the reigning powers."

"And he really succeeded?"

"No doubt of it. The keepers and kept were soon made to exchange places. Not that exactly either—for the madmen had been free, but the keepers were shut up in cells forthwith, and treated, I am sorry to say, in a very cavalier manner."

"But I presume a counter-revolution was soon effected. This condition of things could not have long existed. The country people in the neighborhood-visitors coming to see the establishment—would have given the alarm."

"There you are out. The head rebel was too cunning for that. He admitted no visitors at all—with the exception, one day, of a very stupid-looking young gentleman of whom he had no reason to be afraid. He let him in to see the place—just by way of variety,—to have a little fun with him. As soon as he had gammoned him sufficiently, he let him out, and sent him about his business."

"And how long, then, did the madmen reign?"

"Oh, a very long time, indeed—a month certainly—how much longer I can't precisely say. In the meantime, the lunatics had a jolly season of it—that you may swear. They doffed their own shabby clothes, and made free with the family wardrobe and jewels. The cellars of the chateau were well stocked with wine; and these madmen are just the devils that know how to drink it. They lived well, I can tell you."

"And the treatment—what was the particular species of treatment which the leader of the rebels put into operation?"

"Why, as for that, a madman is not necessarily a fool, as I have already observed; and it is my honest opinion that his treatment was a much better treatment than that which it superseded. It was a very capital system indeed—simple—neat—no trouble at all—in fact it was delicious it was."

Here my host's observations were cut short by another series of yells, of the same character as those which had previously disconcerted us. This time, however, they seemed to proceed from persons rapidly approaching.

"Gracious heavens!" I ejaculated—"the lunatics have most undoubtedly broken loose."

"I very much fear it is so," replied Monsieur Maillard, now becoming excessively pale. He had scarcely finished the sentence, before loud shouts and imprecations were heard beneath the windows; and, immediately afterward, it became evident that some persons outside were endeavoring to gain entrance into the room. The door was beaten with what appeared to be a sledge-hammer, and the shutters were wrenched and shaken with prodigious violence.

A scene of the most terrible confusion ensued. Monsieur Maillard, to my excessive astonishment threw himself under the side-board. I had expected more resolution at his hands. The members of the orchestra, who, for the last fifteen minutes, had been seemingly too much intoxicated to do duty, now sprang all at once to their feet and to their instruments, and, scrambling upon their table, broke out, with one accord, into, "Yankee Doodle," which they performed, if not exactly in tune, at least with an energy superhuman, during the whole of the uproar.

Meantime, upon the main dining-table, among the bottles and glasses, leaped the gentleman who, with such difficulty, had been restrained from leaping there before. As soon as he fairly settled himself, he commenced an oration, which, no doubt, was a very capital one, if it could only have been heard. At the same moment, the man with the teetotum predilection, set himself to spinning around the apartment, with immense energy, and with arms outstretched at right angles with his body; so that he had all the air of a tee-totum in fact, and knocked everybody down that happened to get in his way. And now, too, hearing an incredible popping and fizzing of champagne, I discovered at length, that it proceeded from the person who performed the bottle of that delicate drink during dinner. And then, again, the frog-man croaked away as if the salvation of his soul depended upon every note that he uttered. And, in the midst of all this, the continuous braying of a donkey arose over all. As for my old friend, Madame Joyeuse, I really could have wept for the poor lady, she appeared so terribly perplexed. All she did, however, was to stand up in a corner, by the fireplace, and sing out incessantly at the top of her voice, "Cock-a-doodle-de-dooooooh!"

And now came the climax—the catastrophe of the drama. As no resistance, beyond whooping and yelling and cock-a-doodling, was offered to the encroachments of the party without, the ten windows were very speedily, and almost simultaneously, broken in. But I shall never forget the emotions of wonder and horror with which I gazed, when, leaping through these windows, and down among us pele-mele, fighting, stamping, scratching, and howling, there rushed a perfect army of what I took to be Chimpanzees, Ourang-Outangs, or big black baboons of the Cape of Good Hope.

I received a terrible beating—after which I rolled under a sofa and lay still. After lying there some fifteen minutes, during which time I listened with all my ears to what was going on in the room, I came to same satisfactory denouement of this tragedy. Monsieur Maillard, it appeared, in giving me the account of the lunatic who had excited his fellows to rebellion, had been merely relating his own exploits. This gentleman had, indeed, some two or three years before, been the superintendent of the establishment, but grew crazy himself, and so became a patient. This fact was unknown to the travelling companion who introduced me. The keepers, ten in number, having been suddenly overpowered, were first well tarred, then—carefully feathered, and then shut up in underground cells. They had been so imprisoned for more than a month, during which period Monsieur Maillard had generously allowed them not only the tar and feathers (which constituted his "system"), but some bread and abundance of water. The latter was pumped on them daily. At length, one escaping through a sewer, gave freedom to all the rest.

The "soothing system," with important modifications, has been resumed at the chateau; yet I cannot help agreeing with Monsieur Maillard, that his own "treatment" was a very capital one of its kind. As he justly observed, it was "simple—neat—and gave no trouble at all—not the least."

I have only to add that, although I have searched every library in Europe for the works of Doctor Tarr and Professor Fether, I have, up to the present day, utterly failed in my endeavors at procuring an edition.

THE LITERARY LIFE OF THINGUM BOB, ESQ.

LATE EDITOR OF THE "GOOSETHERUMFOODLE."

By Himself

I AM now growing in years, and—since I understand that Shakespeare and Mr. Emmons are deceased—it is not impossible that I may even die. It has occurred to me, therefore, that I may as well retire from the field of Letters and repose upon my laurels. But I am ambitious of signalizing my abdication of the literary sceptre by some important bequest to posterity; and, perhaps, I cannot do a better thing than just pen for it an account of my earlier career. My name, indeed, has been so long and so constantly before the public eye, that I am not only willing to admit the naturalness of the interest which it has everywhere excited, but ready to satisfy the extreme curiosity which it has inspired. In fact, it is no more than the duty of him who achieves greatness to leave behind him, in his ascent, such landmarks as may guide others to be great. I propose, therefore, in the present paper, (which I had some idea of calling "Memoranda to serve for the Literary History of America,") to give a detail of those important, yet feeble and tottering first steps, by which, at length, I attained the high road to the pinnacle of human renown.

Of one's very remote ancestors it is superfluous to say much. My father, Thomas Bob, Esq., stood for many years at the summit of his profession, which was that of a merchant-barber, in the city of Smug. His warehouse was the resort of all the principal people of the place, and especially of the editorial corps—a body which inspires all about it with profound veneration and awe. For my own part, I regarded them as gods, and drank in with avidity the rich wit and wisdom which continuously flowed from their august mouths during the process of what is styled "lather." My first moment of positive inspiration must be dated from that ever-memorable epoch, when the brilliant conductor of the "Gad-Fly," in the intervals of the important process just mentioned, recited aloud, before a conclave of our apprentices, an inimitable poem in honor of the "Only Genuine Oil-of-Bob," (so called from its talented inventor, my father,) and for which effusion the editor of the "Fly" was remunerated with a regal liberality by the firm of Thomas Bob and company, merchant-barbers.

The genius of the stanzas to the "Oil-of-Bob" first breathed into me, I say, the divine afflatus. I resolved at once to become a great man and to commence by becoming a great poet. That very evening I fell upon my knees at the feet of my father.

"Father," I said, "pardon me!—but I have a soul above lather. It is my firm intention to cut the shop. I would be an editor—I would be a poet—I would pen stanzas to the 'Oil-of-Bob.' Pardon me and aid me to be great!"

"My dear Thingum," replied my father, (I had been christened Thingum after a wealthy relative so surnamed,) "My dear Thingum," he said, raising me from my knees by the ears—"Thingum, my boy, you're a trump, and take after your father in having a soul. You have an immense head, too, and it must hold a great many brains. This I have long seen, and therefore had thoughts of making you a lawyer. The business, however, has grown ungenteel, and that of a politician don't pay. Upon the whole you judge wisely;—the trade of editor is best:—and if you can be a poet at the same time,—as most of the editors are, by the by,—why you will kill two birds with one stone. To encourage you in the beginning of things, I will allow you a garret; pen, ink and paper; a rhyming dictionary; and a copy of the 'Gad-Fly.' I suppose you would scarcely demand any more."

"I would be an ungrateful villain if I did," I replied with enthusiasm. "Your generosity is boundless. I will repay it by making you the father of a genius."

Thus ended my conference with the best of men, and immediately upon its termination, I betook myself with zeal to my poetical labors; as upon these, chiefly, I founded my hopes of ultimate elevation to the editorial chair.

In my first attempts at composition I found the stanzas to "The Oil-of-Bob" rather a draw-back than otherwise. Their splendor more dazzled than enlightened me. The contemplation of their excellence tended, naturally, to discourage me by comparison with my own abortions; so that for a long time I labored in vain. At length there came into my head one of those exquisitely original ideas which now and then will permeate the brain of a man of genius. It was this:—or, rather, thus was it carried into execution. From the rubbish of an old book-stall, in a very remote corner of the town, I got together several antique and altogether unknown or forgotten volumes. The bookseller sold them to me for a song. From one of these, which purported to be a translation of one Dante's "Inferno," I copied with remarkable neatness a long passage about a man named Ugolino, who had a parcel of brats. From another which contained a good many old plays by some person whose name I forget, I extracted in the same manner, and with the same care, a great number of lines about "angels" and "ministers saying grace," and "goblins damned," and more besides of that sort. From a third, which was the composition of some blind man or other, either a Greek or a Choctaw—I cannot be at the pains of remembering every trifle exactly—I took about fifty verses beginning with "Achilles' wrath," and "grease," and something else. From a fourth, which I recollect was also the work of a blind man, I selected a page or two all about "hail" and "holy light"; and although a blind man has no business to write about light, still the verses were sufficiently good in their way.

Having made fair copies of these poems' I signed every one of them "Oppodeldoc," (a fine sonorous name,) and, doing each up nicely in a separate envelope, I despatched one to each of the four principal Magazines, with a request for speedy insertion and prompt pay. The result of this well conceived plan, however, (the success of which would have saved me much trouble in after life,) served to convince me that some editors are not to be bamboozled, and gave the coup-de-grace (as they say in France,) to my nascent hopes, (as they say in the city of the transcendentals.)

The fact is, that each and every one of the Magazines in question, gave Mr. "Oppodeldoc" a complete using-up, in the "Monthly Notices to Correspondents." The "Hum-Drum" gave him a dressing after this fashion:

"'Oppodeldoc,' (whoever he is,) has sent us a long tirade concerning a bedlamite whom he styles 'Ugolino,' who had a great many children that should have been all whipped and sent to bed without their suppers. The whole affair is exceedingly tame—not to say flat. 'Oppodeldoc,' (whoever he is,) is entirely devoid of imagination—and imagination, in our humble opinion, is not only the soul of Poesy, but also its very heart. 'Oppodeldoc,' (whoever he is,) has the audacity to demand of us, for his twattle, a 'speedy insertion and prompt pay.' We neither insert nor purchase any stuff of the sort. There can be no doubt, however, that he would meet with a ready sale for all the balderdash he can scribble, at the office of either the 'Rowdy-Dow,' the 'Lollipop,' or the 'Goosetherumfoodle.'"

All this, it must be acknowledged, was very severe upon "Oppodeldoc"—but the unkindest cut was putting the word Poesy in small caps. In those five pre-eminent letters what a world of bitterness is there not involved!

But "Oppodeldoc" was punished with equal severity in the "Rowdy-Dow," which spoke thus:

"We have received a most singular and insolent communication from a person (whoever he is,) signing himself 'Oppodeldoc'—thus desecrating the greatness of the illustrious Roman Emperor so named. Accompanying the letter of 'Oppodeldoc,' (whoever he is,) we find sundry lines of most disgusting and unmeaning rant about 'angels and ministers of grace'—rant such as no madman short of a Nat Lee, or an 'Oppodeldoc,' could possibly perpetrate. And for this trash of trash, we are modestly requested to 'pay promptly.' No sir—no! We pay for nothing of that sort. Apply to the 'Hum-Drum,' the 'Lollipop,' or the 'Goosetherumfoodle.' These periodicals will undoubtedly accept any literary offal you may send them—and as undoubtedly promise to pay for it."

This was bitter indeed upon poor "Oppodeldoc"; but, in this instance, the weight of the satire falls upon the "Humdrum," the "Lollipop," and the "Goosetherumfoodle," who are pungently styled "periodicals"—in Italics, too—a thing that must have cut them to the heart.

Scarcely less savage was the "Lollipop," which thus discoursed:

"Some individual, who rejoices in the appellation 'Oppodeldoc,' (to what low uses are the names of the illustrious dead too often applied!) has enclosed us some fifty or sixty verses commencing after this fashion:

Achilles' wrath, to Greece the direful spring

Of woes unnumbered, &c., &c., &c., &c.

"'Oppodeldoc,' (whoever he is,) is respectfully informed that there is not a printer's devil in our office who is not in the daily habit of composing better lines. Those of 'Oppodeldoc' will not scan. 'Oppodeldoc' should learn to count. But why he should have conceived the idea that we, (of all others, we!) would disgrace our pages with his ineffable nonsense, is utterly beyond comprehension. Why, the absurd twattle is scarcely good enough for the 'Hum-Drum,' the 'Rowdy-Dow,' the 'Goosetherumfoodle'—things that are in the practice of publishing 'Mother Goose's Melodies' as original lyrics. And 'Oppodeldoc' (whoever he is,) has even the assurance to demand pay for this drivel. Does 'Oppodeldoc,' (whoever he is,) know—is he aware that we could not be paid to insert it?"

As I perused this I felt myself growing gradually smaller and smaller, and when I came to the point at which the editor sneered at the poem as "verses" there was little more than an ounce of me left. As for "Oppodeldoc," I began to experience compassion for the poor fellow. But the "Goosetherumfoodle" showed, if possible, less mercy than the "Lollipop." It was the "Goosetherumfoodle" that said:

"A wretched poetaster, who signs himself 'Oppodeldoc,' is silly enough to fancy that we will print and pay for a medley of incoherent and ungrammatical bombast which he has transmitted to us, and which commences with the following most intelligible line:

'Hail, Holy Light! Offspring of Heaven, first born.'

"We say, 'most intelligible' 'Oppodeldoc,' (whoever he is,) will be kind enough to tell us, perhaps, how 'hail' can be 'holy light' We always regarded it as frozen rain. Will he inform us, also, how frozen rain can be, at one and the same time, both 'holy light,' (whatever that is,) and an 'offspring?'—which latter term, (if we understand any thing about English,) is only employed, with propriety, in reference to small babies of about six weeks old. But it is preposterous to descant upon such absurdity—although 'Oppodeldoc,' (whoever he is,) has the unparalleled effrontery to suppose that we will not only 'insert' his ignorant ravings, but (absolutely) pay for them!

"Now this is fine—it is rich!—and we have half a mind to punish this young scribbler for his egotism, by really publishing his effusion, verbatim et literatim, as he has written it. We could inflict no punishment so severe, and we would inflict it, but for the boredom which we should cause our readers in so doing.

"Let 'Oppodeldoc,' (whoever he is,) send any future composition of like character to the 'Hum-Drum,' the 'Lollipop,' or the 'Rowdy-Dow,' They will 'insert' it. They 'insert' every month just such stuff. Send it to them. WE are not to be insulted with impunity."

This made an end of me; and as for the "HumDrum," the "Rowdy-Dow," and the "Lollipop," I never could comprehend how they survived it. The putting them in the smallest possible minion, (that was the rub—thereby insinuating their lowness—their baseness,) while WE stood looking down upon them in gigantic capitals!—oh it was too bitter!—it was wormwood—it was gall. Had I been either of these periodicals I would have spared no pains to have the "Goosetherumfoodle" prosecuted. It might have been done under the Act for the "Prevention of Cruelty to Animals." As for "Oppodeldoc," (whoever he was), I had by this time lost all patience with the fellow, and sympathized with him no longer. He was a fool, beyond doubt, (whoever he was,) and got not a kick more than he deserved.

The result of my experiment with the old books, convinced me, in the first place, that "honesty is the best policy," and, in the second, that if I could not write better than Mr. Dante, and the two blind men, and the rest of the old set, it would, at least, be a difficult matter to write worse. I took heart, therefore, and determined to prosecute the "entirely original," (as they say on the covers of the magazines,) at whatever cost of study and pains. I again placed before my eyes, as a model, the brilliant stanzas on "The Oil-of-Bob" by the editor of the "Gad-Fly," and resolved to construct an Ode on the same sublime theme, in rivalry of what had already been done.

With my first verse I had no material difficulty. It ran thus: "To pen an Ode upon the 'Oil-of-Bob.'"

Having carefully looked out, however, all the legitimate rhymes to "Bob," I found it impossible to proceed. In this dilemma I had recourse to paternal aid; and, after some hours of mature thought, my father and myself thus constructed the poem:

"To pen an Ode upon the "Oil-of-Bob"

Is all sorts of a job.

(Signed.) Snob.

To be sure, this composition was of no very great length—but I "have yet to learn" as they say in the Edinburgh Review, that the mere extent of a literary work has any thing to do with its merit. As for the Quarterly cant about "sustained effort," it is impossible to see the sense of it. Upon the whole, therefore, I was satisfied with the success of my maiden attempt, and now the only question regarded the disposal I should make of it. My father suggested that I should send it to the "Gad-Fly"—but there were two reasons which operated to prevent me from so doing. I dreaded the jealousy of the editor—and I had ascertained that he did not pay for original contributions. I therefore, after due deliberation, consigned the article to the more dignified pages of the "Lollipop," and awaited the event in anxiety, but with resignation.

In the very next published number I had the proud satisfaction of seeing my poem printed at length, as the leading article, with the following significant words, prefixed in italics and between brackets:

We call the attention of our readers to the subjoined admirable stanza on "The Oil of Bob." We need say nothing of their sublimity, or their pathos:—it is impossible to peruse them without tears. Those who have been nauseated with a sad dose on the same august topic from the goose quill of the editor of the "Gad Fly" will do well to compare the two compositions.

P. S. We are consumed with anxiety to probe the mystery which envelops the evident pseudonym "Snob." May we hope for a personal interview?

All this was scarcely more than justice, but it was, I confess, rather more than I had expected:—I acknowledged this, be it observed, to the everlasting disgrace of my country and of mankind. I lost no time, however, in calling upon the editor of the "Lollipop," and had the good fortune to find this gentleman at home. He saluted me with an air of profound respect, slightly blended with a fatherly and patronizing admiration, wrought in him, no doubt, by my appearance of extreme youth and inexperience. Begging me to be seated, he entered at once upon the subject of my poem;—but modesty will ever forbid me to repeat the thousand compliments which he lavished upon me. The eulogies of Mr. Crab, (such was the editor's name,) were, however, by no means fulsomely indiscriminate. He analyzed my composition with much freedom and great ability—not hesitating to point out a few trivial defects—a circumstance which elevated him highly in my esteem. The "Gad-Fly" was, of course, brought upon the tapis, and I hope never to be subjected to a criticism so searching, or to rebukes so withering, as were bestowed by Mr. Crab upon that unhappy effusion. I had been accustomed to regard the editor of the "Gad-Fly" as something superhuman; but Mr. Crab soon disabused me of that idea. He set the literary as well as the personal character of the Fly (so Mr. C. satirically designated the rival editor,) in its true light. He, the Fly, was very little better than he should be. He had written infamous things. He was a penny-a-liner, and a buffoon. He was a villain. He had composed a tragedy which set the whole country in a guffaw, and a farce which deluged the universe in tears. Besides all this, he had the impudence to pen what he meant for a lampoon upon himself, (Mr. Crab,) and the temerity to style him "an ass." Should I at any time wish to express my opinion of Mr. Fry, the pages of the "Lollipop," Mr. Crab assured me, were at my unlimited disposal. In the meantime, as it was very certain that I would be attacked in the Fly for my attempt at composing a rival poem on the "Oil-of-Bob," he (Mr. Crab,) would take it upon himself to attend, pointedly, to my private and personal interests. If I were not made a man of at once, it should not be the fault of himself, (Mr. Crab.)

Mr. Crab having now paused in his discourse, (the latter portion of which I found it impossible to comprehend,) I ventured to suggest something about the remuneration which I had been taught to expect for my poem, by an announcement on the cover of the "Lollipop," declaring that it, (the "Lollipop,") "insisted upon being permitted to pay exorbitant prices for all accepted contributions;—frequently expending more money for a single brief poem than the whole annual cost of the 'HumDrum,' the 'Rowdy-Dow,' and the 'Goosetherumfoodle' combined."

As I mentioned the word "remuneration," Mr. Crab first opened his eyes, and then his mouth, to quite a remarkable extent; causing his personal appearance to resemble that of a highly-agitated elderly duck in the act of quacking;—and in this condition he remained, (ever and anon pressing his hands tightly to his forehead, as if in a state of desperate bewilderment) until I had nearly made an end of what I had to say.

Upon my conclusion, he sank back into his seat, as if much overcome, letting his arms fall lifelessly by his side, but keeping his mouth still rigorously open, after the fashion of the duck. While I remained in speechless astonishment at behavior so alarming, he suddenly leaped to his feet and made a rush at the bell-rope; but just as he reached this, he appeared to have altered his intention, whatever it was, for he dived under a table and immediately re-appeared with a cudgel. This he was in the act of uplifting, (for what purpose I am at a loss to imagine,) when, all at once, there came a benign smile over his features, and he sank placidly back in his chair.

"Mr. Bob," he said, (for I had sent up my card before ascending myself,) "Mr. Bob, you are a young man, I presume—very?"

I assented; adding that I had not yet concluded my third lustrum.

"Ah!" he replied, "very good! I see how it is—say no more! Touching this matter of compensation, what you observe is very just: in fact it is excessively so. But ah—ah—the first contribution—the first, I say,—it is never the Magazine custom to pay for—you comprehend, eh? The truth is, we are usually the recipients in such case." [Mr. Crab smiled blandly as he emphasized the word "recipients."] "For the most part, we are paid for the insertion of a maiden attempt—especially in verse. In the second place, Mr. Bob, the Magazine rule is never to disburse what we term in France the argent comptant—I have no doubt you understand. In a quarter or two after publication of the article—or in a year or two—we make no objection to giving our note at nine months:—provided always that we can so arrange our affairs as to be quite certain of a 'burst up' in six. I really do hope, Mr. Bob, that you will look upon this explanation as satisfactory." Here Mr. Crab concluded, and the tears stood in his eyes.

Grieved to the soul at having been, however innocently, the cause of pain to so eminent and so sensitive a man, I hastened to apologize, and to reassure him, by expressing my perfect coincidence with his views, as well as my entire appreciation of the delicacy of his position. Having done all this in a neat speech, I took leave.

One fine morning, very shortly afterwards, "I awoke and found myself famous." The extent of my renown will be best estimated by reference to the editorial opinions of the day. These opinions, it will be seen, were embodied in critical notices of the number of the "Lollipop" containing my poem, and are perfectly satisfactory, conclusive and clear with the exception, perhaps, of the hieroglyphical marks, "Sep. 15—1 t." appended to each of the critiques.

The "Owl," a journal of profound sagacity, and well known for the deliberate gravity of its literary decisions—the "Owl," I say, spoke as follows:

"'The Lollipop!' The October number of this delicious Magazine surpasses its predecessors, and sets competition at defiance. In the beauty of its typography and paper—in the number and excellence of its steel plates—as well as in the literary merit of its contributions—the 'Lollipop' compares with its slow-paced rivals as Hyperion with a Satyr. The 'Hum-Drum,' the 'Rowdy-Dow,' and the 'Goosetherumfoodle,' excel, it is true, in braggadocio, but, in all other points, give us the 'Lollipop!' How this celebrated journal can sustain its evidently tremendous expenses, is more than we can understand. To be sure, it has a circulation of 100,000, and its subscription-list has increased one-fourth during the last month; but, on the other hand, the sums it disburses constantly for contributions are inconceivable. It is reported that Mr. Slyass received no less than thirty-seven and a half cents for his inimitable paper on 'Pigs.' With Mr. Crab, as editor, and with such names upon the list of contributors as Snob and Slyass, there can be no such word as 'fail' for the Lollipop.' Go and subscribe. Sep. 15—1 t."

I must say that I was gratified with this high-toned notice from a paper so respectable as the "Owl." The placing my name—that is to say, my nom de guerre—in priority of station to that of the great Slyass, was a compliment as happy as I felt it to be deserved.

My attention was next arrested by these paragraphs in the "Toad"—a print highly distinguished for its uprightness, and independence—for its entire freedom from sycophancy and subservience to the givers of dinners:

"The 'Lollipop' for October is out in advance of all its contemporaries, and infinitely surpasses them, of course, in the splendor of its embellishments, as well as in the richness of its literary contents. The 'Hum-Drum,' the 'Rowdy-Dow,' and the 'Goosetherumfoodle' excel, we admit, in braggadocio, but, in all other points, give us the 'Lollipop. How this celebrated Magazine can sustain its evidently tremendous expenses, is more than we can understand. To be sure, it has a circulation of 200,000, and its subscription list has increased one-third during the last fortnight, but on the other hand, the sums it disburses, monthly, for contributions, are fearfully great. We learn that Mr. Mumblethumb received no less than fifty cents for his late 'Monody in a Mud-Puddle.'

"Among the original contributors to the present number we notice, (besides the eminent editor, Mr. Crab,) such men as Snob, Slyass, and Mumblethumb. Apart from the editorial matter, the most valuable paper, nevertheless, is, we think, a poetical gem by 'Snob, on the 'Oil-of-Bob'—but our readers must not suppose from the title of this incomparable bijou, that it bears any similitude to some balderdash on the same subject by a certain contemptible individual whose name is unmentionable to ears polite. The present poem 'On the Oil-of-Bob,' has excited universal anxiety and curiosity in respect to the owner of the evident pseudonym, 'Snob'—a curiosity which, happily, we have it in our power to satisfy. 'Snob' is the nom de plume of Mr. Thingum Bob, of this city,—a relative of the great Mr. Thingum, (after whom he is named,) and otherwise connected with the most illustrious families of the State. His father, Thomas Bob, Esq., is an opulent merchant in Smug. Sep. 15—1t."

This generous approbation touched me to the heart—the more

especially as it emanated from a source so avowedly—so proverbially pure as the "Toad." The word "balderdash," as applied to the "Oil-of-Bob" of the Fly, I considered singularly pungent and appropriate. The words "gem" and "bijou," however, used in reference to my composition, struck me as being, in some degree, feeble, and seemed to me to be deficient in force. They were not sufficiently prononc?s, (as we have it in France).

I had hardly finished reading the "Toad," when a friend placed in my hands a copy of the "Mole," a daily, enjoying high reputation for the keenness of its perception about matters in general, and for the open, honest, above-ground style of its editorials. The "Mole" spoke of the "Lollipop" as follows:

"We have just received the 'Lollipop' for October, and must say that never before have we perused any single number of any periodical which afforded us a felicity so supreme. We speak advisedly. The 'Hum-Drum,' the 'Rowdy-Dow' and the 'Goosetherumfoodle' must look well to their laurels. These prints, no doubt, surpass every thing in loudness of pretension, but, in all other points, give us the 'Lollipop!' How this celebrated Magazine can sustain its evidently tremendous expenses, is more than we can comprehend. To be sure, it has a circulation of 300,000 and its subscription-list has increased one-half within the last week, but then the sum it disburses, monthly, for contributions, is astoundingly enormous. We have it upon good authority, that Mr. Fatquack received no less than sixty-two cents and a half for his late Domestic Nouvelette, the 'Dish-Clout.'

"The contributors to the number before us are Mr. Crab, (the eminent editor,) Snob, Mumblethumb, Fatquack, and others; but, after the inimitable compositions of the editor himself, we prefer a diamond-like effusion from the pen of a rising poet who writes over the signature 'Snob'—a nom de guerre which we predict will one day extinguish the radiance of 'Boz.' 'Snob,' we learn, is a Mr. Thingum Bob, Esq., sole heir of a wealthy merchant of this city, Thomas Bob, Esq., and a near relative of the distinguished Mr. Thingum. The title of Mr. B.'s admirable poem is the 'Oil-of-Bob'—a somewhat unfortunate name, by-the-by, as some contemptible vagabond connected with the penny press has already disgusted the town with a great deal of drivel upon the same topic. There will be no danger, however, of confounding the compositions. Sep. 15-z t."

The generous approbation of so clear-sighted a journal as the "Mole" penetrated my soul with delight. The only objection which occurred to me was, that the terms "contemptible vagabond" might have been better written "odious and contemptible, wretch, villain and vagabond." This would have sounded more gracefully, I think. "Diamond-like," also, was scarcely, it will be admitted, of sufficient intensity to express what the "Mole" evidently thought of the brilliancy of the "Oil-of-Bob."

On the same afternoon in which I saw these notices in the "Owl," the "Toad," and the "Mole" I happened to meet with a copy of the "Daddy-Long-Legs," a periodical proverbial for the extreme extent of its understanding. And it was the "Daddy-Long-Legs" which spoke thus:

"The 'Lollipop,'! This gorgeous Magazine is already before the public for October. The question of preeminence is forever put to rest, and hereafter it will be excessively preposterous in the 'Hum-Drum,' the 'Rowdy-Dow,' or the 'Goosetherumfoodle,' to make any farther spasmodic attempts at competition. These journals may excel the 'Lollipop' in outcry, but, in all other points, give us the 'Lollipop!' How this celebrated Magazine can sustain its evidently tremendous expenses, is past comprehension. To be sure it has a circulation of precisely half a million, and its subscription-list has increased seventy-five per cent, within the last couple of days; but then the sums it disburses, monthly, for contributions, are scarcely credible; we are cognizant of the fact, that Mademoiselle Cribalittle received no less than eighty-seven cents and a half for her late valuable Revolutionary Tale, entitled 'The York-Town Katy-Did, and the Bunker-Hill Katy-Didn't.'

"The most able papers in the present number, are, of course, those furnished by the editor, (the eminent Mr. Crab,) but there are numerous magnificent contributions from such names as Snob, Mademoiselle Cribalittle, Slyass, Mrs. Fibalittle, Mumblethumb, Mrs. Squibalittle, and last, though not least, Fatquack. The world may well be challenged to produce so rich a galaxy of genius.

"The poem over the signature 'Snob' is, we find, attracting universal commendation, and, we are constrained to say, deserves, if possible, even more applause than it has received. The 'Oil-of-Bob' is the title of this masterpiece of eloquence and art. One or two of our readers may have a very faint, although sufficiently disgusting recollection of a poem (?) similarly entitled, the perpetration of a miserable penny-a-liner, mendicant, and cut-throat, connected in the capacity of scullion, we believe, with one of the indecent prints about the purlieus of the city; we beg them, for God's sake, not to confound the compositions. The author of the 'Oil-of-Bob' is, we hear, Thingum Bob, Esq., a gentleman of high genius, and a scholar. 'Snob' is merely a nom-de-guerre. Sept. 15—1 t."

I could scarcely restrain my indignation while I perused the concluding portions of this diatribe. It was clear to me that the yea-nay manner—not to say the gentleness—the positive forbearance with which the "Daddy-Long-Legs" spoke of that pig, the editor of the "Gad-Fly"—it was evident to me, I say, that this gentleness of speech could proceed from nothing else than a partiality for the Fly—whom it was clearly the intention of the "Daddy-Long-Legs" to elevate into reputation at my expense. Any one, indeed, might perceive, with half an eye, that, had the real design of the "Daddy" been what it wished to appear, it, (the "Daddy,") might have expressed itself in terms more direct, more pungent, and altogether more to the purpose. The words "penny-a-liner," "mendicant," "scullion," and "cut-throat," were epithets so intentionally inexpressive and equivocal, as to be worse than nothing when applied to the author of the very worst stanzas ever penned by one of the human race. We all know what is meant by "damning with faint praise," and, on the other hand, who could fail seeing through the covert purpose of the "Daddy"—that of glorifying with feeble abuse?

What the "Daddy" chose to say of the Fly, however, was no business of mine. What it said of myself was. After the noble manner in which the "Owl," the "Toad," the "Mole," had expressed themselves in respect to my ability, it was rather too much to be coolly spoken of by a thing like the "Daddy-Long-Legs," as merely "a gentleman of high genius and a scholar." Gentleman indeed! I made up my mind at once, either to get a written apology from the "Daddy-Long-Legs," or to call it out.

Full of this purpose, I looked about me to find a friend whom I could entrust with a message to his Daddyship, and as the editor of the "Lollipop" had given me marked tokens of regard, I at length concluded to seek assistance upon the present occasion.

I have never yet been able to account, in a manner satisfactory to my own understanding, for the very peculiar countenance and demeanor with which Mr. Crab listened to me, as I unfolded to him my design. He again went through the scene of the bell-rope and cudgel, and did not omit the duck. At one period I thought he really intended to quack. His fit, nevertheless, finally subsided as before, and he began to act and speak in a rational way. He declined bearing the cartel, however, and in fact, dissuaded me from sending it at all; but was candid enough to admit that the "Daddy-Long-Legs" had been disgracefully in the wrong—more especially in what related to the epithets "gentleman and scholar."

Towards the end of this interview with Mr. Crab, who really appeared to take a paternal interest in my welfare, he suggested to me that I might turn an honest penny, and, at the same time, advance my reputation, by occasionally playing Thomas Hawk for the "Lollipop."

I begged Mr. Crab to inform me who was Mr. Thomas Hawk, and how it was expected that I should play him.

Here Mr. Crab again "made great eyes," (as we say in Germany,) but at length, recovering himself from a profound attack of astonishment, he assured me that he employed the words "Thomas Hawk" to avoid the colloquialism, Tommy, which was low—but that the true idea was Tommy Hawk—or tomahawk—and that by "playing tomahawk" he referred to scalping, brow-beating and otherwise using-up the herd of poor-devil authors.

I assured my patron that, if this was all, I was perfectly resigned to the task of playing Thomas Hawk. Hereupon Mr. Crab desired me to use-up the editor of the "Gad-Fly" forthwith, in the fiercest style within the scope of my ability, and as a specimen of my powers. This I did, upon the spot, in a review of the original "Oil-of-Bob," occupying thirty-six pages of the "Lollipop." I found playing Thomas Hawk, indeed, a far less onerous occupation than poetizing; for I went upon system altogether, and thus it was easy to do the thing thoroughly and well. My practice was this. I bought auction copies (cheap) of "Lord Brougham's Speeches," "Cobbett's Complete Works," the "New Slang-Syllabus," the "Whole Art of Snubbing," "Prentice's Billingsgate," (folio edition,) and "Lewis G. Clarke on Tongue." These works I cut up thoroughly with a currycomb, and then, throwing the shreds into a sieve, sifted out carefully all that might be thought decent, (a mere trifle); reserving the hard phrases, which I threw into a large tin pepper-castor with longitudinal holes, so that an entire sentence could get through without material injury. The mixture was then ready for use. When called upon to play Thomas Hawk, I anointed a sheet of fools-cap with the white of a gander's egg; then, shredding the thing to be reviewed as I had previously shredded the books,—only with more care, so as to get every word separate—I threw the latter shreds in with the former, screwed on the lid of the castor, gave it a shake, and so dusted out the mixture upon the egg'd foolscap; where it stuck. The effect was beautiful to behold. It was captivating. Indeed, the reviews I brought to pass by this simple expedient have never been approached, and were the wonder of the world. At first, through bashfulness—the result of inexperience—I was a little put out by a certain inconsistency—a certain air of the bizarre, (as we say in France,) worn by the composition as a whole. All the phrases did not fit, (as we say in the Anglo-Saxon). Many were quite awry. Some, even, were up-side-down; and there were none of them which were not, in some measure, injured in regard to effect, by this latter species of accident, when it occurred;—with the exception of Mr. Lewis Clarke's paragraphs, which were so vigorous, and altogether stout, that they seemed not particularly disconcerted by any extreme of position, but looked equally happy and satisfactory, whether on their heads, or on their heels.

What became of the editor of the "Gad-Fly," after the publication of my criticism on his "Oil-of-Bob," it is somewhat difficult to determine. The most reasonable conclusion is, that he wept himself to death. At all events he disappeared instantaneously from the face of the earth, and no man has seen even the ghost of him since.

This matter having been properly accomplished, and the Furies appeased, I grew at once into high favor with Mr. Crab. He took me into his confidence, gave me a permanent situation as Thomas Hawk of the "Lollipop," and, as for the present, he could afford me no salary, allowed me to profit, at discretion, by his advice.

"My dear Thingum," said he to me one day after dinner, "I respect your abilities and love you as a son. You shall be my heir. When I die I will bequeath you the 'Lollipop.' In the meantime I will make a man of you—I will—provided always that you follow my counsel. The first thing to do is to get rid of the old bore."

"Boar?" said I inquiringly—"pig, eh?—aper? (as we say in Latin)—who?—where?"

"Your father," said he.

"Precisely," I replied,—"pig."

"You have your fortune to make, Thingum," resumed Mr. Crab, "and that governor of yours is a millstone about your neck. We must cut him at once." [Here I took out my knife.] "We must cut him," continued Mr. Crab, "decidedly and forever. He won't do—he won't. Upon second thoughts, you had better kick him, or cane him, or something of that kind."

"What do you say," I suggested modestly, "to my kicking him in the first instance, caning him afterwards, and winding up by tweaking his nose?"

Mr. Crab looked at me musingly for some moments, and then answered:

"I think, Mr. Bob, that what you propose would answer sufficiently well—indeed remarkably well—that is to say, as far as it went—but barbers are exceedingly hard to cut, and I think, upon the whole, that, having performed upon Thomas Bob the operations you suggest, it would be advisable to blacken, with your fists, both his eyes, very carefully and thoroughly, to prevent his ever seeing you again in fashionable promenades. After doing this, I really do not perceive that you can do any more. However—it might be just as well to roll him once or twice in the gutter, and then put him in charge of the police. Any time the next morning you can call at the watch-house and swear an assault."

I was much affected by the kindness of feeling towards me personally, which was evinced in this excellent advice of Mr. Crab, and I did not fail to profit by it forthwith. The result was, that I got rid of the old bore, and began to feel a little independent and gentleman-like. The want of money, however, was, for a few weeks, a source of some discomfort; but at length, by carefully putting to use my two eyes, and observing how matters went just in front of my nose, I perceived how the thing was to be brought about. I say "thing"—be it observed—for they tell me the Latin for it is rem. By the way, talking of Latin, can any one tell me the meaning of quocunque—or what is the meaning of modo?

My plan was exceedingly simple. I bought, for a song, a sixteenth of the "Snapping-Turtle":—that was all. The thing was done, and I put money in my purse. There were some trivial arrangements afterwards, to be sure; but these formed no portion of the plan. They were a consequence—a result. For example, I bought pen, ink and paper, and put them into furious activity. Having thus completed a Magazine article, I gave it, for appellation, "Fol-Lol, by the Author of 'The Oil-of-Bob,'" and enveloped it to the "Goosetherumfoodle." That journal, however, having pronounced it "twattle" in the "Monthly Notices to Correspondents," I reheaded the paper "'Hey-Diddle-Diddle,' by ThingumBob, Esq., Author of the Ode on 'The Oil-of-Bob,' and Editor of the 'Snapping-Turtle.' "With this amendment, I re-enclosed it to the "Goosetherumfoodle," and, while I awaited a reply, published daily, in the "Turtle," six columns of what may be termed philosophical and analytical investigation of the literary merits of the "Goosetherumfoodle," as well as of the personal character of the editor of the "Goosetherumfoodle." At the end of a week the "Goosetherumfoodle" discovered that it had, by some odd mistake, "confounded a stupid article, headed 'Hey-Diddle-Diddle' and composed by some unknown ignoramus, with a gem of resplendent lustre similarly entitled, the work of Thingum Bob, Esq., the celebrated author of 'The Oil-of-Bob.'" The "Goosetherumfoodle" deeply "regretted this very natural accident," and promised, moreover, an insertion of the genuine "Hey-Diddle-Diddle" in the very next number of the Magazine.

The fact is, I thought—I really thought—I thought at the time—I thought then—and have no reason for thinking otherwise now—that the

"Goosetherumfoodle" did make a mistake. With the best intentions in the world, I never knew any thing that made as many singular mistakes as the "Goosetherumfoodle." From that day I took a liking to the "Goosetherumfoodle," and the result was I soon saw into the very depths of its literary merits, and did not fail to expatiate upon them, in the "Turtle," whenever a fitting opportunity occurred. And it is to be regarded as a very peculiar coincidence—as one of those positively remarkable coincidences which set a man to serious thinking—that just such a total revolution of opinion—just such entire bouleversement, (as we say in French,)—just such thorough topsiturviness, (if I may be permitted to employ a rather forcible term of the Choctaws,) as happened, pro and con, between myself on the one part, and the "Goosetherumfoodle" on the other, did actually again happen, in a brief period afterwards, and with precisely similar circumstances, in the case of myself and the "Rowdy-Dow," and in the case of myself and the "HumDrum."

Thus it was that, by a master-stroke of genius, I at length consummated my triumphs by "putting money in my purse," and thus may be said really and fairly to have commenced that brilliant and eventful career which rendered me illustrious, and which now enables me to say, with Chateaubriand, "I have made history"—"J'ai fait l'histoire."

I have indeed "made history." From the bright epoch which I now record, my actions—my works—are the property of mankind. They are familiar to the world. It is, then, needless for me to detail how, soaring rapidly, I fell heir to the "Lollipop"—how I merged this journal in the "Hum-Drum"—how again I made purchase of the "Rowdy-Dow," thus combining the three periodicals—how, lastly, I effected a bargain for the sole remaining rival, and united all the literature of the country in one magnificent Magazine, known everywhere as the

"Rowdy-Dow, Lollipop, Hum-Drum,

and

goosetherumfoodlb"

Yes; I have made history. My fame is universal. It extends to the uttermost ends of the earth. You cannot take up a common newspaper in which you shall not see some allusion to the immortal Thingum Bob. It is Mr. Thingum Bob said so, and Mr. Thingum Bob wrote this, and Mr. Thingum Bob did that. But I am meek and expire with an humble heart. After all, what is it?—this indescribable something which men will persist in terming "genius?" I agree with Buffon—with Hogarth—it is but diligence after all.

Look at me!—how I labored—how I toiled—how I wrote! Ye Gods, did I not write? I knew not the word "ease." By day I adhered to my desk, and at night, a pale student, I consumed the midnight oil. You should have seen me—you should. I leaned to the right. I leaned to the left. I sat forward. I sat backward. I sat upon end. I sat tete baiss?e, (as they have it in the Kickapoo,) bowing my head close to the alabaster page. And, through all, I—wrote. Through joy and through sorrow, I—wrote. Through hunger and through thirst, I—wrote. Through good report and through ill report, I—wrote. Through sunshine and through moonshine, I—wrote. What I wrote it is unnecessary to say. The style!—that was the thing. I caught it from Fatquack—whizz!—fizz!—— and I am giving you a specimen of it now.

HOW TO WRITE A BLACKWOOD ARTICLE.

"In the name of the Prophet—figs!!"

Cry of the Turkish fig-peddler.

I PRESUME everybody has heard of me. My name is the Signora Psyche Zenobia. This I know to be a fact. Nobody but my enemies ever calls me Suky Snobbs. I have been assured that Suky is but a vulgar corruption of Psyche, which is good Greek, and means "the soul" (that's me, I'm all soul) and sometimes "a butterfly," which latter meaning undoubtedly alludes to my appearance in my new crimson satin dress, with the sky-blue Arabian mantelet, and the trimmings of green agraffas, and the seven flounces of orange-colored auriculas. As for Snobbs—any person who should look at me would be instantly aware that my name wasn't Snobbs. Miss Tabitha Turnip propagated that report through sheer envy. Tabitha Turnip indeed! Oh, the little wretch! But what can we expect from a turnip? Wonder if she remembers the old adage about "blood out of a turnip," &c.? [Mem. put her in mind of it the first opportunity.] [Mem. again—pull her nose.] Where was I? Ah! I have been assured that Snobbs is a mere corruption of Zenobia, and that Zenobia was a queen—(So am I. Dr. Moneypenny always calls me the Queen of the Hearts)—and that Zenobia, as well as Psyche, is good Greek, and that my father was "a Greek," and that consequently I have a right to our patronymic, which is Zenobia and not by any means Snobbs. Nobody but Tabitha Turnip calls me Suky Snobbs. I am the Signora Psyche Zenobia.

As I said before, everybody has heard of me. I am that very Signora Psyche Zenobia, so justly celebrated as corresponding secretary to the "Philadelphia, Regular, Exchange, Tea, Total, Young, Belles, Lettres, Universal, Experimental, Bibliographical, Association, To, Civilize, Humanity." Dr. Moneypenny made the title for us, and says he chose it because it sounded big like an empty rum-puncheon. (A vulgar man that sometimes—but he's deep.) We all sign the initials of the society after our names, in the fashion of the R. S. A., Royal Society of Arts—the S. D. U. K., Society for the Diffusion of Useful

Knowledge, &c, &c. Dr. Moneypenny says that S. stands for stale, and that D. U. K. spells duck, (but it don't,) that S. D. U. K. stands for Stale Duck and not for Lord Brougham's society—but then Dr. Moneypenny is such a queer man that I am never sure when he is telling me the truth. At any rate we always add to our names the initials P. R. E. T. T. Y. B. L. U. E. B. A. T. C. H.—that is to say, Philadelphia, Regular, Exchange, Tea, Total, Young, Belles, Lettres, Universal, Experimental, Bibliographical, Association, To, Civilize, Humanity—one letter for each word, which is a decided improvement upon Lord Brougham. Dr. Moneypenny will have it that our initials give our true character—but for my life I can't see what he means.

Notwithstanding the good offices of the Doctor, and the strenuous exertions of the association to get itself into notice, it met with no very great success until I joined it. The truth is, the members indulged in too flippant a tone of discussion. The papers read every Saturday evening were characterized less by depth than buffoonery. They were all whipped syllabub. There was no investigation of first causes, first principles. There was no investigation of any thing at all. There was no attention paid to that great point, the "fitness of things." In short there was no fine writing like this. It was all low—very! No profundity, no reading, no metaphysics—nothing which the learned call spirituality, and which the unlearned choose to stigmatize as cant. [Dr. M. says I ought to spell "cant" with a capital K—but I know better.]

When I joined the society it was my endeavor to introduce a better style of thinking and writing, and all the world knows how well I have succeeded. We get up as good papers now in the P. R. E. T. T. Y. B. L. U. E. B. A. T. C. H. as any to be found even in Blackwood. I say, Blackwood, because I have been assured that the finest writing, upon every subject, is to be discovered in the pages of that justly celebrated Magazine. We now take it for our model upon all themes, and are getting into rapid notice accordingly. And, after all, it's not so very difficult a matter to compose an article of the genuine Blackwood stamp, if one only goes properly about it. Of course I don't speak of the political articles. Everybody knows how they are managed, since Dr. Moneypenny explained it. Mr. Blackwood has a pair of tailor's-shears, and three apprentices who stand by him for orders. One hands him the "Times," another the "Examiner" and a third a "Culley's New Compendium of Slang-Whang." Mr. B. merely cuts out and intersperses. It is soon done—nothing but "Examiner," "Slang-Whang," and "Times"—then "Times," "Slang-Whang," and "Examiner"—and then "Times," "Examiner," and "Slang-Whang."

But the chief merit of the Magazine lies in its miscellaneous articles; and the best of these come under the head of what Dr. Moneypenny calls the bizarreries (whatever that may mean) and what everybody else calls the intensities. This is a species of writing which I have long known how to appreciate, although it is only since my late visit to Mr. Blackwood (deputed by the society) that I have been made aware of the exact method of composition. This method is very simple, but not so much so as the politics. Upon my calling at Mr. B.'s, and making known to him the wishes of the society, he received me with great civility, took me into his study, and gave me a clear explanation of the whole process.

"My dear madam," said he, evidently struck with my majestic appearance, for I had on the crimson satin, with the green agraffas, and orange-colored auriclas. "My dear madam," said he, "sit down. The matter stands thus: In the first place your writer of intensities must have very black ink, and a very big pen, with a very blunt nib. And, mark me, Miss Psyche Zenobia!" he continued, after a pause, with the most expressive energy and solemnity of manner, "mark me!—that pen—must—never be mended! Herein, madam, lies the secret, the soul, of intensity. I assume upon myself to say, that no individual, of however great genius ever wrote with a good pen—understand me,—a good article. You may take, it for granted, that when manuscript can be read it is never worth reading. This is a leading principle in our faith, to which if you cannot readily assent, our conference is at an end."

He paused. But, of course, as I had no wish to put an end to the conference, I assented to a proposition so very obvious, and one, too, of whose truth I had all along been sufficiently aware. He seemed pleased, and went on with his instructions.

"It may appear invidious in me, Miss Psyche Zenobia, to refer you to any article, or set of articles, in the way of model or study, yet perhaps I may as well call your attention to a few cases. Let me see. There was 'The Dead Alive,' a capital thing!—the record of a gentleman's sensations when entombed before the breath was out of his body—full of tastes, terror, sentiment, metaphysics, and erudition. You would have sworn that the writer had been born and brought up in a coffin. Then we had the 'Confessions of an Opium-eater'—fine, very fine!—glorious imagination—deep philosophy acute speculation—plenty of fire and fury, and a good spicing of the decidedly unintelligible. That was a nice bit of flummery, and went down the throats of the people delightfully. They would have it that Coleridge wrote the paper—but not so. It was composed by my pet baboon, Juniper, over a rummer of Hollands and water, 'hot, without sugar.'" [This I could scarcely have believed had it been anybody but Mr. Blackwood, who assured me of it.] "Then there was 'The Involuntary Experimentalist,' all about a gentleman who got baked in an oven, and came out alive and well, although certainly done to a turn. And then there was 'The Diary of a Late Physician,' where the merit lay in good rant, and indifferent Greek—both of them taking things with the public. And then there was 'The Man in the Bell,' a paper by-the-by, Miss Zenobia, which I cannot sufficiently recommend to your attention. It is the history of a young person who goes to sleep under the clapper of a church bell, and is awakened by its tolling for a funeral. The sound drives him mad, and, accordingly, pulling out his tablets, he gives a record of his sensations. Sensations are the great things after all. Should you ever be drowned or hung, be sure and make a note of your sensations—they will be worth to you ten guineas a sheet. If you wish to write forcibly, Miss Zenobia, pay minute attention to the sensations."

"That I certainly will, Mr. Blackwood," said I.

"Good!" he replied. "I see you are a pupil after my own heart. But I must put you au fait to the details necessary in composing what may be denominated a genuine Blackwood article of the sensation stamp—the kind which you will understand me to say I consider the best for all purposes.

"The first thing requisite is to get yourself into such a scrape as no one ever got into before. The oven, for instance,—that was a good hit. But if you have no oven or big bell, at hand, and if you cannot conveniently tumble out of a balloon, or be swallowed up in an earthquake, or get stuck fast in a chimney, you will have to be contented with simply imagining some similar misadventure. I should prefer, however, that you have the actual fact to bear you out. Nothing so well assists the fancy, as an experimental knowledge of the matter in hand. 'Truth is strange,' you know, 'stranger than fiction'— besides being more to the purpose."

Here I assured him I had an excellent pair of garters, and would go and hang myself forthwith.

"Good!" he replied, "do so;—although hanging is somewhat hacknied. Perhaps you might do better. Take a dose of Brandreth's pills, and then give us your sensations. However, my instructions will apply equally well to any variety of misadventure, and in your way home you may easily get knocked in the head, or run over by an omnibus, or bitten by a mad dog, or drowned in a gutter. But to proceed.

"Having determined upon your subject, you must next consider the tone, or manner, of your narration. There is the tone didactic, the tone enthusiastic, the tone natural—all common—place enough. But then there is the tone laconic, or curt, which has lately come much into use. It consists in short sentences. Somehow thus: Can't be too brief. Can't be too snappish. Always a full stop. And never a paragraph.

"Then there is the tone elevated, diffusive, and interjectional. Some of our best novelists patronize this tone. The words must be all in a whirl, like a humming-top, and make a noise very similar, which answers remarkably well instead of meaning. This is the best of all possible styles where the writer is in too great a hurry to think.

"The tone metaphysical is also a good one. If you know any big words this is your chance for them. Talk of the Ionic and Eleatic schools—of Archytas, Gorgias, and Alcmaeon. Say something about objectivity and subjectivity. Be sure and abuse a man named Locke. Turn up your nose at things in general, and when you let slip any thing a little too absurd, you need not be at the trouble of scratching it out, but just add a footnote and say that you are indebted for the above profound observation to the 'Kritik der reinem

Vernunft,' or to the 'Metaphysithe Anfongsgrunde der Noturwissenchaft.' This would look erudite and—and—and frank.

"There are various other tones of equal celebrity, but I shall mention only two more—the tone transcendental and the tone heterogeneous. In the former the merit consists in seeing into the nature of affairs a very great deal farther than anybody else. This second sight is very efficient when properly managed. A little reading of the 'Dial' will carry you a great way. Eschew, in this case, big words; get them as small as possible, and write them upside down. Look over Channing's poems and quote what he says about a 'fat little man with a delusive show of Can.' Put in something about the Supernal Oneness. Don't say a syllable about the Infernal Twoness. Above all, study innuendo. Hint everything—assert nothing. If you feel inclined to say 'bread and butter,' do not by any means say it outright. You may say any thing and every thing approaching to 'bread and butter.' You may hint at buck-wheat cake, or you may even go so far as to insinuate oat-meal porridge, but if bread and butter be your real meaning, be cautious, my dear Miss Psyche, not on any account to say 'bread and butter!'"

I assured him that I should never say it again as long as I lived. He kissed me and continued:

"As for the tone heterogeneous, it is merely a judicious mixture, in equal proportions, of all the other tones in the world, and is consequently made up of every thing deep, great, odd, piquant, pertinent, and pretty.

"Let us suppose now you have determined upon your incidents and tone. The most important portion—in fact, the soul of the whole business, is yet to be attended to—I allude to the filling up. It is not to be supposed that a lady, or gentleman either, has been leading the life of a book worm. And yet above all things it is necessary that your article have an air of erudition, or at least afford evidence of extensive general reading. Now I'll put you in the way of accomplishing this point. See here!" (pulling down some three or four ordinary-looking volumes, and opening them at random). "By casting your eye down almost any page of any book in the world, you will be able to perceive at once a host of little scraps of either learning or bel-espritism, which are the very thing for the spicing of a Blackwood article. You might as well note down a few while I read them to you. I shall make two divisions: first, Piquant Facts for the Manufacture of Similes, and, second, Piquant Expressions to be introduced as occasion may require. Write now!"—and I wrote as he dictated.

"PIQUANT FACTS FOR SIMILES. 'There were originally but three Muses—Melete, Mneme, Aoede—meditation, memory, and singing.' You may make a good deal of that little fact if properly worked. You see it is not generally known, and looks recherche. You must be careful and give the thing with a downright improviso air.

"Again. 'The river Alpheus passed beneath the sea, and emerged without injury to the purity of its waters.' Rather stale that, to be sure, but, if properly dressed and dished up, will look quite as fresh as ever.

"Here is something better. 'The Persian Iris appears to some persons to possess a sweet and very powerful perfume, while to others it is perfectly scentless.' Fine that, and very delicate! Turn it about a little, and it will do wonders. We'll have some thing else in the botanical line. There's nothing goes down so well, especially with the help of a little Latin. Write!

"'The Epidendrum Flos Aeris, of Java, bears a very beautiful flower, and will live when pulled up by the roots. The natives suspend it by a cord from the ceiling, and enjoy its fragrance for years.' That's capital! That will do for the similes. Now for the Piquant Expressions.

"PIQUANT EXPRESSIONS. 'The Venerable Chinese novel Ju-Kiao-Li.' Good! By introducing these few words with dexterity you will evince your intimate acquaintance with the language and literature of the Chinese. With the aid of this you may either get along without either Arabic, or Sanscrit, or Chickasaw. There is no passing muster, however, without Spanish, Italian, German, Latin, and Greek. I must look you out a little specimen of each. Any scrap will answer, because you must depend upon your own ingenuity to make it fit into your article. Now write!

"'Aussi tendre que Zaire'—as tender as Zaire-French. Alludes to the frequent repetition of the phrase, la tendre Zaire, in the French tragedy of that name. Properly introduced, will show not only your knowledge of the language, but your general reading and wit. You can say, for instance, that the chicken you were eating (write an article about being choked to death by a chicken-bone) was not altogether aussi tendre que Zaire. Write!

'Van muerte tan escondida,

Que no te sienta venir,

Porque el plazer del morir,

No mestorne a dar la vida.'

"That's Spanish—from Miguel de Cervantes. 'Come quickly, O death! but be sure and don't let me see you coming, lest the pleasure I shall feel at your appearance should unfortunately bring me back again to life.' This you may slip in quite a propos when you are struggling in the last agonies with the chicken-bone. Write!

'Il pover 'huomo che non sén era accorto, Andava combattendo, e era morto.'

"That's Italian, you perceive—from Ariosto. It means that a great hero, in the heat of combat, not perceiving that he had been fairly killed, continued to fight valiantly, dead as he was. The application of this to your own case is obvious—for I trust, Miss Psyche, that you will not neglect to kick for at least an hour and a half after you have been choked to death by that chicken-bone. Please to write!

'Und sterb'ich doch, no sterb'ich denn

Durch sie—durch sie!'

"That's German—from Schiller. 'And if I die, at least I die—for thee— for thee!' Here it is clear that you are apostrophizing the cause of your disaster, the chicken. Indeed what gentleman (or lady either) of sense, wouldn't die, I should like to know, for a well fattened capon of the right Molucca breed, stuffed with capers and mushrooms, and served up in a salad-bowl, with orange-jellies en mosaiques. Write! (You can get them that way at Tortoni's)—

Write, if you please!

"Here is a nice little Latin phrase, and rare too, (one can't be too recherche or brief in one's Latin, it's getting so common—ignoratio elenchi. He has committed an ignoratio elenchi—that is to say, he has understood the words of your proposition, but not the idea. The man was a fool, you see. Some poor fellow whom you address while choking with that chicken-bone, and who therefore didn't precisely understand what you were talking about. Throw the ignoratio elenchi in his teeth, and, at once, you have him annihilated. If he dares to reply, you can tell him from Lucan (here it is) that speeches are mere anemonae verborum, anemone words. The anemone, with great brilliancy, has no smell. Or, if he begins to bluster, you may be down upon him with insomnia Jovis, reveries of Jupiter—a phrase which Silius Italicus (see here!) applies to thoughts pompous and inflated. This will be sure and cut him to the heart. He can do nothing but roll over and die. Will you be kind enough to write?

"In Greek we must have some thing pretty—from Demosthenes, for example. [Greek phrase]

[Anerh o pheugoen kai palin makesetai] There is a tolerably good translation of it in Hudibras

'For he that flies may fight again,

Which he can never do that's slain.'

"In a Blackwood article nothing makes so fine a show as your Greek. The very letters have an air of profundity about them. Only observe, madam, the astute look of that Epsilon! That Phi ought certainly to be a bishop! Was ever there a smarter fellow than that Omicron? Just twig that Tau! In short, there is nothing like Greek for a genuine sensation-paper. In the present case your application is the most obvious thing in the world. Rap out the sentence, with a huge oath, and by way of ultimatum at the good-for-nothing dunder-headed villain who couldn't understand your plain English in relation to the chicken-bone. He'll take the hint and be off, you may depend upon it."

These were all the instructions Mr. B. could afford me upon the topic in question, but I felt they would be entirely sufficient. I was, at length, able to write a genuine Blackwood article, and determined to do it forthwith. In taking leave of me, Mr. B. made a proposition for the purchase of the paper when written; but as he could offer me only fifty guineas a sheet, I thought it better to let our society have it, than sacrifice it for so paltry a sum. Notwithstanding this niggardly spirit, however, the gentleman showed his consideration for me in all other respects, and indeed treated me with the greatest civility. His parting words made a deep impression upon my heart, and I hope I shall always remember them with gratitude.

"My dear Miss Zenobia," he said, while the tears stood in his eyes, "is there anything else I can do to promote the success of your laudable undertaking? Let me reflect! It is just possible that you may not be able, so soon as convenient, to—to—get yourself drowned, or—choked with a chicken-bone, or—or hung,—or—bitten by a—but stay! Now I think me of it, there are a couple of very excellent bull-dogs in the yard—fine fellows, I assure you—savage, and all that—indeed just the thing for your money— they'll have you eaten up, auricula and all, in less than five minutes (here's my watch!)—and then only think of the sensations! Here! I say—Tom!—Peter!— Dick, you villain!—let out those"—but as I was really in a great hurry, and had not another moment to spare, I was reluctantly forced to expedite my departure, and accordingly took leave at once—somewhat more abruptly, I admit, than strict courtesy would have otherwise allowed.

It was my primary object upon quitting Mr. Blackwood, to get into some immediate difficulty, pursuant to his advice, and with this view I spent the greater part of the day in wandering about Edinburgh, seeking for desperate adventures—adventures adequate to the intensity of my feelings, and adapted to the vast character of the article I intended to write. In this excursion I was attended by one negro—servant, Pompey, and my little lap-dog Diana, whom I had brought with me from Philadelphia. It was not, however, until late in the afternoon that I fully succeeded in my arduous undertaking. An important event then happened of which the following Blackwood article, in the tone heterogeneous, is the substance and result.

A PREDICAMENT

What chance, good lady, hath bereft you thus?

—COMUS.

IT was a quiet and still afternoon when I strolled forth in the goodly city of Edina. The confusion and bustle in the streets were terrible. Men were talking. Women were screaming. Children were choking. Pigs were whistling. Carts they rattled. Bulls they bellowed. Cows they lowed. Horses they neighed. Cats they caterwauled. Dogs they danced. Danced! Could it then be possible? Danced! Alas, thought I, my dancing days are over! Thus it is ever. What a host of gloomy recollections will ever and anon be awakened in the mind of genius and imaginative contemplation, especially of a genius doomed to the everlasting and eternal, and continual, and, as one might say, the—continued—yes, the continued and continuous, bitter, harassing, disturbing, and, if I may be allowed the expression, the very disturbing influence of the serene, and godlike, and heavenly, and exalted, and elevated, and purifying effect of what may be rightly termed the most enviable, the most truly enviable—nay! the most benignly beautiful, the most deliciously ethereal, and, as it were, the most pretty (if I may use so bold an expression) thing (pardon me, gentle reader!) in the world—but I am always led away by my feelings. In such a mind, I repeat, what a host of recollections are stirred up by a trifle! The dogs danced! I—I could not! They frisked—I wept. They capered—I sobbed aloud. Touching circumstances! which cannot fail to bring to the recollection of the classical reader that exquisite passage in relation to the fitness of things, which is to be found in the commencement of the third volume of that admirable and venerable Chinese novel the Jo-Go-Slow.

In my solitary walk through, the city I had two humble but faithful companions. Diana, my poodle! sweetest of creatures! She had a quantity of hair over her one eye, and a blue ribband tied fashionably around her neck. Diana was not more than five inches in height, but her head was somewhat bigger than her body, and her tail being cut off exceedingly close, gave an air of injured innocence to the interesting animal which rendered her a favorite with all.

And Pompey, my negro!—sweet Pompey! how shall I ever forget thee? I had taken Pompey's arm. He was three feet in height (I like to be particular) and about seventy, or perhaps eighty, years of age. He had bow-legs and was corpulent. His mouth should not be called small, nor his ears short. His teeth, however, were like pearl, and his large full eyes were deliciously white. Nature had endowed him with no neck, and had placed his ankles (as usual with that race) in the middle of the upper portion of the feet. He was clad with a striking simplicity. His sole garments were a stock of nine inches in height, and a nearly—new drab overcoat which had formerly been in the service of the tall, stately, and illustrious Dr. Moneypenny. It was a good overcoat. It was well cut. It was well made. The coat was nearly new. Pompey held it up out of the dirt with both hands.

There were three persons in our party, and two of them have already been the subject of remark. There was a third—that person was myself. I am the Signora Psyche Zenobia. I am not Suky Snobbs. My appearance is commanding. On the memorable occasion of which I speak I was habited in a crimson satin dress, with a sky-blue Arabian mantelet. And the dress had trimmings of green agraffas, and seven graceful flounces of the orange-colored auricula. I thus formed the third of the party. There was the poodle. There was Pompey. There was myself. We were three. Thus it is said there were originally but three Furies—Melty, Nimmy, and Hetty—Meditation, Memory, and Fiddling.

Leaning upon the arm of the gallant Pompey, and attended at a respectable distance by Diana, I proceeded down one of the populous and very pleasant streets of the now deserted Edina. On a sudden, there presented itself to view a church—a Gothic cathedral—vast, venerable, and with a tall steeple, which towered into the sky. What madness now possessed me? Why did I rush upon my fate? I was seized with an uncontrollable desire to ascend the giddy pinnacle, and then survey the immense extent of the city. The door of the cathedral stood invitingly open. My destiny prevailed. I entered the ominous archway. Where then was my guardian angel?—if indeed such angels there be. If! Distressing monosyllable! what world of mystery, and meaning, and doubt, and uncertainty is there involved in thy two letters! I entered the ominous archway! I entered; and, without injury to my orange-colored auriculas, I passed beneath the portal, and emerged within the vestibule. Thus it is said the immense river Alfred passed, unscathed, and unwetted, beneath the sea.

I thought the staircase would never have an end. Round! Yes, they went round and up, and round and up and round and up, until I could not help surmising, with the sagacious Pompey, upon whose supporting arm I leaned in all the confidence of early affection—I could not help surmising that the upper end of the continuous spiral ladder had been accidentally, or perhaps designedly, removed. I paused for breath; and, in the meantime, an accident occurred of too momentous a nature in a moral, and also in a metaphysical point of view, to be passed over without notice. It appeared to me—indeed I was quite confident of the fact—I could not be mistaken—no! I had, for some moments, carefully and anxiously observed the motions of my Diana—I say that I could not be mistaken—Diana smelt a rat! At once I called Pompey's attention to the subject, and he—he agreed with me. There was then no longer any reasonable room for doubt. The rat had been smelled—and by Diana. Heavens! shall I ever forget the intense excitement of the moment? Alas! what is the boasted intellect of man? The rat!—it was there—that is to say, it was somewhere. Diana smelled the rat. I—I could not! Thus it is said the Prussian Isis has, for some persons, a sweet and very powerful perfume, while to others it is perfectly scentless.

The staircase had been surmounted, and there were now only three or four more upward steps intervening between us and the summit. We still ascended, and now only one step remained. One step! One little, little step! Upon one such little step in the great staircase of human life how vast a sum of human happiness or misery depends! I thought of myself, then of Pompey, and then of the mysterious and inexplicable destiny which surrounded us. I thought of Pompey!—alas, I thought of love! I thought of my many false steps which have been taken, and may be taken again. I resolved to be more cautious, more reserved. I abandoned the arm of Pompey, and, without his assistance, surmounted the one remaining step, and gained the chamber of the belfry. I was followed immediately afterward by my poodle. Pompey alone remained behind. I stood at the head of the staircase, and encouraged him to ascend. He stretched forth to me his hand, and unfortunately in so doing was forced to abandon his firm hold upon the overcoat. Will the gods never cease their persecution? The overcoat is dropped, and, with one of his feet, Pompey stepped upon the long and trailing skirt of the overcoat. He stumbled and fell—this consequence was inevitable. He fell forward, and, with his accursed head, striking me full in the—in the breast, precipitated me headlong, together with himself, upon the hard, filthy, and detestable floor of the belfry. But my revenge was sure, sudden, and complete. Seizing him furiously by the wool with both hands, I tore out a vast quantity of black, and crisp, and curling material, and tossed it from me with every manifestation of disdain. It fell among the ropes of the belfry and remained. Pompey arose, and said no word. But he regarded me piteously with his large eyes and— sighed. Ye Gods—that sigh! It sunk into my heart. And the hair—the wool! Could I have reached that wool I would have bathed it with my tears, in testimony of regret. But alas! it was now far beyond my grasp. As it dangled among the cordage of the bell, I fancied it alive. I fancied that it stood on end with indignation. Thus the happy-dandy Flos Aeris of Java bears, it is said, a beautiful flower, which will live when pulled up by the roots. The natives suspend it by a cord from the ceiling and enjoy its fragrance for years.

Our quarrel was now made up, and we looked about the room for an aperture through which to survey the city of Edina. Windows there were none. The sole light admitted into the gloomy chamber proceeded from a square opening, about a foot in diameter, at a height of about seven feet from the floor. Yet what will the energy of true genius not effect? I resolved to clamber up to this hole. A vast quantity of wheels, pinions, and other cabalistic— looking machinery stood opposite the hole, close to it; and through the hole there passed an iron rod from the machinery. Between the wheels and the wall where the hole lay there was barely room for my body—yet I was desperate, and determined to persevere. I called Pompey to my side.

"You perceive that aperture, Pompey. I wish to look through it. You will stand here just beneath the hole—so. Now, hold out one of your hands, Pompey, and let me step upon it—thus. Now, the other hand, Pompey, and with its aid I will get upon your shoulders."

He did every thing I wished, and I found, upon getting up, that I could easily pass my head and neck through the aperture. The prospect was sublime. Nothing could be more magnificent. I merely paused a moment to bid Diana behave herself, and assure Pompey that I would be considerate and bear as lightly as possible upon his shoulders. I told him I would be tender of his feelings—ossi tender que beefsteak. Having done this justice to my faithful friend, I gave myself up with great zest and enthusiasm to the enjoyment of the scene which so obligingly spread itself out before my eyes.

Upon this subject, however, I shall forbear to dilate. I will not describe the city of Edinburgh. Every one has been to the city of Edinburgh. Every one has been to Edinburgh—the classic Edina. I will confine myself to the momentous details of my own lamentable adventure. Having, in some measure, satisfied my curiosity in regard to the extent, situation, and general appearance of the city, I had leisure to survey the church in which I was, and the delicate architecture of the steeple. I observed that the aperture through which I had thrust my head was an opening in the dial-plate of a gigantic clock, and must have appeared, from the street, as a large key-hole, such as we see in the face of the French watches. No doubt the true object was to admit the arm of an attendant, to adjust, when necessary, the hands of the clock from within. I observed also, with surprise, the immense size of these hands, the longest of which could not have been less than ten feet in length, and, where broadest, eight or nine inches in breadth. They were of solid steel apparently, and their edges appeared to be sharp. Having noticed these particulars, and some others, I again turned my eyes upon the glorious prospect below, and soon became absorbed in contemplation.

From this, after some minutes, I was aroused by the voice of Pompey, who declared that he could stand it no longer, and requested that I would be so kind as to come down. This was unreasonable, and I told him so in a speech of some length. He replied, but with an evident misunderstanding of my ideas upon the subject. I accordingly grew angry, and told him in plain words, that he was a fool, that he had committed an ignoramus e-clench-eye, that his notions were mere insommary Bovis, and his words little better than an ennemywerrybor'em. With this he appeared satisfied, and I resumed my contemplations.

It might have been half an hour after this altercation when, as I was deeply absorbed in the heavenly scenery beneath me, I was startled by something very cold which pressed with a gentle pressure on the back of my neck. It is needless to say that I felt inexpressibly alarmed. I knew that Pompey was beneath my feet, and that Diana was sitting, according to my explicit directions, upon her hind legs, in the farthest corner of the room. What could it be? Alas! I but too soon discovered. Turning my head gently to one side, I perceived, to my extreme horror, that the huge, glittering, scimetar-like minute-hand of the clock had, in the course of its hourly revolution, descended upon my neck. There was, I knew, not a second to be lost. I pulled back at once—but it was too late. There was no chance of forcing my head through the mouth of that terrible trap in which it was so fairly caught, and which grew narrower and narrower with a rapidity too horrible to be conceived. The agony of that moment is not to be imagined. I threw up my hands and endeavored, with all my strength, to force upward the ponderous iron bar. I might as well have tried to lift the cathedral itself. Down, down, down it came, closer and yet closer. I screamed to Pompey for aid; but he said that I had hurt his feelings by calling him 'an ignorant old squint-eye:' I yelled to Diana; but she only said 'bow-wow-wow,' and that I had told her 'on no account to stir from the corner.' Thus I had no relief to expect from my associates.

Meantime the ponderous and terrific Scythe of Time (for I now discovered the literal import of that classical phrase) had not stopped, nor was it likely to stop, in its career. Down and still down, it came. It had already buried its sharp edge a full inch in my flesh, and my sensations grew indistinct and confused. At one time I fancied myself in Philadelphia with the stately Dr. Moneypenny, at another in the back parlor of Mr. Blackwood receiving his invaluable instructions. And then again the sweet recollection of better and earlier times came over me, and I thought of that happy period when the world was not all a desert, and Pompey not altogether cruel.

The ticking of the machinery amused me. Amused me, I say, for my sensations now bordered upon perfect happiness, and the most trifling circumstances afforded me pleasure. The eternal click-clak, click-clak, click-clak of the clock was the most melodious of music in my ears, and occasionally even put me in mind of the graceful sermonic harangues of Dr. Ollapod. Then there were the great figures upon the dial-plate—how intelligent how intellectual, they all looked! And presently they took to dancing the Mazurka, and I think it was the figure V. who performed the most to my satisfaction. She was evidently a lady of breeding. None of your swaggerers, and nothing at all indelicate in her motions. She did the pirouette to admiration—whirling round upon her apex. I made an endeavor to hand her a chair, for I saw that she appeared fatigued with her exertions—and it was not until then that I fully perceived my lamentable situation. Lamentable indeed! The bar had buried itself two inches in my neck. I was aroused to a sense of exquisite pain. I prayed for death, and, in the agony of the moment, could not help repeating those exquisite verses of the poet Miguel De Cervantes:

Vanny Buren, tan escondida

Query no te senty venny

Pork and pleasure, delly morry

Nommy, torny, darry, widdy!

But now a new horror presented itself, and one indeed sufficient to startle the strongest nerves. My eyes, from the cruel pressure of the machine, were absolutely starting from their sockets. While I was thinking how I should possibly manage without them, one actually tumbled out of my head, and, rolling down the steep side of the steeple, lodged in the rain gutter which ran along the eaves of the main building. The loss of the eye was not so much as the insolent air of independence and contempt with which it regarded me after it was out. There it lay in the gutter just under my nose, and the airs it gave itself would have been ridiculous had they not been disgusting. Such a winking and b2150linking were never before seen. This behavior on the part of my eye in the gutter was not only irritating on account of its manifest insolence and shameful ingratitude, but was also exceedingly inconvenient on account of the sympathy which always exists between two eyes of the same head, however far apart. I was forced, in a manner, to wink and to b2150link, whether I would or not, in exact concert with the scoundrelly thing that lay just under my nose. I was presently relieved, however, by the dropping out of the other eye. In falling it took the same direction (possibly a concerted plot) as its fellow. Both rolled out of the gutter together, and in truth I was very glad to get rid of them.

The bar was now four inches and a half deep in my neck, and there was only a little bit of skin to cut through. My sensations were those of entire happiness, for I felt that in a few minutes, at farthest, I should be relieved from my disagreeable situation. And in this expectation I was not at all deceived. At twenty-five minutes past five in the afternoon, precisely, the huge minute-hand had proceeded sufficiently far on its terrible revolution to sever the small remainder of my neck. I was not sorry to see the head which had occasioned me so much embarrassment at length make a final separation from my body. It first rolled down the side of the steeple, then lodge, for a few seconds, in the gutter, and then made its way, with a plunge, into the middle of the street.

I will candidly confess that my feelings were now of the most singular— nay, of the most mysterious, the most perplexing and incomprehensible character. My senses were here and there at one and the same moment. With my head I imagined, at one time, that I, the head, was the real Signora Psyche Zenobia—at another I felt convinced that myself, the body, was the proper identity. To clear my ideas on this topic I felt in my pocket for my snuff-box, but, upon getting it, and endeavoring to apply a pinch of its grateful contents in the ordinary manner, I became immediately aware of my peculiar deficiency, and threw the box at once down to my head. It took a pinch with great satisfaction, and smiled me an acknowledgement in return. Shortly afterward it made me a speech, which I could hear but indistinctly without ears. I gathered enough, however, to know that it was astonished at my wishing to remain alive under such circumstances. In the concluding sentences it quoted the noble words of Ariosto—

Il pover hommy che non sera corty

And have a combat tenty erry morty; thus comparing me to the hero who, in the heat of the combat, not perceiving that he was dead, continued to contest the battle with inextinguishable valor. There was nothing now to prevent my getting down from my elevation, and I did so. What it was that Pompey saw so very peculiar in my appearance I have never yet been able to find out. The fellow opened his mouth from ear to ear, and shut his two eyes as if he were endeavoring to crack nuts between the lids. Finally, throwing off his overcoat, he made one spring for the staircase and disappeared. I hurled after the scoundrel these vehement words of Demosthenes—

Andrew O'Phlegethon, you really make haste to fly, and then turned to the darling of my heart, to the one-eyed! the shaggy-haired Diana. Alas! what a horrible vision affronted my eyes? Was that a rat I saw skulking into his hole? Are these the picked bones of the little angel who has been cruelly devoured by the monster? Ye gods! and what do I behold—is that the departed spirit, the shade, the ghost, of my beloved puppy, which I perceive sitting with a grace so melancholy, in the corner? Hearken! for she speaks, and, heavens! it is in the German of Schiller—

> *"Unt stubby duk, so stubby dun*
>
> *Duk she! duk she!"*

> *Alas! and are not her words too true?*

> *"And if I died, at least I died*
>
> *For thee—for thee."*

Sweet creature! she too has sacrificed herself in my behalf. Dogless, niggerless, headless, what now remains for the unhappy Signora Psyche Zenobia? Alas—nothing! I have done.

MYSTIFICATION

Slid, if these be your "passados" and "montantes," I'll have

none o' them.

—NED KNOWLES.

THE BARON RITZNER VON JUNG was a noble Hungarian family, every member of which (at least as far back into antiquity as any certain records extend) was more or less remarkable for talent of some description—the majority for that species of grotesquerie in conception of which Tieck, a scion of the house, has given a vivid, although by no means the most vivid exemplifications. My acquaintance with Ritzner commenced at the magnificent Ch?teau Jung, into which a train of droll adventures, not to be made public, threw a place in his regard, and here, with somewhat more difficulty, a partial insight into his mental conformation. In later days this insight grew more clear, as the intimacy which had at first permitted it became more close; and when, after three years of the character of the Baron Ritzner von Jung.

I remember the buzz of curiosity which his advent excited within the college precincts on the night of the twenty-fifth of June. I remember still more distinctly, that while he was pronounced by all parties at first sight "the most remarkable man in the world," no person made any attempt at accounting for his opinion. That he was unique appeared so undeniable, that it was deemed impertinent to inquire wherein the uniquity consisted. But, letting this matter pass for the present, I will merely observe that, from the first moment of his setting foot within the limits of the university, he began to exercise over the habits, manners, persons, purses, and propensities of the whole community which surrounded him, an influence the most extensive and despotic, yet at the same time the most indefinite and altogether unaccountable. Thus the brief period of his residence at the university forms an era in its annals, and is characterized by all classes of people appertaining to it or its dependencies as "that very extraordinary epoch forming the domination of the Baron Ritzner von Jung." then of no particular age, by which I mean that it was impossible to form a guess respecting his age by any data personally afforded. He might have been fifteen or fifty, and was twenty-one years and seven months. He was by no means a handsome man—perhaps the reverse. The contour of his face was somewhat angular and harsh. His forehead was lofty and very fair; his nose a snub; his eyes large, heavy, glassy, and meaningless. About the mouth there was more to be observed. The lips were gently protruded, and rested the one upon the other, after such a fashion that it is impossible to conceive any, even the most complex, combination of human features, conveying so entirely, and so singly, the idea of unmitigated gravity, solemnity and repose.

It will be perceived, no doubt, from what I have already said, that the Baron was one of those human anomalies now and then to be found, who make the science of mystification the study and the business of their lives. For this science a peculiar turn of mind gave him instinctively the cue, while his physical appearance afforded him unusual facilities for carrying his prospects into effect. I quaintly termed the domination of the Baron Ritzner von Jung, ever rightly entered into the mystery which overshadowed his character. I truly think that no person at the university, with the exception of myself, ever suspected him to be capable of a joke, verbal or practical:—the old bull-dog at the garden-gate would sooner have been accused,—the ghost of Heraclitus,—or the wig of the Emeritus Professor of Theology. This, too, when it was evident that the most egregious and unpardonable of all conceivable tricks, whimsicalities and buffooneries were brought about, if not directly by him, at least plainly through his intermediate agency or connivance. The beauty, if I may so call it, of his art mystifique, lay in that consummate ability (resulting from an almost intuitive knowledge of human nature, and a most wonderful self-possession,) by means of which he never failed to make it appear that the drolleries he was occupied in bringing to a point, arose partly in spite, and partly in consequence of the laudable efforts he was making for their prevention, and for the preservation of the good order and dignity of Alma Mater. The deep, the poignant, the overwhelming mortification, which upon each such failure of his praise worthy endeavors, would suffuse every lineament of his countenance, left not the slightest room for doubt of his sincerity in the bosoms of even his most skeptical companions. The adroitness, too, was no less worthy of observation by which he contrived to shift the sense of the grotesque from the creator to the created—from his own person to the absurdities to which he had given rise. In no instance before that of which I speak, have I known the habitual mystific escape the natural consequence of his manoevres—an attachment of the ludicrous to his own character and person. Continually enveloped in an atmosphere of whim, my friend appeared to live only for the severities of society; and not even his own household have for a moment associated other ideas than those of the rigid and august with the memory of the Baron Ritzner von Jung, the demon of the dolce far niente lay like an incubus upon the university. Nothing, at least, was done beyond eating and drinking and making merry. The apartments of the students were converted into so many pot-houses, and there was no pot-house of them all more famous or more frequented than that of the Baron. Our carousals here were many, and boisterous, and long, and never unfruitful of events.

Upon one occasion we had protracted our sitting until nearly daybreak, and an unusual quantity of wine had been drunk. The company consisted of seven or eight individuals besides the Baron and myself. Most of these were young men of wealth, of high connection, of great family pride, and all alive with an exaggerated sense of honor. They abounded in the most ultra German opinions respecting the duello. To these Quixotic notions some recent Parisian publications, backed by three or four desperate and fatal conversation, during the greater part of the night, had run wild upon the all—engrossing topic of the times. The Baron, who had been unusually silent and abstracted in the earlier portion of the evening, at length seemed to be aroused from his apathy, took a leading part in the discourse, and dwelt upon the benefits, and more especially upon the beauties, of the received code of etiquette in passages of arms with an ardor, an eloquence, an impressiveness, and an affectionateness of manner, which elicited the warmest enthusiasm from his hearers in general, and absolutely staggered even myself, who well knew him to be at heart a ridiculer of those very points for which he contended, and especially to hold the entire fanfaronade of duelling etiquette in the sovereign contempt which it deserves.

Looking around me during a pause in the Baron's discourse (of which my readers may gather some faint idea when I say that it bore resemblance to the fervid, chanting, monotonous, yet musical sermonic manner of Coleridge), I perceived symptoms of even more than the general interest in the countenance of one of the party. This gentleman, whom I shall call Hermann, was an original in every respect—except, perhaps, in the single particular that he was a very great fool. He contrived to bear, however, among a particular set at the university, a reputation for deep metaphysical thinking, and, I believe, for some logical talent. As a duellist he had acquired who had fallen at his hands; but they were many. He was a man of courage undoubtedly. But it was upon his minute acquaintance with the etiquette of the duello, and the nicety of his sense of honor, that he most especially prided himself. These things were a hobby which he rode to the death. To Ritzner, ever upon the lookout for the grotesque, his peculiarities had for a long time past afforded food for mystification. Of this, however, I was not aware; although, in the present instance, I saw clearly that something of a whimsical nature was upon the tapis with my friend, and that Hermann was its especial object.

As the former proceeded in his discourse, or rather monologue I perceived the excitement of the latter momently increasing. At length he spoke; offering some objection to a point insisted upon by R., and giving his reasons in detail. To these the Baron replied at length (still maintaining his exaggerated tone of sentiment) and concluding, in what I thought very bad taste, with a sarcasm and a sneer. The hobby of Hermann now took the bit in his teeth. This I could discern by the studied hair-splitting farrago of his rejoinder. His last words I distinctly remember. "Your opinions, allow me to say, Baron von Jung, although in the main correct, are, in many nice points, discreditable to yourself and to the university of which you are a member. In a few respects they are even unworthy of serious refutation. I would say more than this, sir, were it not for the fear of giving you offence (here the speaker smiled blandly), I would say, sir, that your opinions are not the opinions to be expected from a gentleman."

As Hermann completed this equivocal sentence, all eyes were turned upon the Baron. He became pale, then excessively red; then, dropping his pocket-handkerchief, stooped to recover it, when I caught a glimpse of his countenance, while it could be seen by no one else at the table. It was radiant with the quizzical expression which was its natural character, but which I had never seen it assume except when we were alone together, and when he unbent himself freely. In an instant afterward he stood erect, confronting Hermann; and so total an alteration of countenance in so short a period I certainly never saw before. For a moment I even fancied that I had misconceived him, and that he was in sober earnest. He appeared to be stifling with passion, and his face was cadaverously white. For a short time he remained silent, apparently striving to master his emotion. Having at length seemingly succeeded, he reached a decanter which stood near him, saying as he held it firmly clenched "The language you have thought proper to employ, Mynheer Hermann, in addressing yourself to me, is objectionable in so many particulars, that I have neither temper nor time for specification. That my opinions, however, are not the opinions to be expected from a gentleman, is an observation so directly offensive as to allow me but one line of conduct. Some courtesy, nevertheless, is due to the presence of this company, and to yourself, at this moment, as my guest. You will pardon me, therefore, if, upon this consideration, I deviate slightly from the general usage among gentlemen in similar cases of personal affront. You will forgive me for the moderate tax I shall make upon your imagination, and endeavor to consider, for an instant, the reflection of your person in yonder mirror as the living Mynheer Hermann himself. This being done, there will be no difficulty whatever. I shall discharge this decanter of wine at your image in yonder mirror, and thus fulfil all the spirit, if not the exact letter, of resentment for your insult, while the necessity of physical violence to your real person will be obviated."

With these words he hurled the decanter, full of wine, against the mirror which hung directly opposite Hermann; striking the reflection of his person with great precision, and of course shattering the glass into fragments. The whole company at once started to their feet, and, with the exception of myself and Ritzner, took their departure. As Hermann went out, the Baron whispered me that I should follow him and make an offer of my services. To this I agreed; not knowing precisely what to make of so ridiculous a piece of business.

The duellist accepted my aid with his stiff and ultra recherche air, and, taking my arm, led me to his apartment. I could hardly forbear laughing in his face while he proceeded to discuss, with the profoundest gravity, what he termed "the refinedly peculiar character" of the insult he had received. After a tiresome harangue in his ordinary style, he took down from his book shelves a number of musty volumes on the subject of the duello, and entertained me for a long time with their contents; reading aloud, and commenting earnestly as he read. I can just remember the titles of some of the works. There were the "Ordonnance of Philip le Bel on Single Combat"; the "Theatre of Honor," by Favyn, and a treatise "On the Permission of Duels," by Andiguier. He displayed, also, with much pomposity, Brantome's "Memoirs of Duels,"— published at Cologne, 1666, in the types of Elzevir—a precious and unique vellum-paper volume, with a fine margin, and bound by Derome. But he requested my attention particularly, and with an air of mysterious sagacity, to a thick octavo, written in barbarous Latin by one Hedelin, a Frenchman, and having the quaint title, "Duelli Lex Scripta, et non; aliterque." From this he read me one of the drollest chapters in the world concerning "Injuriae per applicationem, per constructionem, et per se," about half of which, he averred, was strictly applicable to his own "refinedly peculiar" case, although not one syllable of the whole matter could I understand for the life of me. Having finished the chapter, he closed the book, and demanded what I thought necessary to be done. I replied that I had entire confidence in his superior delicacy of feeling, and would abide by what he proposed. With this answer he seemed flattered, and sat down to write a note to the Baron. It ran thus:

Sir,—My friend, M. P.-, will hand you this note. I find it incumbent upon me to request, at your earliest convenience, an explanation of this evening's occurrences at your chambers. In the event of your declining this request, Mr. P. will be happy to arrange, with any friend whom you may appoint, the steps preliminary to a meeting.

With sentiments of perfect respect,

Your most humble servant,

JOHANN HERMAN.

To the Baron Ritzner von Jung,

Not knowing what better to do, I called upon Ritzner with this epistle. He bowed as I presented it; then, with a grave countenance, motioned me to a seat. Having perused the cartel, he wrote the following reply, which I carried to Hermann.

SIR,—Through our common friend, Mr. P., I have received your note of this evening. Upon due reflection I frankly admit the propriety of the explanation you suggest. This being admitted, I still find great difficulty, (owing to the refinedly peculiar nature of our disagreement, and of the personal affront offered on my part,) in so wording what I have to say by way of apology, as to meet all the minute exigencies, and all the variable shadows, of the case. I have great reliance, however, on that extreme delicacy of discrimination, in matters appertaining to the rules of etiquette, for which you have been so long and so pre-eminently distinguished. With perfect certainty, therefore, of being comprehended, I beg leave, in lieu of offering any sentiments of my own, to refer you to the opinions of Sieur Hedelin, as set forth in the ninth paragraph of the chapter of "Injuriae per applicationem, per constructionem, et per se," in his "Duelli Lex scripta, et non; aliterque." The nicety of your discernment in all the matters here treated, will be sufficient, I am assured, to convince you that the mere circumstance of me referring you to this admirable passage, ought to satisfy your request, as a man of honor, for explanation.

With sentiments of profound respect,

Your most obedient servant,

VON JUNG.

The Herr Johann Hermann

Hermann commenced the perusal of this epistle with a scowl, which, however, was converted into a smile of the most ludicrous self-complacency as he came to the rigmarole about Injuriae per applicationem, per constructionem, et per se. Having finished reading, he begged me, with the blandest of all possible smiles, to be seated, while he made reference to the treatise in question. Turning to the passage specified, he read it with great care to himself, then closed the book, and desired me, in my character of confidential acquaintance, to express to the Baron von Jung his exalted sense of his chivalrous behavior, and, in that of second, to assure him that the explanation offered was of the fullest, the most honorable, and the most unequivocally satisfactory nature.

Somewhat amazed at all this, I made my r?treat to the Baron. He seemed to receive Hermann's amicable letter as a matter of course, and after a few words of general conversation, went to an inner room and brought out the everlasting treatise "Duelli Lex scripta, et non; aliterque." He handed me the volume and asked me to look over some portion of it. I did so, but to little purpose, not being able to gather the least particle of meaning. He then took the book himself, and read me a chapter aloud. To my surprise, what he read proved to be a most horribly absurd account of a duel between two baboons. He now explained the mystery; showing that the volume, as it appeared prima facie, was written upon the plan of the nonsense verses of Du Bartas; that is to say, the language was ingeniously framed so as to present to the ear all the outward signs of intelligibility, and even of profundity, while in fact not a shadow of meaning existed. The key to the whole was found in leaving out every second and third word alternately, when there appeared a series of ludicrous quizzes upon a single combat as practised in modern times.

The Baron afterwards informed me that he had purposely thrown the treatise in Hermann's way two or three weeks before the adventure, and that he was satisfied, from the general tenor of his conversation, that he had studied it with the deepest attention, and firmly believed it to be a work of unusual merit. Upon this hint he proceeded. Hermann would have died a thousand deaths rather than acknowledge his inability to understand anything and everything in the universe that had ever been written about the duello.

Littleton Barry.

DIDDLING

CONSIDERED AS ONE OF THE EXACT SCIENCES.

Hey, diddle diddle

The cat and the fiddle

SINCE the world began there have been two Jeremys. The one wrote a Jeremiad about usury, and was called Jeremy Bentham. He has been much admired by Mr. John Neal, and was a great man in a small way. The other gave name to the most important of the Exact Sciences, and was a great man in a great way—I may say, indeed, in the very greatest of ways.

Diddling—or the abstract idea conveyed by the verb to diddle—is sufficiently well understood. Yet the fact, the deed, the thing diddling, is somewhat difficult to define. We may get, however, at a tolerably distinct conception of the matter in hand, by defining—not the thing, diddling, in itself—but man, as an animal that diddles. Had Plato but hit upon this, he would have been spared the affront of the picked chicken.

Very pertinently it was demanded of Plato, why a picked chicken, which was clearly "a biped without feathers," was not, according to his own definition, a man? But I am not to be bothered by any similar query. Man is an animal that diddles, and there is no animal that diddles but man. It will take an entire hen-coop of picked chickens to get over that.

What constitutes the essence, the nare, the principle of diddling is, in fact, peculiar to the class of creatures that wear coats and pantaloons. A crow thieves; a fox cheats; a weasel outwits; a man diddles. To diddle is his destiny. "Man was made to mourn," says the poet. But not so:—he was made to diddle. This is his aim—his object—his end. And for this reason when a man's diddled we say he's "done."

Diddling, rightly considered, is a compound, of which the ingredients are minuteness, interest, perseverance, ingenuity, audacity, nonchalance, originality, impertinence, and grin.

Minuteness:—Your diddler is minute. His operations are upon a small scale. His business is retail, for cash, or approved paper at sight. Should he ever be tempted into magnificent speculation, he then, at once, loses his distinctive features, and becomes what we term "financier." This latter word conveys the diddling idea in every respect except that of magnitude. A diddler may thus be regarded as a banker in petto—a "financial operation," as a diddle at Brobdignag. The one is to the other, as Homer to "Flaccus"—as a Mastodon to a mouse—as the tail of a comet to that of a pig.

Interest:—Your diddler is guided by self-interest. He scorns to diddle for the mere sake of the diddle. He has an object in view—his pocket—and yours. He regards always the main chance. He looks to Number One. You are Number Two, and must look to yourself.

Perseverance:—Your diddler perseveres. He is not readily discouraged. Should even the banks break, he cares nothing about it. He steadily pursues his end, and 'Ut canis a corio nunquam absterrebitur uncto,' so he never lets go of his game.

Ingenuity:—Your diddler is ingenious. He has constructiveness large. He understands plot. He invents and circumvents. Were he not Alexander he would be Diogenes. Were he not a diddler, he would be a maker of patent rat-traps or an angler for trout.

Audacity:—Your diddler is audacious.—He is a bold man. He carries the war into Africa. He conquers all by assault. He would not fear the daggers of Frey Herren. With a little more prudence Dick Turpin would have made a good diddler; with a trifle less blarney, Daniel O'Connell; with a pound or two more brains Charles the Twelfth.

Nonchalance:—Your diddler is nonchalant. He is not at all nervous. He never had any nerves. He is never seduced into a flurry. He is never put out—unless put out of doors. He is cool—cool as a cucumber. He is calm—"calm as a smile from Lady Bury." He is easy—easy as an old glove, or the damsel of ancient Baiae.

Originality:—Your diddler is original—conscientiously so. His thoughts are his own. He would scorn to employ those of another. A stale trick is his aversion. He would return a purse, I am sure, upon discovering that he had obtained it by an unoriginal diddle.

Impertinence.—Your diddler is impertinent. He swaggers. He sets his arms a-kimbo. He thrusts his hands in his trowsers' pockets. He sneers in your face. He treads on your corns. He eats your dinner, he drinks your wine, he borrows your money, he pulls your nose, he kicks your poodle, and he kisses your wife.

Grin:—Your true diddler winds up all with a grin. But this nobody sees but himself. He grins when his daily work is done—when his allotted labors are accomplished—at night in his own closet, and altogether for his own private entertainment. He goes home. He locks his door. He divests himself of his clothes. He puts out his candle. He gets into bed. He places his head upon the pillow. All this done, and your diddler grins. This is no hypothesis. It is a matter of course. I reason a priori, and a diddle would be no diddle without a grin.

The origin of the diddle is referrable to the infancy of the Human Race. Perhaps the first diddler was Adam. At all events, we can trace the science back to a very remote period of antiquity. The moderns, however, have brought it to a perfection never dreamed of by our thick-headed progenitors. Without pausing to speak of the "old saws," therefore, I shall content myself with a compendious account of some of the more "modern instances."

A very good diddle is this. A housekeeper in want of a sofa, for instance, is seen to go in and out of several cabinet warehouses. At length she arrives at one offering an excellent variety. She is accosted, and invited to enter, by a polite and voluble individual at the door. She finds a sofa well adapted to her views, and upon inquiring the price, is surprised and delighted to hear a sum named at least twenty per cent. lower than her expectations. She hastens to make the purchase, gets a bill and receipt, leaves her address, with a request that the article be sent home as speedily as possible, and retires amid a profusion of bows from the shopkeeper. The night arrives and no sofa. A servant is sent to make inquiry about the delay. The whole transaction is denied. No sofa has been sold—no money received—except by the diddler, who played shop-keeper for the nonce.

Our cabinet warehouses are left entirely unattended, and thus afford every facility for a trick of this kind. Visiters enter, look at furniture, and depart unheeded and unseen. Should any one wish to purchase, or to inquire the price of an article, a bell is at hand, and this is considered amply sufficient.

Again, quite a respectable diddle is this. A well-dressed individual enters a shop, makes a purchase to the value of a dollar; finds, much to his vexation, that he has left his pocket-book in another coat pocket; and so says to the shopkeeper—

"My dear sir, never mind; just oblige me, will you, by sending the bundle home? But stay! I really believe that I have nothing less than a five dollar bill, even there. However, you can send four dollars in change with the bundle, you know."

"Very good, sir," replies the shop-keeper, who entertains, at once, a lofty opinion of the high-mindedness of his customer. "I know fellows," he says to himself, "who would just have put the goods under their arm, and walked off with a promise to call and pay the dollar as they came by in the afternoon."

A boy is sent with the parcel and change. On the route, quite accidentally, he is met by the purchaser, who exclaims:

"Ah! This is my bundle, I see—I thought you had been home with it, long ago. Well, go on! My wife, Mrs. Trotter, will give you the five dollars—I left instructions with her to that effect. The change you might as well give to me—I shall want some silver for the Post Office. Very good! One, two, is this a good quarter?—three, four—quite right! Say to Mrs. Trotter that you met me, and be sure now and do not loiter on the way."

The boy doesn't loiter at all—but he is a very long time in getting back from his errand—for no lady of the precise name of Mrs. Trotter is to be discovered. He consoles himself, however, that he has not been such a fool as to leave the goods without the money, and re-entering his shop with a self-satisfied air, feels sensibly hurt and indignant when his master asks him what has become of the change.

A very simple diddle, indeed, is this. The captain of a ship, which is about to sail, is presented by an official looking person with an unusually moderate bill of city charges. Glad to get off so easily, and confused by a hundred duties pressing upon him all at once, he discharges the claim forthwith. In about fifteen minutes, another and less reasonable bill is handed him by one who soon makes it evident that the first collector was a diddler, and the original collection a diddle.

And here, too, is a somewhat similar thing. A steamboat is casting loose from the wharf. A traveller, portmanteau in hand, is discovered running toward the wharf, at full speed. Suddenly, he makes a dead halt, stoops, and picks up something from the ground in a very agitated manner. It is a pocket-book, and—"Has any gentleman lost a pocketbook?" he cries. No one can say that he has exactly lost a pocket-book; but a great excitement ensues, when the treasure trove is found to be of value. The boat, however, must not be detained.

"Time and tide wait for no man," says the captain.

"For God's sake, stay only a few minutes," says the finder of the book—"the true claimant will presently appear."

"Can't wait!" replies the man in authority; "cast off there, d'ye hear?"

"What am I to do?" asks the finder, in great tribulation. "I am about to leave the country for some years, and I cannot conscientiously retain this large amount in my possession. I beg your pardon, sir," [here he addresses a gentleman on shore,] "but you have the air of an honest man. Will you confer upon me the favor of taking charge of this pocket-book—I know I can trust you—and of advertising it? The notes, you see, amount to a very considerable sum. The owner will, no doubt, insist upon rewarding you for your trouble—

"Me!—no, you!—it was you who found the book."

"Well, if you must have it so—I will take a small reward—just to satisfy

111

your scruples. Let me see—why these notes are all hundreds—bless my soul! a hundred is too much to take—fifty would be quite enough, I am sure—

"Cast off there!" says the captain.

"But then I have no change for a hundred, and upon the whole, you had better—

"Cast off there!" says the captain.

"Never mind!" cries the gentleman on shore, who has been examining his own pocket-book for the last minute or so—"never mind! I can fix it—here is a fifty on the Bank of North America—throw the book."

And the over-conscientious finder takes the fifty with marked reluctance, and throws the gentleman the book, as desired, while the steamboat fumes and fizzes on her way. In about half an hour after her departure, the "large amount" is seen to be a "counterfeit presentment," and the whole thing a capital diddle.

A bold diddle is this. A camp-meeting, or something similar, is to be held at a certain spot which is accessible only by means of a free bridge. A diddler stations himself upon this bridge, respectfully informs all passers by of the new county law, which establishes a toll of one cent for foot passengers, two for horses and donkeys, and so forth, and so forth. Some grumble but all submit, and the diddler goes home a wealthier man by some fifty or sixty dollars well earned. This taking a toll from a great crowd of people is an excessively troublesome thing.

A neat diddle is this. A friend holds one of the diddler's promises to pay filled up and signed in due form, upon the ordinary blanks printed in red ink. The diddler purchases one or two dozen of these blanks, and every day dips one of them in his soup, makes his dog jump for it, and finally gives it to him as a bonne bouche. The note arriving at maturity, the diddler, with the diddler's dog, calls upon the friend, and the promise to pay is made the topic of discussion. The friend produces it from his escritoire, and is in the act of reaching it to the diddler, when up jumps the diddler's dog and devours it forthwith. The diddler is not only surprised but vexed and incensed at the absurd behavior of his dog, and expresses his entire readiness to cancel the obligation at any moment when the evidence of the obligation shall be forthcoming.

A very mean diddle is this. A lady is insulted in the street by a diddler's accomplice. The diddler himself flies to her assistance, and, giving his friend a comfortable thrashing, insists upon attending the lady to her own door. He bows, with his hand upon his heart, and most respectfully bids her adieu. She entreats him, as her deliverer, to walk in and be introduced to her big brother and her papa. With a sigh, he declines to do so. "Is there no way, then, sir," she murmurs, "in which I may be permitted to testify my gratitude?"

"Why, yes, madam, there is. Will you be kind enough to lend me a couple of shillings?"

In the first excitement of the moment the lady decides upon fainting outright. Upon second thought, however, she opens her purse-strings and delivers the specie. Now this, I say, is a diddle minute—for one entire moiety of the sum borrowed has to be paid to the gentleman who had the trouble of performing the insult, and who had then to stand still and be thrashed for performing it.

Rather a small but still a scientific diddle is this. The diddler approaches the bar of a tavern, and demands a couple of twists of tobacco. These are handed to him, when, having slightly examined them, he says:

"I don't much like this tobacco. Here, take it back, and give me a glass of brandy and water in its place." The brandy and water is furnished and imbibed, and the diddler makes his way to the door. But the voice of the tavern-keeper arrests him.

"I believe, sir, you have forgotten to pay for your brandy and water."

"Pay for my brandy and water!—didn't I give you the tobacco for the brandy and water? What more would you have?"

"But, sir, if you please, I don't remember that you paid me for the tobacco."

"What do you mean by that, you scoundrel?—Didn't I give you back your tobacco? Isn't that your tobacco lying there? Do you expect me to pay for what I did not take?"

"But, sir," says the publican, now rather at a loss what to say, "but sir-"

"But me no buts, sir," interrupts the diddler, apparently in very high dudgeon, and slamming the door after him, as he makes his escape.—"But me no buts, sir, and none of your tricks upon travellers."

Here again is a very clever diddle, of which the simplicity is not its least recommendation. A purse, or pocket-book, being really lost, the loser inserts in one of the daily papers of a large city a fully descriptive advertisement.

Whereupon our diddler copies the facts of this advertisement, with a change of heading, of general phraseology and address. The original, for instance, is long, and verbose, is headed "A Pocket-Book Lost!" and requires the treasure, when found, to be left at No. 1 Tom Street. The copy is brief, and being headed with "Lost" only, indicates No. 2 Dick, or No. 3 Harry Street, as the locality at which the owner may be seen. Moreover, it is inserted in at least five or six of the daily papers of the day, while in point of time, it makes its appearance only a few hours after the original. Should it be read by the loser of the purse, he would hardly suspect it to have any reference to his own misfortune. But, of course, the chances are five or six to one, that the finder will repair to the address given by the diddler, rather than to that pointed out by the rightful proprietor. The former pays the reward, pockets the treasure and decamps.

Quite an analogous diddle is this. A lady of ton has dropped, some where in the street, a diamond ring of very unusual value. For its recovery, she offers some forty or fifty dollars reward—giving, in her advertisement, a very minute description of the gem, and of its settings, and declaring that, on its restoration at No. so and so, in such and such Avenue, the reward would be paid instanter, without a single question being asked. During the lady's absence from home, a day or two afterwards, a ring is heard at the door of No. so and so, in such and such Avenue; a servant appears; the lady of the house is asked for and is declared to be out, at which astounding information, the visitor expresses the most poignant regret. His business is of importance and concerns the lady herself. In fact, he had the good fortune to find her diamond ring. But perhaps it would be as well that he should call again. "By no means!" says the servant; and "By no means!" says the lady's sister and the lady's sister-in-law, who are summoned forthwith. The ring is clamorously identified, the reward is paid, and the finder nearly thrust out of doors. The lady returns and expresses some little dissatisfaction with her sister and sister-in-law, because they happen to have paid forty or fifty dollars for a fac-simile of her diamond ring—a fac-simile made out of real pinch-beck and unquestionable paste.

But as there is really no end to diddling, so there would be none to this essay, were I even to hint at half the variations, or inflections, of which this science is susceptible. I must bring this paper, perforce, to a conclusion, and this I cannot do better than by a summary notice of a very decent, but rather elaborate diddle, of which our own city was made the theatre, not very long ago, and which was subsequently repeated with success, in other still more verdant localities of the Union. A middle-aged gentleman arrives in town from parts unknown. He is remarkably precise, cautious, staid, and deliberate in his demeanor. His dress is scrupulously neat, but plain, unostentatious. He wears a white cravat, an ample waistcoat, made with an eye to comfort alone; thick-soled cosy-looking shoes, and pantaloons without straps. He has the whole air, in fact, of your well-to-do, sober-sided, exact, and respectable "man of business," Par excellence—one of the stern and outwardly hard, internally soft, sort of people that we see in the crack high comedies—fellows whose words are so many bonds, and who are noted for giving away guineas, in charity, with the one hand, while, in the way of mere bargain, they exact the uttermost fraction of a farthing with the other.

He makes much ado before he can get suited with a boarding house. He dislikes children. He has been accustomed to quiet. His habits are methodical—and then he would prefer getting into a private and respectable small family, piously inclined. Terms, however, are no object—only he must insist upon settling his bill on the first of every month, (it is now the second) and begs his landlady, when he finally obtains one to his mind, not on any account to forget his instructions upon this point—but to send in a bill, and receipt, precisely at ten o'clock, on the first day of every month, and under no circumstances to put it off to the second.

These arrangements made, our man of business rents an office in a reputable rather than a fashionable quarter of the town. There is nothing he more despises than pretense. "Where there is much show," he says, "there is seldom any thing very solid behind"—an observation which so profoundly impresses his landlady's fancy, that she makes a pencil memorandum of it forthwith, in her great family Bible, on the broad margin of the Proverbs of Solomon.

The next step is to advertise, after some such fashion as this, in the principal business six-pennies of the city—the pennies are eschewed as not "respectable"—and as demanding payment for all advertisements in advance. Our man of business holds it as a point of his faith that work should never be paid for until done.

"WANTED—The advertisers, being about to commence extensive business operations in this city, will require the services of three or four intelligent and competent clerks, to whom a liberal salary will be paid. The very best recommendations, not so much for capacity, as for integrity, will be expected. Indeed, as the duties to be performed involve high responsibilities, and large amounts of money must necessarily pass through the hands of those engaged, it is deemed advisable to demand a deposit of fifty dollars from each clerk employed. No person need apply, therefore, who is not prepared to leave this sum in the possession of the advertisers, and who cannot furnish the most satisfactory testimonials of morality. Young gentlemen piously inclined will be preferred. Application should be made between the hours of ten and eleven A. M., and four and five P. M., of Messrs.

"Bogs, Hogs Logs, Frogs & Co.,

"No. 110 Dog Street"

By the thirty-first day of the month, this advertisement has brought to the office of Messrs. Bogs, Hogs, Logs, Frogs, and Company, some fifteen or twenty young gentlemen piously inclined. But our man of business is in no hurry to conclude a contract with any—no man of business is ever precipitate—and it is not until the most rigid catechism in respect to the piety of each young gentleman's inclination, that his services are engaged and his fifty dollars receipted for, just by way of proper precaution, on the part of the respectable firm of Bogs, Hogs, Logs, Frogs, and Company. On the morning of the first day of the next month, the landlady does not present her bill, according to promise—a piece of neglect for which the comfortable head of the house ending in ogs would no doubt have chided her severely, could he have been prevailed upon to remain in town a day or two for that purpose.

As it is, the constables have had a sad time of it, running hither and thither, and all they can do is to declare the man of business most emphatically, a "hen knee high"—by which some persons imagine them to imply that, in fact, he is n. e. i.—by which again the very classical phrase non est inventus, is supposed to be understood. In the meantime the young gentlemen, one and all, are somewhat less piously inclined than before, while the landlady purchases a shilling's worth of the Indian rubber, and very carefully obliterates the pencil memorandum that some fool has made in her great family Bible, on the broad margin of the Proverbs of Solomon.

THE ANGEL OF THE ODD

AN EXTRAVAGANZA.

IT was a chilly November afternoon. I had just consummated an unusually hearty dinner, of which the dyspeptic truffe formed not the least important item, and was sitting alone in the dining-room, with my feet upon the fender, and at my elbow a small table which I had rolled up to the fire, and upon which were some apologies for dessert, with some miscellaneous bottles of wine, spirit and liqueur. In the morning I had been reading Glover's "Leonidas," Wilkie's "Epigoniad," Lamartine's "Pilgrimage," Barlow's "Columbiad," Tuckermann's "Sicily," and Griswold's "Curiosities"; I am willing to confess, therefore, that I now felt a little stupid. I made effort to arouse myself by aid of frequent Lafitte, and, all failing, I betook myself to a stray newspaper in despair. Having carefully perused the column of "houses to let," and the column of "dogs lost," and then the two columns of "wives and apprentices runaway," I attacked with great resolution the editorial matter, and, reading it from beginning to end without understanding a syllable, conceived the possibility of its being Chinese, and so re-read it from the end to the beginning, but with no more satisfactory result. I was about throwing away, in disgust,

> *"This folio of four pages, happy work*
>
> *Which not even critics criticise,"*

when I felt my attention somewhat aroused by the paragraph which follows:

"The avenues to death are numerous and strange. A London paper mentions the decease of a person from a singular cause. He was playing at 'puff the dart,' which is played with a long needle inserted in some worsted, and blown at a target through a tin tube. He placed the needle at the wrong end of the tube, and drawing his breath strongly to puff the dart forward with force, drew the needle into his throat. It entered the lungs, and in a few days killed him."

Upon seeing this I fell into a great rage, without exactly knowing why. "This thing," I exclaimed, "is a contemptible falsehood—a poor hoax—the lees of the invention of some pitiable penny-a-liner—of some wretched concoctor of accidents in Cocaigne. These fellows, knowing the extravagant gullibility of the age, set their wits to work in the imagination of improbable possibilities—-of odd accidents, as they term them; but to a reflecting intellect (like mine," I added, in parenthesis, putting my forefinger unconsciously to the side of my nose,) "to a contemplative understanding such as I myself possess, it seems evident at once that the marvelous increase of late in these 'odd accidents' is by far the oddest accident of all. For my own part, I intend to believe nothing henceforward that has anything of the 'singular' about it."

"Mein Gott, den, vat a vool you bees for dat!" replied one of the most remarkable voices I ever heard. At first I took it for a rumbling in my ears— such as a man sometimes experiences when getting very drunk—but, upon second thought, I considered the sound as more nearly resembling that which proceeds from an empty barrel beaten with a big stick; and, in fact, this I should have concluded it to be, but for the articulation of the syllables and words. I am by no means naturally nervous, and the very few glasses of Lafitte which I had sipped served to embolden me no little, so that I felt nothing of trepidation, but merely uplifted my eyes with a leisurely movement, and looked carefully around the room for the intruder. I could not, however, perceive any one at all.

"Humph!" resumed the voice, as I continued my survey, "you mus pe so dronk as de pig, den, for not zee me as I zit here at your zide."

Hereupon I bethought me of looking immediately before my nose, and there, sure enough, confronting me at the table sat a personage nondescript, although not altogether indescribable. His body was a wine-pipe, or a rum-puncheon, or something of that character, and had a truly Falstaffian air. In its nether extremity were inserted two kegs, which seemed to answer all the purposes of legs. For arms there dangled from the upper portion of the carcass two tolerably long bottles, with the necks outward for hands. All the head that I saw the monster possessed of was one of those Hessian canteens which resemble a large snuff-box with a hole in the middle of the lid. This canteen (with a funnel on its top, like a cavalier cap slouched over the eyes) was set on edge upon the puncheon, with the hole toward myself; and through this hole, which seemed puckered up like the mouth of a very precise old maid, the creature was emitting certain rumbling and grumbling noises which he evidently intended for intelligible talk.

"I zay," said he, "you mos pe dronk as de pig, vor zit dare and not zee me zit ere; and I zay, doo, you mos pe pigger vool as de goose, vor to dispelief vat iz print in de print. 'Tiz de troof—-dat it iz—eberry vord ob it."

"Who are you, pray?" said I, with much dignity, although somewhat puzzled; "how did you get here? and what is it you are talking about?"

"Az vor ow I com'd ere," replied the figure, "dat iz none of your pizzness; and as vor vat I be talking apout, I be talk apout vat I tink proper; and as vor who I be, vy dat is de very ting I com'd here for to let you zee for yourzelf."

"You are a drunken vagabond," said I, "and I shall ring the bell and order my footman to kick you into the street."

"He! he! he!" said the fellow, "hu! hu! hu! dat you can't do."

"Can't do!" said I, "what do you mean?—I can't do what?"

"Ring de pell;" he replied, attempting a grin with his little villanous mouth.

Upon this I made an effort to get up, in order to put my threat into execution; but the ruffian just reached across the table very deliberately, and hitting me a tap on the forehead with the neck of one of the long bottles, knocked me back into the arm-chair from which I had half arisen. I was utterly astounded; and, for a moment, was quite at a loss what to do. In the meantime, he continued his talk.

"You zee," said he, "it iz te bess vor zit still; and now you shall know who I pe. Look at me! zee! I am te Angel ov te Odd."

"And odd enough, too," I ventured to reply; "but I was always under the impression that an angel had wings."

"Te wing!" he cried, highly incensed, "vat I pe do mit te wing? Mein Gott! do you take me vor a shicken?"

"No—oh no!" I replied, much alarmed, "you are no chicken—certainly not."

"Well, den, zit still and pehabe yourself, or I'll rap you again mid me vist. It iz te shicken ab te wing, und te owl ab te wing, und te imp ab te wing, und te head-teuffel ab te wing. Te angel ab not te wing, and I am te Angel ov te Odd."

"And your business with me at present is—is"—

"My pizzness!" ejaculated the thing, "vy vat a low bred buppy you mos pe vor to ask a gentleman und an angel apout his pizziness!"

This language was rather more than I could bear, even from an angel; so, plucking up courage, I seized a salt-cellar which lay within reach, and hurled it at the head of the intruder. Either he dodged, however, or my aim was inaccurate; for all I accomplished was the demolition of the crystal which protected the dial of the clock upon the mantel-piece. As for the Angel, he evinced his sense of my assault by giving me two or three hard consecutive raps upon the forehead as before. These reduced me at once to submission, and I am almost ashamed to confess that either through pain or vexation, there came a few tears into my eyes.

"Mein Gott!" said the Angel of the Odd, apparently much softened at my distress; "mein Gott, te man is eder ferry dronk or ferry zorry. You mos not trink it so strong—you mos put te water in te wine. Here, trink dis, like a goot veller, und don't gry now—don't!"

Hereupon the Angel of the Odd replenished my goblet (which was about a third full of Port) with a colorless fluid that he poured from one of his hand bottles. I observed that these bottles had labels about their necks, and that these labels were inscribed "Kirschenwasser."

The considerate kindness of the Angel mollified me in no little measure;

and, aided by the water with which he diluted my Port more than once, I at length regained sufficient temper to listen to his very extraordinary discourse. I cannot pretend to recount all that he told me, but I gleaned from what he said that he was the genius who presided over the contretemps of mankind, and whose business it was to bring about the odd accidents which are continually astonishing the skeptic. Once or twice, upon my venturing to express my total incredulity in respect to his pretensions, he grew very angry indeed, so that at length I considered it the wiser policy to say nothing at all, and let him have his own way. He talked on, therefore, at great length, while I merely leaned back in my chair with my eyes shut, and amused myself with munching raisins and filliping the stems about the room. But, by-and-by, the Angel suddenly construed this behavior of mine into contempt. He arose in a terrible passion, slouched his funnel down over his eyes, swore a vast oath, uttered a threat of some character which I did not precisely comprehend, and finally made me a low bow and departed, wishing me, in the language of the archbishop in Gil-Blas, "beaucoup de bonheur et un peu plus de bon sens."

His departure afforded me relief. The very few glasses of Lafitte that I had sipped had the effect of rendering me drowsy, and I felt inclined to take a nap of some fifteen or twenty minutes, as is my custom after dinner. At six I had an appointment of consequence, which it was quite indispensable that I should keep. The policy of insurance for my dwelling house had expired the day before; and, some dispute having arisen, it was agreed that, at six, I should meet the board of directors of the company and settle the terms of a renewal. Glancing upward at the clock on the mantel-piece, (for I felt too drowsy to take out my watch), I had the pleasure to find that I had still twenty-five minutes to spare. It was half past five; I could easily walk to the insurance office in five minutes; and my usual siestas had never been known to exceed five and twenty. I felt sufficiently safe, therefore, and composed myself to my slumbers forthwith.

Having completed them to my satisfaction, I again looked toward the time-piece and was half inclined to believe in the possibility of odd accidents when I found that, instead of my ordinary fifteen or twenty minutes, I had been dozing only three; for it still wanted seven and twenty of the appointed hour. I betook myself again to my nap, and at length a second time awoke, when, to my utter amazement, it still wanted twenty-seven minutes of six. I jumped up to examine the clock, and found that it had ceased running. My watch informed me that it was half past seven; and, of course, having slept two hours, I was too late for my appointment. "It will make no difference," I said: "I can call at the office in the morning and apologize; in the meantime what can be the matter with the clock?" Upon examining it I discovered that one of the raisin stems which I had been filliping about the room during the discourse of the Angel of the Odd, had flown through the fractured crystal, and lodging, singularly enough, in the key-hole, with an end projecting outward, had thus arrested the revolution of the minute hand.

"Ah!" said I, "I see how it is. This thing speaks for itself. A natural accident, such as will happen now and then!"

I gave the matter no further consideration, and at my usual hour retired to bed. Here, having placed a candle upon a reading stand at the bed head, and having made an attempt to peruse some pages of the "Omnipresence of the Deity," I unfortunately fell asleep in less than twenty seconds, leaving the light burning as it was.

My dreams were terrifically disturbed by visions of the Angel of the Odd. Methought he stood at the foot of the couch, drew aside the curtains, and, in the hollow, detestable tones of a rum puncheon, menaced me with the bitterest vengeance for the contempt with which I had treated him. He concluded a long harangue by taking off his funnel-cap, inserting the tube into my gullet, and thus deluging me with an ocean of Kirschenw?sser, which he poured, in a continuous flood, from one of the long necked bottles that stood him instead of an arm. My agony was at length insufferable, and I awoke just in time to perceive that a rat had ran off with the lighted candle from the stand, but not in season to prevent his making his escape with it through the hole. Very soon, a strong suffocating odor assailed my nostrils; the house, I clearly perceived, was on fire. In a few minutes the blaze broke forth with violence, and in an incredibly brief period the entire building was wrapped in flames. All egress from my chamber, except through a window, was cut off. The crowd, however, quickly procured and raised a long ladder. By means of this I was descending rapidly, and in apparent safety, when a huge hog, about whose rotund stomach, and indeed about whose whole air and physiognomy, there was something which reminded me of the Angel of the Odd,—when this hog, I say, which hitherto had been quietly slumbering in the mud, took it suddenly into his head that his left shoulder needed scratching, and could find no more convenient rubbing-post than that afforded by the foot of the ladder. In an instant I was precipitated and had the misfortune to fracture my arm.

This accident, with the loss of my insurance, and with the more serious loss of my hair, the whole of which had been singed off by the fire, predisposed me to serious impressions, so that, finally, I made up my mind to take a wife. There was a rich widow disconsolate for the loss of her seventh husband, and to her wounded spirit I offered the balm of my vows. She yielded a reluctant consent to my prayers. I knelt at her feet in gratitude and adoration. She blushed and bowed her luxuriant tresses into close contact with those supplied me, temporarily, by Grandjean. I know not how the entanglement took place, but so it was. I arose with a shining pate, wigless; she in disdain and wrath, half buried in alien hair. Thus ended my hopes of the widow by an accident which could not have been anticipated, to be sure, but which the natural sequence of events had brought about.

Without despairing, however, I undertook the siege of a less implacable heart. The fates were again propitious for a brief period; but again a trivial incident interfered. Meeting my betrothed in an avenue thronged with the ?lite of the city, I was hastening to greet her with one of my best considered bows, when a small particle of some foreign matter, lodging in the corner of my eye, rendered me, for the moment, completely blind. Before I could recover my sight, the lady of my love had disappeared—irreparably affronted at what she chose to consider my premeditated rudeness in passing her by ungreeted. While I stood bewildered at the suddenness of this accident, (which might have happened, nevertheless, to any one under the sun), and while I still continued incapable of sight, I was accosted by the Angel of the Odd, who proffered me his aid with a civility which I had no reason to expect. He examined my disordered eye with much gentleness and skill, informed me that I had a drop in it, and (whatever a "drop" was) took it out, and afforded me relief.

I now considered it high time to die, (since fortune had so determined to persecute me,) and accordingly made my way to the nearest river. Here, divesting myself of my clothes, (for there is no reason why we cannot die as we were born), I threw myself headlong into the current; the sole witness of my fate being a solitary crow that had been seduced into the eating of brandy-saturated corn, and so had staggered away from his fellows. No sooner had I entered the water than this bird took it into its head to fly away with the most indispensable portion of my apparel. Postponing, therefore, for the present, my suicidal design, I just slipped my nether extremities into the sleeves of my coat, and betook myself to a pursuit of the felon with all the nimbleness which the case required and its circumstances would admit. But my evil destiny attended me still. As I ran at full speed, with my nose up in the atmosphere, and intent only upon the purloiner of my property, I suddenly perceived that my feet rested no longer upon terra-firma; the fact is, I had thrown myself over a precipice, and should inevitably have been dashed to pieces but for my good fortune in grasping the end of a long guide-rope, which depended from a passing balloon.

As soon as I sufficiently recovered my senses to comprehend the terrific predicament in which I stood or rather hung, I exerted all the power of my lungs to make that predicament known to the ?ronaut overhead. But for a long time I exerted myself in vain. Either the fool could not, or the villain would not perceive me. Meantime the machine rapidly soared, while my strength even more rapidly failed. I was soon upon the point of resigning myself to my fate, and dropping quietly into the sea, when my spirits were suddenly revived by hearing a hollow voice from above, which seemed to be lazily humming an opera air. Looking up, I perceived the Angel of the Odd. He was leaning with his arms folded, over the rim of the car; and with a pipe in his mouth, at which he puffed leisurely, seemed to be upon excellent terms with himself and the universe. I was too much exhausted to speak, so I merely regarded him with an imploring air.

For several minutes, although he looked me full in the face, he said nothing. At length removing carefully his meerschaum from the right to the left corner of his mouth, he condescended to speak.

"Who pe you," he asked, "und what der teuffel you pe do dare?"

To this piece of impudence, cruelty and affectation, I could reply only by ejaculating the monosyllable "Help!"

"Elp!" echoed the ruffian—"not I. Dare iz te pottle—elp yourself, und pe tam'd!"

With these words he let fall a heavy bottle of Kirschenwasser which, dropping precisely upon the crown of my head, caused me to imagine that my brains were entirely knocked out. Impressed with this idea, I was about to relinquish my hold and give up the ghost with a good grace, when I was arrested by the cry of the Angel, who bade me hold on.

"Old on!" he said; "don't pe in te urry—don't. Will you pe take de odder pottle, or ave you pe got zober yet and come to your zenzes?"

I made haste, hereupon, to nod my head twice—once in the negative, meaning thereby that I would prefer not taking the other bottle at present—and once in the affirmative, intending thus to imply that I was sober and had positively come to my senses. By these means I somewhat softened the Angel.

"Und you pelief, ten," he inquired, "at te last? You pelief, ten, in te possibilty of te odd?"

I again nodded my head in assent.

"Und you ave pelief in me, te Angel of te Odd?"

I nodded again.

"Und you acknowledge tat you pe te blind dronk and te vool?"

I nodded once more.

"Put your right hand into your left hand preeches pocket, ten, in token ov your vull zubmizzion unto te Angel ov te Odd."

This thing, for very obvious reasons, I found it quite impossible to do.

In the first place, my left arm had been broken in my fall from the ladder, and, therefore, had I let go my hold with the right hand, I must have let go altogether. In the second place, I could have no breeches until I came across the crow. I was therefore obliged, much to my regret, to shake my head in the negative—intending thus to give the Angel to understand that I found it inconvenient, just at that moment, to comply with his very reasonable demand! No sooner, however, had I ceased shaking my head than—

"Go to der teuffel, ten!" roared the Angel of the Odd.

In pronouncing these words, he drew a sharp knife across the guide-rope by which I was suspended, and as we then happened to be precisely over my own house, (which, during my peregrinations, had been handsomely rebuilt,) it so occurred that I tumbled headlong down the ample chimney and alit upon the dining-room hearth.

Upon coming to my senses, (for the fall had very thoroughly stunned me,) I found it about four o'clock in the morning. I lay outstretched where I had fallen from the balloon. My head grovelled in the ashes of an extinguished fire, while my feet reposed upon the wreck of a small table, overthrown, and amid the fragments of a miscellaneous dessert, intermingled with a newspaper, some broken glass and shattered bottles, and an empty jug of the Schiedam Kirschenwasser. Thus revenged himself the Angel of the Odd.

[Mabbott states that Griswold "obviously had a revised form" for use in the 1856 volume of Poe's works. Mabbott does not substantiate this claim, but it is surely not unreasonable. An editor, and even typographical errors, may have produced nearly all of the very minor changes made in this version. (Indeed, two very necessary words were clearly dropped by accident.) An editor might have corrected "Wickliffe's 'Epigoniad'" to "Wilkie's 'Epigoniad'," but is unlikely to have added "Tuckerman's 'Sicily'" to the list of books read by the narrator. Griswold was not above forgery (in Poe's letters) when it suited his purpose, but would have too little to gain by such an effort in this instance.]

MELLONTA TAUTA

TO THE EDITORS OF THE LADY'S BOOK:

I have the honor of sending you, for your magazine, an article which I hope you will be able to comprehend rather more distinctly than I do myself. It is a translation, by my friend, Martin Van Buren Mavis, (sometimes called the "Poughkeepsie Seer") of an odd-looking MS. which I found, about a year ago, tightly corked up in a jug floating in the Mare Tenebrarum—a sea well described by the Nubian geographer, but seldom visited now-a-days, except for the transcendentalists and divers for crotchets.

Truly yours,

EDGAR A. POE

{this paragraph not in the volume—ED}

ON BOARD BALLOON "SKYLARK"

April, 1, 2848

NOW, my dear friend—now, for your sins, you are to suffer the infliction of a long gossiping letter. I tell you distinctly that I am going to punish you for all your impertinences by being as tedious, as discursive, as incoherent and as unsatisfactory as possible. Besides, here I am, cooped up in a dirty balloon, with some one or two hundred of the canaille, all bound on a pleasure excursion, (what a funny idea some people have of pleasure!) and I have no prospect of touching terra firma for a month at least. Nobody to talk to. Nothing to do. When one has nothing to do, then is the time to correspond with ones friends. You perceive, then, why it is that I write you this letter—it is on account of my ennui and your sins.

Get ready your spectacles and make up your mind to be annoyed. I mean to write at you every day during this odious voyage.

Heigho! when will any Invention visit the human pericranium? Are we forever to be doomed to the thousand inconveniences of the balloon? Will nobody contrive a more expeditious mode of progress? The jog-trot movement, to my thinking, is little less than positive torture. Upon my word we have not made more than a hundred miles the hour since leaving home! The very birds beat us—at least some of them. I assure you that I do not exaggerate at all. Our motion, no doubt, seems slower than it actually is—this on account of our having no objects about us by which to estimate our velocity, and on account of our going with the wind. To be sure, whenever we meet a balloon we have a chance of perceiving our rate, and then, I admit, things do not appear so very bad. Accustomed as I am to this mode of travelling, I cannot get over a kind of giddiness whenever a balloon passes us in a current directly overhead. It always seems to me like an immense bird of prey about to pounce upon us and carry us off in its claws. One went over us this morning about sunrise, and so nearly overhead that its drag-rope actually brushed the network suspending our car, and caused us very serious apprehension. Our captain said that if the material of the bag had been the trumpery varnished "silk" of five hundred or a thousand years ago, we should inevitably have been damaged. This silk, as he explained it to me, was a fabric composed of the entrails of a species of earth-worm. The worm was carefully fed on mulberries—kind of fruit resembling a water-melon—and, when sufficiently fat, was crushed in a mill. The paste thus arising was called papyrus in its primary state, and went through a variety of processes until it finally became "silk." Singular to relate, it was once much admired as an article of female dress! Balloons were also very generally constructed from it. A better kind of material, it appears, was subsequently found in the down surrounding the seed-vessels of a plant vulgarly called euphorbium, and at that time botanically termed milk-weed. This latter kind of silk was designated as silk-buckingham, on account of its superior durability, and was usually prepared for use by being varnished with a solution of gum caoutchouc—a substance which in some respects must have resembled the gutta percha now in common use. This caoutchouc was occasionally called Indian rubber or rubber of twist, and was no doubt one of the numerous fungi. Never tell me again that I am not at heart an antiquarian.

Talking of drag-ropes—our own, it seems, has this moment knocked a man overboard from one of the small magnetic propellers that swarm in ocean below us—a boat of about six thousand tons, and, from all accounts, shamefully crowded. These diminutive barques should be prohibited from carrying more than a definite number of passengers. The man, of course, was not permitted to get on board again, and was soon out of sight, he and his life-preserver. I rejoice, my dear friend, that we live in an age so enlightened that no such a thing as an individual is supposed to exist. It is the mass for which the true Humanity cares. By-the-by, talking of Humanity, do you know that our immortal Wiggins is not so original in his views of the Social Condition and so forth, as his contemporaries are inclined to suppose? Pundit assures me that the same ideas were put nearly in the same way, about a thousand years ago, by an Irish philosopher called Furrier, on account of his keeping a retail shop for cat peltries and other furs. Pundit knows, you know; there can be no mistake about it. How very wonderfully do we see verified every day, the profound observation of the Hindoo Aries Tottle (as quoted by Pundit)— "Thus must we say that, not once or twice, or a few times, but with almost infinite repetitions, the same opinions come round in a circle among men."

April 2.—Spoke to-day the magnetic cutter in charge of the middle section of floating telegraph wires. I learn that when this species of telegraph was first put into operation by Horse, it was considered quite impossible to convey the wires over sea, but now we are at a loss to comprehend where the difficulty lay! So wags the world. Tempora mutantur—excuse me for quoting the Etruscan. What would we do without the Atalantic telegraph? (Pundit says Atlantic was the ancient adjective.) We lay to a few minutes to ask the cutter some questions, and learned, among other glorious news, that civil war is raging in Africa, while the plague is doing its good work beautifully both in Yurope and Ayesher. Is it not truly remarkable that, before the magnificent light shed upon philosophy by Humanity, the world was accustomed to regard War and Pestilence as calamities? Do you know that prayers were actually offered up in the ancient temples to the end that these evils (!) might not be visited upon mankind? Is it not really difficult to comprehend upon what principle of interest our forefathers acted? Were they so blind as not to perceive that the destruction of a myriad of individuals is only so much positive advantage to the mass!

April 3.—It is really a very fine amusement to ascend the rope-ladder leading to the summit of the balloon-bag, and thence survey the surrounding world. From the car below you know the prospect is not so comprehensive— you can see little vertically. But seated here (where I write this) in the luxuriously-cushioned open piazza of the summit, one can see everything that is going on in all directions. Just now there is quite a crowd of balloons in sight, and they present a very animated appearance, while the air is resonant with the hum of so many millions of human voices. I have heard it asserted that when Yellow or (Pundit will have it) Violet, who is supposed to have been the first aeronaut, maintained the practicability of traversing the atmosphere in all directions, by merely ascending or descending until a favorable current was attained, he was scarcely hearkened to at all by his contemporaries, who looked upon him as merely an ingenious sort of madman, because the philosophers (?) of the day declared the thing impossible. Really now it does seem to me quite unaccountable how any thing so obviously feasible could have escaped the sagacity of the ancient savans. But in all ages the great obstacles to advancement in Art have been opposed by the so-called men of science. To be sure, our men of science are not quite so bigoted as those of old:—oh, I have something so queer to tell you on this topic. Do you know that it is not more than a thousand years ago since the metaphysicians consented to relieve the people of the singular fancy that there existed but two possible roads for the attainment of Truth! Believe it if you can! It appears that long, long ago, in the night of Time, there lived a Turkish philosopher (or Hindoo possibly) called Aries Tottle. This person introduced, or at all events propagated what was termed the deductive or a priori mode of investigation. He started with what he maintained to be axioms or "self-evident truths," and thence proceeded "logically" to results. His greatest disciples were one Neuclid, and one Cant. Well, Aries Tottle flourished supreme until advent of one Hog, surnamed the "Ettrick Shepherd," who preached an entirely different system, which he called the a posteriori or inductive. His plan referred altogether to Sensation. He proceeded by observing, analyzing, and classifying facts- instantiae naturae, as they were affectedly called—into general laws. Aries Tottle's mode, in a word, was based on noumena; Hog's on phenomena. Well, so great was the admiration excited by this latter system that, at its first introduction, Aries Tottle fell into disrepute; but finally he recovered ground and was permitted to divide the realm of Truth with his more modern rival. The savans now maintained the Aristotelian and Baconian roads were the sole possible avenues to knowledge. "Baconian," you must know, was an adjective invented as equivalent to Hog-ian and more euphonious and dignified.

Now, my dear friend, I do assure you, most positively, that I represent this matter fairly, on the soundest authority and you can easily understand how a notion so absurd on its very face must have operated to retard the progress of all true knowledge—which makes its advances almost invariably by intuitive bounds. The ancient idea confined investigations to crawling; and for hundreds of years so great was the infatuation about Hog especially, that a virtual end was put to all thinking, properly so called. No man dared utter a truth to which he felt himself indebted to his Soul alone. It mattered not whether the truth was even demonstrably a truth, for the bullet-headed savans of the time regarded only the road by which he had attained it. They would not even look at the end. "Let us see the means," they cried, "the means!" If, upon investigation of the means, it was found to come under neither the category Aries (that is to say Ram) nor under the category Hog, why then the savans went no farther, but pronounced the "theorist" a fool, and would have nothing to do with him or his truth.

Now, it cannot be maintained, even, that by the crawling system the greatest amount of truth would be attained in any long series of ages, for the repression of imagination was an evil not to be compensated for by any superior certainty in the ancient modes of investigation. The error of these Jurmains, these Vrinch, these Inglitch, and these Amriccans (the latter, by the way, were our own immediate progenitors), was an error quite analogous with that of the wiseacre who fancies that he must necessarily see an object the better the more closely he holds it to his eyes. These people blinded themselves by details. When they proceeded Hoggishly, their "facts" were by no means always facts—a matter of little consequence had it not been for assuming that they were facts and must be facts because they appeared to be such. When they proceeded on the path of the Ram, their course was scarcely as straight as a ram's horn, for they never had an axiom which was an axiom at all. They must have been very blind not to see this, even in their own day; for even in their own day many of the long "established" axioms had been rejected. For example—"Ex nihilo nihil fit"; "a body cannot act where it is not"; "there cannot exist antipodes"; "darkness cannot come out of light"— all these, and a dozen other similar propositions, formerly admitted without hesitation as axioms, were, even at the period of which I speak, seen to be untenable. How absurd in these people, then, to persist in putting faith in "axioms" as immutable bases of Truth! But even out of the mouths of their soundest reasoners it is easy to demonstrate the futility, the impalpability of their axioms in general. Who was the soundest of their logicians? Let me see! I will go and ask Pundit and be back in a minute.... Ah, here we have it! Here is a book written nearly a thousand years ago and lately translated from the Inglitch—which, by the way, appears to have been the rudiment of the Amriccan. Pundit says it is decidedly the cleverest ancient work on its topic, Logic. The author (who was much thought of in his day) was one Miller, or Mill; and we find it recorded of him, as a point of some importance, that he had a mill-horse called Bentham. But let us glance at the treatise!

Ah!—"Ability or inability to conceive," says Mr. Mill, very properly, "is in no case to be received as a criterion of axiomatic truth." What modern in his senses would ever think of disputing this truism? The only wonder with us must be, how it happened that Mr. Mill conceived it necessary even to hint at any thing so obvious. So far good—but let us turn over another paper. What have we here?—"Contradictories cannot both be true—that is, cannot co-exist in nature." Here Mr. Mill means, for example, that a tree must be either a tree or not a tree—that it cannot be at the same time a tree and not a tree. Very well; but I ask him why. His reply is this—and never pretends to be any thing else than this—"Because it is impossible to conceive that contradictories can both be true." But this is no answer at all, by his own showing, for has he not just admitted as a truism that "ability or inability to conceive is in no case to be received as a criterion of axiomatic truth."

Now I do not complain of these ancients so much because their logic is, by their own showing, utterly baseless, worthless and fantastic altogether, as because of their pompous and imbecile proscription of all other roads of Truth, of all other means for its attainment than the two preposterous paths—the one of creeping and the one of crawling—to which they have dared to confine the Soul that loves nothing so well as to soar.

By the by, my dear friend, do you not think it would have puzzled these ancient dogmaticians to have determined by which of their two roads it was that the most important and most sublime of all their truths was, in effect, attained? I mean the truth of Gravitation. Newton owed it to Kepler. Kepler admitted that his three laws were guessed at—these three laws of all laws which led the great Inglitch mathematician to his principle, the basis of all physical principle—to go behind which we must enter the Kingdom of Metaphysics. Kepler guessed—that is to say imagined. He was essentially a "theorist"—that word now of so much sanctity, formerly an epithet of contempt. Would it not have puzzled these old moles too, to have explained by which of the two "roads" a cryptographist unriddles a cryptograph of more than usual secrecy, or by which of the two roads Champollion directed mankind to those enduring and almost innumerable truths which resulted from his deciphering the Hieroglyphics.

One word more on this topic and I will be done boring you. Is it not passing strange that, with their eternal prattling about roads to Truth, these bigoted people missed what we now so clearly perceive to be the great highway—that of Consistency? Does it not seem singular how they should have failed to deduce from the works of God the vital fact that a perfect consistency must be an absolute truth! How plain has been our progress since the late announcement of this proposition! Investigation has been taken out of the hands of the ground-moles and given, as a task, to the true and only true thinkers, the men of ardent imagination. These latter theorize. Can you not fancy the shout of scorn with which my words would be received by our progenitors were it possible for them to be now looking over my shoulder? These men, I say, theorize; and their theories are simply corrected, reduced, systematized—cleared, little by little, of their dross of inconsistency—until, finally, a perfect consistency stands apparent which even the most stolid admit, because it is a consistency, to be an absolute and an unquestionable truth.

April 4.—The new gas is doing wonders, in conjunction with the new improvement with gutta percha. How very safe, commodious, manageable, and in every respect convenient are our modern balloons! Here is an immense one approaching us at the rate of at least a hundred and fifty miles an hour. It seems to be crowded with people—perhaps there are three or four hundred passengers—and yet it soars to an elevation of nearly a mile, looking down upon poor us with sovereign contempt. Still a hundred or even two hundred miles an hour is slow travelling after all. Do you remember our flight on the railroad across the Kanadaw continent?—fully three hundred miles the hour—that was travelling. Nothing to be seen though—nothing to be done but flirt, feast and dance in the magnificent saloons. Do you remember what an odd sensation was experienced when, by chance, we caught a glimpse of external objects while the cars were in full flight? Every thing seemed unique—in one mass. For my part, I cannot say but that I preferred the travelling by the slow train of a hundred miles the hour. Here we were permitted to have glass windows—even to have them open—and something like a distinct view of the country was attainable.... Pundit says that the route for the great Kanadaw railroad must have been in some measure marked out about nine hundred years ago! In fact, he goes so far as to assert that actual traces of a road are still discernible—traces referable to a period quite as remote as that mentioned. The track, it appears was double only; ours, you know, has twelve paths; and three or four new ones are in preparation. The ancient rails were very slight, and placed so close together as to be, according to modern notions, quite frivolous, if not dangerous in the extreme. The present width of track—fifty feet—is considered, indeed, scarcely secure enough. For my part, I make no doubt that a track of some sort must have existed in very remote times, as Pundit asserts; for nothing can be clearer, to my mind, than that, at some period—not less than seven centuries ago, certainly—the Northern and Southern Kanadaw continents were united; the Kanawdians, then, would have been driven, by necessity, to a great railroad across the continent.

April 5.—I am almost devoured by ennui. Pundit is the only conversible person on board; and he, poor soul! can speak of nothing but antiquities. He has been occupied all the day in the attempt to convince me that the ancient Amriccans governed themselves!—did ever anybody hear of such an absurdity?—that they existed in a sort of every-man-for-himself confederacy, after the fashion of the "prairie dogs" that we read of in fable. He says that they started with the queerest idea conceivable, viz: that all men are born free and equal—this in the very teeth of the laws of gradation so visibly impressed upon all things both in the moral and physical universe. Every man "voted," as they called it—that is to say meddled with public affairs—until at length, it was discovered that what is everybody's business is nobody's, and that the "Republic" (so the absurd thing was called) was without a government at all. It is related, however, that the first circumstance which disturbed, very particularly, the self-complacency of the philosophers who constructed this "Republic," was the startling discovery that universal suffrage gave opportunity for fraudulent schemes, by means of which any desired number of votes might at any time be polled, without the possibility of prevention or even detection, by any party which should be merely villainous enough not to be ashamed of the fraud. A little reflection upon this discovery sufficed to render evident the consequences, which were that rascality must predominate—in a word, that a republican government could never be any thing but a rascally one. While the philosophers, however, were busied in blushing at their stupidity in not having foreseen these inevitable evils, and intent upon the invention of new theories, the matter was put to an abrupt issue by a fellow of the name of Mob, who took every thing into his own hands and set up a despotism, in comparison with which those of the fabulous Zeros and Hellofagabaluses were respectable and delectable. This Mob (a foreigner, by-the-by), is said to have been the most odious of all men that ever encumbered the earth. He was a giant in stature—insolent, rapacious, filthy, had the gall of a bullock with the heart of a hyena and the brains of a peacock. He died, at length, by dint of his own energies, which exhausted him. Nevertheless, he had his uses, as every thing has, however vile, and taught mankind a lesson which to this day it is in no danger of forgetting—never to run directly contrary to the natural analogies. As for Republicanism, no analogy could be found for it upon the face of the earth—unless we except the case of the "prairie dogs," an exception which seems to demonstrate, if anything, that democracy is a very admirable form of government—for dogs.

April 6.—Last night had a fine view of Alpha Lyrae, whose disk, through our captain's spy-glass, subtends an angle of half a degree, looking very much as our sun does to the naked eye on a misty day. Alpha Lyrae, although so very much larger than our sun, by the by, resembles him closely as regards its spots, its atmosphere, and in many other particulars. It is only within the last century, Pundit tells me, that the binary relation existing between these two orbs began even to be suspected. The evident motion of our system in the heavens was (strange to say!) referred to an orbit about a prodigious star in the centre of the galaxy. About this star, or at all events about a centre of gravity common to all the globes of the Milky Way and supposed to be near Alcyone in the Pleiades, every one of these globes was declared to be revolving, our own performing the circuit in a period of 117,000,000 of years! We, with our present lights, our vast telescopic improvements, and so forth, of course find it difficult to comprehend the ground of an idea such as this. Its first propagator was one Mudler. He was led, we must presume, to this wild hypothesis by mere analogy in the first instance; but, this being the case, he should have at least adhered to analogy in its development. A great central orb was, in fact, suggested; so far Mudler was consistent. This central orb, however, dynamically, should have been greater than all its surrounding orbs taken together. The question might then have been asked—"Why do we not see it?"—we, especially, who occupy the mid region of the cluster—the very locality near which, at least, must be situated this inconceivable central sun. The astronomer, perhaps, at this point, took refuge in the suggestion of non-luminosity; and here analogy was suddenly let fall. But even admitting the central orb non-luminous, how did he manage to explain its failure to be rendered visible by the incalculable host of glorious suns glaring in all directions about it? No doubt what he finally maintained was merely a centre of gravity common to all the revolving orbs—but here again analogy must have been let fall. Our system revolves, it is true, about a common centre of gravity, but it does this in connection with and in consequence of a material sun whose mass more than counterbalances the rest of the system. The mathematical circle is a curve composed of an infinity of straight lines; but this idea of the circle—this idea of it which, in regard to all earthly geometry, we consider as merely the mathematical, in contradistinction from the practical, idea—is, in sober fact, the practical conception which alone we have any right to entertain in respect to those Titanic circles with which we have to deal, at least in fancy, when we suppose our system, with its fellows, revolving about a point in the centre of the galaxy. Let the most vigorous of human imaginations but attempt to take a single step toward the comprehension of a circuit so unutterable! I would scarcely be paradoxical to say that a flash of lightning itself, travelling forever upon the circumference of this inconceivable circle, would still forever be travelling in a straight line. That the path of our sun along such a circumference—that the direction of our system in such an orbit—would, to any human perception, deviate in the slightest degree from a straight line even in a million of years, is a proposition not to be entertained; and yet these ancient astronomers were absolutely cajoled, it appears, into believing that a decisive curvature had become apparent during the brief period of their astronomical history—during the mere point—during the utter nothingness of two or three thousand years! How incomprehensible, that considerations such as this did not at once indicate to them the true state of affairs—that of the binary revolution of our sun and Alpha Lyrae around a common centre of gravity!

April 7.—Continued last night our astronomical amusements. Had a fine view of the five Neptunian asteroids, and watched with much interest the putting up of a huge impost on a couple of lintels in the new temple at Daphnis in the moon. It was amusing to think that creatures so diminutive as the lunarians, and bearing so little resemblance to humanity, yet evinced a mechanical ingenuity so much superior to our own. One finds it difficult, too, to conceive the vast masses which these people handle so easily, to be as light as our own reason tells us they actually are.

April 8.—Eureka! Pundit is in his glory. A balloon from Kanadaw spoke us to-day and threw on board several late papers; they contain some exceedingly curious information relative to Kanawdian or rather Amriccan antiquities. You know, I presume, that laborers have for some months been employed in preparing the ground for a new fountain at Paradise, the Emperor's principal pleasure garden. Paradise, it appears, has been, literally speaking, an island time out of mind—that is to say, its northern boundary was always (as far back as any record extends) a rivulet, or rather a very narrow arm of the sea. This arm was gradually widened until it attained its present breadth—a mile. The whole length of the island is nine miles; the breadth varies materially. The entire area (so Pundit says) was, about eight hundred years ago, densely packed with houses, some of them twenty stories high; land (for some most unaccountable reason) being considered as especially precious just in this vicinity. The disastrous earthquake, however, of the year 2050, so totally uprooted and overwhelmed the town (for it was almost too large to be called a village) that the most indefatigable of our antiquarians have never yet been able to obtain from the site any sufficient data (in the shape of coins, medals or inscriptions) wherewith to build up even the ghost of a theory concerning the manners, customs, &c., &c., &c., of the aboriginal inhabitants. Nearly all that we have hitherto known of them is, that they were a portion of the Knickerbocker tribe of savages infesting the continent at its first discovery by Recorder Riker, a knight of the Golden Fleece. They were by no means uncivilized, however, but cultivated various arts and even sciences after a fashion of their own. It is related of them that they were acute in many respects, but were oddly afflicted with monomania for building what, in the ancient Amriccan, was denominated "churches"—a kind of pagoda instituted for the worship of two idols that went by the names of Wealth and Fashion. In the end, it is said, the island became, nine tenths of it, church. The women, too, it appears, were oddly deformed by a natural protuberance of the region just below the small of the back—although, most unaccountably, this deformity was looked upon altogether in the light of a beauty. One or two pictures of these singular women have in fact, been miraculously preserved. They look very odd, very—like something between a turkey-cock and a dromedary.

Well, these few details are nearly all that have descended to us respecting the ancient Knickerbockers. It seems, however, that while digging in the centre of the emperors garden, (which, you know, covers the whole island), some of the workmen unearthed a cubical and evidently chiseled block of granite, weighing several hundred pounds. It was in good preservation, having received, apparently, little injury from the convulsion which entombed it. On one of its surfaces was a marble slab with (only think of it!) an inscription—a legible inscription. Pundit is in ecstacies. Upon detaching the slab, a cavity appeared, containing a leaden box filled with various coins, a long scroll of names, several documents which appear to resemble newspapers, with other matters of intense interest to the antiquarian! There can be no doubt that all these are genuine Amriccan relics belonging to the tribe called Knickerbocker. The papers thrown on board our balloon are filled with fac-similes of the coins, MSS., typography, &c., &c. I copy for your amusement the Knickerbocker inscription on the marble slab:—

This Corner Stone of a Monument to

The Memory of

GEORGE WASHINGTON

Was Laid With Appropriate Ceremonies

on the

19th Day of October, 1847

The anniversary of the surrender of

Lord Cornwallis

to General Washington at Yorktown

A. D. 1781

Under the Auspices of the

Washington Monument Association of

the city of New York

This, as I give it, is a verbatim translation done by Pundit himself, so there can be no mistake about it. From the few words thus preserved, we glean several important items of knowledge, not the least interesting of which is the fact that a thousand years ago actual monuments had fallen into disuse—as was all very proper—the people contenting themselves, as we do now, with a mere indication of the design to erect a monument at some future time; a corner-stone being cautiously laid by itself "solitary and alone" (excuse me for quoting the great American poet Benton!), as a guarantee of the magnanimous intention. We ascertain, too, very distinctly, from this admirable inscription, the how as well as the where and the what, of the great surrender in question. As to the where, it was Yorktown (wherever that was), and as to the what, it was General Cornwallis (no doubt some wealthy dealer in corn). He was surrendered. The inscription commemorates the surrender of—what? why, "of Lord Cornwallis." The only question is what could the savages wish him surrendered for. But when we remember that these savages were undoubtedly cannibals, we are led to the conclusion that they intended him for sausage. As to the how of the surrender, no language can be more explicit. Lord Cornwallis was surrendered (for sausage) "under the auspices of the Washington Monument Association"—no doubt a charitable institution for the depositing of corner-stones.—But, Heaven bless me! what is the matter? Ah, I see—the balloon has collapsed, and we shall have a tumble into the sea. I have, therefore, only time enough to add that, from a hasty inspection of the fac-similes of newspapers, &c., &c., I find that the great men in those days among the Amriccans, were one John, a smith, and one Zacchary, a tailor.

Good-bye, until I see you again. Whether you ever get this letter or not is point of little importance, as I write altogether for my own amusement. I shall cork the MS. up in a bottle, however, and throw it into the sea.

Yours everlastingly,

PUNDITA.

THE DUC DE L'OMELETTE.

And stepped at once into a cooler clime.—Cowper

KEATS fell by a criticism. Who was it died of "The Andromache"? {*1}
Ignoble souls!—De L'Omelette perished of an ortolan. L'histoire en est br?ve.
Assist me, Spirit of Apicius!

A golden cage bore the little winged wanderer, enamored, melting,
indolent, to the Chauss?e D'Antin, from its home in far Peru. From its
queenly possessor La Bellissima, to the Duc De L'Omelette, six peers of the
empire conveyed the happy bird.

That night the Duc was to sup alone. In the privacy of his bureau he
reclined languidly on that ottoman for which he sacrificed his loyalty in
outbidding his king—the notorious ottoman of Cadet.

He buries his face in the pillow. The clock strikes! Unable to restrain his
feelings, his Grace swallows an olive. At this moment the door gently opens
to the sound of soft music, and lo! the most delicate of birds is before the
most enamored of men! But what inexpressible dismay now overshadows the
countenance of the Duc?—"Horreur!—chien! Baptiste!—l'oiseau! ah, bon
Dieu! cet oiseau modeste que tu as d?shabill? de ses plumes, et que tu as servi
sans papier!" It is superfluous to say more:—the Duc expired in a paroxysm
of disgust.

"Ha! ha! ha!" said his Grace on the third day after his decease.

"He! he! he!" replied the Devil faintly, drawing himself up with an air
of hauteur.

"Why, surely you are not serious," retorted De L'Omelette. "I have
sinned—c'est vrai—but, my good sir, consider!—you have no actual intention
of putting such—such barbarous threats into execution."

"No what?" said his majesty—"come, sir, strip!"

"Strip, indeed! very pretty i' faith! no, sir, I shall not strip. Who are you, pray, that I, Duc De L'Omelette, Prince de Foie-Gras, just come of age, author of the 'Mazurkiad,' and Member of the Academy, should divest myself at your bidding of the sweetest pantaloons ever made by Bourdon, the daintiest robe-de-chambre ever put together by Rombert—to say nothing of the taking my hair out of paper—not to mention the trouble I should have in drawing off my gloves?"

"Who am I?—ah, true! I am Baal-Zebub, Prince of the Fly. I took thee, just now, from a rose-wood coffin inlaid with ivory. Thou wast curiously scented, and labelled as per invoice. Belial sent thee,—my Inspector of Cemeteries. The pantaloons, which thou sayest were made by Bourdon, are an excellent pair of linen drawers, and thy robe-de-chambre is a shroud of no scanty dimensions."

"Sir!" replied the Duc, "I am not to be insulted with impunity!—Sir! I shall take the earliest opportunity of avenging this insult!—Sir! you shall hear from me! in the meantime au revoir!"—and the Duc was bowing himself out of the Satanic presence, when he was interrupted and brought back by a gentleman in waiting. Hereupon his Grace rubbed his eyes, yawned, shrugged his shoulders, reflected. Having become satisfied of his identity, he took a bird's eye view of his whereabouts.

The apartment was superb. Even De L'Omelette pronounced it bien comme il faut. It was not its length nor its breadth,—but its height—ah, that was appalling!—There was no ceiling—certainly none—but a dense whirling mass of fiery-colored clouds. His Grace's brain reeled as he glanced upward. From above, hung a chain of an unknown blood-red metal—its upper end lost, like the city of Boston, parmi les nues. From its nether extremity swung a large cresset. The Duc knew it to be a ruby; but from it there poured a light so intense, so still, so terrible, Persia never worshipped such—Gheber never imagined such—Mussulman never dreamed of such when, drugged with opium, he has tottered to a bed of poppies, his back to the flowers, and his face to the God Apollo. The Duc muttered a slight oath, decidedly approbatory.

The corners of the room were rounded into niches. Three of these were filled with statues of gigantic proportions. Their beauty was Grecian, their deformity Egyptian, their tout ensemble French. In the fourth niche the statue was veiled; it was not colossal. But then there was a taper ankle, a sandalled foot. De L'Omelette pressed his hand upon his heart, closed his eyes, raised them, and caught his Satanic Majesty—in a blush.

But the paintings!—Kupris! Astarte! Astoreth!—a thousand and the same! And Rafaelle has beheld them! Yes, Rafaelle has been here, for did he not paint the—? and was he not consequently damned? The paintings—the paintings! O luxury! O love!—who, gazing on those forbidden beauties, shall have eyes for the dainty devices of the golden frames that besprinkled, like stars, the hyacinth and the porphyry walls?

But the Duc's heart is fainting within him. He is not, however, as you suppose, dizzy with magnificence, nor drunk with the ecstatic breath of those innumerable censers. C'est vrai que de toutes ces choses il a pense beaucoup—mais! The Duc De L'Omelette is terror-stricken; for, through the lurid vista which a single uncurtained window is affording, lo! gleams the most ghastly of all fires!

Le pauvre Duc! He could not help imagining that the glorious, the voluptuous, the never-dying melodies which pervaded that hall, as they passed filtered and transmuted through the alchemy of the enchanted window-panes, were the wailings and the howlings of the hopeless and the damned! And there, too!—there!—upon the ottoman!—who could he be?—he, the petitma?tre—no, the Deity—who sat as if carved in marble, et qui sourit, with his pale countenance, si am?rement?

Mais il faut agir—that is to say, a Frenchman never faints outright. Besides, his Grace hated a scene—De L'Omelette is himself again. There were some foils upon a table—some points also. The Duc s'?chapper. He measures two points, and, with a grace inimitable, offers his Majesty the choice. Horreur! his Majesty does not fence!

Mais il joue!—how happy a thought!—but his Grace had always an excellent memory. He had dipped in the "Diable" of Abb? Gualtier. Therein it is said "que le Diable n'ose pas refuser un jeu d'?carte."

144

But the chances—the chances! True—desperate: but scarcely more desperate than the Duc. Besides, was he not in the secret?—had he not skimmed over P?re Le Brun?—was he not a member of the Club Vingt-un? "Si je perds," said he, "je serai deux fois perdu—I shall be doubly dammed—voil? tout! (Here his Grace shrugged his shoulders.) Si je gagne, je reviendrai a mes ortolans—que les cartes soient pr?par?es!"

His Grace was all care, all attention—his Majesty all confidence. A spectator would have thought of Francis and Charles. His Grace thought of his game. His Majesty did not think; he shuffled. The Duc cut.

The cards were dealt. The trump is turned—it is—it is—the king! No—it was the queen. His Majesty cursed her masculine habiliments. De L'Omelette placed his hand upon his heart.

They play. The Duc counts. The hand is out. His Majesty counts heavily, smiles, and is taking wine. The Duc slips a card.

"C'est ? vous ? faire," said his Majesty, cutting. His Grace bowed, dealt, and arose from the table en presentant le Roi.

His Majesty looked chagrined.

Had Alexander not been Alexander, he would have been Diogenes; and the Duc assured his antagonist in taking leave, "que s'il n'e?t ?t? De L'Omelette il n'aurait point d'objection d'?tre le Diable."

THE OBLONG BOX.

SOME years ago, I engaged passage from Charleston, S. C, to the city of New York, in the fine packet-ship "Independence," Captain Hardy. We were to sail on the fifteenth of the month (June), weather permitting; and on the fourteenth, I went on board to arrange some matters in my state-room.

I found that we were to have a great many passengers, including a more than usual number of ladies. On the list were several of my acquaintances, and among other names, I was rejoiced to see that of Mr. Cornelius Wyatt, a young artist, for whom I entertained feelings of warm friendship. He had been with me a fellow-student at C— University, where we were very much together. He had the ordinary temperament of genius, and was a compound of misanthropy, sensibility, and enthusiasm. To these qualities he united the warmest and truest heart which ever beat in a human bosom.

I observed that his name was carded upon three state-rooms; and, upon again referring to the list of passengers, I found that he had engaged passage for himself, wife, and two sisters—his own. The state-rooms were sufficiently roomy, and each had two berths, one above the other. These berths, to be sure, were so exceedingly narrow as to be insufficient for more than one person; still, I could not comprehend why there were three state-rooms for these four persons. I was, just at that epoch, in one of those moody frames of mind which make a man abnormally inquisitive about trifles: and I confess, with shame, that I busied myself in a variety of ill-bred and preposterous conjectures about this matter of the supernumerary state-room. It was no business of mine, to be sure, but with none the less pertinacity did I occupy myself in attempts to resolve the enigma. At last I reached a conclusion which wrought in me great wonder why I had not arrived at it before. "It is a servant of course," I said; "what a fool I am, not sooner to have thought of so obvious a solution!" And then I again repaired to the list—but here I saw distinctly that no servant was to come with the party, although, in fact, it had been the original design to bring one—for the words "and servant" had been first written and then overscored. "Oh, extra baggage, to be sure," I now said to myself—"something he wishes not to be put in the hold—something to be kept under his own eye—ah, I have it—a painting or so—and this is what he has been bargaining about with Nicolino, the Italian Jew." This idea satisfied me, and I dismissed my curiosity for the nonce.

Wyatt's two sisters I knew very well, and most amiable and clever girls they were. His wife he had newly married, and I had never yet seen her. He had often talked about her in my presence, however, and in his usual style of enthusiasm. He described her as of surpassing beauty, wit, and accomplishment. I was, therefore, quite anxious to make her acquaintance.

On the day in which I visited the ship (the fourteenth), Wyatt and party were also to visit it—so the captain informed me—and I waited on board an hour longer than I had designed, in hope of being presented to the bride, but then an apology came. "Mrs. W. was a little indisposed, and would decline coming on board until to-morrow, at the hour of sailing."

The morrow having arrived, I was going from my hotel to the wharf, when Captain Hardy met me and said that, "owing to circumstances" (a stupid but convenient phrase), "he rather thought the 'Independence' would not sail for a day or two, and that when all was ready, he would send up and let me know." This I thought strange, for there was a stiff southerly breeze; but as "the circumstances" were not forthcoming, although I pumped for them with much perseverance, I had nothing to do but to return home and digest my impatience at leisure.

I did not receive the expected message from the captain for nearly a week. It came at length, however, and I immediately went on board. The ship was crowded with passengers, and every thing was in the bustle attendant upon making sail. Wyatt's party arrived in about ten minutes after myself. There were the two sisters, the bride, and the artist—the latter in one of his customary fits of moody misanthropy. I was too well used to these, however, to pay them any special attention. He did not even introduce me to his wife—this courtesy devolving, per force, upon his sister Marian—a very sweet and intelligent girl, who, in a few hurried words, made us acquainted.

Mrs. Wyatt had been closely veiled; and when she raised her veil, in acknowledging my bow, I confess that I was very profoundly astonished. I should have been much more so, however, had not long experience advised me not to trust, with too implicit a reliance, the enthusiastic descriptions of my friend, the artist, when indulging in comments upon the loveliness of woman. When beauty was the theme, I well knew with what facility he soared into the regions of the purely ideal.

The truth is, I could not help regarding Mrs. Wyatt as a decidedly plain-looking woman. If not positively ugly, she was not, I think, very far from it. She was dressed, however, in exquisite taste—and then I had no doubt that she had captivated my friend's heart by the more enduring graces of the intellect and soul. She said very few words, and passed at once into her state-room with Mr. W.

My old inquisitiveness now returned. There was no servant—that was a settled point. I looked, therefore, for the extra baggage. After some delay, a cart arrived at the wharf, with an oblong pine box, which was every thing that seemed to be expected. Immediately upon its arrival we made sail, and in a short time were safely over the bar and standing out to sea.

The box in question was, as I say, oblong. It was about six feet in length by two and a half in breadth; I observed it attentively, and like to be precise. Now this shape was peculiar; and no sooner had I seen it, than I took credit to myself for the accuracy of my guessing. I had reached the conclusion, it will be remembered, that the extra baggage of my friend, the artist, would prove to be pictures, or at least a picture; for I knew he had been for several weeks in conference with Nicolino:—and now here was a box, which, from its shape, could possibly contain nothing in the world but a copy of Leonardo's "Last Supper;" and a copy of this very "Last Supper," done by Rubini the younger, at Florence, I had known, for some time, to be in the possession of Nicolino. This point, therefore, I considered as sufficiently settled. I chuckled excessively when I thought of my acumen. It was the first time I had ever known Wyatt to keep from me any of his artistical secrets; but here he evidently intended to steal a march upon me, and smuggle a fine picture to New York, under my very nose; expecting me to know nothing of the matter. I resolved to quiz him well, now and hereafter.

One thing, however, annoyed me not a little. The box did not go into the extra state-room. It was deposited in Wyatt's own; and there, too, it remained, occupying very nearly the whole of the floor—no doubt to the exceeding discomfort of the artist and his wife;—this the more especially as the tar or paint with which it was lettered in sprawling capitals, emitted a strong, disagreeable, and, to my fancy, a peculiarly disgusting odor. On the lid were painted the words—"Mrs. Adelaide Curtis, Albany, New York. Charge of Cornelius Wyatt, Esq. This side up. To be handled with care."

Now, I was aware that Mrs. Adelaide Curtis, of Albany, was the artist's wife's mother,—but then I looked upon the whole address as a mystification, intended especially for myself. I made up my mind, of course, that the box and contents would never get farther north than the studio of my misanthropic friend, in Chambers Street, New York.

For the first three or four days we had fine weather, although the wind was dead ahead; having chopped round to the northward, immediately upon our losing sight of the coast. The passengers were, consequently, in high spirits and disposed to be social. I must except, however, Wyatt and his sisters, who behaved stiffly, and, I could not help thinking, uncourteously to the rest of the party. Wyatt's conduct I did not so much regard. He was gloomy, even beyond his usual habit—in fact he was morose—but in him I was prepared for eccentricity. For the sisters, however, I could make no excuse. They secluded themselves in their staterooms during the greater part of the passage, and absolutely refused, although I repeatedly urged them, to hold communication with any person on board.

Mrs. Wyatt herself was far more agreeable. That is to say, she was chatty; and to be chatty is no slight recommendation at sea. She became excessively intimate with most of the ladies; and, to my profound astonishment, evinced no equivocal disposition to coquet with the men. She amused us all very much. I say "amused"—and scarcely know how to explain myself. The truth is, I soon found that Mrs. W. was far oftener laughed at than with. The gentlemen said little about her; but the ladies, in a little while, pronounced her "a good-hearted thing, rather indifferent looking, totally uneducated, and decidedly vulgar." The great wonder was, how Wyatt had been entrapped into such a match. Wealth was the general solution—but this I knew to be no solution at all; for Wyatt had told me that she neither brought him a dollar nor had any expectations from any source whatever. "He had married," he said, "for love, and for love only; and his bride was far more than worthy of his love." When I thought of these expressions, on the part of my friend, I confess that I felt indescribably puzzled. Could it be possible that he was taking leave of his senses? What else could I think? He, so refined, so intellectual, so fastidious, with so exquisite a perception of the faulty, and so keen an appreciation of the beautiful! To be sure, the lady seemed especially fond of him—particularly so in his absence—when she made herself ridiculous by frequent quotations of what had been said by her "beloved husband, Mr. Wyatt." The word "husband" seemed forever—to use one of her own delicate expressions— forever "on the tip of her tongue." In the meantime, it was observed by all on board, that he avoided her in the most pointed manner, and, for the most part, shut himself up alone in his state-room, where, in fact, he might have been said to live altogether, leaving his wife at full liberty to amuse herself as she thought best, in the public society of the main cabin.

My conclusion, from what I saw and heard, was, that, the artist, by some unaccountable freak of fate, or perhaps in some fit of enthusiastic and fanciful passion, had been induced to unite himself with a person altogether beneath him, and that the natural result, entire and speedy disgust, had ensued. I pitied him from the bottom of my heart—but could not, for that reason, quite forgive his incommunicativeness in the matter of the "Last Supper." For this I resolved to have my revenge.

One day he came upon deck, and, taking his arm as had been my wont, I sauntered with him backward and forward. His gloom, however (which I considered quite natural under the circumstances), seemed entirely unabated. He said little, and that moodily, and with evident effort. I ventured a jest or two, and he made a sickening attempt at a smile. Poor fellow!—as I thought of his wife, I wondered that he could have heart to put on even the semblance of mirth. I determined to commence a series of covert insinuations, or innuendoes, about the oblong box—just to let him perceive, gradually, that I was not altogether the butt, or victim, of his little bit of pleasant mystification. My first observation was by way of opening a masked battery. I said something about the "peculiar shape of that box-," and, as I spoke the words, I smiled knowingly, winked, and touched him gently with my forefinger in the ribs.

The manner in which Wyatt received this harmless pleasantry convinced me, at once, that he was mad. At first he stared at me as if he found it impossible to comprehend the witticism of my remark; but as its point seemed slowly to make its way into his brain, his eyes, in the same proportion, seemed protruding from their sockets. Then he grew very red—then hideously pale—then, as if highly amused with what I had insinuated, he began a loud and boisterous laugh, which, to my astonishment, he kept up, with gradually increasing vigor, for ten minutes or more. In conclusion, he fell flat and heavily upon the deck. When I ran to uplift him, to all appearance he was dead.

I called assistance, and, with much difficulty, we brought him to himself. Upon reviving he spoke incoherently for some time. At length we bled him and put him to bed. The next morning he was quite recovered, so far as regarded his mere bodily health. Of his mind I say nothing, of course. I avoided him during the rest of the passage, by advice of the captain, who seemed to coincide with me altogether in my views of his insanity, but cautioned me to say nothing on this head to any person on board.

Several circumstances occurred immediately after this fit of Wyatt which contributed to heighten the curiosity with which I was already possessed. Among other things, this: I had been nervous—drank too much strong green tea, and slept ill at night—in fact, for two nights I could not be properly said to sleep at all. Now, my state-room opened into the main cabin, or dining-room, as did those of all the single men on board. Wyatt's three rooms were in the after-cabin, which was separated from the main one by a slight sliding door, never locked even at night. As we were almost constantly on a wind, and the breeze was not a little stiff, the ship heeled to leeward very considerably; and whenever her starboard side was to leeward, the sliding door between the cabins slid open, and so remained, nobody taking the trouble to get up and shut it. But my berth was in such a position, that when my own state-room door was open, as well as the sliding door in question (and my own door was always open on account of the heat,) I could see into the after-cabin quite distinctly, and just at that portion of it, too, where were situated the state-rooms of Mr. Wyatt. Well, during two nights (not consecutive) while I lay awake, I clearly saw Mrs. W., about eleven o'clock upon each night, steal cautiously from the state-room of Mr. W., and enter the extra room, where she remained until daybreak, when she was called by her husband and went back. That they were virtually separated was clear. They had separate apartments—no doubt in contemplation of a more permanent divorce; and here, after all I thought was the mystery of the extra state-room.

There was another circumstance, too, which interested me much. During the two wakeful nights in question, and immediately after the disappearance of Mrs. Wyatt into the extra state-room, I was attracted by certain singular cautious, subdued noises in that of her husband. After listening to them for some time, with thoughtful attention, I at length succeeded perfectly in translating their import. They were sounds occasioned by the artist in prying open the oblong box, by means of a chisel and mallet—the latter being apparently muffled, or deadened, by some soft woollen or cotton substance in which its head was enveloped.

In this manner I fancied I could distinguish the precise moment when he fairly disengaged the lid—also, that I could determine when he removed it altogether, and when he deposited it upon the lower berth in his room; this latter point I knew, for example, by certain slight taps which the lid made in striking against the wooden edges of the berth, as he endeavored to lay it down very gently—there being no room for it on the floor. After this there was a dead stillness, and I heard nothing more, upon either occasion, until nearly daybreak; unless, perhaps, I may mention a low sobbing, or murmuring sound, so very much suppressed as to be nearly inaudible—if, indeed, the whole of this latter noise were not rather produced by my own imagination. I say it seemed to resemble sobbing or sighing—but, of course, it could not have been either. I rather think it was a ringing in my own ears. Mr. Wyatt, no doubt, according to custom, was merely giving the rein to one of his hobbies—indulging in one of his fits of artistic enthusiasm. He had opened his oblong box, in order to feast his eyes on the pictorial treasure within. There was nothing in this, however, to make him sob. I repeat, therefore, that it must have been simply a freak of my own fancy, distempered by good Captain Hardy's green tea. Just before dawn, on each of the two nights of which I speak, I distinctly heard Mr. Wyatt replace the lid upon the oblong box, and force the nails into their old places by means of the muffled mallet. Having done this, he issued from his state-room, fully dressed, and proceeded to call Mrs. W. from hers.

We had been at sea seven days, and were now off Cape Hatteras, when there came a tremendously heavy blow from the southwest. We were, in a measure, prepared for it, however, as the weather had been holding out threats for some time. Every thing was made snug, alow and aloft; and as the wind steadily freshened, we lay to, at length, under spanker and foretopsail, both double-reefed.

In this trim we rode safely enough for forty-eight hours—the ship proving herself an excellent sea-boat in many respects, and shipping no water of any consequence. At the end of this period, however, the gale had freshened into a hurricane, and our after—sail split into ribbons, bringing us so much in the trough of the water that we shipped several prodigious seas, one immediately after the other. By this accident we lost three men overboard with the caboose, and nearly the whole of the larboard bulwarks. Scarcely had we recovered our senses, before the foretopsail went into shreds, when we got up a storm stay—sail and with this did pretty well for some hours, the ship heading the sea much more steadily than before.

The gale still held on, however, and we saw no signs of its abating. The rigging was found to be ill-fitted, and greatly strained; and on the third day of the blow, about five in the afternoon, our mizzen-mast, in a heavy lurch to windward, went by the board. For an hour or more, we tried in vain to get rid of it, on account of the prodigious rolling of the ship; and, before we had succeeded, the carpenter came aft and announced four feet of water in the hold. To add to our dilemma, we found the pumps choked and nearly useless.

All was now confusion and despair—but an effort was made to lighten

153

the ship by throwing overboard as much of her cargo as could be reached, and by cutting away the two masts that remained. This we at last accomplished—but we were still unable to do any thing at the pumps; and, in the meantime, the leak gained on us very fast.

At sundown, the gale had sensibly diminished in violence, and as the sea went down with it, we still entertained faint hopes of saving ourselves in the boats. At eight P. M., the clouds broke away to windward, and we had the advantage of a full moon—a piece of good fortune which served wonderfully to cheer our drooping spirits.

After incredible labor we succeeded, at length, in getting the longboat over the side without material accident, and into this we crowded the whole of the crew and most of the passengers. This party made off immediately, and, after undergoing much suffering, finally arrived, in safety, at Ocracoke Inlet, on the third day after the wreck.

Fourteen passengers, with the captain, remained on board, resolving to trust their fortunes to the jolly-boat at the stern. We lowered it without difficulty, although it was only by a miracle that we prevented it from swamping as it touched the water. It contained, when afloat, the captain and his wife, Mr. Wyatt and party, a Mexican officer, wife, four children, and myself, with a negro valet.

We had no room, of course, for any thing except a few positively necessary instruments, some provisions, and the clothes upon our backs. No one had thought of even attempting to save any thing more. What must have been the astonishment of all, then, when having proceeded a few fathoms from the ship, Mr. Wyatt stood up in the stern-sheets, and coolly demanded of Captain Hardy that the boat should be put back for the purpose of taking in his oblong box!

"Sit down, Mr. Wyatt," replied the captain, somewhat sternly, "you will capsize us if you do not sit quite still. Our gunwhale is almost in the water now."

"The box!" vociferated Mr. Wyatt, still standing—"the box, I say!

154

Captain Hardy, you cannot, you will not refuse me. Its weight will be but a trifle—it is nothing—mere nothing. By the mother who bore you—for the love of Heaven—by your hope of salvation, I implore you to put back for the box!"

The captain, for a moment, seemed touched by the earnest appeal of the artist, but he regained his stern composure, and merely said:

"Mr. Wyatt, you are mad. I cannot listen to you. Sit down, I say, or you will swamp the boat. Stay—hold him—seize him!—he is about to spring overboard! There—I knew it—he is over!"

As the captain said this, Mr. Wyatt, in fact, sprang from the boat, and, as we were yet in the lee of the wreck, succeeded, by almost superhuman exertion, in getting hold of a rope which hung from the fore-chains. In another moment he was on board, and rushing frantically down into the cabin.

In the meantime, we had been swept astern of the ship, and being quite out of her lee, were at the mercy of the tremendous sea which was still running. We made a determined effort to put back, but our little boat was like a feather in the breath of the tempest. We saw at a glance that the doom of the unfortunate artist was sealed.

As our distance from the wreck rapidly increased, the madman (for as such only could we regard him) was seen to emerge from the companion—way, up which by dint of strength that appeared gigantic, he dragged, bodily, the oblong box. While we gazed in the extremity of astonishment, he passed, rapidly, several turns of a three-inch rope, first around the box and then around his body. In another instant both body and box were in the sea—disappearing suddenly, at once and forever.

We lingered awhile sadly upon our oars, with our eyes riveted upon the spot. At length we pulled away. The silence remained unbroken for an hour. Finally, I hazarded a remark.

"Did you observe, captain, how suddenly they sank? Was not that an exceedingly singular thing? I confess that I entertained some feeble hope of his final deliverance, when I saw him lash himself to the box, and commit himself to the sea."

"They sank as a matter of course," replied the captain, "and that like a shot. They will soon rise again, however—but not till the salt melts."

"The salt!" I ejaculated.

"Hush!" said the captain, pointing to the wife and sisters of the deceased. "We must talk of these things at some more appropriate time."

We suffered much, and made a narrow escape, but fortune befriended us, as well as our mates in the long-boat. We landed, in fine, more dead than alive, after four days of intense distress, upon the beach opposite Roanoke Island. We remained here a week, were not ill-treated by the wreckers, and at length obtained a passage to New York.

About a month after the loss of the "Independence," I happened to meet Captain Hardy in Broadway. Our conversation turned, naturally, upon the disaster, and especially upon the sad fate of poor Wyatt. I thus learned the following particulars.

The artist had engaged passage for himself, wife, two sisters and a servant. His wife was, indeed, as she had been represented, a most lovely, and most accomplished woman. On the morning of the fourteenth of June (the day in which I first visited the ship), the lady suddenly sickened and died. The young husband was frantic with grief—but circumstances imperatively forbade the deferring his voyage to New York. It was necessary to take to her mother the corpse of his adored wife, and, on the other hand, the universal prejudice which would prevent his doing so openly was well known. Nine-tenths of the passengers would have abandoned the ship rather than take passage with a dead body.

In this dilemma, Captain Hardy arranged that the corpse, being first partially embalmed, and packed, with a large quantity of salt, in a box of suitable dimensions, should be conveyed on board as merchandise. Nothing was to be said of the lady's decease; and, as it was well understood that Mr. Wyatt had engaged passage for his wife, it became necessary that some person should personate her during the voyage. This the deceased lady's-maid was easily prevailed on to do. The extra state-room, originally engaged for this girl during her mistress' life, was now merely retained. In this state-room the pseudo-wife, slept, of course, every night. In the daytime she performed, to the best of her ability, the part of her mistress—whose person, it had been carefully ascertained, was unknown to any of the passengers on board.

My own mistake arose, naturally enough, through too careless, too inquisitive, and too impulsive a temperament. But of late, it is a rare thing that I sleep soundly at night. There is a countenance which haunts me, turn as I will. There is an hysterical laugh which will forever ring within my ears.

LOSS OF BREATH

O Breathe not, etc.   —*Moore's Melodies*

THE MOST notorious ill-fortune must in the end yield to the untiring courage of philosophy—as the most stubborn city to the ceaseless vigilance of an enemy. Shalmanezer, as we have it in holy writings, lay three years before Samaria; yet it fell. Sardanapalus—see Diodorus—maintained himself seven in Nineveh; but to no purpose. Troy expired at the close of the second lustrum; and Azoth, as Aristaeus declares upon his honour as a gentleman, opened at last her gates to Psammetichus, after having barred them for the fifth part of a century....

"Thou wretch!—thou vixen!—thou shrew!" said I to my wife on the morning after our wedding; "thou witch!—thou hag!—thou whippersnapper—thou sink of iniquity!—thou fiery-faced quintessence of all that is abominable!—thou—thou-" here standing upon tiptoe, seizing her by the throat, and placing my mouth close to her ear, I was preparing to launch forth a new and more decided epithet of opprobrium, which should not fail, if ejaculated, to convince her of her insignificance, when to my extreme horror and astonishment I discovered that I had lost my breath.

The phrases "I am out of breath," "I have lost my breath," etc., are often enough repeated in common conversation; but it had never occurred to me that the terrible accident of which I speak could bona fide and actually happen! Imagine—that is if you have a fanciful turn—imagine, I say, my wonder—my consternation—my despair!

There is a good genius, however, which has never entirely deserted me. In my most ungovernable moods I still retain a sense of propriety, et le chemin des passions me conduit—as Lord Edouard in the "Julie" says it did him—a la philosophie veritable.

Although I could not at first precisely ascertain to what degree the occurrence had affected me, I determined at all events to conceal the matter from my wife, until further experience should discover to me the extent of this my unheard of calamity. Altering my countenance, therefore, in a moment, from its bepuffed and distorted appearance, to an expression of arch and coquettish benignity, I gave my lady a pat on the one cheek, and a kiss on the other, and without saying one syllable (Furies! I could not), left her astonished at my drollery, as I pirouetted out of the room in a Pas de Zephyr.

Behold me then safely ensconced in my private boudoir, a fearful instance of the ill consequences attending upon irascibility—alive, with the qualifications of the dead—dead, with the propensities of the living—an anomaly on the face of the earth—being very calm, yet breathless.

Yes! breathless. I am serious in asserting that my breath was entirely gone. I could not have stirred with it a feather if my life had been at issue, or sullied even the delicacy of a mirror. Hard fate!—yet there was some alleviation to the first overwhelming paroxysm of my sorrow. I found, upon trial, that the powers of utterance which, upon my inability to proceed in the conversation with my wife, I then concluded to be totally destroyed, were in fact only partially impeded, and I discovered that had I, at that interesting crisis, dropped my voice to a singularly deep guttural, I might still have continued to her the communication of my sentiments; this pitch of voice (the guttural) depending, I find, not upon the current of the breath, but upon a certain spasmodic action of the muscles of the throat.

Throwing myself upon a chair, I remained for some time absorbed in meditation. My reflections, be sure, were of no consolatory kind. A thousand vague and lachrymatory fancies took possession of my soul—and even the idea of suicide flitted across my brain; but it is a trait in the perversity of human nature to reject the obvious and the ready, for the far-distant and equivocal. Thus I shuddered at self-murder as the most decided of atrocities while the tabby cat purred strenuously upon the rug, and the very water dog wheezed assiduously under the table, each taking to itself much merit for the strength of its lungs, and all obviously done in derision of my own pulmonary incapacity.

Oppressed with a tumult of vague hopes and fears, I at length heard the footsteps of my wife descending the staircase. Being now assured of her absence, I returned with a palpitating heart to the scene of my disaster.

Carefully locking the door on the inside, I commenced a vigorous search. It was possible, I thought, that, concealed in some obscure corner, or lurking in some closet or drawer, might be found the lost object of my inquiry. It might have a vapory—it might even have a tangible form. Most philosophers, upon many points of philosophy, are still very unphilosophical. William Godwin, however, says in his "Mandeville," that "invisible things are the only realities," and this, all will allow, is a case in point. I would have the judicious reader pause before accusing such asseverations of an undue quantum of absurdity. Anaxagoras, it will be remembered, maintained that snow is black, and this I have since found to be the case.

Long and earnestly did I continue the investigation: but the contemptible reward of my industry and perseverance proved to be only a set of false teeth, two pair of hips, an eye, and a bundle of billets-doux from Mr. Windenough to my wife. I might as well here observe that this confirmation of my lady's partiality for Mr. W. occasioned me little uneasiness. That Mrs. Lackobreath should admire anything so dissimilar to myself was a natural and necessary evil. I am, it is well known, of a robust and corpulent appearance, and at the same time somewhat diminutive in stature. What wonder, then, that the lath-like tenuity of my acquaintance, and his altitude, which has grown into a proverb, should have met with all due estimation in the eyes of Mrs. Lackobreath. But to return.

My exertions, as I have before said, proved fruitless. Closet after closet—drawer after drawer—corner after corner—were scrutinized to no purpose. At one time, however, I thought myself sure of my prize, having, in rummaging a dressing-case, accidentally demolished a bottle of Grandjean's Oil of Archangels—which, as an agreeable perfume, I here take the liberty of recommending.

With a heavy heart I returned to my boudoir—there to ponder upon some method of eluding my wife's penetration, until I could make arrangements prior to my leaving the country, for to this I had already made up my mind. In a foreign climate, being unknown, I might, with some probability of success, endeavor to conceal my unhappy calamity—a calamity calculated, even more than beggary, to estrange the affections of the multitude, and to draw down upon the wretch the well-merited indignation of the virtuous and the happy. I was not long in hesitation. Being naturally quick, I committed to memory the entire tragedy of "Metamora." I had the good fortune to recollect that in the accentuation of this drama, or at least of such portion of it as is allotted to the hero, the tones of voice in which I found myself deficient were altogether unnecessary, and the deep guttural was expected to reign monotonously throughout.

I practised for some time by the borders of a well frequented marsh;—herein, however, having no reference to a similar proceeding of Demosthenes, but from a design peculiarly and conscientiously my own. Thus armed at all points, I determined to make my wife believe that I was suddenly smitten with a passion for the stage. In this, I succeeded to a miracle; and to every question or suggestion found myself at liberty to reply in my most frog-like and sepulchral tones with some passage from the tragedy—any portion of which, as I soon took great pleasure in observing, would apply equally well to any particular subject. It is not to be supposed, however, that in the delivery of such passages I was found at all deficient in the looking asquint—the showing my teeth—the working my knees—the shuffling my feet—or in any of those unmentionable graces which are now justly considered the characteristics of a popular performer. To be sure they spoke of confining me in a strait-jacket—but, good God! they never suspected me of having lost my breath.

Having at length put my affairs in order, I took my seat very early one morning in the mail stage for—, giving it to be understood, among my acquaintances, that business of the last importance required my immediate personal attendance in that city.

The coach was crammed to repletion; but in the uncertain twilight the features of my companions could not be distinguished. Without making any effectual resistance, I suffered myself to be placed between two gentlemen of colossal dimensions; while a third, of a size larger, requesting pardon for the liberty he was about to take, threw himself upon my body at full length, and falling asleep in an instant, drowned all my guttural ejaculations for relief, in a snore which would have put to blush the roarings of the bull of Phalaris. Happily the state of my respiratory faculties rendered suffocation an accident entirely out of the question.

As, however, the day broke more distinctly in our approach to the outskirts of the city, my tormentor, arising and adjusting his shirt-collar, thanked me in a very friendly manner for my civility. Seeing that I remained motionless (all my limbs were dislocated and my head twisted on one side), his apprehensions began to be excited; and arousing the rest of the passengers, he communicated, in a very decided manner, his opinion that a dead man had been palmed upon them during the night for a living and responsible fellow-traveller; here giving me a thump on the right eye, by way of demonstrating the truth of his suggestion.

Hereupon all, one after another (there were nine in company), believed it their duty to pull me by the ear. A young practising physician, too, having applied a pocket-mirror to my mouth, and found me without breath, the assertion of my persecutor was pronounced a true bill; and the whole party expressed a determination to endure tamely no such impositions for the future, and to proceed no farther with any such carcasses for the present.

I was here, accordingly, thrown out at the sign of the "Crow" (by which tavern the coach happened to be passing), without meeting with any farther accident than the breaking of both my arms, under the left hind wheel of the vehicle. I must besides do the driver the justice to state that he did not forget to throw after me the largest of my trunks, which, unfortunately falling on my head, fractured my skull in a manner at once interesting and extraordinary.

The landlord of the "Crow," who is a hospitable man, finding that my trunk contained sufficient to indemnify him for any little trouble he might take in my behalf, sent forthwith for a surgeon of his acquaintance, and delivered me to his care with a bill and receipt for ten dollars.

The purchaser took me to his apartments and commenced operations immediately. Having cut off my ears, however, he discovered signs of animation. He now rang the bell, and sent for a neighboring apothecary with whom to consult in the emergency. In case of his suspicions with regard to my existence proving ultimately correct, he, in the meantime, made an incision in my stomach, and removed several of my viscera for private dissection.

The apothecary had an idea that I was actually dead. This idea I endeavored to confute, kicking and plunging with all my might, and making the most furious contortions—for the operations of the surgeon had, in a measure, restored me to the possession of my faculties. All, however, was attributed to the effects of a new galvanic battery, wherewith the apothecary, who is really a man of information, performed several curious experiments, in which, from my personal share in their fulfillment, I could not help feeling deeply interested. It was a course of mortification to me, nevertheless, that although I made several attempts at conversation, my powers of speech were so entirely in abeyance, that I could not even open my mouth; much less, then, make reply to some ingenious but fanciful theories of which, under other circumstances, my minute acquaintance with the Hippocratian pathology would have afforded me a ready confutation.

Not being able to arrive at a conclusion, the practitioners remanded me for farther examination. I was taken up into a garret; and the surgeon's lady having accommodated me with drawers and stockings, the surgeon himself fastened my hands, and tied up my jaws with a pocket-handkerchief—then bolted the door on the outside as he hurried to his dinner, leaving me alone to silence and to meditation.

I now discovered to my extreme delight that I could have spoken had not my mouth been tied up with the pocket-handkerchief. Consoling myself with this reflection, I was mentally repeating some passages of the "Omnipresence of the Deity," as is my custom before resigning myself to sleep, when two cats, of a greedy and vituperative turn, entering at a hole in the wall, leaped up with a flourish a la Catalani, and alighting opposite one another on my visage, betook themselves to indecorous contention for the paltry consideration of my nose.

But, as the loss of his ears proved the means of elevating to the throne of Cyrus, the Magian or Mige-Gush of Persia, and as the cutting off his nose gave

Zopyrus possession of Babylon, so the loss of a few ounces of my countenance proved the salvation of my body. Aroused by the pain, and burning with indignation, I burst, at a single effort, the fastenings and the bandage. Stalking across the room I cast a glance of contempt at the belligerents, and throwing open the sash to their extreme horror and disappointment, precipitated myself, very dexterously, from the window. The mail-robber W---, to whom I bore a singular resemblance, was at this moment passing from the city jail to the scaffold erected for his execution in the suburbs. His extreme infirmity and long continued ill health had obtained him the privilege of remaining unmanacled; and habited in his gallows costume—one very similar to my own,—he lay at full length in the bottom of the hangman's cart (which happened to be under the windows of the surgeon at the moment of my precipitation) without any other guard than the driver, who was asleep, and two recruits of the sixth infantry, who were drunk.

As ill-luck would have it, I alit upon my feet within the vehicle. immediately, he bolted out behind, and turning down an alley, was out of sight in the twinkling of an eye. The recruits, aroused by the bustle, could not exactly comprehend the merits of the transaction. Seeing, however, a man, the precise counterpart of the felon, standing upright in the cart before their eyes, they were of (so they expressed themselves,) and, having communicated this opinion to one another, they took each a dram, and then knocked me down with the butt-ends of their muskets.

It was not long ere we arrived at the place of destination. Of course nothing could be said in my defence. Hanging was my inevitable fate. I resigned myself thereto with a feeling half stupid, half acrimonious. Being little of a cynic, I had all the sentiments of a dog. The hangman, however, adjusted the noose about my neck. The drop fell.

I forbear to depict my sensations upon the gallows; although here, undoubtedly, I could speak to the point, and it is a topic upon which nothing has been well said. In fact, to write upon such a theme it is necessary to have been hanged. Every author should confine himself to matters of experience. Thus Mark Antony composed a treatise upon getting drunk.

I may just mention, however, that die I did not. My body was, but I had no breath to be, suspended; and but for the knot under my left ear (which had the feel of a military stock) I dare say that I should have experienced very little inconvenience. As for the jerk given to my neck upon the falling of the drop, it merely proved a corrective to the twist afforded me by the fat gentleman in the coach.

For good reasons, however, I did my best to give the crowd the worth of their trouble. My convulsions were said to be extraordinary. My spasms it would have been difficult to beat. The populace encored. Several gentlemen swooned; and a multitude of ladies were carried home in hysterics. Pinxit availed himself of the opportunity to retouch, from a sketch taken upon the spot, his admirable painting of the "Marsyas flayed alive."

When I had afforded sufficient amusement, it was thought proper to remove my body from the gallows;—this the more especially as the real culprit had in the meantime been retaken and recognized, a fact which I was so unlucky as not to know.

Much sympathy was, of course, exercised in my behalf, and as no one made claim to my corpse, it was ordered that I should be interred in a public vault.

Here, after due interval, I was deposited. The sexton departed, and I was left alone. A line of Marston's "Malcontent"—

Death's a good fellow and keeps open house—struck me at that moment as a palpable lie.

I knocked off, however, the lid of my coffin, and stepped out. The place was dreadfully dreary and damp, and I became troubled with ennui. By way of amusement, I felt my way among the numerous coffins ranged in order around. I lifted them down, one by one, and breaking open their lids, busied myself in speculations about the mortality within.

"This," I soliloquized, tumbling over a carcass, puffy, bloated, and rotund—"this has been, no doubt, in every sense of the word, an unhappy—an unfortunate man. It has been his terrible lot not to walk but to waddle—to pass through life not like a human being, but like an elephant—not like a man, but like a rhinoceros.

"His attempts at getting on have been mere abortions, and his circumgyratory proceedings a palpable failure. Taking a step forward, it has been his misfortune to take two toward the right, and three toward the left. His studies have been confined to the poetry of Crabbe. He can have no idea of the wonder of a pirouette. To him a pas de papillon has been an abstract conception. He has never ascended the summit of a hill. He has never viewed from any steeple the glories of a metropolis. Heat has been his mortal enemy. In the dog-days his days have been the days of a dog. Therein, he has dreamed of flames and suffocation—of mountains upon mountains—of Pelion upon Ossa. He was short of breath—to say all in a word, he was short of breath. He thought it extravagant to play upon wind instruments. He was the inventor of self-moving fans, wind-sails, and ventilators. He patronized Du Pont the bellows-maker, and he died miserably in attempting to smoke a cigar. His was a case in which I feel a deep interest—a lot in which I sincerely sympathize.

"But here,"—said I—"here"—and I dragged spitefully from its receptacle a gaunt, tall and peculiar-looking form, whose remarkable appearance struck me with a sense of unwelcome familiarity—"here is a wretch entitled to no earthly commiseration." Thus saying, in order to obtain a more distinct view of my subject, I applied my thumb and forefinger to its nose, and causing it to assume a sitting position upon the ground, held it thus, at the length of my arm, while I continued my soliloquy.

"Entitled," I repeated, "to no earthly commiseration. Who indeed would think of compassioning a shadow? Besides, has he not had his full share of the blessings of mortality? He was the originator of tall monuments—shot-towers—lightning-rods—Lombardy poplars. His treatise upon "Shades and Shadows" has immortalized him. He edited with distinguished ability the last edition of "South on the Bones." He went early to college and studied pneumatics. He then came home, talked eternally, and played upon the French-horn. He patronized the bagpipes. Captain Barclay, who walked against Time, would not walk against him. Windham and Allbreath were his favorite writers,—his favorite artist, Phiz. He died gloriously while inhaling gas—levique flatu corrupitur, like the fama pudicitae in Hieronymus. {*1} He was indubitably a"—

"How can you?—how—can—you?"—interrupted the object of my animadversions, gasping for breath, and tearing off, with a desperate exertion, the bandage around its jaws—"how can you, Mr. Lackobreath, be so infernally cruel as to pinch me in that manner by the nose? Did you not see how they had fastened up my mouth—and you must know—if you know any thing—how vast a superfluity of breath I have to dispose of! If you do not know, however, sit down and you shall see. In my situation it is really a great relief to be able to open ones mouth—to be able to expatiate—to be able to communicate with a person like yourself, who do not think yourself called upon at every period to interrupt the thread of a gentleman's discourse. Interruptions are annoying and should undoubtedly be abolished—don't you think so?—no reply, I beg you,—one person is enough to be speaking at a time.—I shall be done by and by, and then you may begin.—How the devil sir, did you get into this place?—not a word I beseech you—been here some time myself— terrible accident!—heard of it, I suppose?—awful calamity!—walking under your windows—some short while ago—about the time you were stage-struck—horrible occurrence!—heard of "catching one's breath," eh?—hold your tongue I tell you!—I caught somebody elses!—had always too much of my own—met Blab at the corner of the street—wouldn't give me a chance for a word—couldn't get in a syllable edgeways—attacked, consequently, with epilepsis—Blab made his escape—damn all fools!—they took me up for dead, and put me in this place—pretty doings all of them!—heard all you said about me—every word a lie—horrible!—wonderful—outrageous!— hideous!—incomprehensible!—et cetera—et cetera—et cetera—et cetera-"

It is impossible to conceive my astonishment at so unexpected a discourse, or the joy with which I became gradually convinced that the breath so fortunately caught by the gentleman (whom I soon recognized as my neighbor Windenough) was, in fact, the identical expiration mislaid by myself in the conversation with my wife. Time, place, and circumstances rendered it a matter beyond question. I did not at least during the long period in which the inventor of Lombardy poplars continued to favor me with his explanations.

In this respect I was actuated by that habitual prudence which has ever been my predominating trait. I reflected that many difficulties might still lie in the path of my preservation which only extreme exertion on my part would be able to surmount. Many persons, I considered, are prone to estimate commodities in their possession—however valueless to the then proprietor—however troublesome, or distressing—in direct ratio with the advantages to be derived by others from their attainment, or by themselves from their abandonment. Might not this be the case with Mr. Windenough? In displaying anxiety for the breath of which he was at present so willing to get rid, might I not lay myself open to the exactions of his avarice? There are scoundrels in this world, I remembered with a sigh, who will not scruple to take unfair opportunities with even a next door neighbor, and (this remark is from Epictetus) it is precisely at that time when men are most anxious to throw off the burden of their own calamities that they feel the least desirous of relieving them in others.

Upon considerations similar to these, and still retaining my grasp upon the nose of Mr. W., I accordingly thought proper to model my reply.

"Monster!" I began in a tone of the deepest indignation—"monster and double-winded idiot!—dost thou, whom for thine iniquities it has pleased heaven to accurse with a two-fold respimtion—dost thou, I say, presume to address me in the familiar language of an old acquaintance?—'I lie,' forsooth! and 'hold my tongue,' to be sure!—pretty conversation indeed, to a gentleman with a single breath!—all this, too, when I have it in my power to relieve the calamity under which thou dost so justly suffer—to curtail the superfluities of thine unhappy respiration."

Like Brutus, I paused for a reply—with which, like a tornado, Mr. Windenough immediately overwhelmed me. Protestation followed upon protestation, and apology upon apology. There were no terms with which he was unwilling to comply, and there were none of which I failed to take the fullest advantage.

Preliminaries being at length arranged, my acquaintance delivered me the respiration; for which (having carefully examined it) I gave him afterward a receipt.

I am aware that by many I shall be held to blame for speaking in a manner so cursory, of a transaction so impalpable. It will be thought that I should have entered more minutely, into the details of an occurrence by which—and this is very true—much new light might be thrown upon a highly interesting branch of physical philosophy.

To all this I am sorry that I cannot reply. A hint is the only answer which I am permitted to make. There were circumstances—but I think it much safer upon consideration to say as little as possible about an affair so delicate—so delicate, I repeat, and at the time involving the interests of a third party whose sulphurous resentment I have not the least desire, at this moment, of incurring.

We were not long after this necessary arrangement in effecting an escape from the dungeons of the sepulchre. The united strength of our resuscitated voices was soon sufficiently apparent. Scissors, the Whig editor, republished a treatise upon "the nature and origin of subterranean noises." A reply—rejoinder—confutation—and justification—followed in the columns of a Democratic Gazette. It was not until the opening of the vault to decide the controversy, that the appearance of Mr. Windenough and myself proved both parties to have been decidedly in the wrong.

I cannot conclude these details of some very singular passages in a life at all times sufficiently eventful, without again recalling to the attention of the reader the merits of that indiscriminate philosophy which is a sure and ready shield against those shafts of calamity which can neither be seen, felt nor fully understood. It was in the spirit of this wisdom that, among the ancient Hebrews, it was believed the gates of Heaven would be inevitably opened to that sinner, or saint, who, with good lungs and implicit confidence, should vociferate the word "Amen!" It was in the spirit of this wisdom that, when a great plague raged at Athens, and every means had been in vain attempted for its removal, Epimenides, as Laertius relates, in his second book, of that philosopher, advised the erection of a shrine and temple "to the proper God."

LYTTLETON BARRY.

THE MAN THAT WAS USED UP.

A TALE OF THE LATE BUGABOO AND KICKAPOO CAMPAIGN.

Pleurez, pleurez, mes yeux, et fondez vous en eau!

La moiti?; de ma vie a mis l' autre au tombeau.

CORNEILLE.

I CANNOT just now remember when or where I first made the acquaintance of that truly fine-looking fellow, Brevet Brigadier General John A. B. C. Smith. Some one did introduce me to the gentleman, I am sure—at some public meeting, I know very well—held about something of great importance, no doubt—at some place or other, I feel convinced,—whose name I have unaccountably forgotten. The truth is—that the introduction was attended, upon my part, with a degree of anxious embarrassment which operated to prevent any definite impressions of either time or place. I am constitutionally nervous—this, with me, is a family failing, and I can't help it. In especial, the slightest appearance of mystery—of any point I cannot exactly comprehend—puts me at once into a pitiable state of agitation.

There was something, as it were, remarkable—yes, remarkable, although this is but a feeble term to express my full meaning—about the entire individuality of the personage in question. He was, perhaps, six feet in height, and of a presence singularly commanding. There was an air distingu? pervading the whole man, which spoke of high breeding, and hinted at high birth. Upon this topic—the topic of Smith's personal appearance—I have a kind of melancholy satisfaction in being minute. His head of hair would have done honor to a Brutus;—nothing could be more richly flowing, or possess a brighter gloss. It was of a jetty black;—which was also the color, or more properly the no color of his unimaginable whiskers. You perceive I cannot speak of these latter without enthusiasm; it is not too much to say that they were the handsomest pair of whiskers under the sun. At all events, they encircled, and at times partially overshadowed, a mouth utterly unequalled. Here were the most entirely even, and the most brilliantly white of all conceivable teeth. From between them, upon every proper occasion, issued a voice of surpassing clearness, melody, and strength. In the matter of eyes, also, my acquaintance was pre-eminently endowed. Either one of such a pair was worth a couple of the ordinary ocular organs. They were of a deep hazel, exceedingly large and lustrous; and there was perceptible about them, ever and anon, just that amount of interesting obliquity which gives pregnancy to expression.

The bust of the General was unquestionably the finest bust I ever saw. For your life you could not have found a fault with its wonderful proportion. This rare peculiarity set off to great advantage a pair of shoulders which would have called up a blush of conscious inferiority into the countenance of the marble Apollo. I have a passion for fine shoulders, and may say that I never beheld them in perfection before. The arms altogether were admirably modelled. Nor were the lower limbs less superb. These were, indeed, the ne plus ultra of good legs. Every connoisseur in such matters admitted the legs to be good. There was neither too much flesh, nor too little,—neither rudeness nor fragility. I could not imagine a more graceful curve than that of the os femoris, and there was just that due gentle prominence in the rear of the fibula which goes to the conformation of a properly proportioned calf. I wish to God my young and talented friend Chiponchipino, the sculptor, had but seen the legs of Brevet Brigadier General John A. B. C. Smith.

But although men so absolutely fine-looking are neither as plenty as reasons or blackberries, still I could not bring myself to believe that the remarkable something to which I alluded just now,—that the odd air of je ne sais quoi which hung about my new acquaintance,—lay altogether, or indeed at all, in the supreme excellence of his bodily endowments. Perhaps it might be traced to the manner;—yet here again I could not pretend to be positive. There was a primness, not to say stiffness, in his carriage—a degree of measured, and, if I may so express it, of rectangular precision, attending his every movement, which, observed in a more diminutive figure, would have had the least little savor in the world, of affectation, pomposity or constraint, but which noticed in a gentleman of his undoubted dimensions, was readily placed to the account of reserve, hauteur—of a commendable sense, in short, of what is due to the dignity of colossal proportion.

The kind friend who presented me to General Smith whispered in my ear some few words of comment upon the man. He was a remarkable man—a very remarkable man—indeed one of the most remarkable men of the age. He was an especial favorite, too, with the ladies—chiefly on account of his high reputation for courage.

"In that point he is unrivalled—indeed he is a perfect desperado—a down-right fire-eater, and no mistake," said my friend, here dropping his voice excessively low, and thrilling me with the mystery of his tone.

"A downright fire-eater, and no mistake. Showed that, I should say, to some purpose, in the late tremendous swamp-fight away down South, with the Bugaboo and Kickapoo Indians." [Here my friend opened his eyes to some extent.] "Bless my soul!—blood and thunder, and all that!—prodigies of valor!—heard of him of course?—you know he's the man"—

"Man alive, how do you do? why, how are ye? very glad to see ye, indeed!" here interrupted the General himself, seizing my companion by the hand as he drew near, and bowing stiffly, but profoundly, as I was presented. I then thought, (and I think so still,) that I never heard a clearer nor a stronger voice, nor beheld a finer set of teeth: but I must say that I was sorry for the interruption just at that moment, as, owing to the whispers and insinuations aforesaid, my interest had been greatly excited in the hero of the Bugaboo and Kickapoo campaign.

However, the delightfully luminous conversation of Brevet Brigadier General John A. B. C. Smith soon completely dissipated this chagrin. My friend leaving us immediately, we had quite a long t?te-?-t?te, and I was not only pleased but really—instructed. I never heard a more fluent talker, or a man of greater general information. With becoming modesty, he forebore, nevertheless, to touch upon the theme I had just then most at heart—I mean the mysterious circumstances attending the Bugaboo war—and, on my own part, what I conceive to be a proper sense of delicacy forbade me to broach the subject; although, in truth, I was exceedingly tempted to do so. I perceived, too, that the gallant soldier preferred topics of philosophical interest, and that he delighted, especially, in commenting upon the rapid march of mechanical invention. Indeed, lead him where I would, this was a point to which he invariably came back.

"There is nothing at all like it," he would say; "we are a wonderful people, and live in a wonderful age. Parachutes and rail-roads—man-traps and spring-guns! Our steam-boats are upon every sea, and the Nassau balloon packet is about to run regular trips (fare either way only twenty pounds sterling) between London and Timbuctoo. And who shall calculate the immense influence upon social life—upon arts—upon commerce— upon literature—which will be the immediate result of the great principles of electro magnetics! Nor, is this all, let me assure you! There is really no end to the march of invention. The most wonderful—the most ingenious—and let me add, Mr.—Mr.—Thompson, I believe, is your name—let me add, I say, the most useful—the most truly useful mechanical contrivances, are daily springing up like mushrooms, if I may so express myself, or, more figuratively, like—ah—grasshoppers—like grasshoppers, Mr. Thompson—about us and ah—ah—ah—around us!"

Thompson, to be sure, is not my name; but it is needless to say that I left General Smith with a heightened interest in the man, with an exalted opinion of his conversational powers, and a deep sense of the valuable privileges we enjoy in living in this age of mechanical invention. My curiosity, however, had not been altogether satisfied, and I resolved to prosecute immediate inquiry among my acquaintances touching the Brevet Brigadier General himself, and particularly respecting the tremendous events quorum pars magna fuit, during the Bugaboo and Kickapoo campaign.

The first opportunity which presented itself, and which (horresco referens) I did not in the least scruple to seize, occurred at the Church of the Reverend Doctor Drummummupp, where I found myself established, one Sunday, just at sermon time, not only in the pew, but by the side, of that worthy and communicative little friend of mine, Miss Tabitha T. Thus seated, I congratulated myself, and with much reason, upon the very flattering state of affairs. If any person knew anything about Brevet Brigadier General John

A. B. C. Smith, that person, it was clear to me, was Miss Tabitha T. We telegraphed a few signals, and then commenced, soto voce, a brisk t?te-?-t?te.

"Smith!" said she, in reply to my very earnest inquiry; "Smith!—why, not General John A. B. C.? Bless me, I thought you knew all about him! This is a wonderfully inventive age! Horrid affair that!—a bloody set of wretches, those Kickapoos!—fought like a hero—prodigies of valor—immortal renown. Smith!—Brevet Brigadier General John A. B. C.! why, you know he's the man"—

"Man," here broke in Doctor Drummummupp, at the top of his voice, and with a thump that came near knocking the pulpit about our ears; "man that is born of a woman hath but a short time to live; he cometh up and is cut down like a flower!" I started to the extremity of the pew, and perceived by the animated looks of the divine, that the wrath which had nearly proved fatal to the pulpit had been excited by the whispers of the lady and myself. There was no help for it; so I submitted with a good grace, and listened, in all the martyrdom of dignified silence, to the balance of that very capital discourse.

Next evening found me a somewhat late visitor at the Rantipole theatre, where I felt sure of satisfying my curiosity at once, by merely stepping into the box of those exquisite specimens of affability and omniscience, the Misses Arabella and Miranda Cognoscenti. That fine tragedian, Climax, was doing Iago to a very crowded house, and I experienced some little difficulty in making my wishes understood; especially, as our box was next the slips, and completely overlooked the stage.

"Smith?" said Miss Arabella, as she at length comprehended the purport of my query; "Smith?—why, not General John A. B. C.?"

"Smith?" inquired Miranda, musingly. "God bless me, did you ever behold a finer figure?"

"Never, madam, but do tell me"—

"Or so inimitable grace?"

"Never, upon my word!—But pray inform me"—

"Or so just an appreciation of stage effect?"

"Madam!"

"Or a more delicate sense of the true beauties of Shakespeare? Be so good as to look at that leg!"

"The devil!" and I turned again to her sister.

"Smith?" said she, "why, not General John A. B. C.? Horrid affair that, wasn't it?—great wretches, those Bugaboos—savage and so on—but we live in a wonderfully inventive age!—Smith!—O yes! great man!—perfect desperado—immortal renown—prodigies of valor! Never heard!" [This was given in a scream.] "Bless my soul! why, he's the man"—

"——mandragora

Nor all the drowsy syrups of the world

Shall ever medicine thee to that sweet sleep

Which thou owd'st yesterday!"

here roared our Climax just in my ear, and shaking his fist in my face all the time, in a way that I couldn't stand, and I wouldn't. I left the Misses Cognoscenti immediately, went behind the scenes forthwith, and gave the beggarly scoundrel such a thrashing as I trust he will remember to the day of his death.

At the soir?e of the lovely widow, Mrs. Kathleen O'Trump, I was confident that I should meet with no similar disappointment. Accordingly, I was no sooner seated at the card-table, with my pretty hostess for a vis-?-vis, than I propounded those questions the solution of which had become a matter so essential to my peace.

"Smith?" said my partner, "why, not General John A. B. C.? Horrid affair that, wasn't it?—diamonds, did you say?—terrible wretches those Kickapoos!—we are playing whist, if you please, Mr. Tattle—however, this is the age of invention, most certainly the age, one may say—the age par excellence—speak French?—oh, quite a hero—perfect desperado!—no hearts,

175

Mr. Tattle? I don't believe it!—immortal renown and all that!—prodigies of valor! Never heard!!—why, bless me, he's the man"—

"Mann?—Captain Mann?" here screamed some little feminine interloper from the farthest corner of the room. "Are you talking about Captain Mann and the duel?—oh, I must hear—do tell—go on, Mrs. O'Trump!—do now go on!" And go on Mrs. O'Trump did—all about a certain Captain Mann, who was either shot or hung, or should have been both shot and hung. Yes! Mrs. O'Trump, she went on, and I—I went off. There was no chance of hearing anything farther that evening in regard to Brevet Brigadier General John A. B. C. Smith.

Still I consoled myself with the reflection that the tide of ill luck would not run against me forever, and so determined to make a bold push for information at the rout of that bewitching little angel, the graceful Mrs. Pirouette.

"Smith?" said Mrs. P., as we twirled about together in a pas de zephyr, "Smith?—why, not General John A. B. C.? Dreadful business that of the Bugaboos, wasn't it?—dreadful creatures, those Indians!—do turn out your toes! I really am ashamed of you—man of great courage, poor fellow!—but this is a wonderful age for invention—O dear me, I'm out of breath—quite a desperado—prodigies of valor—never heard!!—can't believe it—I shall have to sit down and enlighten you—Smith! why, he's the man"—

"Man-Fred, I tell you!" here bawled out Miss Bas-Bleu, as I led Mrs. Pirouette to a seat. "Did ever anybody hear the like? It's Man-Fred, I say, and not at all by any means Man-Friday." Here Miss Bas-Bleu beckoned to me in a very peremptory manner; and I was obliged, will I nill I, to leave Mrs. P. for the purpose of deciding a dispute touching the title of a certain poetical drama of Lord Byron's. Although I pronounced, with great promptness, that the true title was Man-Friday, and not by any means Man-Fred, yet when I returned to seek Mrs. Pirouette she was not to be discovered, and I made my r?treat from the house in a very bitter spirit of animosity against the whole race of the Bas-Bleus.

Matters had now assumed a really serious aspect, and I resolved to call at once upon my particular friend, Mr. Theodore Sinivate; for I knew that here at least I should get something like definite information.

"Smith?" said he, in his well-known peculiar way of drawling out his syllables; "Smith?—why, not General John A. B. C.? Savage affair that with the Kickapo-o-o-os, wasn't it? Say! don't you think so?—perfect despera-a-ado—great pity, 'pon my honor!—wonderfully inventive age!—pro-o-odigies of valor! By the by, did you ever hear about Captain Ma-a-a-a-n?"

"Captain Mann be d—d!" said I; "please to go on with your story."

"Hem!—oh well!—quite la m?me cho-o-ose, as we say in France. Smith, eh? Brigadier-General John A. B. C.? I say"—[here Mr. S. thought proper to put his finger to the side of his nose]—"I say, you don't mean to insinuate now, really and truly, and conscientiously, that you don't know all about that affair of Smith's, as well as I do, eh? Smith? John A-B-C.? Why, bless me, he's the ma-a-an"—

"Mr. Sinivate," said I, imploringly, "is he the man in the mask?"

"No-o-o!" said he, looking wise, "nor the man in the mo-o-on."

This reply I considered a pointed and positive insult, and so left the house at once in high dudgeon, with a firm resolve to call my friend, Mr. Sinivate, to a speedy account for his ungentlemanly conduct and ill-breeding.

In the meantime, however, I had no notion of being thwarted touching the information I desired. There was one resource left me yet. I would go to the fountain-head. I would call forthwith upon the General himself, and demand, in explicit terms, a solution of this abominable piece of mystery. Here, at least, there should be no chance for equivocation. I would be plain, positive, peremptory—as short as pie-crust—as concise as Tacitus or Montesquieu.

It was early when I called, and the General was dressing; but I pleaded urgent business, and was shown at once into his bed-room by an old negro valet, who remained in attendance during my visit. As I entered the chamber, I looked about, of course, for the occupant, but did not immediately perceive him. There was a large and exceedingly odd-looking bundle of something which lay close by my feet on the floor, and, as I was not in the best humor in the world, I gave it a kick out of the way.

"Hem! ahem! rather civil that, I should say!" said the bundle, in one of the smallest, and altogether the funniest little voices, between a squeak and a whistle, that I ever heard in all the days of my existence.

"Ahem! rather civil that, I should observe."

I fairly shouted with terror, and made off, at a tangent, into the farthest extremity of the room.

"God bless me! my dear fellow," here again whistled the bundle, "what—what—what—why, what is the matter? I really believe you don't know me at all."

What could I say to all this—what could I? I staggered into an arm-chair, and, with staring eyes and open mouth, awaited the solution of the wonder.

"Strange you shouldn't know me though, isn't it?" presently re-squeaked the nondescript, which I now perceived was performing, upon the floor, some inexplicable evolution, very analogous to the drawing on of a stocking. There was only a single leg, however, apparent.

"Strange you shouldn't know me, though, isn't it? Pompey, bring me that leg!" Here Pompey handed the bundle, a very capital cork leg, already dressed, which it screwed on in a trice; and then it stood up before my eyes.

"And a bloody action it was," continued the thing, as if in a soliloquy; "but then one mustn't fight with the Bugaboos and Kickapoos, and think of coming off with a mere scratch. Pompey, I'll thank you now for that arm. Thomas" [turning to me] "is decidedly the best hand at a cork leg; but if you should ever want an arm, my dear fellow, you must really let me recommend you to Bishop." Here Pompey screwed on an arm.

"We had rather hot work of it, that you may say. Now, you dog, slip on my shoulders and bosom! Pettitt makes the best shoulders, but for a bosom you will have to go to Ducrow."

"Bosom!" said I.

"Pompey, will you never be ready with that wig? Scalping is a rough process after all; but then you can procure such a capital scratch at De L'Orme's."

"Scratch!"

"Now, you nigger, my teeth! For a good set of these you had better go to Parmly's at once; high prices, but excellent work. I swallowed some very capital articles, though, when the big Bugaboo rammed me down with the butt end of his rifle."

"Butt end! ram down!! my eye!!"

"O yes, by-the-by, my eye—here, Pompey, you scamp, screw it in! Those Kickapoos are not so very slow at a gouge; but he's a belied man, that Dr. Williams, after all; you can't imagine how well I see with the eyes of his make."

I now began very clearly to perceive that the object before me was nothing more nor less than my new acquaintance, Brevet Brigadier General John A. B. C. Smith. The manipulations of Pompey had made, I must confess, a very striking difference in the appearance of the personal man. The voice, however, still puzzled me no little; but even this apparent mystery was speedily cleared up.

"Pompey, you black rascal," squeaked the General, "I really do believe you would let me go out without my palate."

Hereupon, the negro, grumbling out an apology, went up to his master, opened his mouth with the knowing air of a horse-jockey, and adjusted therein a somewhat singular-looking machine, in a very dexterous manner, that I could not altogether comprehend. The alteration, however, in the entire expression of the General's countenance was instantaneous and surprising. When he again spoke, his voice had resumed all that rich melody and strength which I had noticed upon our original introduction.

"D—n the vagabonds!" said he, in so clear a tone that I positively started at the change, "D—n the vagabonds! they not only knocked in the roof of my mouth, but took the trouble to cut off at least seven-eighths of my tongue. There isn't Bonfanti's equal, however, in America, for really good articles of this description. I can recommend you to him with confidence," [here the General bowed,] "and assure you that I have the greatest pleasure in so doing."

I acknowledged his kindness in my best manner, and took leave of him at once, with a perfect understanding of the true state of affairs—with a full comprehension of the mystery which had troubled me so long. It was evident. It was a clear case. Brevet Brigadier General John A. B. C. Smith was the man—was the man that was used up.

THE BUSINESS MAN

Method is the soul of business.—OLD SAYING.

I AM a business man. I am a methodical man. Method is the thing, after all. But there are no people I more heartily despise than your eccentric fools who prate about method without understanding it; attending strictly to its letter, and violating its spirit. These fellows are always doing the most out-of-the-way things in what they call an orderly manner. Now here, I conceive, is a positive paradox. True method appertains to the ordinary and the obvious alone, and cannot be applied to the outre. What definite idea can a body attach to such expressions as "methodical Jack o' Dandy," or "a systematical Will o' the Wisp"?

My notions upon this head might not have been so clear as they are, but for a fortunate accident which happened to me when I was a very little boy. A good-hearted old Irish nurse (whom I shall not forget in my will) took me up one day by the heels, when I was making more noise than was necessary, and swinging me round two or knocked my head into a cocked hat against the bedpost. This, I say, decided my fate, and made my fortune. A bump arose at once on my sinciput, and turned out to be as pretty an organ of order as one shall see on a summer's day. Hence that positive appetite for system and regularity which has made me the distinguished man of business that I am.

If there is any thing on earth I hate, it is a genius. Your geniuses are all arrant asses—the greater the genius the greater the ass—and to this rule there is no exception whatever. Especially, you cannot make a man of business out of a genius, any more than money out of a Jew, or the best nutmegs out of pine-knots. The creatures are always going off at a tangent into some fantastic employment, or ridiculous speculation, entirely at variance with the "fitness of things," and having no business whatever to be considered as a business at all. Thus you may tell these characters immediately by the nature of their occupations. If you ever perceive a man setting up as a merchant or a manufacturer, or going into the cotton or tobacco trade, or any of those eccentric pursuits; or getting to be a drygoods dealer, or soap-boiler, or something of that kind; or pretending to be a lawyer, or a blacksmith, or a physician—any thing out of the usual way—you may set him down at once as a genius, and then, according to the rule-of-three, he's an ass.

Now I am not in any respect a genius, but a regular business man. My Day-book and Ledger will evince this in a minute. They are well kept, though I say it myself; and, in my general habits of accuracy and punctuality, I am not to be beat by a clock. Moreover, my occupations have been always made to chime in with the ordinary habitudes of my fellowmen. Not that I feel the least indebted, upon this score, to my exceedingly weak-minded parents, who, beyond doubt, would have made an arrant genius of me at last, if my guardian angel had not come, in good time, to the rescue. In biography the truth is every thing, and in autobiography it is especially so—yet I scarcely hope to be believed when I state, however solemnly, that my poor father put me, when I was about fifteen years of age, into the counting-house of what be termed "a respectable hardware and commission merchant doing a capital bit of business!" A capital bit of fiddlestick! However, the consequence of this folly was, that in two or three days, I had to be sent home to my button-headed family in a high state of fever, and with a most violent and dangerous pain in the sinciput, all around about my organ of order. It was nearly a gone case with me then—just touch-and-go for six weeks—the physicians giving me up and all that sort of thing. But, although I suffered much, I was a thankful boy in the main. I was saved from being a "respectable hardware and commission merchant, doing a capital bit of business," and I felt grateful to the protuberance which had been the means of my salvation, as well as to the kindhearted female who had originally put these means within my reach.

The most of boys run away from home at ten or twelve years of age, but I waited till I was sixteen. I don't know that I should have gone even then, if I had not happened to hear my old mother talk about setting me up on my own hook in the grocery way. The grocery way!—only think of that! I resolved to be off forthwith, and try and establish myself in some decent occupation, without dancing attendance any longer upon the caprices of these eccentric old people, and running the risk of being made a genius of in the end. In this project I succeeded perfectly well at the first effort, and by the time I was fairly eighteen, found myself doing an extensive and profitable business in the Tailor's Walking-Advertisement line.

I was enabled to discharge the onerous duties of this profession, only by that rigid adherence to system which formed the leading feature of my mind. A scrupulous method characterized my actions as well as my accounts. In my case it was method—not money—which made the man: at least all of him that was not made by the tailor whom I served. At nine, every morning, I called upon that individual for the clothes of the day. Ten o'clock found me in some fashionable promenade or other place of public amusement. The precise regularity with which I turned my handsome person about, so as to bring successively into view every portion of the suit upon my back, was the admiration of all the knowing men in the trade. Noon never passed without my bringing home a customer to the house of my employers, Messrs. Cut & Comeagain. I say this proudly, but with tears in my eyes—for the firm proved themselves the basest of ingrates. The little account, about which we quarreled and finally parted, cannot, in any item, be thought overcharged, by gentlemen really conversant with the nature of the business. Upon this point, however, I feel a degree of proud satisfaction in permitting the reader to judge for himself. My bill ran thus:

Messrs. Cut & Comeagain, Merchant Tailors.

To Peter Proffit, Walking Advertiser, Drs.

JULY 10.—to promenade, as usual and customer brought home... $00 25

JULY 11.—To do do do 25

JULY 12.—To one lie, second class; damaged black cloth sold for invisible green.. 25

JULY 13.—To one lie, first class, extra quality and size; recommended milled satinet as broadcloth...................... 75

183

JULY 20.—To purchasing bran new paper shirt collar or dickey, to

set off gray Petersham.................................. 02

AUG. 15.—To wearing double-padded bobtail frock, (thermometer 106

in the shade)... 25

AUG. 16.—Standing on one leg three hours, to show off new-style

strapped pants at 12 1/2 cents per leg per hour............. 37 1/2

AUG. 17.—To promenade, as usual, and large customer brought (fat

man)... 50

AUG. 18.—To do do (medium size)................. 25

AUG. 19.—To do do (small man and bad pay)....... 06

TOTAL [sic] $2 95 1/2

The item chiefly disputed in this bill was the very moderate charge of two pennies for the dickey. Upon my word of honor, this was not an unreasonable price for that dickey. It was one of the cleanest and prettiest little dickeys I ever saw; and I have good reason to believe that it effected the sale of three Petershams. The elder partner of the firm, however, would allow me only one penny of the charge, and took it upon himself to show in what manner four of the same sized conveniences could be got out of a sheet of foolscap. But it is needless to say that I stood upon the principle of the thing. Business is business, and should be done in a business way. There was no system whatever in swindling me out of a penny—a clear fraud of fifty per cent—no method in any respect. I left at once the employment of Messrs. Cut & Comeagain, and set up in the Eye-Sore line by myself—one of the most lucrative, respectable, and independent of the ordinary occupations.

My strict integrity, economy, and rigorous business habits, here again came into play. I found myself driving a flourishing trade, and soon became a marked man upon 'Change. The truth is, I never dabbled in flashy matters, but jogged on in the good old sober routine of the calling—a calling in which I should, no doubt, have remained to the present hour, but for a little accident which happened to me in the prosecution of one of the usual business operations of the profession. Whenever a rich old hunks or prodigal heir or bankrupt corporation gets into the notion of putting up a palace, there is no such thing in the world as stopping either of them, and this every intelligent person knows. The fact in question is indeed the basis of the Eye-Sore trade. As soon, therefore, as a building-project is fairly afoot by one of these parties, we merchants secure a nice corner of the lot in contemplation, or a prime little situation just adjoining, or tight in front. This done, we wait until the palace is half-way up, and then we pay some tasty architect to run us up an ornamental mud hovel, right against it; or a Down-East or Dutch Pagoda, or a pig-sty, or an ingenious little bit of fancy work, either Esquimau, Kickapoo, or Hottentot. Of course we can't afford to take these structures down under a bonus of five hundred per cent upon the prime cost of our lot and plaster. Can we? I ask the question. I ask it of business men. It would be irrational to suppose that we can. And yet there was a rascally corporation which asked me to do this very thing—this very thing! I did not reply to their absurd proposition, of course; but I felt it a duty to go that same night, and lamp-black the whole of their palace. For this the unreasonable villains clapped me into jail; and the gentlemen of the Eye-Sore trade could not well avoid cutting my connection when I came out.

The Assault-and-Battery business, into which I was now forced to adventure for a livelihood, was somewhat ill-adapted to the delicate nature of my constitution; but I went to work in it with a good heart, and found my account here, as heretofore, in those stern habits of methodical accuracy which had been thumped into me by that delightful old nurse—I would indeed be the basest of men not to remember her well in my will. By observing, as I say, the strictest system in all my dealings, and keeping a well-regulated set of books, I was enabled to get over many serious difficulties, and, in the end, to establish myself very decently in the profession. The truth is, that few individuals, in any line, did a snugger little business than I. I will just copy a page or so out of my Day-Book; and this will save me the necessity of blowing my own trumpet—a contemptible practice of which no high-minded man will be guilty. Now, the Day-Book is a thing that don't lie.

"Jan. 1.—New Year's Day. Met Snap in the street, groggy. Mem—he'll do. Met Gruff shortly afterward, blind drunk. Mem—he'll answer, too. Entered both gentlemen in my Ledger, and opened a running account with each.

"Jan. 2.—Saw Snap at the Exchange, and went up and trod on his toe. Doubled his fist and knocked me down. Good!—got up again. Some trifling difficulty with Bag, my attorney. I want the damages at a thousand, but he says that for so simple a knock down we can't lay them at more than five hundred. Mem—must get rid of Bag—no system at all.

"Jan. 3—Went to the theatre, to look for Gruff. Saw him sitting in a side box, in the second tier, between a fat lady and a lean one. Quizzed the whole party through an opera-glass, till I saw the fat lady blush and whisper to G. Went round, then, into the box, and put my nose within reach of his hand. Wouldn't pull it—no go. Blew it, and tried again—no go. Sat down then, and winked at the lean lady, when I had the high satisfaction of finding him lift me up by the nape of the neck, and fling me over into the pit. Neck dislocated, and right leg capitally splintered. Went home in high glee, drank a bottle of champagne, and booked the young man for five thousand. Bag says it'll do.

"Feb. 15—Compromised the case of Mr. Snap. Amount entered in Journal—fifty cents—which see.

"Feb. 16.—Cast by that ruffian, Gruff, who made me a present of five dollars. Costs of suit, four dollars and twenty-five cents. Nett profit,—see Journal,—seventy-five cents."

Now, here is a clear gain, in a very brief period, of no less than one dollar and twenty-five cents—this is in the mere cases of Snap and Gruff; and I solemnly assure the reader that these extracts are taken at random from my Day-Book.

It's an old saying, and a true one, however, that money is nothing in comparison with health. I found the exactions of the profession somewhat too much for my delicate state of body; and, discovering, at last, that I was knocked all out of shape, so that I didn't know very well what to make of the matter, and so that my friends, when they met me in the street, couldn't tell that I was Peter Proffit at all, it occurred to me that the best expedient I could adopt was to alter my line of business. I turned my attention, therefore, to Mud-Dabbling, and continued it for some years.

The worst of this occupation is, that too many people take a fancy to it, and the competition is in consequence excessive. Every ignoramus of a fellow who finds that he hasn't brains in sufficient quantity to make his way as a walking advertiser, or an eye-sore prig, or a salt-and-batter man, thinks, of course, that he'll answer very well as a dabbler of mud. But there never was entertained a more erroneous idea than that it requires no brains to mud-dabble. Especially, there is nothing to be made in this way without method. I did only a retail business myself, but my old habits of system carried me swimmingly along. I selected my street-crossing, in the first place, with great deliberation, and I never put down a broom in any part of the town but that. I took care, too, to have a nice little puddle at hand, which I could get at in a minute. By these means I got to be well known as a man to be trusted; and this is one-half the battle, let me tell you, in trade. Nobody ever failed to pitch me a copper, and got over my crossing with a clean pair of pantaloons. And, as my business habits, in this respect, were sufficiently understood, I never met with any attempt at imposition. I wouldn't have put up with it, if I had. Never imposing upon any one myself, I suffered no one to play the possum with me. The frauds of the banks of course I couldn't help. Their suspension put me to ruinous inconvenience. These, however, are not individuals, but corporations; and corporations, it is very well known, have neither bodies to be kicked nor souls to be damned.

I was making money at this business when, in an evil moment, I was induced to merge it in the Cur-Spattering—a somewhat analogous, but, by no means, so respectable a profession. My location, to be sure, was an excellent one, being central, and I had capital blacking and brushes. My little dog, too, was quite fat and up to all varieties of snuff. He had been in the trade a long time, and, I may say, understood it. Our general routine was this:—Pompey, having rolled himself well in the mud, sat upon end at the shop door, until he observed a dandy approaching in bright boots. He then proceeded to meet him, and gave the Wellingtons a rub or two with his wool. Then the dandy swore very much, and looked about for a boot-black. There I was, full in his view, with blacking and brushes. It was only a minute's work, and then came a sixpence. This did moderately well for a time;—in fact, I was not avaricious, but my dog was. I allowed him a third of the profit, but he was advised to insist upon half. This I couldn't stand—so we quarrelled and parted.

I next tried my hand at the Organ-Grinding for a while, and may say that I made out pretty well. It is a plain, straightforward business, and requires no particular abilities. You can get a music-mill for a mere song, and to put it in order, you have but to open the works, and give them three or four smart raps with a hammer. In improves the tone of the thing, for business purposes, more than you can imagine. This done, you have only to stroll along, with the mill on your back, until you see tanbark in the street, and a knocker wrapped up in buckskin. Then you stop and grind; looking as if you meant to stop and grind till doomsday. Presently a window opens, and somebody pitches you a sixpence, with a request to "Hush up and go on," etc. I am aware that some grinders have actually afforded to "go on" for this sum; but for my part, I found the necessary outlay of capital too great to permit of my "going on" under a shilling.

At this occupation I did a good deal; but, somehow, I was not quite satisfied, and so finally abandoned it. The truth is, I labored under the disadvantage of having no monkey—and American streets are so muddy, and a Democratic rabble is so obstrusive, and so full of demnition mischievous little boys.

I was now out of employment for some months, but at length succeeded, by dint of great interest, in procuring a situation in the Sham-Post. The duties, here, are simple, and not altogether unprofitable. For example:—very early in the morning I had to make up my packet of sham letters. Upon the inside of each of these I had to scrawl a few lines on any subject which occurred to me as sufficiently mysterious—signing all the epistles Tom Dobson, or Bobby Tompkins, or anything in that way. Having folded and sealed all, and stamped them with sham postmarks—New Orleans, Bengal, Botany Bay, or any other place a great way off—I set out, forthwith, upon my daily route, as if in a very great hurry. I always called at the big houses to deliver the letters, and receive the postage. Nobody hesitates at paying for a letter—especially for a double one—people are such fools—and it was no trouble to get round a corner before there was time to open the epistles. The worst of this profession was, that I had to walk so much and so fast; and so frequently to vary my route. Besides, I had serious scruples of conscience. I can't bear to hear innocent individuals abused—and the way the whole town took to cursing Tom Dobson and Bobby Tompkins was really awful to hear. I washed my hands of the matter in disgust.

My eighth and last speculation has been in the Cat-Growing way. I have found that a most pleasant and lucrative business, and, really, no trouble at all. The country, it is well known, has become infested with cats—so much so of late, that a petition for relief, most numerously and respectably signed, was brought before the Legislature at its late memorable session. The Assembly, at this epoch, was unusually well-informed, and, having passed many other wise and wholesome enactments, it crowned all with the Cat-Act. In its original form, this law offered a premium for cat-heads (fourpence a-piece), but the Senate succeeded in amending the main clause, so as to substitute the word "tails" for "heads." This amendment was so obviously proper, that the House concurred in it nem. con.

As soon as the governor had signed the bill, I invested my whole estate in the purchase of Toms and Tabbies. At first I could only afford to feed them upon mice (which are cheap), but they fulfilled the scriptural injunction at so marvellous a rate, that I at length considered it my best policy to be liberal, and so indulged them in oysters and turtle. Their tails, at a legislative price, now bring me in a good income; for I have discovered a way, in which, by means of Macassar oil, I can force three crops in a year. It delights me to find, too, that the animals soon get accustomed to the thing, and would rather have the appendages cut off than otherwise. I consider myself, therefore, a made man, and am bargaining for a country seat on the Hudson.

THE LANDSCAPE GARDEN

The garden like a lady fair was cut

That lay as if she slumbered in delight,

And to the open skies her eyes did shut;

The azure fields of heaven were 'sembled right

In a large round set with flow'rs of light:

The flowers de luce and the round sparks of dew

That hung upon their azure leaves, did show

Like twinkling stars that sparkle in the ev'ning blue.

—GILES FLETCHER

NO MORE remarkable man ever lived than my friend, the young Ellison. He was remarkable in the entire and continuous profusion of good gifts ever lavished upon him by fortune. From his cradle to his grave, a gale of the blandest prosperity bore him along. Nor do I use the word Prosperity in its mere wordly or external sense. I mean it as synonymous with happiness. The person of whom I speak, seemed born for the purpose of foreshadowing the wild doctrines of Turgot, Price, Priestley, and Condorcet—of exemplifying, by individual instance, what has been deemed the mere chimera of the perfectionists. In the brief existence of Ellison, I fancy, that I have seen refuted the dogma—that in man's physical and spiritual nature, lies some hidden principle, the antagonist of Bliss. An intimate and anxious examination of his career, has taught me to understand that, in general, from the violation of a few simple laws of Humanity, arises the Wretchedness of mankind; that, as a species, we have in our possession the as yet unwrought elements of Content,—and that even now, in the present blindness and darkness of all idea on the great question of the Social Condition, it is not impossible that Man, the individual, under certain unusual and highly fortuitous conditions, may be happy.

With opinions such as these was my young friend fully imbued; and thus is it especially worthy of observation that the uninterrupted enjoyment which distinguished his life was in great part the result of preconcert. It is, indeed evident, that with less of the instinctive philosophy which, now and then, stands so well in the stead of experience, Mr. Ellison would have found himself precipitated, by the very extraordinary successes of his life, into the common vortex of Unhappiness which yawns for those of preeminent endowments. But it is by no means my present object to pen an essay on Happiness. The ideas of my friend may be summed up in a few words. He admitted but four unvarying laws, or rather elementary principles, of Bliss. That which he considered chief, was (strange to say!) the simple and purely physical one of free exercise in the open air. "The health," he said, "attainable by other means than this is scarcely worth the name." He pointed to the tillers of the earth—the only people who, as a class, are proverbially more happy than others—and then he instanced the high ecstasies of the fox-hunter. His second principle was the love of woman. His third was the contempt of ambition. His fourth was an object of unceasing pursuit; and he held that, other things being equal, the extent of happiness was proportioned to the spirituality of this object.

I have said that Ellison was remarkable in the continuous profusion of good gifts lavished upon him by Fortune. In personal grace and beauty he exceeded all men. His intellect was of that order to which the attainment of knowledge is less a labor than a necessity and an intuition. His family was one of the most illustrious of the empire. His bride was the loveliest and most devoted of women. His possessions had been always ample; but, upon the attainment of his one and twentieth year, it was discovered that one of those extraordinary freaks of Fate had been played in his behalf which startle the whole social world amid which they occur, and seldom fail radically to alter the entire moral constitution of those who are their objects. It appears that about one hundred years prior to Mr. Ellison's attainment of his majority, there had died, in a remote province, one Mr. Seabright Ellison. This gentlemen had amassed a princely fortune, and, having no very immediate connexions, conceived the whim of suffering his wealth to accumulate for a century after his decease. Minutely and sagaciously directing the various modes of investment, he bequeathed the aggregate amount to the nearest of blood, bearing the name Ellison, who should be alive at the end of the hundred years. Many futile attempts had been made to set aside this singular bequest; their ex post facto character rendered them abortive; but the attention of a jealous government was aroused, and a decree finally obtained, forbidding all similar accumulations. This act did not prevent young Ellison, upon his twenty-first birth-day, from entering into possession, as the heir of his ancestor, Seabright, of a fortune of four hundred and fifty millions of dollars. {*1}

When it had become definitely known that such was the enormous wealth inherited, there were, of course, many speculations as to the mode of its disposal. The gigantic magnitude and the immediately available nature of the sum, dazzled and bewildered all who thought upon the topic. The possessor of any appreciable amount of money might have been imagined to perform any one of a thousand things. With riches merely surpassing those of any citizen, it would have been easy to suppose him engaging to supreme excess in the fashionable extravagances of his time; or busying himself with political intrigues; or aiming at ministerial power, or purchasing increase of nobility, or devising gorgeous architectural piles; or collecting large specimens of Virtu; or playing the munificent patron of Letters and Art; or endowing and bestowing his name upon extensive institutions of charity. But, for the inconceivable wealth in the actual possession of the young heir, these objects and all ordinary objects were felt to be inadequate. Recourse was had to figures; and figures but sufficed to confound. It was seen, that even at three per cent, the annual income of the inheritance amounted to no less than thirteen millions and five hundred thousand dollars; which was one million and one hundred and twenty-five thousand per month; or thirty-six thousand, nine hundred and eighty-six per day, or one thousand five hundred and forty-one per hour, or six and twenty dollars for every minute that flew. Thus the usual track of supposition was thoroughly broken up. Men knew not what to imagine. There were some who even conceived that Mr. Ellison would divest himself forthwith of at least two-thirds of his fortune as of utterly superfluous opulence; enriching whole troops of his relatives by division of his superabundance.

I was not surprised, however, to perceive that he had long made up his mind upon a topic which had occasioned so much of discussion to his friends. Nor was I greatly astonished at the nature of his decision. In the widest and noblest sense, he was a poet. He comprehended, moreover, the true character, the august aims, the supreme majesty and dignity of the poetic sentiment. The proper gratification of the sentiment he instinctively felt to lie in the creation of novel forms of Beauty. Some peculiarities, either in his early education, or in the nature of his intellect, had tinged with what is termed materialism the whole cast of his ethical speculations; and it was this bias, perhaps, which imperceptibly led him to perceive that the most advantageous, if not the sole legitimate field for the exercise of the poetic sentiment, was to be found in the creation of novel moods of purely physical loveliness. Thus it happened that he became neither musician nor poet; if we use this latter term in its every—day acceptation. Or it might have been that he became neither the one nor the other, in pursuance of an idea of his which I have already mentioned—the idea, that in the contempt of ambition lay one of the essential principles of happiness on earth. Is it not, indeed, possible that while a high order of genius is necessarily ambitious, the highest is invariably above that which is termed ambition? And may it not thus happen that many far greater than Milton, have contentedly remained "mute and inglorious?" I believe the world has never yet seen, and that, unless through some series of accidents goading the noblest order of mind into distasteful exertion, the world will never behold, that full extent of triumphant execution, in the richer productions of Art, of which the human nature is absolutely capable.

Mr. Ellison became neither musician nor poet; although no man lived more profoundly enamored both of Music and the Muse. Under other circumstances than those which invested him, it is not impossible that he would have become a painter. The field of sculpture, although in its nature rigidly poetical, was too limited in its extent and in its consequences, to have occupied, at any time, much of his attention. And I have now mentioned all the provinces in which even the most liberal understanding of the poetic sentiment has declared this sentiment capable of expatiating. I mean the most liberal public or recognized conception of the idea involved in the phrase "poetic sentiment." But Mr. Ellison imagined that the richest, and altogether the most natural and most suitable province, had been blindly neglected. No definition had spoken of the Landscape-Gardener, as of the poet; yet my friend could not fail to perceive that the creation of the Landscape-Garden offered to the true muse the most magnificent of opportunities. Here was, indeed, the fairest field for the display of invention, or imagination, in the endless combining of forms of novel Beauty; the elements which should enter into combination being, at all times, and by a vast superiority, the most glorious which the earth could afford. In the multiform of the tree, and in the multicolor of the flower, he recognized the most direct and the most energetic efforts of Nature at physical loveliness. And in the direction or concentration of this effort, or, still more properly, in its adaption to the eyes which were to behold it upon earth, he perceived that he should be employing the best means—laboring to the greatest advantage—in the fulfilment of his destiny as Poet.

"Its adaptation to the eyes which were to behold it upon earth." In his explanation of this phraseology, Mr. Ellison did much towards solving what has always seemed to me an enigma. I mean the fact (which none but the ignorant dispute,) that no such combinations of scenery exist in Nature as the painter of genius has in his power to produce. No such Paradises are to be found in reality as have glowed upon the canvass of Claude. In the most enchanting of natural landscapes, there will always be found a defect or an excess—many excesses and defects. While the component parts may exceed, individually, the highest skill of the artist, the arrangement of the parts will always be susceptible of improvement. In short, no position can be attained, from which an artistical eye, looking steadily, will not find matter of offence, in what is technically termed the composition of a natural landscape. And yet how unintelligible is this! In all other matters we are justly instructed to regard Nature as supreme. With her details we shrink from competition. Who shall presume to imitate the colors of the tulip, or to improve the proportions of the lily of the valley? The criticism which says, of sculpture or of portraiture, that "Nature is to be exalted rather than imitated," is in error. No pictorial or sculptural combinations of points of human loveliness, do more than approach the living and breathing human beauty as it gladdens our daily path. Byron, who often erred, erred not in saying, I've seen more living beauty, ripe and real, than all the nonsense of their stone ideal. In landscape alone is the principle of the critic true; and, having felt its truth here, it is but the headlong spirit of generalization which has induced him to pronounce it true throughout all the domains of Art. Having, I say, felt its truth here. For the feeling is no affectation or chimera. The mathematics afford no more absolute demonstrations, than the sentiment of his Art yields to the artist. He not only believes, but positively knows, that such and such apparently arbitrary arrangements of matter, or form, constitute, and alone constitute, the true Beauty. Yet his reasons have not yet been matured into expression. It remains for a more profound analysis than the world has yet seen, fully to investigate and express them. Nevertheless is he confirmed in his instinctive opinions, by the concurrence of all his compeers. Let a composition be defective, let an emendation be wrought in its mere arrangement of form; let this emendation be submitted to every artist in the world; by each will its necessity be admitted. And even far more than this, in remedy of the defective composition, each insulated member of the fraternity will suggest the identical emendation.

I repeat that in landscape arrangements, or collocations alone, is the physical Nature susceptible of "exaltation" and that, therefore, her susceptibility of improvement at this one point, was a mystery which, hitherto I had been unable to solve. It was Mr. Ellison who first suggested the idea that what we regarded as improvement or exaltation of the natural beauty, was really such, as respected only the mortal or human point of view; that each alteration or disturbance of the primitive scenery might possibly effect a blemish in the picture, if we could suppose this picture viewed at large from some remote point in the heavens. "It is easily understood," says Mr. Ellison, "that what might improve a closely scrutinized detail, might, at the same time, injure a general and more distantly—observed effect." He spoke upon this topic with warmth: regarding not so much its immediate or obvious importance, (which is little,) as the character of the conclusions to which it might lead, or of the collateral propositions which it might serve to corroborate or sustain. There might be a class of beings, human once, but now to humanity invisible, for whose scrutiny and for whose refined appreciation of the beautiful, more especially than for our own, had been set in order by God the great landscape-garden of the whole earth.

In the course of our discussion, my young friend took occasion to quote some passages from a writer who has been supposed to have well treated this theme.

"There are, properly," he writes, "but two styles of landscape-gardening, the natural and the artificial. One seeks to recall the original beauty of the country, by adapting its means to the surrounding scenery; cultivating trees in harmony with the hills or plain of the neighboring land; detecting and bringing into practice those nice relations of size, proportion and color which, hid from the common observer, are revealed everywhere to the experienced student of nature. The result of the natural style of gardening, is seen rather in the absence of all defects and incongruities—in the prevalence of a beautiful harmony and order, than in the creation of any special wonders or miracles. The artificial style has as many varieties as there are different tastes to gratify. It has a certain general relation to the various styles of building. There are the stately avenues and retirements of Versailles; Italian terraces; and a various mixed old English style, which bears some relation to the domestic Gothic or English Elizabethan architecture. Whatever may be said against the abuses of the artificial landscape-gardening, a mixture of pure art in a garden scene, adds to it a great beauty. This is partly pleasing to the eye, by the show of order and design, and partly moral. A terrace, with an old moss-covered balustrade, calls up at once to the eye, the fair forms that have passed there in other days. The slightest exhibition of art is an evidence of care and human interest."

"From what I have already observed," said Mr. Ellison, "you will understand that I reject the idea, here expressed, of 'recalling the original beauty of the country.' The original beauty is never so great as that which may be introduced. Of course, much depends upon the selection of a spot with capabilities. What is said in respect to the 'detecting and bringing into practice those nice relations of size, proportion and color,' is a mere vagueness of speech, which may mean much, or little, or nothing, and which guides in no degree. That the true 'result of the natural style of gardening is seen rather in the absence of all defects and incongruities, than in the creation of any special wonders or miracles,' is a proposition better suited to the grovelling apprehension of the herd, than to the fervid dreams of the man of genius. The merit suggested is, at best, negative, and appertains to that hobbling criticism which, in letters, would elevate Addison into apotheosis. In truth, while that merit which consists in the mere avoiding demerit, appeals directly to the understanding, and can thus be foreshadowed in Rule, the loftier merit, which breathes and flames in invention or creation, can be apprehended solely in its results. Rule applies but to the excellences of avoidance—to the virtues which deny or refrain. Beyond these the critical art can but suggest. We may be instructed to build an Odyssey, but it is in vain that we are told how to conceive a 'Tempest,' an 'Inferno,' a 'Prometheus Bound,' a 'Nightingale,' such as that of Keats, or the 'Sensitive Plant' of Shelley. But, the thing done, the wonder accomplished, and the capacity for apprehension becomes universal. The sophists of the negative school, who, through inability to create, have scoffed at creation, are now found the loudest in applause. What, in its chrysalis condition of principle, affronted their demure reason, never fails, in its maturity of accomplishment, to extort admiration from their instinct of the beautiful or of the sublime.

"Our author's observations on the artificial style of gardening," continued Mr. Ellison, "are less objectionable. 'A mixture of pure art in a garden scene, adds to it a great beauty.' This is just; and the reference to the sense of human interest is equally so. I repeat that the principle here expressed, is incontrovertible; but there may be something even beyond it. There may be an object in full keeping with the principle suggested—an object unattainable by the means ordinarily in possession of mankind, yet which, if attained, would lend a charm to the landscape-garden immeasurably surpassing that which a merely human interest could bestow. The true poet possessed of very unusual pecuniary resources, might possibly, while retaining the necessary idea of art or interest or culture, so imbue his designs at once with extent and novelty of Beauty, as to convey the sentiment of spiritual interference. It will be seen that, in bringing about such result, he secures all the advantages of interest or design, while relieving his work of all the harshness and technicality of Art. In the most rugged of wildernesses—in the most savage of the scenes of pure

Nature—there is apparent the art of a Creator; yet is this art apparent only to reflection; in no respect has it the obvious force of a feeling. Now, if we imagine this sense of the Almighty Design to be harmonized in a measurable degree, if we suppose a landscape whose combined strangeness, vastness, definitiveness, and magnificence, shall inspire the idea of culture, or care, or superintendence, on the part of intelligences superior yet akin to humanity— then the sentiment of interest is preserved, while the Art is made to assume the air of an intermediate or secondary Nature—a Nature which is not God, nor an emanation of God, but which still is Nature, in the sense that it is the handiwork of the angels that hover between man and God."

It was in devoting his gigantic wealth to the practical embodiment of a vision such as this—in the free exercise in the open air, which resulted from personal direction of his plans—in the continuous and unceasing object which these plans afford—in the contempt of ambition which it enabled him more to feel than to affect—and, lastly, it was in the companionship and sympathy of a devoted wife, that Ellison thought to find, and found, an exemption from the ordinary cares of Humanity, with a far greater amount of positive happiness than ever glowed in the rapt day-dreams of De Stael.

MAELZEL'S CHESS-PLAYER

PERHAPS no exhibition of the kind has ever elicited so general attention as the Chess-Player of Maelzel. Wherever seen it has been an object of intense curiosity, to all persons who think. Yet the question of its modus operandi is still undetermined. Nothing has been written on this topic which can be considered as decisive—and accordingly we find every where men of mechanical genius, of great general acuteness, and discriminative understanding, who make no scruple in pronouncing the Automaton a pure machine, unconnected with human agency in its movements, and consequently, beyond all comparison, the most astonishing of the inventions of mankind. And such it would undoubtedly be, were they right in their supposition. Assuming this hypothesis, it would be grossly absurd to compare with the Chess-Player, any similar thing of either modern or ancient days. Yet there have been many and wonderful automata. In Brewster's Letters on Natural Magic, we have an account of the most remarkable. Among these may be mentioned, as having beyond doubt existed, firstly, the coach invented by M. Camus for the amusement of Louis XIV when a child. A table, about four feet square, was introduced, into the room appropriated for the exhibition. Upon this table was placed a carriage, six inches in length, made of wood, and drawn by two horses of the same material. One window being down, a lady was seen on the back seat. A coachman held the reins on the box, and a footman and page were in their places behind. M. Camus now touched a spring; whereupon the coachman smacked his whip, and the horses proceeded in a natural manner, along the edge of the table, drawing after them the carriage. Having gone as far as possible in this direction, a sudden turn was made to the left, and the vehicle was driven at right angles to its former course, and still closely along the edge of the table. In this way the coach proceeded until it arrived opposite the chair of the young prince. It then stopped, the page descended and opened the door, the lady alighted, and presented a petition to her sovereign. She then re-entered. The page put up the steps, closed the door, and resumed his station. The coachman whipped his horses, and the carriage was driven back to its original position.

The magician of M. Maillardet is also worthy of notice. We copy the following account of it from the Letters before mentioned of Dr. B., who derived his information principally from the Edinburgh Encyclopaedia.

"One of the most popular pieces of mechanism which we have seen, Is the Magician constructed by M. Maillardet, for the purpose of answering certain given questions. A figure, dressed like a magician, appears seated at the bottom of a wall, holding a wand in one hand, and a book in the other A number of questions, ready prepared, are inscribed on oval medallions, and the spectator takes any of these he chooses and to which he wishes an answer, and having placed it in a drawer ready to receive it, the drawer shuts with a spring till the answer is returned. The magician then arises from his seat, bows his head, describes circles with his wand, and consulting the book as If in deep thought, he lifts it towards his face. Having thus appeared to ponder over the proposed question he raises his wand, and striking with it the wall above his head, two folding doors fly open, and display an appropriate answer to the question. The doors again close, the magician resumes his original position, and the drawer opens to return the medallion. There are twenty of these medallions, all containing different questions, to which the magician returns the most suitable and striking answers. The medallions are thin plates of brass, of an elliptical form, exactly resembling each other. Some of the medallions have a question inscribed on each side, both of which the magician answered in succession. If the drawer is shut without a medallion being put into it, the magician rises, consults his book, shakes his head, and resumes his seat. The folding doors remain shut, and the drawer is returned empty. If two medallions are put into the drawer together, an answer is returned only to the lower one. When the machinery is wound up, the movements continue about an hour, during which time about fifty questions may be answered. The inventor stated that the means by which the different medallions acted upon the machinery, so as to produce the proper answers to the questions which they contained, were extremely simple."

The duck of Vaucanson was still more remarkable. It was of the size of life, and so perfect an imitation of the living animal that all the spectators were deceived. It executed, says Brewster, all the natural movements and gestures, it ate and drank with avidity, performed all the quick motions of the head and throat which are peculiar to the duck, and like it muddled the water which it drank with its bill. It produced also the sound of quacking in the most natural manner. In the anatomical structure the artist exhibited the highest skill. Every bone in the real duck had its representative In the automaton, and its wings were anatomically exact. Every cavity, apophysis, and curvature was imitated, and each bone executed its proper movements. When corn was thrown down before it, the duck stretched out its neck to pick it up, swallowed, and digested it. {*1}

But if these machines were ingenious, what shall we think of the calculating machine of Mr. Babbage? What shall we think of an engine of wood and metal which can not only compute astronomical and navigation tables to any given extent, but render the exactitude of its operations mathematically certain through its power of correcting its possible errors? What shall we think of a machine which can not only accomplish all this, but actually print off its elaborate results, when obtained, without the slightest intervention of the intellect of man? It will, perhaps, be said, in reply, that a machine such as we have described is altogether above comparison with the Chess-Player of Maelzel. By no means—it is altogether beneath it—that is to say provided we assume (what should never for a moment be assumed) that the Chess-Player is a pure machine, and performs its operations without any immediate human agency. Arithmetical or algebraical calculations are, from their very nature, fixed and determinate. Certain data being given, certain results necessarily and inevitably follow. These results have dependence upon nothing, and are influenced by nothing but the data originally given. And the question to be solved proceeds, or should proceed, to its final determination, by a succession of unerring steps liable to no change, and subject to no modification. This being the case, we can without difficulty conceive the possibility of so arranging a piece of mechanism, that upon starting In accordance with the data of the question to be solved, it should continue its movements regularly, progressively, and undeviatingly towards the required solution, since these movements, however complex, are never imagined to be otherwise than finite and determinate. But the case is widely different with the Chess-Player. With him there is no determinate progression. No one move in chess necessarily follows upon any one other. From no particular disposition of the men at one period of a game can we predicate their disposition at a different period. Let us place the first move in a game of chess, in juxta-position with the data of an algebraical question, and their great difference will be immediately perceived. From the latter—from the data—the second step of the question, dependent thereupon, inevitably follows. It is modelled by the data. It must be thus and not otherwise. But from the first move in the game of chess no especial second move follows of necessity. In the algebraical question, as it proceeds towards solution, the certainty of its operations remains altogether unimpaired. The second step having been a consequence of the data, the third step is equally a consequence of the second, the fourth of the third, the fifth of the fourth, and so on, and not possibly otherwise, to the end. But in proportion to the progress made in a game of chess, is the uncertainty of each ensuing move. A few moves having been made, no step is certain. Different spectators of the game would advise different moves. All is then dependent upon the variable judgment of the players. Now even granting (what should not be granted) that the movements of the Automaton Chess-Player were in themselves determinate, they would be necessarily interrupted and disarranged by the indeterminate will of his antagonist. There is then no analogy whatever between the operations of the Chess-Player, and those of the calculating machine of Mr. Babbage, and if we choose to call the former a pure machine we must be prepared to admit that it is, beyond all comparison, the most wonderful of the inventions of mankind. Its original projector, however, Baron Kempelen, had no scruple in declaring it to be a "very ordinary piece of mechanism—a bagatelle whose effects appeared so marvellous only from the boldness of the conception, and the fortunate choice of the methods adopted for promoting the illusion." But it is needless to dwell upon this point. It is quite certain that the operations of the Automaton are regulated by mind, and by nothing else. Indeed this matter is susceptible of a mathematical demonstration, a priori. The only question then is of the manner in which human agency is brought to bear. Before entering upon this subject it would be as well to give a brief history and description of the Chess-Player for the benefit of such of our readers as may never have had an opportunity of witnessing Mr. Maelzel's exhibition.

The Automaton Chess-Player was invented in 1769, by Baron Kempelen, a nobleman of Presburg, in Hungary, who afterwards disposed of it, together with the secret of its operations, to its present possessor. {2*} Soon after its completion it was exhibited in Presburg, Paris, Vienna, and other continental cities. In 1783 and 1784, it was taken to London by Mr. Maelzel. Of late years it has visited the principal towns in the United States. Wherever seen, the most intense curiosity was excited by its appearance, and numerous have been the attempts, by men of all classes, to fathom the mystery of its evolutions. The cut on this page gives a tolerable representation of the figure as seen by the citizens of Richmond a few weeks ago. The right arm, however, should lie more at length upon the box, a chess-board should appear upon it, and the cushion should not be seen while the pipe is held. Some immaterial alterations have been made in the costume of the player since it came into the possession of Maelzel—the plume, for example, was not originally worn.
{image of automaton}

At the hour appointed for exhibition, a curtain is withdrawn, or folding doors are thrown open, and the machine rolled to within about twelve feet of the nearest of the spectators, between whom and it (the machine) a rope is stretched. A figure is seen habited as a Turk, and seated, with its legs crossed, at a large box apparently of maple wood, which serves it as a table. The exhibiter will, if requested, roll the machine to any portion of the room, suffer it to remain altogether on any designated spot, or even shift its location repeatedly during the progress of a game. The bottom of the box is elevated considerably above the floor by means of the castors or brazen rollers on which it moves, a clear view of the surface immediately beneath the Automaton being thus afforded to the spectators. The chair on which the figure sits is affixed permanently to the box. On the top of this latter is a chess-board, also permanently affixed. The right arm of the Chess-Player is extended at full length before him, at right angles with his body, and lying, in an apparently careless position, by the side of the board. The back of the hand is upwards. The board itself is eighteen inches square. The left arm of the figure is bent at the elbow, and in the left hand is a pipe. A green drapery conceals the back of the Turk, and falls partially over the front of both shoulders. To judge from the external appearance of the box, it is divided into five compartments—three cupboards of equal dimensions, and two drawers occupying that portion of the chest lying beneath the cupboards. The foregoing observations apply to the appearance of the Automaton upon its first introduction into the presence of the spectators.

Maelzel now informs the company that he will disclose to their view the mechanism of the machine. Taking from his pocket a bunch of keys he unlocks with one of them, door marked ⁓ in the cut above, and throws the cupboard fully open to the inspection of all present. Its whole interior is apparently filled with wheels, pinions, levers, and other machinery, crowded very closely together, so that the eye can penetrate but a little distance into the mass. Leaving this door open to its full extent, he goes now round to the back of the box, and raising the drapery of the figure, opens another door situated precisely in the rear of the one first opened. Holding a lighted candle at this door, and shifting the position of the whole machine repeatedly at the same time, a bright light is thrown entirely through the cupboard, which is now clearly seen to be full, completely full, of machinery. The spectators being satisfied of this fact, Maelzel closes the back door, locks it, takes the key from the lock, lets fall the drapery of the figure, and comes round to the front. The door marked I, it will be remembered, is still open. The exhibiter now proceeds to open the drawer which lies beneath the cupboards at the bottom of the box—for although there are apparently two drawers, there is really only one—the two handles and two key holes being intended merely for ornament. Having opened this drawer to its full extent, a small cushion, and a set of chessmen, fixed in a frame work made to support them perpendicularly, are discovered. Leaving this drawer, as well as cupboard No. 1 open, Maelzel now unlocks door No. 2, and door No. 3, which are discovered to be folding doors, opening into one and the same compartment. To the right of this compartment, however, (that is to say the spectators' right) a small division, six inches wide, and filled with machinery, is partitioned off. The main compartment itself (in speaking of that portion of the box visible upon opening doors 2 and 3, we shall always call it the main compartment) is lined with dark cloth and contains no machinery whatever beyond two pieces of steel, quadrant-shaped, and situated one in each of the rear top corners of the compartment. A small protuberance about eight inches square, and also covered with dark cloth, lies on the floor of the compartment near the rear corner on the spectators' left hand. Leaving doors No. 2 and No. 3 open as well as the drawer, and door No. I, the exhibiter now goes round to the back of the main compartment, and, unlocking another door there, displays clearly all the interior of the main compartment, by introducing a candle behind it and within it. The whole box being thus apparently disclosed to the scrutiny of the company, Maelzel, still leaving the doors and drawer open, rolls the Automaton entirely round, and exposes the back of the Turk by lifting up the drapery. A door about ten inches square is thrown open in the loins of the figure, and a smaller one also in the left thigh. The interior of the figure, as seen through these apertures, appears to be crowded with machinery. In general, every spectator is now thoroughly satisfied of having beheld and completely scrutinized, at one and the same time, every individual portion of the Automaton, and the idea of any person being concealed in the interior, during so complete an exhibition of that interior, if ever entertained, is immediately dismissed as preposterous in the extreme.

M. Maelzel, having rolled the machine back into its original position, now informs the company that the Automaton will play a game of chess with any one disposed to encounter him. This challenge being accepted, a small table is prepared for the antagonist, and placed close by the rope, but on the spectators' side of it, and so situated as not to prevent the company from obtaining a full view of the Automaton. From a drawer in this table is taken a set of chess-men, and Maelzel arranges them generally, but not always, with his own hands, on the chess board, which consists merely of the usual number of squares painted upon the table. The antagonist having taken his seat, the exhibiter approaches the drawer of the box, and takes therefrom the cushion, which, after removing the pipe from the hand of the Automaton, he places under its left arm as a support. Then taking also from the drawer the Automaton's set of chess-men, he arranges them upon the chessboard before the figure. He now proceeds to close the doors and to lock them—leaving the bunch of keys in door No. 1. He also closes the drawer, and, finally, winds up the machine, by applying a key to an aperture in the left end (the spectators' left) of the box. The game now commences—the Automaton taking the first move. The duration of the contest is usually limited to half an hour, but if it be not finished at the expiration of this period, and the antagonist still contend that he can beat the Automaton, M. Maelzel has seldom any objection to continue it. Not to weary the company, is the ostensible, and no doubt the real object of the limitation. It Wits of course be understood that when a move is made at his own table, by the antagonist, the corresponding move is made at the box of the Automaton, by Maelzel himself, who then acts as the representative of the antagonist. On the other hand, when the Turk moves, the corresponding move is made at the table of the antagonist, also by M. Maelzel, who then acts as the representative of the Automaton. In this manner it is necessary that the exhibiter should often pass from one table to the other. He also frequently goes in rear of the figure to remove the chessmen which it has taken, and which it deposits, when taken, on the box to the left (to its own left) of the board. When the Automaton hesitates in relation to its move, the exhibiter is occasionally seen to place himself very near its right side, and to lay his hand, now and then, in a careless manner upon the box. He has also a peculiar shuffle with his feet, calculated to induce suspicion of collusion with the machine in minds which are more cunning than sagacious. These peculiarities are, no doubt, mere mannerisms of M. Maelzel, or, if he is aware of them at all, he puts them in practice with a view of exciting in the spectators a false idea of the pure mechanism in the Automaton.

The Turk plays with his left hand. All the movements of the arm are at right angles. In this manner, the hand (which is gloved and bent in a natural way,) being brought directly above the piece to be moved, descends finally upon it, the fingers receiving it, in most cases, without difficulty. Occasionally, however, when the piece is not precisely in its proper situation, the Automaton fails in his attempt at seizing it. When this occurs, no second effort is made, but the arm continues its movement in the direction originally intended, precisely as if the piece were in the fingers. Having thus designated the spot whither the move should have been made, the arm returns to its cushion, and Maelzel performs the evolution which the Automaton pointed out. At every movement of the figure machinery is heard in motion. During the progress of the game, the figure now and then rolls its eyes, as if surveying the board, moves its head, and pronounces the word echec (check) when necessary. {*3} If a false move be made by his antagonist, he raps briskly on the box with the fingers of his right hand, shakes his head roughly, and replacing the piece falsely moved, in its former situation, assumes the next move himself. Upon beating the game, he waves his head with an air of triumph, looks round complacently upon the spectators, and drawing his left arm farther back than usual, suffers his fingers alone to rest upon the cushion. In general, the Turk is victorious—once or twice he has been beaten. The game being ended, Maelzel will again if desired, exhibit the mechanism of the box, in the same manner as before. The machine is then rolled back, and a curtain hides it from the view of the company.

There have been many attempts at solving the mystery of the Automaton. The most general opinion in relation to it, an opinion too not unfrequently adopted by men who should have known better, was, as we have before said, that no immediate human agency was employed—in other words, that the machine was purely a machine and nothing else. Many, however maintained that the exhibiter himself regulated the movements of the figure by mechanical means operating through the feet of the box. Others again, spoke confidently of a magnet. Of the first of these opinions we shall say nothing at present more than we have already said. In relation to the second it is only necessary to repeat what we have before stated, that the machine is rolled about on castors, and will, at the request of a spectator, be moved to and fro to any portion of the room, even during the progress of a game. The supposition of the magnet is also untenable—for if a magnet were the agent, any other magnet in the pocket of a spectator would disarrange the entire mechanism. The exhibiter, however, will suffer the most powerful loadstone to remain even upon the box during the whole of the exhibition.

The first attempt at a written explanation of the secret, at least the first attempt of which we ourselves have any knowledge, was made in a large pamphlet printed at Paris in 1785. The author's hypothesis amounted to this—that a dwarf actuated the machine. This dwarf he supposed to conceal himself during the opening of the box by thrusting his legs into two hollow cylinders, which were represented to be (but which are not) among the machinery in the cupboard No. I, while his body was out of the box entirely, and covered by the drapery of the Turk. When the doors were shut, the dwarf was enabled to bring his body within the box—the noise produced by some portion of the machinery allowing him to do so unheard, and also to close the door by which he entered. The interior of the automaton being then exhibited, and no person discovered, the spectators, says the author of this pamphlet, are satisfied that no one is within any portion of the machine. This whole hypothesis was too obviously absurd to require comment, or refutation, and accordingly we find that it attracted very little attention.

In 1789 a book was published at Dresden by M. I. F. Freyhere in which another endeavor was made to unravel the mystery. Mr. Freyhere's book was a pretty large one, and copiously illustrated by colored engravings. His supposition was that "a well-taught boy very thin and tall of his age (sufficiently so that he could be concealed in a drawer almost immediately under the chess-board") played the game of chess and effected all the evolutions of the Automaton. This idea, although even more silly than that of the Parisian author, met with a better reception, and was in some measure believed to be the true solution of the wonder, until the inventor put an end to the discussion by suffering a close examination of the top of the box.

These bizarre attempts at explanation were followed by others equally bizarre. Of late years however, an anonymous writer, by a course of reasoning exceedingly unphilosophical, has contrived to blunder upon a plausible solution—although we cannot consider it altogether the true one. His Essay was first published in a Baltimore weekly paper, was illustrated by cuts, and was entitled "An attempt to analyze the Automaton Chess-Player of M. Maelzel." This Essay we suppose to have been the original of the pamphlet to which Sir David Brewster alludes in his letters on Natural Magic, and which he has no hesitation in declaring a thorough and satisfactory explanation. The results of the analysis are undoubtedly, in the main, just; but we can only account for Brewster's pronouncing the Essay a thorough and satisfactory explanation, by supposing him to have bestowed upon it a very cursory and inattentive perusal. In the compendium of the Essay, made use of in the Letters on Natural Magic, it is quite impossible to arrive at any distinct conclusion in regard to the adequacy or inadequacy of the analysis, on account of the gross misarrangement and deficiency of the letters of reference employed. The same fault is to be found in the "Attempt &c.," as we originally saw it. The solution consists in a series of minute explanations, (accompanied by wood-cuts, the whole occupying many pages) in which the object is to show the possibility of so shifting the partitions of the box, as to allow a human being, concealed in the interior, to move portions of his body from one part of the box to another, during the exhibition of the mechanism—thus eluding the scrutiny of the spectators. There can be no doubt, as we have before observed, and as we will presently endeavor to show, that the principle, or rather the result, of this solution is the true one. Some person is concealed in the box during the whole time of exhibiting the interior. We object, however, to the whole verbose description of the manner in which the partitions are shifted, to accommodate the movements of the person concealed. We object to it as a mere theory assumed in the first place, and to which circumstances are afterwards made to adapt themselves. It was not, and could not have been, arrived at by any inductive reasoning. In whatever way the shifting is managed, it is of course concealed at every step from observation. To show that certain movements might possibly be effected in a certain way, is very far from showing that they are actually so effected. There may be an infinity of other methods by which the same results may be obtained. The probability of the one assumed proving the correct one is then as unity to infinity. But, in reality, this particular point, the shifting of the partitions, is of no consequence whatever. It was altogether unnecessary to devote seven or eight pages for the purpose of proving what no one in his senses would deny—viz: that the wonderful mechanical genius of Baron Kempelen could invent the necessary means for shutting a door or slipping aside a pannel, with a human agent too at his service in actual contact with the pannel or the door, and the whole operations carried on, as the author of the Essay himself shows, and as we shall attempt to show more fully hereafter, entirely out of reach of the observation of the spectators.

In attempting ourselves an explanation of the Automaton, we will, in the first place, endeavor to show how its operations are effected, and afterwards describe, as briefly as possible, the nature of the observations from which we have deduced our result.

It will be necessary for a proper understanding of the subject, that we repeat here in a few words, the routine adopted by the exhibiter in disclosing the interior of the box—a routine from which he never deviates in any material particular. In the first place he opens the door No. I. Leaving this open, he goes round to the rear of the box, and opens a door precisely at the back of door No. I. To this back door he holds a lighted candle. He then closes the back door, locks it, and, coming round to the front, opens the drawer to its full extent. This done, he opens the doors No. 2 and No. 3, (the folding doors) and displays the interior of the main compartment. Leaving open the main compartment, the drawer, and the front door of cupboard No. I, he now goes to the rear again, and throws open the back door of the main compartment. In shutting up the box no particular order is observed, except that the folding doors are always closed before the drawer.

Now, let us suppose that when the machine is first rolled into the presence of the spectators, a man is already within it. His body is situated behind the dense machinery in cupboard No. T. (the rear portion of which machinery is so contrived as to slip en masse, from the main compartment to the cupboard No. I, as occasion may require,) and his legs lie at full length in the main compartment. When Maelzel opens the door No. I, the man within is not in any danger of discovery, for the keenest eye cannot penetrate more than about two inches into the darkness within. But the case is otherwise when the back door of the cupboard No. I, is opened. A bright light then pervades the cupboard, and the body of the man would be discovered if it were there. But it is not. The putting the key in the lock of the back door was a signal on hearing which the person concealed brought his body forward to an angle as acute as possible—throwing it altogether, or nearly so, into the main compartment. This, however, is a painful position, and cannot be long maintained. Accordingly we find that Maelzel closes the back door. This being done, there is no reason why the body of the man may not resume its former situation—for the cupboard is again so dark as to defy scrutiny. The drawer is now opened, and the legs of the person within drop down behind it in the space it formerly occupied. {*4} There is, consequently, now no longer any part of the man in the main compartment—his body being behind the machinery in cupboard No. 1, and his legs in the space occupied by the drawer. The exhibiter, therefore, finds himself at liberty to display the main compartment. This he does—opening both its back and front doors—and no person Is discovered. The spectators are now satisfied that the whole of the box is exposed to view—and exposed too, all portions of it at one and the same time. But of course this is not the case. They neither see the space behind the drawer, nor the interior of cupboard No. 1—the front door of which latter the exhibiter virtually shuts in shutting its back door. Maelzel, having now rolled the machine around, lifted up the drapery of the Turk, opened the doors in his back and thigh, and shown his trunk to be full of machinery, brings the whole back into its original position, and closes the doors. The man within is now at liberty to move about. He gets up into the body of the Turk just so high as to bring his eyes above the level of the chess-board. It is very probable that he seats himself upon the little square block or protuberance which is seen in a corner of the main compartment when the doors are open. In this position he sees the chess-board through the bosom of the Turk which is of gauze. Bringing his right arm across his breast he actuates the little machinery necessary to guide the left arm and the fingers of the figure. This machinery is situated just beneath the left shoulder of the Turk, and is consequently easily reached by the right hand of the man concealed, if we suppose his right arm brought across the breast. The motions of the head and eyes, and of the right arm of the figure, as well as the sound echec are produced by other mechanism in the interior, and actuated at will by the man within. The whole of this mechanism—that is to say all the mechanism essential to the machine—is most probably contained within the little cupboard (of about six inches in breadth) partitioned off at the right (the spectators' right) of the main compartment.

In this analysis of the operations of the Automaton, we have purposely avoided any allusion to the manner in which the partitions are shifted, and it will now be readily comprehended that this point is a matter of no importance, since, by mechanism within the ability of any common carpenter, it might be effected in an infinity of different ways, and since we have shown that, however performed, it is performed out of the view of the spectators. Our result is founded upon the following observations taken during frequent visits to the exhibition of Maelzel. {*5}

I. The moves of the Turk are not made at regular intervals of time, but accommodate themselves to the moves of the antagonist—although this point (of regularity) so important in all kinds of mechanical contrivance, might have been readily brought about by limiting the time allowed for the moves of the antagonist. For example, if this limit were three minutes, the moves of the Automaton might be made at any given intervals longer than three minutes. The fact then of irregularity, when regularity might have been so easily attained, goes to prove that regularity is unimportant to the action of the Automaton—in other words, that the Automaton is not a pure machine.

2. When the Automaton is about to move a piece, a distinct motion is observable just beneath the left shoulder, and which motion agitates in a slight degree, the drapery covering the front of the left shoulder. This motion invariably precedes, by about two seconds, the movement of the arm itself—and the arm never, in any instance, moves without this preparatory motion in the shoulder. Now let the antagonist move a piece, and let the corresponding move be made by Maelzel, as usual, upon the board of the Automaton. Then let the antagonist narrowly watch the Automaton, until he detect the preparatory motion in the shoulder. Immediately upon detecting this motion, and before the arm itself begins to move, let him withdraw his piece, as if perceiving an error in his manoeuvre. It will then be seen that the movement of the arm, which, in all other cases, immediately succeeds the motion in the shoulder, is withheld—is not made—although Maelzel has not yet performed, on the board of the Automaton, any move corresponding to the withdrawal of the antagonist. In this case, that the Automaton was about to move is evident—and that he did not move, was an effect plainly produced by the withdrawal of the antagonist, and without any intervention of Maelzel.

This fact fully proves, 1—that the intervention of Maelzel, in performing the moves of the antagonist on the board of the Automaton, is not essential to the movements of the Automaton, 2—that its movements are regulated by mind—by some person who sees the board of the antagonist, 3—that its movements are not regulated by the mind of Maelzel, whose back was turned towards the antagonist at the withdrawal of his move.

3. The Automaton does not invariably win the game. Were the machine a pure machine this would not be the case—it would always win. The principle being discovered by which a machine can be made to play a game of chess, an extension of the same principle would enable it to win a game—a farther extension would enable it to win all games—that is, to beat any possible game of an antagonist. A little consideration will convince any one that the difficulty of making a machine beat all games, Is not in the least degree greater, as regards the principle of the operations necessary, than that of making it beat a single game. If then we regard the Chess-Player as a machine, we must suppose, (what is highly improbable,) that its inventor preferred leaving it incomplete to perfecting it—a supposition rendered still more absurd, when we reflect that the leaving it incomplete would afford an argument against the possibility of its being a pure machine—the very argument we now adduce.

4. When the situation of the game is difficult or complex, we never perceive the Turk either shake his head or roll his eyes. It is only when his next move is obvious, or when the game is so circumstanced that to a man in the Automaton's place there would be no necessity for reflection. Now these peculiar movements of the head and eyes are movements customary with persons engaged in meditation, and the ingenious Baron Kempelen would have adapted these movements (were the machine a pure machine) to occasions proper for their display—that is, to occasions of complexity. But the reverse is seen to be the case, and this reverse applies precisely to our supposition of a man in the interior. When engaged in meditation about the game he has no time to think of setting in motion the mechanism of the Automaton by which are moved the head and the eyes. When the game, however, is obvious, he has time to look about him, and, accordingly, we see the head shake and the eyes roll.

5. When the machine is rolled round to allow the spectators an examination of the back of the Turk, and when his drapery is lifted up and the doors in the trunk and thigh thrown open, the interior of the trunk is seen to be crowded with machinery. In scrutinizing this machinery while the Automaton was in motion, that is to say while the whole machine was moving

on the castors, it appeared to us that certain portions of the mechanism changed their shape and position in a degree too great to be accounted for by the simple laws of perspective; and subsequent examinations convinced us that these undue alterations were attributable to mirrors in the interior of the trunk. The introduction of mirrors among the machinery could not have been intended to influence, in any degree, the machinery itself. Their operation, whatever that operation should prove to be, must necessarily have reference to the eye of the spectator. We at once concluded that these mirrors were so placed to multiply to the vision some few pieces of machinery within the trunk so as to give it the appearance of being crowded with mechanism. Now the direct inference from this is that the machine is not a pure machine. For if it were, the inventor, so far from wishing its mechanism to appear complex, and using deception for the purpose of giving it this appearance, would have been especially desirous of convincing those who witnessed his exhibition, of the simplicity of the means by which results so wonderful were brought about.

6. The external appearance, and, especially, the deportment of the Turk, are, when we consider them as imitations of life, but very indifferent imitations. The countenance evinces no ingenuity, and is surpassed, in its resemblance to the human face, by the very commonest of wax-works. The eyes roll unnaturally in the head, without any corresponding motions of the lids or brows. The arm, particularly, performs its operations in an exceedingly stiff, awkward, jerking, and rectangular manner. Now, all this is the result either of inability in Maelzel to do better, or of intentional neglect—accidental neglect being out of the question, when we consider that the whole time of the ingenious proprietor is occupied in the improvement of his machines. Most assuredly we must not refer the unlife-like appearances to inability—for all the rest of Maelzel's automata are evidence of his full ability to copy the motions and peculiarities of life with the most wonderful exactitude. The rope-dancers, for example, are inimitable. When the clown laughs, his lips, his eyes, his eye-brows, and eyelids—indeed, all the features of his countenance—are imbued with their appropriate expressions. In both him and his companion, every gesture is so entirely easy, and free from the semblance of artificiality, that, were it not for the diminutiveness of their size,

and the fact of their being passed from one spectator to another previous to their exhibition on the rope, it would be difficult to convince any assemblage of persons that these wooden automata were not living creatures. We cannot, therefore, doubt Mr. Maelzel's ability, and we must necessarily suppose that he intentionally suffered his Chess Player to remain the same artificial and unnatural figure which Baron Kempelen (no doubt also through design) originally made it. What this design was it is not difficult to conceive. Were the Automaton life-like in its motions, the spectator would be more apt to attribute its operations to their true cause, (that is, to human agency within) than he is now, when the awkward and rectangular manoeuvres convey the idea of pure and unaided mechanism.

7. When, a short time previous to the commencement of the game, the Automaton is wound up by the exhibiter as usual, an ear in any degree accustomed to the sounds produced in winding up a system of machinery, will not fail to discover, instantaneously, that the axis turned by the key in the box of the Chess-Player, cannot possibly be connected with either a weight, a spring, or any system of machinery whatever. The inference here is the same as in our last observation. The winding up is inessential to the operations of the Automaton, and is performed with the design of exciting in the spectators the false idea of mechanism.

8. When the question is demanded explicitly of Maelzel—"Is the Automaton a pure machine or not?" his reply is invariably the same—"I will say nothing about it." Now the notoriety of the Automaton, and the great curiosity it has every where excited, are owing more especially to the prevalent opinion that it is a pure machine, than to any other circumstance. Of course, then, it is the interest of the proprietor to represent it as a pure machine. And what more obvious, and more effectual method could there be of impressing the spectators with this desired idea, than a positive and explicit declaration to that effect? On the other hand, what more obvious and effectual method could there be of exciting a disbelief in the Automaton's being a pure machine, than by withholding such explicit declaration? For, people will naturally reason thus,—It is Maelzel's interest to represent this thing a pure machine—he refuses to do so, directly, in words, although he

does not scruple, and is evidently anxious to do so, indirectly by actions—were it actually what he wishes to represent it by actions, he would gladly avail himself of the more direct testimony of words—the inference is, that a consciousness of its not being a pure machine, is the reason of his silence—his actions cannot implicate him in a falsehood—his words may.

9. When, in exhibiting the interior of the box, Maelzel has thrown open the door No. I, and also the door immediately behind it, he holds a lighted candle at the back door (as mentioned above) and moves the entire machine to and fro with a view of convincing the company that the cupboard No. 1 is entirely filled with machinery. When the machine is thus moved about, it will be apparent to any careful observer, that whereas that portion of the machinery near the front door No. 1, is perfectly steady and unwavering, the portion farther within fluctuates, in a very slight degree, with the movements of the machine. This circumstance first aroused in us the suspicion that the more remote portion of the machinery was so arranged as to be easily slipped, en masse, from its position when occasion should require it. This occasion we have already stated to occur when the man concealed within brings his body into an erect position upon the closing of the back door.

10. Sir David Brewster states the figure of the Turk to be of the size of life—but in fact it is far above the ordinary size. Nothing is more easy than to err in our notions of magnitude. The body of the Automaton is generally insulated, and, having no means of immediately comparing it with any human form, we suffer ourselves to consider it as of ordinary dimensions. This mistake may, however, be corrected by observing the Chess-Player when, as is sometimes the case, the exhibiter approaches it. Mr. Maelzel, to be sure, is not very tall, but upon drawing near the machine, his head will be found at least eighteen inches below the head of the Turk, although the latter, it will be remembered, is in a sitting position.

11. The box behind which the Automaton is placed, is precisely three feet six inches long, two feet four inches deep, and two feet six inches high. These dimensions are fully sufficient for the accommodation of a man very much above the common size—and the main compartment alone is capable of holding any ordinary man in the position we have mentioned as assumed

by the person concealed. As these are facts, which any one who doubts them may prove by actual calculation, we deem it unnecessary to dwell upon them. We will only suggest that, although the top of the box is apparently a board of about three inches in thickness, the spectator may satisfy himself by stooping and looking up at it when the main compartment is open, that it is in reality very thin. The height of the drawer also will be misconceived by those who examine it in a cursory manner. There is a space of about three inches between the top of the drawer as seen from the exterior, and the bottom of the cupboard—a space which must be included in the height of the drawer. These contrivances to make the room within the box appear less than it actually is, are referrible to a design on the part of the inventor, to impress the company again with a false idea, viz. that no human being can be accommodated within the box.

12. The interior of the main compartment is lined throughout with cloth. This cloth we suppose to have a twofold object. A portion of it may form, when tightly stretched, the only partitions which there is any necessity for removing during the changes of the man's position, viz: the partition between the rear of the main compartment and the rear of the cupboard No. 1, and the partition between the main compartment, and the space behind the drawer when open. If we imagine this to be the case, the difficulty of shifting the partitions vanishes at once, if indeed any such difficulty could be supposed under any circumstances to exist. The second object of the cloth is to deaden and render indistinct all sounds occasioned by the movements of the person within.

13. The antagonist (as we have before observed) is not suffered to play at the board of the Automaton, but is seated at some distance from the machine. The reason which, most probably, would be assigned for this circumstance, if the question were demanded, is, that were the antagonist otherwise situated, his person would intervene between the machine and the spectators, and preclude the latter from a distinct view. But this difficulty might be easily obviated, either by elevating the seats of the company, or by turning the end of the box towards them during the game. The true cause of the restriction is, perhaps, very different. Were the antagonist seated in contact with the

box, the secret would be liable to discovery, by his detecting, with the aid of a quick car, the breathings of the man concealed.

14. Although M. Maelzel, in disclosing the interior of the machine, sometimes slightly deviates from the routine which we have pointed out, yet reeler in any instance does he so deviate from it as to interfere with our solution. For example, he has been known to open, first of all, the drawer—but he never opens the main compartment without first closing the back door of cupboard No. 1—he never opens the main compartment without first pulling out the drawer—he never shuts the drawer without first shutting the main compartment—he never opens the back door of cupboard No. 1 while the main compartment is open—and the game of chess is never commenced until the whole machine is closed. Now if it were observed that never, in any single instance, did M. Maelzel differ from the routine we have pointed out as necessary to our solution, it would be one of the strongest possible arguments in corroboration of it—but the argument becomes infinitely strengthened if we duly consider the circumstance that he does occasionally deviate from the routine but never does so deviate as to falsify the solution.

15. There are six candles on the board of the Automaton during exhibition. The question naturally arises—"Why are so many employed, when a single candle, or, at farthest, two, would have been amply sufficient to afford the spectators a clear view of the board, in a room otherwise so well lit up as the exhibition room always is—when, moreover, if we suppose the machine a pure machine, there can be no necessity for so much light, or indeed any light at all, to enable it to perform its operations—and when, especially, only a single candle is placed upon the table of the antagonist?" The first and most obvious inference is, that so strong a light is requisite to enable the man within to see through the transparent material (probably fine gauze) of which the breast of the Turk is composed. But when we consider the arrangement of the candles, another reason immediately presents itself. There are six lights (as we have said before) in all. Three of these are on each side of the figure. Those most remote from the spectators are the longest—those in the middle are about two inches shorter—and those nearest the company about two inches shorter still—and the candles on one side differ in height

from the candles respectively opposite on the other, by a ratio different from two inches—that is to say, the longest candle on one side is about three inches shorter than the longest candle on the other, and so on. Thus it will be seen that no two of the candles are of the same height, and thus also the difficulty of ascertaining the material of the breast of the figure (against which the light is especially directed) is greatly augmented by the dazzling effect of the complicated crossings of the rays—crossings which are brought about by placing the centres of radiation all upon different levels.

16. While the Chess-Player was in possession of Baron Kempelen, it was more than once observed, first, that an Italian in the suite of the Baron was never visible during the playing of a game at chess by the Turk, and, secondly, that the Italian being taken seriously ill, the exhibition was suspended until his recovery. This Italian professed a total ignorance of the game of chess, although all others of the suite played well. Similar observations have been made since the Automaton has been purchased by Maelzel. There is a man, Schlumberoer, who attends him wherever he goes, but who has no ostensible occupation other than that of assisting in the packing and unpacking of the automata. This man is about the medium size, and has a remarkable stoop in the shoulders. Whether he professes to play chess or not, we are not informed. It is quite certain, however, that he is never to be seen during the exhibition of the Chess-Player, although frequently visible just before and just after the exhibition. Moreover, some years ago Maelzel visited Richmond with his automata, and exhibited them, we believe, in the house now occupied by M. Bossieux as a Dancing Academy. Schlumberger was suddenly taken ill, and during his illness there was no exhibition of the Chess-Player. These facts are well known to many of our citizens. The reason assigned for the suspension of the Chess-Player's performances, was not the illness of Schlumberger. The inferences from all this we leave, without farther comment, to the reader.

17. The Turk plays with his left arm. A circumstance so remarkable cannot be accidental. Brewster takes no notice of it whatever beyond a mere statement, we believe, that such is the fact. The early writers of treatises on the Automaton, seem not to have observed the matter at all, and have no reference to it. The author of the pamphlet alluded to by Brewster, mentions

it, but acknowledges his inability to account for it. Yet it is obviously from such prominent discrepancies or incongruities as this that deductions are to be made (if made at all) which shall lead us to the truth.

The circumstance of the Automaton's playing with his left hand cannot have connexion with the operations of the machine, considered merely as such. Any mechanical arrangement which would cause the figure to move, in any given manner, the left arm—could, if reversed, cause it to move, in the same manner, the right. But these principles cannot be extended to the human organization, wherein there is a marked and radical difference in the construction, and, at all events, in the powers, of the right and left arms. Reflecting upon this latter fact, we naturally refer the incongruity noticeable in the Chess-Player to this peculiarity in the human organization. If so, we must imagine some reversion—for the Chess-Player plays precisely as a man would not. These ideas, once entertained, are sufficient of themselves, to suggest the notion of a man in the interior. A few more imperceptible steps lead us, finally, to the result. The Automaton plays with his left arm, because under no other circumstances could the man within play with his right—a desideratum of course. Let us, for example, imagine the Automaton to play with his right arm. To reach the machinery which moves the arm, and which we have before explained to lie just beneath the shoulder, it would be necessary for the man within either to use his right arm in an exceedingly painful and awkward position, (viz. brought up close to his body and tightly compressed between his body and the side of the Automaton,) or else to use his left arm brought across his breast. In neither case could he act with the requisite ease or precision. On the contrary, the Automaton playing, as it actually does, with the left arm, all difficulties vanish. The right arm of the man within is brought across his breast, and his right fingers act, without any constraint, upon the machinery in the shoulder of the figure.

We do not believe that any reasonable objections can be urged against this solution of the Automaton Chess-Player.

THE POWER OF WORDS

OINOS. Pardon, Agathos, the weakness of a spirit new-fledged with immortality!

AGATHOS. You have spoken nothing, my Oinos, for which pardon is to be demanded. Not even here is knowledge thing of intuition. For wisdom, ask of the angels freely, that it may be given!

OINOS. But in this existence, I dreamed that I should be at once cognizant of all things, and thus at once be happy in being cognizant of all.

AGATHOS. Ah, not in knowledge is happiness, but in the acquisition of knowledge! In for ever knowing, we are for ever blessed; but to know all were the curse of a fiend.

OINOS. But does not The Most High know all?

AGATHOS. That (since he is The Most Happy) must be still the one thing unknown even to Him.

OINOS. But, since we grow hourly in knowledge, must not at last all things be known?

AGATHOS. Look down into the abysmal distances!—attempt to force the gaze down the multitudinous vistas of the stars, as we sweep slowly through them thus—and thus—and thus! Even the spiritual vision, is it not at all points arrested by the continuous golden walls of the universe?—the walls of the myriads of the shining bodies that mere number has appeared to blend into unity?

OINOS. I clearly perceive that the infinity of matter is no dream.

AGATHOS. There are no dreams in Aidenn—but it is here whispered that, of this infinity of matter, the sole purpose is to afford infinite springs, at which the soul may allay the thirst to know, which is for ever unquenchable within it—since to quench it, would be to extinguish the soul's self. Question me then, my Oinos, freely and without fear. Come! we will leave to the left the loud harmony of the Pleiades, and swoop outward from the throne into the starry meadows beyond Orion, where, for pansies and violets, and heart's—ease, are the beds of the triplicate and triple—tinted suns.

OINOS. And now, Agathos, as we proceed, instruct me!—speak to me in the earth's familiar tones. I understand not what you hinted to me, just now, of the modes or of the method of what, during mortality, we were accustomed to call Creation. Do you mean to say that the Creator is not God?

AGATHOS. I mean to say that the Deity does not create.

OINOS. Explain.

AGATHOS. In the beginning only, he created. The seeming creatures which are now, throughout the universe, so perpetually springing into being, can only be considered as the mediate or indirect, not as the direct or immediate results of the Divine creative power.

OINOS. Among men, my Agathos, this idea would be considered heretical in the extreme.

AGATHOS. Among angels, my Oinos, it is seen to be simply true.

OINOS. I can comprehend you thus far—that certain operations of what we term Nature, or the natural laws, will, under certain conditions, give rise to that which has all the appearance of creation. Shortly before the final overthrow of the earth, there were, I well remember, many very successful experiments in what some philosophers were weak enough to denominate the creation of animalculae.

AGATHOS. The cases of which you speak were, in fact, instances of the secondary creation—and of the only species of creation which has ever been, since the first word spoke into existence the first law.

OINOS. Are not the starry worlds that, from the abyss of nonentity, burst hourly forth into the heavens—are not these stars, Agathos, the immediate handiwork of the King?

AGATHOS. Let me endeavor, my Oinos, to lead you, step by step, to the conception I intend. You are well aware that, as no thought can perish, so no act is without infinite result. We moved our hands, for example, when we were dwellers on the earth, and, in so doing, gave vibration to the atmosphere which engirdled it. This vibration was indefinitely extended, till it gave impulse to every particle of the earth's air, which thenceforward, and for ever, was actuated by the one movement of the hand. This fact the mathematicians of our globe well knew. They made the special effects, indeed, wrought in the fluid by special impulses, the subject of exact calculation—so that it became easy to determine in what precise period an impulse of given extent would engirdle the orb, and impress (for ever) every atom of the atmosphere circumambient. Retrograding, they found no difficulty, from a given effect, under given conditions, in determining the value of the original impulse. Now the mathematicians who saw that the results of any given impulse were absolutely endless—and who saw that a portion of these results were accurately traceable through the agency of algebraic analysis—who saw, too, the facility of the retrogradation—these men saw, at the same time, that this species of analysis itself, had within itself a capacity for indefinite progress—that there were no bounds conceivable to its advancement and applicability, except within the intellect of him who advanced or applied it. But at this point our mathematicians paused.

OINOS. And why, Agathos, should they have proceeded?

AGATHOS. Because there were some considerations of deep interest beyond. It was deducible from what they knew, that to a being of infinite understanding—one to whom the perfection of the algebraic analysis lay unfolded—there could be no difficulty in tracing every impulse given the air—and the ether through the air—to the remotest consequences at any even infinitely remote epoch of time. It is indeed demonstrable that every such impulse given the air, must, in the end, impress every individual thing that exists within the universe;—and the being of infinite understanding—the being whom we have imagined—might trace the remote undulations of the impulse—trace them upward and onward in their influences upon all particles of an matter—upward and onward for ever in their modifications of old forms—or, in other words, in their creation of new—until he found them reflected—unimpressive at last—back from the throne of the Godhead. And not only could such a thing do this, but at any epoch, should a given result be afforded him—should one of these numberless comets, for example, be presented to his inspection—he could have no difficulty in determining, by the analytic retrogradation, to what original impulse it was due. This power of retrogradation in its absolute fulness and perfection—this faculty of referring at all epochs, all effects to all causes—is of course the prerogative of the Deity alone—but in every variety of degree, short of the absolute perfection, is the power itself exercised by the whole host of the Angelic intelligences.

OINOS. But you speak merely of impulses upon the air.

AGATHOS. In speaking of the air, I referred only to the earth; but the general proposition has reference to impulses upon the ether—which, since it pervades, and alone pervades all space, is thus the great medium of creation.

OINOS. Then all motion, of whatever nature, creates?

AGATHOS. It must: but a true philosophy has long taught that the source of all motion is thought—and the source of all thought is—

OINOS. God.

AGATHOS. I have spoken to you, Oinos, as to a child of the fair Earth which lately perished—of impulses upon the atmosphere of the Earth.

OINOS. You did.

AGATHOS. And while I thus spoke, did there not cross your mind some thought of the physical power of words? Is not every word an impulse on the air?

OINOS. But why, Agathos, do you weep—and why, oh why do your wings droop as we hover above this fair star—which is the greenest and yet most terrible of all we have encountered in our flight? Its brilliant flowers look like a fairy dream—but its fierce volcanoes like the passions of a turbulent heart.

AGATHOS. They are!—they are! This wild star—it is now three

centuries since, with clasped hands, and with streaming eyes, at the feet of my beloved—I spoke it—with a few passionate sentences—into birth. Its brilliant flowers are the dearest of all unfulfilled dreams, and its raging volcanoes are the passions of the most turbulent and unhallowed of hearts.

THE COLLOQUY OF MONOS AND UNA

"These; things are in the future."

Sophocles—Antig:

Una. "Born again?"

Monos. Yes, fairest and best beloved Una, "born again." These were the words upon whose mystical meaning I had so long pondered, rejecting the explanations of the priesthood, until Death himself resolved for me the secret.

Una. Death!

Monos. How strangely, sweet Una, you echo my words! I observe, too, a vacillation in your step—a joyous inquietude in your eyes. You are confused and oppressed by the majestic novelty of the Life Eternal. Yes, it was of Death I spoke. And here how singularly sounds that word which of old was wont to bring terror to all hearts—throwing a mildew upon all pleasures!

Una. Ah, Death, the spectre which sate at all feasts! How often, Monos, did we lose ourselves in speculations upon its nature! How mysteriously did it act as a check to human bliss—saying unto it "thus far, and no farther!" That earnest mutual love, my own Monos, which burned within our bosoms how vainly did we flatter ourselves, feeling happy in its first up-springing, that our happiness would strengthen with its strength! Alas! as it grew, so grew in our hearts the dread of that evil hour which was hurrying to separate us forever! Thus, in time, it became painful to love. Hate would have been mercy then.

Monos. Speak not here of these griefs, dear Una—mine, mine, forever now!

Una. But the memory of past sorrow—is it not present joy? I have much to say yet of the things which have been. Above all, I burn to know the incidents of your own passage through the dark Valley and Shadow.

Monos. And when did the radiant Una ask anything of her Monos in vain? I will be minute in relating all—but at what point shall the weird narrative begin?

Una. At what point?

Monos. You have said.

Una. Monos, I comprehend you. In Death we have both learned the propensity of man to define the indefinable. I will not say, then, commence with the moment of life's cessation—but commence with that sad, sad instant when, the fever having abandoned you, you sank into a breathless and motionless torpor, and I pressed down your pallid eyelids with the passionate fingers of love.

Monos. One word first, my Una, in regard to man's general condition at this epoch. You will remember that one or two of the wise among our forefathers—wise in fact, although not in the world's esteem—had ventured to doubt the propriety of the term "improvement," as applied to the progress of our civilization. There were periods in each of the five or six centuries immediately preceding our dissolution, when arose some vigorous intellect, boldly contending for those principles whose truth appears now, to our disenfranchised reason, so utterly obvious—principles which should have taught our race to submit to the guidance of the natural laws, rather than attempt their control. At long intervals some masterminds appeared, looking upon each advance in practical science as a retro-gradation in the true utility. Occasionally the poetic intellect—that intellect which we now feel to have been the most exalted of all—since those truths which to us were of the most enduring importance could only be reached by that analogy which speaks in proof tones to the imagination alone and to the unaided reason bears no weight—occasionally did this poetic intellect proceed a step farther in the evolving of the vague idea of the philosophic, and find in the mystic parable that tells of the tree of knowledge, and of its forbidden fruit, death-producing, a distinct intimation that knowledge was not meet for man in the infant condition of his soul. And these men—the poets—living and perishing amid the scorn of the "utilitarians"—of rough pedants, who arrogated to themselves a title which could have been properly applied only to the scorned—these men, the poets, pondered piningly, yet not unwisely, upon the ancient days when our wants were not more simple than our enjoyments were keen—days when mirth was a word unknown, so solemnly deep-toned was happiness—holy, august and blissful days, when blue rivers ran undammed, between hills unhewn, into far forest solitudes, prim?val, odorous, and unexplored.

Yet these noble exceptions from the general misrule served but to strengthen it by opposition. Alas! we had fallen upon the most evil of all our evil days. The great "movement"—that was the cant term—went on: a diseased commotion, moral and physical. Art—the Arts—arose supreme, and, once enthroned, cast chains upon the intellect which had elevated them to power. Man, because he could not but acknowledge the majesty of Nature, fell into childish exultation at his acquired and still-increasing dominion over her elements. Even while he stalked a God in his own fancy, an infantine imbecility came over him. As might be supposed from the origin of his disorder, he grew infected with system, and with abstraction. He enwrapped himself in generalities. Among other odd ideas, that of universal equality gained ground; and in the face of analogy and of God—in despite of the loud warning voice of the laws of gradation so visibly pervading all things in Earth an Heaven—wild attempts at an omni-prevalent Democracy were made. Yet this evil sprang necessarily from the leading evil, Knowledge. Man could not both know and succumb. Meantime huge smoking cities arose, innumerable. Green leaves shrank before the hot breath of furnaces. The fair face of Nature was deformed as with the ravages of some loathsome disease. And methinks, sweet Una, even our slumbering sense of the forced and of the far-fetched might have arrested us here. But now it appears that we had worked out our own destruction in the perversion of our taste, or rather in the blind neglect of its culture in the schools. For, in truth, it was at this crisis that taste alone—that faculty which, holding a middle position between the pure intellect and the moral sense, could never safely have been disregarded—it was now that taste alone could have led us gently back to Beauty, to Nature, and to Life. But alas for the pure contemplative spirit and majestic intuition of Plato! Alas for the which he justly regarded as an all-sufficient education for the soul! Alas for him and for it!—since both were most desperately needed when both were most entirely forgotten or despised. {*1}

Pascal, a philosopher whom we both love, has said, how truly!—"que tout notre raisonnement se r?duit ? c?der au sentiment;" and it is not impossible that the sentiment of the natural, had time permitted it, would have regained its old ascendancy over the harsh mathematical reason of the schools. But this thing was not to be. Prematurely induced by intemperance of knowledge the old age of the world drew on. This the mass of mankind saw not, or, living lustily although unhappily, affected not to see. But, for myself, the Earth's records had taught me to look for widest ruin as the price of highest civilization. I had imbibed a prescience of our Fate from comparison of China the simple and enduring, with Assyria the architect, with Egypt the astrologer, with Nubia, more crafty than either, the turbulent mother of all Arts. In history {*2} of these regions I met with a ray from the Future. The individual artificialities of the three latter were local diseases of the Earth, and in their individual overthrows we had seen local remedies applied; but for the infected world at large I could anticipate no regeneration save in death. That man, as a race, should not become extinct, I saw that he must be "born again."

And now it was, fairest and dearest, that we wrapped our spirits, daily, in dreams. Now it was that, in twilight, we discoursed of the days to come, when the Art-scarred surface of the Earth, having undergone that purification {*3} which alone could efface its rectangular obscenities, should clothe itself anew in the verdure and the mountain-slopes and the smiling waters of Paradise, and be rendered at length a fit dwelling-place for man:—for man the Death purged—for man to whose now exalted intellect there should be poison in knowledge no more—for the redeemed, regenerated, blissful, and now immortal, but still for the material, man.

Una. Well do I remember these conversations, dear Monos; but the epoch of the fiery overthrow was not so near at hand as we believed, and as the corruption you indicate did surely warrant us in believing. Men lived; and died individually. You yourself sickened, and passed into the grave; and thither your constant Una speedily followed you. And though the century which has since elapsed, and whose conclusion brings us thus together once more, tortured our slumbering senses with no impatience of duration, yet, my Monos, it was a century still.

Monos. Say, rather, a point in the vague infinity. Unquestionably, it was in the Earth's dotage that I died. Wearied at heart with anxieties which had their origin in the general turmoil and decay, I succumbed to the fierce fever. After some few days of pain, and many of dreamy delirium replete with ecstasy, the manifestations of which you mistook for pain, while I longed but was impotent to undeceive you—after some days there came upon me, as you have said, a breathless and motionless torpor; and this was termed Death by those who stood around me.

Words are vague things. My condition did not deprive me of sentience. It appeared to me not greatly dissimilar to the extreme quiescence of him, who, having slumbered long and profoundly, lying motionless and fully prostrate in a midsummer noon, begins to steal slowly back into consciousness, through the mere sufficiency of his sleep, and without being awakened by external disturbances.

I breathed no longer. The pulses were still. The heart had ceased to beat. Volition had not departed, but was powerless. The senses were unusually active, although eccentrically so—assuming often each other's functions at random. The taste and the smell were inextricably confounded, and became one sentiment, abnormal and intense. The rose-water with which your tenderness had moistened my lips to the last, affected me with sweet fancies of flowers—fantastic flowers, far more lovely than any of the old Earth, but whose prototypes we have here blooming around us. The eyelids, transparent and bloodless, offered no complete impediment to vision. As volition was in abeyance, the balls could not roll in their sockets but all objects within the range of the visual hemisphere were seen with more or less distinctness; the rays which fell upon the external retina, or into the corner of the eye, producing a more vivid effect than those which struck the front or interior surface. Yet, in the former instance, this effect was so far anomalous that I appreciated it only as sound—sound sweet or discordant as the matters presenting themselves at my side were light or dark in shade—curved or angular in outline. The hearing, at the same time, although excited in degree, was not irregular in action—estimating real sounds with an extravagance of precision, not less than of sensibility. Touch had undergone a modification more peculiar. Its impressions were tardily received, but pertinaciously retained, and resulted always in the highest physical pleasure. Thus the pressure of your sweet fingers upon my eyelids, at first only recognised through vision, at length, long after their removal, filled my whole being with a sensual delight immeasurable. I say with a sensual delight. All my perceptions were purely sensual. The materials furnished the passive brain by the senses were not in the least degree wrought into shape by the deceased understanding. Of pain there was some little; of pleasure there was much; but of moral pain or pleasure none at all. Thus your wild sobs floated into my ear with all their mournful cadences, and were appreciated in their every variation of sad tone; but they were soft musical sounds and no more; they conveyed to the extinct reason no intimation of the sorrows which gave them birth; while the large and constant tears which fell upon my face, telling the bystanders of a heart which broke, thrilled every fibre of my frame with ecstasy alone. And this was in truth the Death of which these bystanders spoke reverently, in low whispers—you, sweet Una, gaspingly, with loud cries.

They attired me for the coffin—three or four dark figures which flitted busily to and fro. As these crossed the direct line of my vision they affected me as forms; but upon passing to my side their images impressed me with the idea of shrieks, groans, and other dismal expressions of terror, of horror, or of wo. You alone, habited in a white robe, passed in all directions musically about me.

The day waned; and, as its light faded away, I became possessed by a vague uneasiness—an anxiety such as the sleeper feels when sad real sounds fall continuously within his ear—low distant bell-tones, solemn, at long but equal intervals, and mingling with melancholy dreams. Night arrived; and with its shadows a heavy discomfort. It oppressed my limbs with the oppression of some dull weight, and was palpable. There was also a moaning sound, not unlike the distant reverberation of surf, but more continuous, which, beginning with the first twilight, had grown in strength with the darkness. Suddenly lights were brought into the room, and this reverberation became forthwith interrupted into frequent unequal bursts of the same sound, but less dreary and less distinct. The ponderous oppression was in a great measure relieved; and, issuing from the flame of each lamp, (for there were many,) there flowed unbrokenly into my ears a strain of melodious monotone. And when now, dear Una, approaching the bed upon which I lay outstretched, you sat gently by my side, breathing odor from your sweet lips, and pressing them upon my brow, there arose tremulously within my bosom, and mingling with the merely physical sensations which circumstances had called forth, a something akin to sentiment itself—a feeling that, half appreciating, half responded to your earnest love and sorrow; but this feeling took no root in the pulseless heart, and seemed indeed rather a shadow than a reality, and faded quickly away, first into extreme quiescence, and then into a purely sensual pleasure as before.

And now, from the wreck and the chaos of the usual senses, there appeared to have arisen within me a sixth, all perfect. In its exercise I found a wild delight—yet a delight still physical, inasmuch as the understanding had in it no part. Motion in the animal frame had fully ceased. No muscle quivered; no nerve thrilled; no artery throbbed. But there seemed to have sprung up in the brain, that of which no words could convey to the merely human intelligence even an indistinct conception. Let me term it a mental pendulous pulsation. It was the moral embodiment of man's abstract idea of Time. By the absolute equalization of this movement—or of such as this— had the cycles of the firmamental orbs themselves, been adjusted. By its aid I measured the irregularities of the clock upon the mantel, and of the watches of the attendants. Their tickings came sonorously to my ears. The slightest deviations from the true proportion—and these deviations were omni-pr?valent—affected me just as violations of abstract truth were wont, on earth, to affect the moral sense. Although no two of the time-pieces in the chamber struck the individual seconds accurately together, yet I had no difficulty in holding steadily in mind the tones, and the respective momentary errors of each. And this—this keen, perfect, self-existing sentiment of duration—this sentiment existing (as man could not possibly have conceived it to exist) independently of any succession of events—this idea—this sixth sense, upspringing from the ashes of the rest, was the first obvious and certain step of the intemporal soul upon the threshold of the temporal Eternity.

It was midnight; and you still sat by my side. All others had departed from the chamber of Death. They had deposited me in the coffin. The lamps burned flickeringly; for this I knew by the tremulousness of the monotonous strains. But, suddenly these strains diminished in distinctness and in volume. Finally they ceased. The perfume in my nostrils died away. Forms affected my vision no longer. The oppression of the Darkness uplifted itself from my bosom. A dull shock like that of electricity pervaded my frame, and was followed by total loss of the idea of contact. All of what man has termed sense was merged in the sole consciousness of entity, and in the one abiding sentiment of duration. The mortal body had been at length stricken with the hand of the deadly Decay.

Yet had not all of sentience departed; for the consciousness and the sentiment remaining supplied some of its functions by a lethargic intuition. I appreciated the direful change now in operation upon the flesh, and, as the dreamer is sometimes aware of the bodily presence of one who leans over him, so, sweet Una, I still dully felt that you sat by my side. So, too, when the noon of the second day came, I was not unconscious of those movements which displaced you from my side, which confined me within the coffin, which deposited me within the hearse, which bore me to the grave, which lowered me within it, which heaped heavily the mould upon me, and which thus left me, in blackness and corruption, to my sad and solemn slumbers with the worm.

And here, in the prison-house which has few secrets to disclose, there rolled away days and weeks and months; and the soul watched narrowly each second as it flew, and, without effort, took record of its flight—without effort and without object.

A year passed. The consciousness of being had grown hourly more indistinct, and that of mere locality had, in great measure, usurped its position. The idea of entity was becoming merged in that of place. The narrow space immediately surrounding what had been the body, was now growing to be the body itself. At length, as often happens to the sleeper (by sleep and its world alone is Death imaged)—at length, as sometimes happened on Earth to the deep slumberer, when some flitting light half startled him into awaking, yet left him half enveloped in dreams—so to me, in the strict embrace of the Shadow came that light which alone might have had power to startle—the light of enduring Love. Men toiled at the grave in which I lay darkling. They upthrew the damp earth. Upon my mouldering bones there descended the coffin of Una.

And now again all was void. That nebulous light had been extinguished. That feeble thrill had vibrated itself into quiescence. Many lustra had supervened. Dust had returned to dust. The worm had food no more. The sense of being had at length utterly departed, and there reigned in its stead—instead of all things—dominant and perpetual—the autocrats Place and Time. For that which was not—for that which had no form—for that which had no thought—for that which had no sentience—for that which was soulless, yet of which matter formed no portion—for all this nothingness, yet for all this immortality, the grave was still a home, and the corrosive hours, co-mates.

THE CONVERSATION OF EIROS AND CHARMION

I will bring fire to thee.

Euripides—Androm:

EIROS.

Why do you call me Eiros?

CHARMION

So henceforward will you always be called. You must forget too, my earthly name, and speak to me as Charmion.

EIROS.

This is indeed no dream!

CHARMION.

Dreams are with us no more;—but of these mysteries anon. I rejoice to see you looking life-like and rational. The film of the shadow has already passed from off your eyes. Be of heart and fear nothing. Your allotted days of stupor have expired and, to-morrow, I will myself induct you into the full joys and wonders of your novel existence.

EIROS.

True—I feel no stupor—none at all. The wild sickness and the terrible darkness have left me, and I hear no longer that mad, rushing, horrible sound, like the "voice of many waters." Yet my senses are bewildered, Charmion, with the keenness of their perception of the new.

CHARMION.

A few days will remove all this;—but I fully understand you, and feel for you. It is now ten earthly years since I underwent what you undergo—yet the remembrance of it hangs by me still. You have now suffered all of pain, however, which you will suffer in Aidenn.

EIROS.

In Aidenn?

CHARMION.

In Aidenn.

EIROS.

Oh God!—pity me, Charmion!—I am overburthened with the majesty of all things—of the unknown now known—of the speculative Future merged in the august and certain Present.

CHARMION.

Grapple not now with such thoughts. To-morrow we will speak of this. Your mind wavers, and its agitation will find relief in the exercise of simple memories. Look not around, nor forward—but back. I am burning with anxiety to hear the details of that stupendous event which threw you among us. Tell me of it. Let us converse of familiar things, in the old familiar language of the world which has so fearfully perished.

EIROS.

Most fearfully, fearfully!—this is indeed no dream.

CHARMION.

Dreams are no more. Was I much mourned, my Eiros?

EIROS.

Mourned, Charmion?—oh deeply. To that last hour of all, there hung a cloud of intense gloom and devout sorrow over your household.

CHARMION.

And that last hour—speak of it. Remember that, beyond the naked fact of the catastrophe itself, I know nothing. When, coming out from among mankind, I passed into Night through the Grave—at that period, if I remember aright, the calamity which overwhelmed you was utterly unanticipated. But, indeed, I knew little of the speculative philosophy of the day.

EIROS.

The individual calamity was as you say entirely unanticipated; but analogous misfortunes had been long a subject of discussion with astronomers. I need scarce tell you, my friend, that, even when you left us, men had agreed to understand those passages in the most holy writings which speak of the final destruction of all things by fire, as having reference to the orb of the earth alone. But in regard to the immediate agency of the ruin, speculation had been at fault from that epoch in astronomical knowledge in which the comets were divested of the terrors of flame. The very moderate density of these bodies had been well established. They had been observed to pass among the satellites of Jupiter, without bringing about any sensible alteration either in the masses or in the orbits of these secondary planets. We had long regarded the wanderers as vapory creations of inconceivable tenuity, and as altogether incapable of doing injury to our substantial globe, even in the event of contact. But contact was not in any degree dreaded; for the elements of all the comets were accurately known. That among them we should look for the agency of the threatened fiery destruction had been for many years considered an inadmissible idea. But wonders and wild fancies had been, of late days, strangely rife among mankind; and, although it was only with a few of the ignorant that actual apprehension prevailed, upon the announcement by astronomers of a new comet, yet this announcement was generally received with I know not what of agitation and mistrust.

The elements of the strange orb were immediately calculated, and it was at once conceded by all observers, that its path, at perihelion, would bring it into very close proximity with the earth. There were two or three astronomers, of secondary note, who resolutely maintained that a contact was inevitable. I cannot very well express to you the effect of this intelligence upon the people. For a few short days they would not believe an assertion which their intellect so long employed among worldly considerations could not in any manner grasp. But the truth of a vitally important fact soon makes its way into the understanding of even the most stolid. Finally, all men saw that astronomical knowledge lied not, and they awaited the comet. Its approach was not, at first, seemingly rapid; nor was its appearance of very unusual character. It was of a dull red, and had little perceptible train. For seven or eight days we saw no material increase in its apparent diameter, and but a partial alteration in its color. Meantime, the ordinary affairs of men were discarded and all interests absorbed in a growing discussion, instituted by the philosophic, in respect to the cometary nature. Even the grossly ignorant aroused their sluggish capacities to such considerations. The learned now gave their intellect—their soul—to no such points as the allaying of fear, or to the sustenance of loved theory. They sought—they panted for right views. They groaned for perfected knowledge. Truth arose in the purity of her strength and exceeding majesty, and the wise bowed down and adored.

That material injury to our globe or to its inhabitants would result from the apprehended contact, was an opinion which hourly lost ground among the wise; and the wise were now freely permitted to rule the reason and the fancy of the crowd. It was demonstrated, that the density of the comet's nucleus was far less than that of our rarest gas; and the harmless passage of a similar visitor among the satellites of Jupiter was a point strongly insisted upon, and which served greatly to allay terror. Theologists with an earnestness fear-enkindled, dwelt upon the biblical prophecies, and expounded them to the people with a directness and simplicity of which no previous instance had been known. That the final destruction of the earth must be brought about by the agency of fire, was urged with a spirit that enforced every where conviction; and that the comets were of no fiery nature (as all men now knew) was a truth which relieved all, in a great measure, from the apprehension of the great calamity foretold. It is noticeable that the popular prejudices and vulgar errors in regard to pestilences and wars—errors which were wont to prevail upon every appearance of a comet—were now altogether unknown. As if by some sudden convulsive exertion, reason had at once hurled superstition from her throne. The feeblest intellect had derived vigor from excessive interest.

What minor evils might arise from the contact were points of elaborate question. The learned spoke of slight geological disturbances, of probable alterations in climate, and consequently in vegetation, of possible magnetic and electric influences. Many held that no visible or perceptible effect would in any manner be produced. While such discussions were going on, their subject gradually approached, growing larger in apparent diameter, and of a more brilliant lustre. Mankind grew paler as it came. All human operations were suspended.

There was an epoch in the course of the general sentiment when the comet had attained, at length, a size surpassing that of any previously recorded visitation. The people now, dismissing any lingering hope that the astronomers were wrong, experienced all the certainty of evil. The chimerical aspect of their terror was gone. The hearts of the stoutest of our race beat violently within their bosoms. A very few days sufficed, however, to merge even such feelings in sentiments more unendurable We could no longer apply to the strange orb any accustomed thoughts. Its historical attributes had disappeared. It oppressed us with a hideous novelty of emotion. We saw it not as an astronomical phenomenon in the heavens, but as an incubus upon our hearts, and a shadow upon our brains. It had taken, with inconceivable rapidity, the character of a gigantic mantle of rare flame, extending from horizon to horizon.

Yet a day, and men breathed with greater freedom. It was clear that we were already within the influence of the comet; yet we lived. We even felt an unusual elasticity of frame and vivacity of mind. The exceeding tenuity of the object of our dread was apparent; for all heavenly objects were plainly visible through it. Meantime, our vegetation had perceptibly altered; and we gained faith, from this predicted circumstance, in the foresight of the wise. A wild luxuriance of foliage, utterly unknown before, burst out upon every vegetable thing.

Yet another day—and the evil was not altogether upon us. It was now evident that its nucleus would first reach us. A wild change had come over all men; and the first sense of pain was the wild signal for general lamentation and horror. This first sense of pain lay in a rigorous constriction of the breast and lungs, and an insufferable dryness of the skin. It could not be denied that our atmosphere was radically affected; the conformation of this atmosphere and the possible modifications to which it might be subjected, were now the topics of discussion. The result of investigation sent an electric thrill of the intensest terror through the universal heart of man.

It had been long known that the air which encircled us was a compound of oxygen and nitrogen gases, in the proportion of twenty-one measures of oxygen, and seventy-nine of nitrogen in every one hundred of the atmosphere. Oxygen, which was the principle of combustion, and the vehicle of heat, was absolutely necessary to the support of animal life, and was the most powerful and energetic agent in nature. Nitrogen, on the contrary, was incapable of supporting either animal life or flame. An unnatural excess of oxygen would result, it had been ascertained in just such an elevation of the animal spirits as we had latterly experienced. It was the pursuit, the extension of the idea, which had engendered awe. What would be the result of a total extraction of the nitrogen? A combustion irresistible, all-devouring, omni-prevalent, immediate;—the entire fulfilment, in all their minute and terrible details, of the fiery and horror-inspiring denunciations of the prophecies of the Holy Book.

Why need I paint, Charmion, the now disenchained frenzy of mankind? That tenuity in the comet which had previously inspired us with hope, was now the source of the bitterness of despair. In its impalpable gaseous character we clearly perceived the consummation of Fate. Meantime a day again passed—bearing away with it the last shadow of Hope. We gasped in the rapid modification of the air. The red blood bounded tumultuously through its strict channels. A furious delirium possessed all men; and, with arms rigidly outstretched towards the threatening heavens, they trembled and shrieked aloud. But the nucleus of the destroyer was now upon us;— even here in Aidenn, I shudder while I speak. Let me be brief—brief as the ruin that overwhelmed. For a moment there was a wild lurid light alone, visiting and penetrating all things. Then—let us bow down Charmion, before the excessive majesty of the great God!—then, there came a shouting and pervading sound, as if from the mouth itself of HIM; while the whole incumbent mass of ether in which we existed, burst at once into a species of intense flame, for whose surpassing brilliancy and all-fervid heat even the angels in the high Heaven of pure knowledge have no name. Thus ended all.

SHADOW—A PARABLE

Yea, though I walk through the valley of the Shadow:

—Psalm of David.

YE who read are still among the living; but I who write shall have long since gone my way into the region of shadows. For indeed strange things shall happen, and secret things be known, and many centuries shall pass away, ere these memorials be seen of men. And, when seen, there will be some to disbelieve, and some to doubt, and yet a few who will find much to ponder upon in the characters here graven with a stylus of iron.

The year had been a year of terror, and of feelings more intense than terror for which there is no name upon the earth. For many prodigies and signs had taken place, and far and wide, over sea and land, the black wings of the Pestilence were spread abroad. To those, nevertheless, cunning in the stars, it was not unknown that the heavens wore an aspect of ill; and to me, the Greek Oinos, among others, it was evident that now had arrived the alternation of that seven hundred and ninety-fourth year when, at the entrance of Aries, the planet Jupiter is conjoined with the red ring of the terrible Saturnus. The peculiar spirit of the skies, if I mistake not greatly, made itself manifest, not only in the physical orb of the earth, but in the souls, imaginations, and meditations of mankind.

Over some flasks of the red Chian wine, within the walls of a noble hall, in a dim city called Ptolemais, we sat, at night, a company of seven. And to our chamber there was no entrance save by a lofty door of brass: and the door was fashioned by the artisan Corinnos, and, being of rare workmanship, was fastened from within. Black draperies, likewise, in the gloomy room, shut out from our view the moon, the lurid stars, and the peopleless streets—but the boding and the memory of Evil they would not be so excluded. There were things around us and about of which I can render no distinct account—things material and spiritual—heaviness in the atmosphere—a sense of suffocation—

anxiety—and, above all, that terrible state of existence which the nervous experience when the senses are keenly living and awake, and meanwhile the powers of thought lie dormant. A dead weight hung upon us. It hung upon our limbs—upon the household furniture—upon the goblets from which we drank; and all things were depressed, and borne down thereby—all things save only the flames of the seven lamps which illumined our revel. Uprearing themselves in tall slender lines of light, they thus remained burning all pallid and motionless; and in the mirror which their lustre formed upon the round table of ebony at which we sat, each of us there assembled beheld the pallor of his own countenance, and the unquiet glare in the downcast eyes of his companions. Yet we laughed and were merry in our proper way—which was hysterical; and sang the songs of Anacreon—which are madness; and drank deeply—although the purple wine reminded us of blood. For there was yet another tenant of our chamber in the person of young Zoilus. Dead, and at full length he lay, enshrouded; the genius and the demon of the scene. Alas! he bore no portion in our mirth, save that his countenance, distorted with the plague, and his eyes, in which Death had but half extinguished the fire of the pestilence, seemed to take such interest in our merriment as the dead may haply take in the merriment of those who are to die. But although I, Oinos, felt that the eyes of the departed were upon me, still I forced myself not to perceive the bitterness of their expression, and gazing down steadily into the depths of the ebony mirror, sang with a loud and sonorous voice the songs of the son of Teios. But gradually my songs they ceased, and their echoes, rolling afar off among the sable draperies of the chamber, became weak, and undistinguishable, and so faded away. And lo! from among those sable draperies where the sounds of the song departed, there came forth a dark and undefined shadow—a shadow such as the moon, when low in heaven, might fashion from the figure of a man: but it was the shadow neither of man nor of God, nor of any familiar thing. And quivering awhile among the draperies of the room, it at length rested in full view upon the surface of the door of brass. But the shadow was vague, and formless, and indefinite, and was the shadow neither of man nor of God—neither God of Greece, nor God of Chaldaea, nor any Egyptian God. And the shadow rested upon the brazen doorway, and under the arch of the entablature of the door, and moved not, nor spoke any word, but there became stationary and remained. And the door whereupon the shadow rested was, if I remember aright, over against the feet of the young Zoilus enshrouded. But we, the seven there assembled, having seen the shadow as it came out from among the draperies, dared not steadily behold it, but cast down our eyes, and gazed continually into the depths of the mirror of ebony. And at length I, Oinos, speaking some low words, demanded of the shadow its dwelling and its appellation. And the shadow answered, "I am SHADOW, and my dwelling is near to the Catacombs of Ptolemais, and hard by those dim plains of Helusion which border upon the foul Charonian canal." And then did we, the seven, start from our seats in horror, and stand trembling, and shuddering, and aghast, for the tones in the voice of the shadow were not the tones of any one being, but of a multitude of beings, and, varying in their cadences from syllable to syllable fell duskly upon our ears in the well-remembered and familiar accents of many thousand departed friends.

About Author

Poe was born in Boston, the second child of actors David and Elizabeth "Eliza" Arnold Hopkins Poe. His father abandoned the family in 1810, and his mother died the following year. Thus orphaned, the child was taken in by John and Frances Allan of Richmond, Virginia. They never formally adopted him, but he was with them well into young adulthood. Tension developed later as John Allan and Poe repeatedly clashed over debts, including those incurred by gambling, and the cost of Poe's secondary education. He attended the University of Virginia but left after a year due to lack of money. Poe quarreled with Allan over the funds for his education and enlisted in the Army in 1827 under an assumed name. It was at this time that his publishing career began with the anonymous collection Tamerlane and Other Poems (1827), credited only to "a Bostonian". Poe and Allan reached a temporary rapprochement after the death of Frances Allan in 1829. Poe later failed as an officer cadet at West Point, declaring a firm wish to be a poet and writer, and he ultimately parted ways with John Allan.

Poe switched his focus to prose and spent the next several years working for literary journals and periodicals, becoming known for his own style of literary criticism. His work forced him to move among several cities, including Baltimore, Philadelphia, and New York City. He married Virginia Clemm in 1836, his 13-year-old cousin. In January 1845, Poe published his poem "The Raven" to instant success, but Virginia died of tuberculosis two years after its publication.

Poe planned for years to produce his own journal The Penn (later renamed The Stylus), but he died before it could be produced. He died in Baltimore on October 7, 1849, at age 40; the cause of his death is unknown and has been variously attributed to alcohol, "brain congestion", cholera, drugs, heart disease, rabies, suicide, tuberculosis, and other causes.

Poe and his works influenced literature around the world, as well as specialized fields such as cosmology and cryptography. He and his work appear throughout popular culture in literature, music, films, and television. A number of his homes are dedicated museums today. The Mystery Writers of America present an annual award known as the Edgar Award for distinguished work in the mystery genre.

Life and career

Early life

He was born Edgar Poe in Boston on January 19, 1809, the second child of English-born actress Elizabeth Arnold Hopkins Poe and actor David Poe Jr. He had an elder brother William Henry Leonard Poe and a younger sister Rosalie Poe. Their grandfather David Poe Sr. had immigrated from County Cavan, Ireland around 1750. Edgar may have been named after a character in William Shakespeare's King Lear which the couple were performing in 1809. His father abandoned the family in 1810, and his mother died a year later from consumption (pulmonary tuberculosis). Poe was then taken into the home of John Allan, a successful merchant in Richmond, Virginia who dealt in a variety of goods, including tobacco, cloth, wheat, tombstones, and slaves. The Allans served as a foster family and gave him the name "Edgar Allan Poe", though they never formally adopted him.

The Allan family had Poe baptized in the Episcopal Church in 1812. John Allan alternately spoiled and aggressively disciplined his foster son. The family sailed to Britain in 1815, and Poe attended the grammar school for a short period in Irvine, Scotland (where John Allan was born) before rejoining the family in London in 1816. There he studied at a boarding school in Chelsea until summer 1817. He was subsequently entered at the Reverend John Bransby's Manor House School at Stoke Newington, then a suburb 4 miles (6 km) north of London.

Poe moved with the Allans back to Richmond, Virginia in 1820. In 1824, he served as the lieutenant of the Richmond youth honor guard as Richmond celebrated the visit of the Marquis de Lafayette. In March 1825, John Allan's uncle and business benefactor William Galt died, who was said to be one of the wealthiest men in Richmond, leaving Allan several acres of real estate. The inheritance was estimated at $750,000 (equivalent to $17,000,000 in 2018). By summer 1825, Allan celebrated his expansive wealth by purchasing a two-story brick home named Moldavia.

Poe may have become engaged to Sarah Elmira Royster before he registered at the University of Virginia in February 1826 to study ancient and modern languages. The university was in its infancy, established on the ideals of its founder Thomas Jefferson. It had strict rules against gambling, horses, guns, tobacco, and alcohol, but these rules were generally ignored. Jefferson had enacted a system of student self-government, allowing students to choose their own studies, make their own arrangements for boarding, and report all wrongdoing to the faculty. The unique system was still in chaos, and there was a high dropout rate. During his time there, Poe lost touch with Royster and also became estranged from his foster father over gambling debts. He claimed that Allan had not given him sufficient money to register for classes, purchase texts, and procure and furnish a dormitory. Allan did send additional money and clothes, but Poe's debts increased. He gave up on the university after a year but did not feel welcome returning to Richmond, especially when he learned that his sweetheart Royster had married Alexander Shelton. He traveled to Boston in April 1827, sustaining himself with odd jobs as a clerk and newspaper writer, and he started using the pseudonym Henri Le Rennet during this period.

Military career

Poe was unable to support himself, so he enlisted in the United States Army as a private on May 27, 1827, using the name "Edgar A. Perry". He claimed that he was 22 years old even though he was 18. He first served at Fort Independence in Boston Harbor for five dollars a month. That same year, he released his first book, a 40-page collection of poetry titled Tamerlane and Other Poems, attributed with the byline "by a Bostonian". Only 50 copies were printed, and the book received virtually no attention. Poe's regiment was posted to Fort Moultrie in Charleston, South Carolina and traveled by ship on the brig Waltham on November 8, 1827. Poe was promoted to "artificer", an enlisted tradesman who prepared shells for artillery, and had his monthly pay doubled. He served for two years and attained the rank of Sergeant Major for Artillery (the highest rank that a noncommissioned officer could achieve); he then sought to end his five-year enlistment early. He revealed his real name and his circumstances to his commanding officer, Lieutenant Howard. Howard would only allow Poe to be discharged if he reconciled with John Allan and wrote a letter to Allan, who was unsympathetic. Several months passed and pleas to Allan were ignored; Allan may not have written to Poe even to make him aware of his foster mother's illness. Frances Allan died on February 28, 1829, and Poe visited the day after her burial. Perhaps softened by his wife's death, John Allan agreed to support Poe's attempt to be discharged in order to receive an appointment to the United States Military Academy at West Point.

Poe was finally discharged on April 15, 1829, after securing a replacement to finish his enlisted term for him. Before entering West Point, Poe moved back to Baltimore for a time to stay with his widowed aunt Maria Clemm, her daughter Virginia Eliza Clemm (Poe's first cousin), his brother Henry, and his invalid grandmother Elizabeth Cairnes Poe. Meanwhile, Poe published his second book Al Aaraaf, Tamerlane and Minor Poems in Baltimore in 1829.

Poe traveled to West Point and matriculated as a cadet on July 1, 1830. In October 1830, John Allan married his second wife Louisa Patterson. The marriage and bitter quarrels with Poe over the children born to Allan out of affairs led to the foster father finally disowning Poe. Poe decided to leave West Point by purposely getting court-martialed. On February 8, 1831, he was tried for gross neglect of duty and disobedience of orders for refusing to attend formations, classes, or church. Poe tactically pleaded not guilty to induce dismissal, knowing that he would be found guilty.

He left for New York in February 1831 and released a third volume of poems, simply titled Poems. The book was financed with help from his fellow cadets at West Point, many of whom donated 75 cents to the cause, raising a total of $170. They may have been expecting verses similar to the satirical ones that Poe had been writing about commanding officers. It was printed by Elam Bliss of New York, labeled as "Second Edition," and including a page saying, "To the U.S. Corps of Cadets this volume is respectfully dedicated". The book once again reprinted the long poems "Tamerlane" and "Al Aaraaf" but also six previously unpublished poems, including early versions of "To Helen", "Israfel", and "The City in the Sea". He returned to Baltimore to his aunt, brother, and cousin in March 1831. His elder brother Henry had been in ill health, in part due to problems with alcoholism, and he died on August 1, 1831.

Publishing career

After his brother's death, Poe began more earnest attempts to start his career as a writer, but he chose a difficult time in American publishing to do so. He was one of the first Americans to live by writing alone and was hampered by the lack of an international copyright law. American publishers often produced unauthorized copies of British works rather than paying for new work by Americans. The industry was also particularly hurt by the Panic of 1837. There was a booming growth in American periodicals around this time, fueled in part by new technology, but many did not last beyond a few issues. Publishers often refused to pay their writers or paid them much later than they promised, and Poe repeatedly resorted to humiliating pleas for money and other assistance.

After his early attempts at poetry, Poe had turned his attention to prose. He placed a few stories with a Philadelphia publication and began work on his only drama Politian. The Baltimore Saturday Visiter awarded him a prize in October 1833 for his short story "MS. Found in a Bottle". The story brought him to the attention of John P. Kennedy, a Baltimorean of considerable means. He helped Poe place some of his stories, and introduced him to Thomas W. White, editor of the Southern Literary Messenger in Richmond, Virginia. Poe became assistant editor of the periodical in August 1835, but White discharged him within a few weeks for being drunk on the job. Poe returned to Baltimore where he obtained a license to marry his cousin Virginia on September 22, 1835, though it is unknown if they were married at that time. He was 26 and she was 13.

He was reinstated by White after promising good behavior, and he went back to Richmond with Virginia and her mother. He remained at the Messenger until January 1837. During this period, Poe claimed that its circulation increased from 700 to 3,500. He published several poems, book reviews, critiques, and stories in the paper. On May 16, 1836, he and Virginia held a Presbyterian wedding ceremony at their Richmond boarding house, with a witness falsely attesting Clemm's age as 21.

The Narrative of Arthur Gordon Pym of Nantucket was published and widely reviewed in 1838. In the summer of 1839, Poe became assistant editor of Burton's Gentleman's Magazine. He published numerous articles, stories, and reviews, enhancing his reputation as a trenchant critic which he had established at the Southern Literary Messenger. Also in 1839, the collection Tales of the Grotesque and Arabesque was published in two volumes, though he made little money from it and it received mixed reviews. Poe left Burton's after about a year and found a position as assistant at Graham's Magazine.

In June 1840, Poe published a prospectus announcing his intentions to start his own journal called The Stylus, although he originally intended to call it The Penn, as it would have been based in Philadelphia. He bought advertising space for his prospectus in the June 6, 1840 issue of Philadelphia's Saturday Evening Post: "Prospectus of the Penn Magazine, a Monthly Literary journal to be edited and published in the city of Philadelphia by Edgar A. Poe." The journal was never produced before Poe's death.

Around this time, he attempted to secure a position within the administration of President Tyler, claiming that he was a member of the Whig Party. He hoped to be appointed to the Custom House in Philadelphia with help from President Tyler's son Robert, an acquaintance of Poe's friend Frederick Thomas. Poe failed to show up for a meeting with Thomas to discuss the appointment in mid-September 1842, claiming to have been sick, though Thomas believed that he had been drunk. Poe was promised an appointment, but all positions were filled by others.

One evening in January 1842, Virginia showed the first signs of consumption, now known as tuberculosis, while singing and playing the piano, which Poe described as breaking a blood vessel in her throat. She only partially recovered, and Poe began to drink more heavily under the stress of her illness. He left Graham's and attempted to find a new position, for a time angling for a government post. He returned to New York where he worked briefly at the Evening Mirror before becoming editor of the Broadway Journal, and later its owner. There he alienated himself from other writers by publicly accusing Henry Wadsworth Longfellow of plagiarism, though Longfellow never responded. On January 29, 1845, his poem "The Raven" appeared in the Evening Mirror and became a popular sensation. It made Poe a household name almost instantly, though he was paid only $9 for its publication. It was concurrently published in The American Review: A Whig Journal under the pseudonym "Quarles".

The Broadway Journal failed in 1846, and Poe moved to a cottage in Fordham, New York in what is now the Bronx. That home is now known as the Edgar Allan Poe Cottage, relocated to a park near the southeast corner of the Grand Concourse and Kingsbridge Road. Nearby, he befriended the Jesuits at St. John's College, now Fordham University. Virginia died at the cottage on January 30, 1847. Biographers and critics often suggest that Poe's frequent theme of the "death of a beautiful woman" stems from the repeated loss of women throughout his life, including his wife.

Poe was increasingly unstable after his wife's death. He attempted to court poet Sarah Helen Whitman who lived in Providence, Rhode Island. Their engagement failed, purportedly because of Poe's drinking and erratic behavior. There is also strong evidence that Whitman's mother intervened and did much to derail their relationship. Poe then returned to Richmond and resumed a relationship with his childhood sweetheart Sarah Elmira Royster.

Death

On October 3, 1849, Poe was found delirious on the streets of Baltimore, "in great distress, and… in need of immediate assistance", according to Joseph W. Walker who found him. He was taken to the Washington Medical College where he died on Sunday, October 7, 1849 at 5:00 in the morning. He was not coherent long enough to explain how he came to be in his dire condition and, oddly, was wearing clothes that were not his own. He is said to have repeatedly called out the name "Reynolds" on the night before his death, though it is unclear to whom he was referring. Some sources say that Poe's final words were "Lord help my poor soul". All medical records have been lost, including his death certificate.

Newspapers at the time reported Poe's death as "congestion of the brain" or "cerebral inflammation", common euphemisms for death from disreputable causes such as alcoholism. The actual cause of death remains a mystery. Speculation has included delirium tremens, heart disease, epilepsy, syphilis, meningeal inflammation, cholera, and rabies. One theory dating from 1872 suggests that cooping was the cause of Poe's death, a form of electoral fraud in which citizens were forced to vote for a particular candidate, sometimes leading to violence and even murder.

Griswold's "Memoir"

The day that Edgar Allan Poe was buried, a long obituary appeared in the New York Tribune signed "Ludwig". It was soon published throughout the country. The piece began, "Edgar Allan Poe is dead. He died in Baltimore the day before yesterday. This announcement will startle many, but few will be grieved by it." "Ludwig" was soon identified as Rufus Wilmot Griswold, an editor, critic, and anthologist who had borne a grudge against Poe since 1842. Griswold somehow became Poe's literary executor and attempted to destroy his enemy's reputation after his death.

Griswold wrote a biographical article of Poe called "Memoir of the Author", which he included in an 1850 volume of the collected works. He depicted Poe as a depraved, drunken, drug-addled madman and included Poe's letters as evidence. Many of his claims were either lies or distorted half-truths. For example, it is now known that Poe was not a drug addict. Griswold's book was denounced by those who knew Poe well, but it became a popularly accepted biographical source. This occurred in part because it was the only full biography available and was widely reprinted, and in part because readers thrilled at the thought of reading works by an "evil" man. Letters that Griswold presented as proof were later revealed to be forgeries.

Literary style and themes

Genres

Poe's best known fiction works are Gothic, a genre that he followed to appease the public taste. His most recurring themes deal with questions of death, including its physical signs, the effects of decomposition, concerns of premature burial, the reanimation of the dead, and mourning. Many of his works are generally considered part of the dark romanticism genre, a literary reaction to transcendentalism which Poe strongly disliked. He referred to followers of the transcendental movement as "Frog-Pondians", after the pond on Boston Common, and ridiculed their writings as "metaphor—run mad," lapsing into "obscurity for obscurity's sake" or "mysticism for mysticism's sake". Poe once wrote in a letter to Thomas Holley Chivers that he did not dislike Transcendentalists, "only the pretenders and sophists among them".

Beyond horror, Poe also wrote satires, humor tales, and hoaxes. For comic effect, he used irony and ludicrous extravagance, often in an attempt to liberate the reader from cultural conformity. "Metzengerstein" is the first story that Poe is known to have published and his first foray into horror, but it was originally intended as a burlesque satirizing the popular genre. Poe also reinvented science fiction, responding in his writing to emerging technologies such as hot air balloons in "The Balloon-Hoax".

Poe wrote much of his work using themes aimed specifically at mass-market tastes. To that end, his fiction often included elements of popular pseudosciences, such as phrenology and physiognomy.

Literary theory

Poe's writing reflects his literary theories, which he presented in his criticism and also in essays such as "The Poetic Principle". He disliked didacticism and allegory, though he believed that meaning in literature should be an undercurrent just beneath the surface. Works with obvious meanings, he wrote, cease to be art. He believed that work of quality should be brief and focus on a specific single effect. To that end, he believed that the writer should carefully calculate every sentiment and idea.

Poe describes his method in writing "The Raven" in the essay "The Philosophy of Composition", and he claims to have strictly followed this method. It has been questioned whether he really followed this system, however. T.S. Eliot said: "It is difficult for us to read that essay without reflecting that if Poe plotted out his poem with such calculation, he might have taken a little more pains over it: the result hardly does credit to the method." Biographer Joseph Wood Krutch described the essay as "a rather highly ingenious exercise in the art of rationalization".

Legacy

Influence

During his lifetime, Poe was mostly recognized as a literary critic. Fellow critic James Russell Lowell called him "the most discriminating, philosophical, and fearless critic upon imaginative works who has written in America", suggesting—rhetorically—that he occasionally used prussic acid instead of ink. Poe's caustic reviews earned him the reputation of being a "tomahawk man". A favorite target of Poe's criticism was Boston's acclaimed poet Henry Wadsworth Longfellow, who was often defended by his literary friends in what was later called "The Longfellow War". Poe accused Longfellow of "the heresy of the didactic", writing poetry that was preachy, derivative, and thematically plagiarized. Poe correctly predicted that Longfellow's reputation and style of poetry would decline, concluding, "We grant him high qualities, but deny him the Future".

Poe was also known as a writer of fiction and became one of the first American authors of the 19th century to become more popular in Europe than in the United States. Poe is particularly respected in France, in part due to early translations by Charles Baudelaire. Baudelaire's translations became definitive renditions of Poe's work throughout Europe.

Poe's early detective fiction tales featuring C. Auguste Dupin laid the groundwork for future detectives in literature. Sir Arthur Conan Doyle said, "Each [of Poe's detective stories] is a root from which a whole literature has developed.... Where was the detective story until Poe breathed the breath of life into it?" The Mystery Writers of America have named their awards for excellence in the genre the "Edgars". Poe's work also influenced science fiction, notably Jules Verne, who wrote a sequel to Poe's novel The Narrative of Arthur Gordon Pym of Nantucket called An Antarctic Mystery, also known as The Sphinx of the Ice Fields. Science fiction author H.G. Wells noted, "Pym tells what a very intelligent mind could imagine about the south polar region a century ago." In 2013, The Guardian cited The Narrative of Arthur Gordon Pym of Nantucket as one of the greatest novels ever written in the English language, and noted its influence on later authors such as Henry James, Arthur Conan Doyle, B. Traven, and David Morrell. Alfred Hitchcock once said "It's because I liked Edgar Allan Poe's stories so much that I began to make suspense films."

Like many famous artists, Poe's works have spawned imitators. One trend among imitators of Poe has been claims by clairvoyants or psychics to be "channeling" poems from Poe's spirit. One of the most notable of these was Lizzie Doten, who published Poems from the Inner Life in 1863, in which she claimed to have "received" new compositions by Poe's spirit. The compositions were re-workings of famous Poe poems such as "The Bells", but which reflected a new, positive outlook.

Even so, Poe has received not only praise, but criticism as well. This is partly because of the negative perception of his personal character and its influence upon his reputation. William Butler Yeats was occasionally critical of Poe and once called him "vulgar". Transcendentalist Ralph Waldo Emerson reacted to "The Raven" by saying, "I see nothing in it", and derisively referred to Poe as "the jingle man". Aldous Huxley wrote that Poe's writing "falls into vulgarity" by being "too poetical"—the equivalent of wearing a diamond ring on every finger.

It is believed that only 12 copies have survived of Poe's first book Tamerlane and Other Poems. In December 2009, one copy sold at Christie's, New York for $662,500, a record price paid for a work of American literature.

Physics and cosmology

Eureka: A Prose Poem, an essay written in 1848, included a cosmological theory that presaged the Big Bang theory by 80 years, as well as the first plausible solution to Olbers' paradox. Poe eschewed the scientific method in Eureka and instead wrote from pure intuition. For this reason, he considered it a work of art, not science, but insisted that it was still true and considered it to be his career masterpiece. Even so, Eureka is full of scientific errors. In particular, Poe's suggestions ignored Newtonian principles regarding the density and rotation of planets.

Cryptography

Poe had a keen interest in cryptography. He had placed a notice of his abilities in the Philadelphia paper Alexander's Weekly (Express) Messenger, inviting submissions of ciphers which he proceeded to solve. In July 1841, Poe had published an essay called "A Few Words on Secret Writing" in Graham's Magazine. Capitalizing on public interest in the topic, he wrote "The Gold-Bug" incorporating ciphers as an essential part of the story. Poe's success with cryptography relied not so much on his deep knowledge of that field (his method was limited to the simple substitution cryptogram) as on his knowledge of the magazine and newspaper culture. His keen analytical abilities, which were so evident in his detective stories, allowed him to see that the general public was largely ignorant of the methods by which a simple substitution cryptogram can be solved, and he used this to his advantage. The sensation that Poe created with his cryptography stunts played a major role in popularizing cryptograms in newspapers and magazines.

Poe had an influence on cryptography beyond increasing public interest during his lifetime. William Friedman, America's foremost cryptologist, was heavily influenced by Poe. Friedman's initial interest in cryptography came from reading "The Gold-Bug" as a child, an interest that he later put to use in deciphering Japan's PURPLE code during World War II. (Source: Wikipedia)

Printed in June 2019
by Rotomail Italia S.p.A., Vignate (MI) - Italy